Spice

Dan O'Connor

Waterton Press

Danville,
California • Koloa
Hawaii • Alberta
Canada

Internal Text & Cover Design by: Dan O'Connor, Author

Cover Illustration by: Shelagh Armstrong
          Toronto, Ontario, Canada

Story Editor: Jacquelyn Powers
          Sedona, Arizona

Copy Editor: Carol O'Hara
          Folsom, California
          cattale@worldnet.att.net

Published by Waterton Press.

ISBN: 0-9667235-5-4   Library of Congress number pending

To order additional copies of this publication, or report errors, contact:
          Waterton Press
          PO Box 847
          Danville, CA   94526-0847
          (925) 838-4102
          Fax: (925) 838-8034
          email: spice@watertonpress.com
          website: www.watertonpress.com

This book is dedicated to

Richard Austin, Reverend & Attorney

Residing in: St. Croix

U.S. Virgin Islands

My best friend in law school

and to his yellow Porsche 356C convertible
(That we used to cruise around in on weekends,
. . . whenever we had a chance to take a moment away from our
studies.)

Disclaimer

This entire story, including its components, is

fiction.

The resemblance of any characters, description or narration to actual people, circumstances, or events is coincidental and unintended.

Likewise, the names and descriptions of actual locations, brand names, historical figures and such have been used only to give the story a greater sense of reality and to promote credibility in the minds of the readers as to the fictional world thus created. Scene descriptions may be accurate, or they may have been intentionally, or unintentionally, altered to better suit the events in the story. No historical accuracy is intended, nor implied.

The names of actual persons have been used in a few instances in cameo roles to honor and immortalize them. This was done with their permission and any resemblance to the actual person(s) is coincidental and unintended.

To those who at times appear to be eager to misinterpret the nature of the author's stories: "This novel is fiction. Try to understand the differences among art, historical fact and a press release."

Part I

Barbados

1994

Chapter One

We tried to slip into our hotel room without being noticed. It had stark white stucco walls with a big round window, cleverly placed window seats, a cylindrical shower stall, strange and varying angles between the wall and ceiling components and most of all a breathtaking view of the ocean. We found it charming.

We made it clear from the beginning that we didn't welcome any intrusion from the maids and my companion periodically went down to the common dining area by himself and brought back all of our meals to the room. I knew from the outset that I was using him but decided in advance to enjoy myself for a brief respite before doing what it was I came here to do.

The proprietor was kind enough to supply us with any number of books to read. They were packed away on a convenient little bookshelf to our left, just as we entered the room. My companion had brought his own reading material. We spent a considerable length of time reading and enjoying our books and magazines.

My companion and I hadn't brought any luggage except for our gym bags and I made sure early on that his fit fully into mine.

We played chess. We conversed about the weather, about our jobs—where we worked for a common employer—about the small and trivial things in life that tend to bind couples and make them feel connected. There was no television in the room and no telephone but no one could call us there anyway because my companion had left a false identity with the receptionist. I had stolen a credit card with plenty of credit line and told him it was on loan to me while my "lost or stolen" one was being replaced. He registered us in the name of the cardholder and his wife, and I was confident the owner would not catch on until after our rendezvous had ended.

It was not long until we slipped off one another's clothing, one delicious piece of apparel at a time. I eagerly pulled down his pants and got him very much into the mood. After that we couldn't wait to get my clothes off and we had intercourse repeatedly with vehemence and passion. I knew this was not to be a long-term relationship but there was something about human intimacy, the sex act itself, that I found enthralling. The feeling of his sweaty body against mine, mine against his, the shrill high pitched roar of an orgasm, the promises, the entreaties, the ritual, the hopes, the dreams, even the deception was a wonderful aphrodisiac.

We did it. And we did it again, staying in our underwear all the while, in case either of us got the desire for more. We made a pact that if either of us wanted to do something nasty the other would oblige without question.

Other than that we mostly ate—delicious, light, nutritious meals brought to us by my lover. We read books and continued our one and only chess game. My companion was very clever when it came to chess and I could see his checkmate coming. I had already been in check three times and knew that an evasive maneuver was in order, so as not to lose the game. I stalled and refused to play until it was nearly time to checkout on the last day.

We decided to have one last encounter before we left the room to return to the real world and our workaday responsibilities. "I'm sorry I don't have time to finish the chess game," I said. "But I'll make time for one more roll in the hay." It was only midmorning and he was under the impression we were staying until late afternoon so I told him that I had just remembered a pressing responsibility I had to attend to. In fact I had one forthcoming and was so nervous about it that I had skipped eating breakfast.

He climbed onto the bed and waited for me while I went into the bathroom and took off my panties. I freshened my lipstick and eye shadow. I found that the ritual of painting my face steadied my nerves for our next encounter. When I approached him from behind he waited for me to do something nasty. Instead I put my arm around his neck and choked him until he gasped for air and flailed in panic and surprise.

He writhed in a similar manner to when we had made love and I found it erotic. The business had to be done before I weakened and gave in to the feelings I had developed for him. When I yanked and twisted his neck I could hear it snap. I flipped him onto his back, slit his throat and cut him from his chin to his navel with a steak knife I had lifted from the breakfast dishes on a tray that we later placed outside the door. I left the knife inserted at the end of the incision. The blood oozed and gushed until his heart stopped beating. The sight of it was exhilarating. I had to be extremely careful not to get it all over me. What blood did come my way, I soon rinsed off in the circular shower.

I dipped my index finger into his blood, took the warm crimson liquid and wrote across the pure white walls. I had to hurry. Yet I couldn't resist the compulsion to express my feelings about what we had done together.

Then I cleaned and scrubbed with the supplies obligingly left by the maids. I made sure there were no fingerprints, neither mine, nor his. No hair. I had been very careful of that. No clothing fragments. No residue from anything we had brought in except, of course, for my lover and his stains. I gathered all of our things, which didn't amount to much and stuffed them into my gym bag. At no small exertion I lugged my victim to the window and left him until I had a chance to make the bed. *Mustn't be untidy.* The quilt was green, white and yellow and had two bright yellow and green Macaws on it.

I wiped a Bajan dollar coin clean with a tissue, dropped it onto the bed and watched it bounce. I knew the proprietor's husband and all the hotel guests were out until evening on a cove and castle nature walk, which was part of their regular schedule of events. The staff had Sunday mornings off after nine a.m. The only one left to contend with was the proprietor and there were no check-ins expected that morning. My companion had inquired about that on the way in when he asked for a late checkout. No lunch was served on Sundays. In short she wouldn't miss us if we departed early and you *could* say that my companion had already departed.

I watched from the window ledge with the body just inches below, partially covered by a towel I had put over his face. He looked so forlorn otherwise. Like clockwork I could see the proprietor walk from the reception area to the kitchen to begin preparations for a lavish dinner they would be serving tonight in advance of their star gazing show and astronomical discussion. Through struggle and sadness I lifted the modestly heavy frame of my lover's still supple body and shoved him out the window. His corpse plummeted to the ground below. I tossed the key on the bed, made sure I had my gym bag in hand, looked to be sure the breakfast dishes had been removed for cleaning and locked the door behind me.

When I got to the ground I could see that his blood had splattered onto the wall on his descent but there was nothing I could do about that. I hurriedly dragged the corpse to the small circular hot tub adjacent to the pool. I grabbed a fallen palm frond and brushed the path from the wall to the spa of footprints. I was careful not to step in any blood.

I turned on the hot tub and set the thermostat as high as it would go. I removed the knife from the body, severed the testicles from my victim and pushed his body into the spa. I tossed the knife into the pool. When I did so I could see the blood swirl into a cloud before it dispersed into the water. The hot tub, on the other hand, looked more like a Roman bath.

It was then that I noticed there were windsurfers just off the rocky shores near the pool. I had not counted on them but doubted any of them could see me clearly or guess what invigorating task I had been up to on this bright, sunny Sunday morning.

I kissed the tips of my fingers, transferred the kiss to the top of my lover's head and ran back to the car. I was in such a hurry that I didn't pay particular attention to whether or not the proprietor might see me. Instead I held my upper arm over my face. I put the gym bag into the trunk, jumped into the front seat and sped away.

On the way back to my abode I took the car, which the decedent had obligingly rented with the stolen credit card, to a remote area of Welchman Hall Gully, poured gasoline on it, as well as on the gym bag and its contents, and set it ablaze. The next morning I read in *The Daily Advocate* that the body had been identified and that Lili Kaleo was the last known person to have seen him alive other than Mrs. Margaret Loveridge, the proprietor of the Peach n Quiet Resort.

* * *

Lili Kaleo arrived in Barbados several months before the murder. She stayed at a quaint little place called the Tower Hotel, which was a misnomer in that it was a wood frame low rise near Paradise Beach, consisting of two small buildings that looked more like converted houses than part of a hotel complex. She didn't bring much luggage, only a small satchel, in that she had left home in haste and been grieving to the point of not caring much about life's incidental amenities, least of all her appearance.

When she first got there she spent most of her time alone in her room, quiet and reflective, feeling sorry for herself, wondering whether or not it made any sense to go on. She would have been happy to stay in her room quilting, sewing and reading but the man who managed the front desk and brought her her meals wouldn't leave her alone.

"It's no good to stay holed up in your room all the time," he said. "You've got to come out and get some sunshine, swim in the pool, meet the rest of the guests."

At first she argued with him. "It's my business what I do with my time. You have no idea, no idea whatsoever what I've been through. You just don't understand."

Yet he was persistent. "It's for your own good, Mum. You're not eating enough to nourish a bananaquit. You must've lost ten kilos since you've been here." He put the service tray down on her table and said, "Come over here and look in the mirror."

She refused. But after he left the room and closed the door she did as he suggested. "*Mon Dieu*, Lili Kaleo," she said to herself. "Two more weeks like this and there'll be nothing left of you!"

* * *

That night with considerable reluctance, she joined the nightly gathering around the big round table on the porch of the auxiliary building. It was nothing more than a big wooden spool that used to hold electrical or telephone cable. It had been painted dark green and placed on its side to host cocktails, hors d'oeuvres and light dinner fair.

As she climbed the steps to the porch, Hans Jenkins, a man who introduced himself as a radio operator from the Netherlands working on a cargo ship out of Antigua said, "I've seen you skulkin' 'round here in the hallways," as the soft white suds from his ale spilled over the edge of his mug onto his heavily tattooed hand. He wiped his hand with his handkerchief and shook hers. The beer was pungent.

"I'm Lili . . . Lili Kaleo," she said as she returned his handshake and sat down. "Some people call me 'Sugar.'"

Hans had a terrible burn mark on the side of his cheek, a large potbelly and enormous, perfectly spherical blue eyes protruding from his heavily wrinkled skin, in much the same fashion as those of a crocodile. "What's a gorgeous creature like you doin' hidin' in your room?"

She responded with a glare as brittle as the island coral. "I'm not hiding, Mr. Jenkins. I spend the days in my room reading and sewing, writing letters, tending to my affairs."

"And, if you don't mind me askin', Miss Kaleo, why are you doing that when you could be bustling about with the rest of the tourists?"

"Oh, but I'm not a tourist." *And, who said I didn't mind you askin'?*

"What brings you here, then, Missy?" the sailor asked. There are people who can ask impertinent and prying questions and get away with it and there are people who can't. Hans Jenkins was one who could. In spite of his brash nature there was an aura of kindness beneath his crusty exterior.

Lili paused. "Business," she said in an almost imperceptible tone. "I have some personal business to attend to."

Mr. Appleby—one-hundred-twenty kilos, at least, with flushed fair skin—chimed in. "Pardon him young lady." He glowered at Hans. "I'm sure Miss Kaleo doesn't want to share her business with everyone who comes along. If she has something to tell us, I'm sure she will. Don't mind him, Miss Kaleo. We're just glad you've chosen to join us. We were worried about you."

Monique Appleby, a plump matronly woman from Marseille, said, "Yes, I've seen you about. I tried to get your attention the other day but you jumped back into your room as quick as a cricket. Do you remember?"

"Was that you? I apologize," Lili answered. "I've been through a lot lately. I'm afraid I haven't been myself. I haven't felt up to doing much."

Mr. Appleby nodded in empathy. "I know how that goes. This heat is stifling. It's enough to sap anyone's ambition." He fanned his face with a cardboard coaster.

"It's gorgeous around here, though," mused Monique as she gazed off into the sunset over the clear turquoise waters of the Caribbean.

"Monique. Monique, dear. You're not supposed to look directly into the sun. You might be blinded," Mr. Appleby reminded her. He still had on a white hat with a black band which kept his bushy gray hair corralled just below the brim, next to his mutton chop sideburns. He took off his thick, dark sunglasses and handed them to his wife.

Mr. Appleby continued, "Enough of this depressing talk," he said. "Where's the minkee? Has anyone here seen Sea Cat? And *where's* his minkee?"

Sea Cat, the man who rousted Lili from her room, was also the waiter, housecleaning supervisor, maintenance man and Casanova *extraordinaire*, whenever he found enough time off from work to walk down the Spring Garden Highway to the wharf to entertain the bored single women overnighting from the cruise ships.

"What's a minkee?" the radio operator asked.

"You know, a minkee," Mr. Appleby said, as he wiped the sweat from his brow. "The kind that climbs trees."

Just then Sea Cat appeared with a tray full of tropical drinks, including the specialty of the house, rum punch with lots of grenadine, a cherry and a little umbrella stuck into a slice of orange peel.

"There it is right there," Mr. Appleby said, much to his own delight. "There's the little minkee."

Perched on Sea Cat's shoulder was a baby green monkey with dark brown, almost black eyes and a long tail with a crook in the end that formed a curl.

"Come here, *mon petit* minkee," Mr. Appleby said. He reached into the center of the table and pulled a peanut, still in its shell, from a bowl and held it out in the palm of his hand, fingers bowed downward.

The monkey alighted from Sea Cat's shoulder and in an instant, retrieved, shelled and ate the nut. Jack, the "minkee," knew he was not allowed to fraternize with the guests unless invited, or beg for food in any case. But when treats were offered, he never risked waiting for a second invitation.

Sea Cat, who wore a white smock with vertical waist high pockets in which his hands often sought refuge, passed out drinks, shared pleasantries and flattered the ladies, whenever he got a chance. For a lady charmer Sea Cat wasn't what you'd call dashing. He was stocky with a mild complexion problem but he had a winning smile and a way about him that helped him slide in and out of easy conversation with anyone. Meanwhile Jack scurried up and down the pillars which led to the roof and then leapt from the latticework around one pillar to another with the ease and grace of a trapeze artist. He may not have been allowed to beg from the tourists but he was allowed to entertain them and snatch the rewards tossed his way with joyful abandon.

Mrs. Appleby, in a tiny, affectionate voice, said, "Here, little minkee, here's some fruit for you my little itty-bitty friend." She collected the fruit from inside her drink and stuck it into the soft tissue of a peeled banana which she had removed and unwrapped from a napkin inside her purse. Jack instantly devoured this delightful cocktail while holding fast to the side of one of the pillars with his feet.

"Cute little minkee, eh?" Mr. Appleby said.

And so it went day after day, night after night, when the hotel guests gathered around the large, round wooden table. As guests came and went new occupants regularly filled its empty seats. According to Sea Cat, the "all-arounder," the strand of nightly conversation at the table had started "nearly twenty-five years ago" and remained unbroken with only the bearers of the torch changing identity. The lamp of continuity had never gone out, not even during the earthquakes and threatened tidal waves from Kick 'Em Jenny, a volcano off the coast of nearby Grenada.

* * *

Then one day, along with her breakfast, Sea Cat brought her a telegram from her lawyer, Izzy Kawamoto. Her brother's house was going into foreclosure proceedings and it became clear that if she didn't resolve her problems soon and resume making his mortgage payments for him, it was likely that it wouldn't be long before he and his family would be out on the street. Mimo had been undernourished as a child and, while strong of body and industrious, lacked the mental acuity of a normal adult. Consequently he had a difficult time securing and holding employment. His wife had her hands full with their children. Mimo was Lili's only living sibling and she felt great affection and sympathy for him and his condition. She loved his wife, Ruth, and their children as though they were her own.

Lili decided there was no more time for mourning. It was a luxury she couldn't afford. It was time to slip into town—a move that didn't go unnoticed by Sea Cat and her fellow guests. She didn't cruise there in a Mini Moke, like the tourists. Instead she walked the hundred or so paces up the little lane to the street, pointed her finger down at the asphalt and thereby called the bus to a halt.

Most of the people on the bus were of African descent. As a brown person, which is how she viewed herself, she stood out but not such that she felt noticed immediately or the focus of attention. At one stop a Scandinavian woman with fair skin, faint blue eyes and long blond hair got on the bus and hardly anyone could quit staring. A little girl sitting behind the woman stroked her hair with her fingertips as the bus drove on a few feet to the next corner, came to a sharp halt and everyone swayed back and forth as the driver jockeyed the bus into position. The road, which rimmed the southern tip of the island, was not much wider than an alley in south Chicago.

But the neighborhoods were kept up much better. The chattel houses along the bus route were various shades of pastel. They were like little gingerbread houses, all neatly lined up, freshly painted and brimming with cleanliness. They were not much bigger than a concession stand at a ballpark, and, like a concession stand, one wall would flip down to form a ledge upon which business—the sale of fish, a warm meal served, imported fine linen embroidery, or perhaps even a bookie operation might be conducted. None of the houses were numbered. The fire department knew them only by their names, which reflected something about their occupants, their business or—in many instances—the setting.

Lili's business, however, was not along the bus route but in the center of town. Once the bus stopped, it let out its remaining passengers at Cheapside, across from the old Saint Mary's Church. Uncertain of what to expect from the people around her she walked swiftly through the burgeoning morning shopping trade. Then she turned up one of the many narrow lanes which spurred away from Broad Street in the downtown area. She walked up a side street and into a white building that resembled a medieval fortress, complete with a tunnel entry and a sentry. A Bajan police officer, smartly dressed in a gray shirt, navy trousers with red stripes down his pant legs and circling the rim of his hat, stood guard—as dignified and with as much pomp as if he were standing in front of Buckingham Palace.

"Good morning, Mum," he said to her as she approached.

"Aloha," she said without thinking. "I mean good morning. Good morning to you, sir." The crackling in her voice belied her tension.

"Your business, Mum?"

"Well, I'm not sure what you'd call it. It has to do with a crime that I think—have reason to believe that is— was committed here a long time ago."

"See the duty officer," he said. "Up the stairs to the left."

The Central Police Station was tidier than it was mighty. The duty officer was busy gathering the details of a car theft from the only Asian man Lili had seen since she'd arrived in Barbados. She found this humorous since virtually all the cars that she'd seen had been made in Asia.

Behind her stood an old wooden sign, sitting on the floor, which outlined the mission of the "Royal Barbados Police Force." Lili read the block red letters: "Cap. 167: 1. To preserve and advance the principals of democracy . . . and so on down to number 10. To maintain the highest standards of integrity." The floor of the building was wooden and there wasn't a speck of dirt anywhere to be seen. All sorts of people, most of them black, were scurrying every which way and interrupted the dispatch officer with their needs and requests. The Asian man pulled out a small red passport and handed it to the officer as he signed a statement summarizing his version of the theft.

Lili took this opportunity to slip out into the courtyard because she had noticed that almost everyone ahead of her was being turned away or told to come back later. She never thought she'd actually have to sneak into a police battalion. Around the perimeter of the atrium into which the tunnel from the outside led, there were risers of wooden stairs which she assumed led to offices on the higher floors. She selected one of them at random and boldly climbed the stairs.

At the top there was a room marked "International Drivers' Licenses." Lili could see through the Venetian blinds that even at this early hour there was a long line of people, most of them white, leading to two or three clerks—all of them black, who were busy typing while the people stood in the queue, talked to one another or read the morning paper. *Not there,* she thought.

There was another room across the hall with gold block letters on the door that said "Austin C. Williams, Inspector." Why not? She thought, and twisted the polished brass knob on the rickety door to enter. It stuck, as she opened it and when it finally broke free it made a loud noise.

"Who let you in here?" a deep, gruff voice from behind a desk said. "No one gets in to see me without an appointment."

Lili couldn't see the person who was speaking to her. Her eyes were still adjusting to the darkness of the dimly lit room. "I let myself in. I need help."

"We could all use a little help." The brash voice reverberated. "But, you'll have to make an appointment and come back to see me . . . later, say in a week or two. How about you call me on Friday morning at around ten a.m. and we'll set something up?"

Gradually, as her eyes adjusted to the light, the man's face developed like an image on film. His teeth became prominent and one of them had a gold border with the letter "L" on it. As his image became clearer she made out the periodic blinking of his eyes. His uniform was adorned with silver buttons down the front and silver numbers on the collar. Now she could associate the voice—the strong, sturdy, reverberating voice—with the frame of an African Bajan man, the police inspector.

Finally she could see him well. He had coarsely hewed, high cheekbones, thick bushy black eyebrows, tightly furrowed, a large billowing chest and arms that seemed to bulge at the sleeves in spite of the thickness of his jacket. He had a strong, sturdy, muscular appearance.

Except for the color of his skin—dark brown his portrait reminded her of a Hawaiian warrior. The man stood up and it was a joy to her to be in the presence of a man who was taller than she was. She was embarrassed it had taken her so long to adjust to the light and see him clearly and had not immediately noticed how handsome he was. Instead she focused on the black hair on his hands, how it seemed to form little wisps of curl. The curls reminded her of her son Christian.

The man had on trousers with vertical stripes, just like the sentry, only his pants were black in contrast to his white coat and shiny silver buttons. She forced herself not to fixate on his appearance, not to drool over his appearance, because she was here on important business. Yet, the sweet smell of lime cologne tickled her nose and drew her closer, as did his expression, which she found inviting in spite of his gruffness. An air of self-assuredness resonated in his voice.

It was rich, deep and harmonic. The walls of the police station seemed to resonate along with it. "To whom do I owe the pleasure of this interruption to the start of a man's day?" He bellowed.

"My name is Lili Kaleo."

He paused, as though it was necessary for him to translate her words into his dialect. "And where are you from, Miss Kaleo? You don't sound like it's from anywhere around here."

"I'm from Hawaii."

"Hawaii." The man scratched his chin and took a step to the side of his desk, leaned against it and folded his arms. "Hawaii? I've heard of Hawaii, but I've never actually met anyone from there." He took a step forward and held out his hand to shake hers. "Austin Clyde Williams. Inspector Williams. Are you a Hawaiian?"

"About as much as anyone these days," she answered. She trembled at the feel of his hand. His grip was firm, yet not crushing.

"Just where is Hawaii?"

"Why it's in the Pacific … the Pacific Ocean. It's on the way to Australia."

"Pacific? You don't say. Well, this is the Caribbean, Miss Kaleo. Are you sure you're in the right precinct?"

"I've been accused of a crime. Well, I was found innocent, but I've got to clear my name, find out where money was laundered. I need to know how to trace it through your banks, but I'm confused and need help."

The man grimaced, then laughed and shook his head.

Lili, who had done her best to hold herself together, lost her composure and the next moment the African Bajan police inspector was holding her in his large, burly arms. "I need help," she continued. "I'm here by myself. My visa's running out. I'm almost broke and I need help. People are depending on me. Can you help me?"

She wasn't one to break down but her losses and grieving had extracted a heavy toll. Tears spilled down her distraught face.

The inspector held her back far enough to look into her eyes. "So this is all about money laundering?" he asked, as he reached one hand into his desk drawer for some tissues without letting go of her with the other. "You must be thinking of St. Vincent or Antigua, Miss Kaleo. We don't permit money laundering here in Barbados. Shirt laundering and pants laundering, maybe—but not money laundering."

Lili laughed. The inspector's unexpected humor broke her somber mood. Then just as suddenly she realized he was touching her. She stepped back and retreated to the other side of his desk.

"Sit down," he said, as he put the Kleenex back into his drawer and closed it. He straightened his uniform, pressed the wrinkles with his large, basket like hands, went behind his desk and sat down. "I'm working at Government House today. Got to keep myself looking sharp." He motioned for her to sit, then folded his hands together and put them on the desk.

Lili sat down in the highly polished wooden armchair in front of his desk, pushed the hair out of her eyes and dabbed at her tears. "Please excuse me," she said. "I've been through a lot lately." There was also something about this man that had thrown her off balance but she had no time to pause and define it.

He stared at her while she tried to get herself together. His large billowing chest drew in and out, as he breathed in rhythm through his broad nostrils. As she calmed down she became aware of his breathing. The strength and predictability of it made her feel secure—a feeling she had felt in the presence of only a handful of men over her thirty-plus years on the planet. She cherished this feeling because it contrasted so sharply with her life's experiences.

After Lili had regained her composure, he said, "Look, you walk in here off the street. You don't know me from Colonel Sanders. You accuse our banks of money laundering. You fall apart. You start crying. . . . You wrinkle my uniform. By the way, I just got it pressed . . ." He reached down and straightened it again.

"I know. I'm sorry. I won't bother—" She got up and no sooner had she done so than he motioned for her to sit back down.

His phone rang and he took a call. "Yes, yes. I'll be right there. I have someone with me now but I'll be right there."

He hung up the phone and turned to her. He spoke in a lower voice than he had been using. "How do you know I'm not on the take?"

Lili blushed.

He leaned forward as he spoke. "That's right. Even if we did allow money laundering here in Barbados, which we don't, how do you know I'm not on the take?"

Suddenly Lili realized how foolish she had been. *Why didn't I think of that? He could be on the take.* "I don't—"

The inspector stretched his arms. "Look, if I were on the take or involved in money laundering, there would be, as of this moment, no chance whatsoever that you would ever find out the first bit of information about whatever it is you're looking for. You couldn't have done a better job of making an announcement if you'd shot a cannon ball over the swing bridge and into the middle of The Constitution River."

Lili shuddered at his commanding voice. She stood up to leave and responded in a resolute, somber tone, "You're right. I shouldn't have come here. Can you tell me where I can find the Grand Barbadian Bank?"

"And what? You're going to go marching in there and tell them you want to know if any of them have been laundering money?"

The tears came back. Out popped the Kleenex.

She sat back down. "I feel like a fool. So much has happened to me lately I can't think clearly. I don't know where to start."

The inspector stood up, placed his hands on the top of the desk, leaned on them, peered into her eyes and said, "Look, I'd like to help you. But, you have to understand. I'm the youngest police inspector this island has ever seen. My father, Clyde Williams, was a legendary traffic cop and my brother has already made deputy superintendent—still on the sunny side of forty-five. But if I don't take my young ass from behind this desk and get over to Government House and take care of my duties, I'm also going to be the youngest police inspector ever to get sacked."

Lili felt dejected. The conversation had begun to seem so promising.

"I'll tell you what, Miss Kaleo. Where are you staying?"

She looked at him quizzically.

"You can trust me," he said. "I'm *not* on the take."

She fought her bedraggled feeling and smiled. "I'm staying at The Tower Hotel. It's over in St. Michael."

"I know where The Tower is, Miss Kaleo. Tonight around ten go down to the Paradise Hotel and get a table next to the dance floor. Perhaps we can talk more freely there. You never know," he said, as he gazed around the room. "The walls may have ears."

On the way out of the station she looked around. On a clerk's desk near the reception area was a police brochure. It depicted a number of bills of various denominations on a clothesline, being showered by a garden hose and was entitled, "What is Money Laundering?" She picked it up and thumbed through it as she left. It spoke only of problems in Barbados and said nothing about St. Vincent or Antigua.

* * *

That night just before sunset, Lili, who had begun joining her fellow guests a few nights before, left her seat empty at the big round table at The Tower. Instead, she took one at The Paradise, underneath a covered porch between the dance floor and the beach. Looking toward the bandstand Lili could see the stars through the open wooden slats which formed the roof. *What am I doing here? Can I trust him? And what about that "no money laundering **here**" business?* Yet a warm tropical breeze caressed her skin and left her with sensations of magic and serenity.

Ten o'clock came and went and no one even looked in her direction. In between sets she could hear the clear waves against the shore, lapping ever so gently, shimmering in the moonlight. They soothed her. She watched the men—honeymooners or crooners, she wasn't sure which—clutching and pawing their companions, whenever the beat slowed from reggae to Calypso. *Men, who needs them? They're so juvenile, so one dimensional, so predictable.*

Shortly after the band announced its last set and about the time she was ready to get up from the table and walk back up the dark, narrow lane to her hotel, the police inspector came to her table and sat down. *This can't be the same man I met this morning. This man is dashing!*

His physique, defined more closely by street clothes and moonlight, disclosed a trim, athletic appearance. He had approached from the beach in a sleek and agile fashion. He was casually dressed with his shirttail out and his collar open. Two gold chains contrasted with his dark, shiny skin—but he wore no medallion as was the popular fashion. She had not taken in the full effect of the man's appearance when she was in his arms—only the support of his frame and the comfort of his gentle strength.

"I'm sorry I'm late," he said. "I had some family business to take care of."

"Oh, do you have a family?" she asked.

The band had just started up again and the steel drums were raging. He spoke over the din as if he hadn't heard her. "What can I do for you?" he said. "Tell me about your problem. I think we can talk here."

"And not in the police station?"

"I sometimes wonder about the police station," she thought she heard him mumble.

She told him about how she had been accused of accepting a bribe. How she had weathered the trial, how terrified she had been that she might be convicted and go to prison. And that they had never caught the person or persons who gave her, or rather her former husband, the bribe that led to the trial and a Swiss bank account that led to Barbados and brought her here.

Lili said, "I'm here to find the source of the bribe money so I can clear my reputation and take care of some legal problems back in Hawaii. The county is suing me for more than a million dollars in punitive damages for allegedly misusing public funds. They claim the bribe money technically belonged to them."

The inspector looked attentive and seemed to be listening intently, above the din of the music. He ordered rum punches for each of them without first asking her.

Lili didn't object. "I spent some of it, unwittingly, from my checking account. Unless I can find out who arranged the payment and expose them, I'm facing financial ruin, and so are my relatives who depend on me. My attorney, Izzy Kawamoto, has had to answer disbarment charges for accepting what the state called 'bribe money' from me for his retainer. But the voters are behind me. I know it! I was once the mayor of Kaua'i, the oldest and most wonderful of the Hawaiian Islands, and I'd like to run for governor and think I could win but I've got to get this cleared up first."

The inspector appeared to listen to all she had to say, raised his glass to his lips and finished his drink. He shook the ice against his glass, took a piece out every now and then and champed on it while appearing to listen all the while.

"Can you help me? Can you point me in the right direction?" She had to yell over the sound of the steel drums.

"Perhaps I can," he said, as he got up from his chair, reached out his hand and escorted her to the dance floor.

She had not expected this. She thought they would sit and discuss the ins and outs of public trust, banking and politics and she would be able to mine him for information about a place to begin her investigation. But the inspector had different ideas. She thought about resisting, in fact stiffened and held back, but his hand provided a counterforce, like that of a stubborn and forceful tide. It reminded her of the tide she had fought as a child in an effort to save her mother but this was a tide of a different sea. She felt as though she were entering a harbor, a harbor free from the torrents of the outside world. She flowed into it, hesitantly at first, but its lure became more pronounced as the evening progressed. She enjoyed the feel of the inspector's steady hand on her waist and the strength in his arms as he rhythmically guided her through an array of Caribbean dance steps.

She tried on several occasions to return to the subject of how to learn more about local banking practices, about whom to trust, about where would be a good place to start. Instead of responding to her questions, he promised to call her soon for further discussions. She found herself drawn in by his charm, his impeccable manners and politeness. The accent of his lime cologne, mixed with the smell of fresh salt air disarmed her. And for whatever reason, with no known basis in fact, she had the feeling his lure was wholesome and forthright. She wanted desperately to trust him. She decided to swim with the tide.

The moonlight cast shadows through the beamed trellis that overhung the circular dance floor. The incessant beat of steel drums reverberated. The rhythm and authority with which he guided her dance step made her feel ethereal. He was mesmerizing, bold and forceful. She liked him and found an unspoken mystery about him. *What deep, dark secrets does he hold?* There were few words but a magnetism that drew her close to the ebb and tide of his being. When the music stopped neither of them noticed as they kept dancing, marking time to their own private rhythm.

There was no one at the big round table when she passed back across the front porch of The Tower on the way back to her room. During the night she could not understand how she had spent so much time with this man and never once been able to revisit the subject for which she had traveled almost seven thousand miles. Instead she had been drawn into a tide pool of magic and intrigue that she did not fully understand—could not distill or define. It was delicious and she wanted desperately to pour it out and taste it. Two distant oceans linked through a tiny isthmus. Feverish bodies clutched together in the silver glow of a full Bajan moon, first on the dance floor and then in her room.

In the morning when she reached out to touch him, he was gone.

Chapter Two

The following day Lili didn't come out of her room. Instead, she sat on the porch facing the lane to Paradise Beach and ate her cheese and pickle spread sandwiches, while she pondered the events of the night before. Will he call me? . . . Am I a fool? . . . Will he help me find the laundered money? . . . Can I trust him? These were her thoughts *du jour*.

Tired of wading in the day's pool of confusion, when evening came she got up and went downstairs to join the nightly gathering at the big round table. A gold prospector from Guyana, a slight image of a man, always fidgeting, even in the heat of Barbados, asked her, "Where were you last night, Sugar? We missed you."

Lili shrugged and looked at a newlywed couple from Birmingham, England who spent almost as much time in their room as she had. The joke at the table was that their room rocked like a ship in a gale.

"I was in my room," Lili replied. "I didn't feel well last night."

"A pity," the gold prospector's return-to-nature looking girlfriend said. "A pity you don't get out more often. Look at you, you're so pale I could mistake you for a frangipani—a wilted one at that, I daresay."

One of the honeymooners looked at the other and said, "Spending time in your room is not all that bad." They both giggled.

"But alone, Honey, just think about it." The wife winked at her husband. "That would be no fun at all. Miss Kaleo, we're so glad you decided to come and join us."

In the midst of this interchange, Sea Cat showed up with drinks. The monkey jumped off his shoulder and claimed an errant nut off the floor. "You were alone last night, huh? I thought I heard footsteps on the porch at around midnight. It must have been a shadow." He winked at her, as he set down the drinks. "In fact I could have sworn I heard you talking with someone."

Lili blushed. "You're mistaken, Sea Cat. It must have been someone else." Her eyes pleaded for him to drop the subject, and he did.

The conversation, yes, that had taken place, a peck on the cheek, a handshake and a warm good-bye. But the intimacy, the invitation into her room, their togetherness into the wee hours—that had all been a fantasy, an interlude she had entertained only in the shadows of her mind.

* * *

A few days later Lili's spirits were buoyed by a call from the inspector requesting a meeting. All of a sudden Lili felt blissful—an unanticipated reaction to an unexpected event. There was a spring in her step and a wicker basket in her hand as she traipsed off to the nearby Convenience Mart. She couldn't get over the brightly colored money and how much she could acquire in exchange for U.S. Dollars—two Bajan dollars for every one U.S. The bread may have been marked four dollars but the funny yellow-and-brown pen-and-ink graphics on the thin white paper she handed the clerk didn't seem like money, well like Monopoly money maybe, but not like real money. The bills were noticeably smaller than she was used to. She laughed. "Here, take all you want." She dropped a few crumpled bills on the counter.

"I got you a job," a voice said from behind her. She got goose bumps down her arms and didn't have to look around to see who it was. She knew the voice belonged to Inspector Williams, the African Bajan policeman, the man who had ignited her torch when she had thought there was nothing combustible left inside her. The man who had continued to waltz with her and danced in her mind long after the music had stopped.

Lili turned to face him. "I don't need a job, thank you. Aunty Fay wired me money just this morning. I have more than enough to pay my expenses." She lied. In fact Aunty Fay had just told her that her funds had run out and the bank was threatening to repossess her Quonset hut. Lili didn't want to be in anyone's debt anyway. The two of them stopped and spoke by a white picnic table under a large sandbox tree.

"Oh, I think you'll want this job," the inspector said. "It's with the Bank of Barbados. Not the Grand Barbadian Bank you asked about, but if there's any money laundering being done on this island, and I'm not saying there is, that's where I would look for it. Besides, the two banks are in the process of merging."

"Why did you do this for me? I didn't expect—"

"You don't have to thank me. Let's just say I did it for international relations."

She very much wanted the job ventured her hand and put it on his chest. Beneath his breastplate she could feel the faint thump of his heart with her fingertips, under the smooth press of his everyday navy blue uniform. She suddenly noticed her hand and pulled it back as if she had been surprised to find it there. She did not feel the closeness they had had on the dance floor. He seemed more distant. *Maybe it's just that he's on duty.*

"When do I start?" she asked.

"A week from Tuesday," the inspector replied. "That's the first time they could fit you in, the beginning of a pay period. I had to pull some strings for you."

"But what about my visa? It expires in less than two weeks and says I'm not allowed to work while I'm here."

He handed her a new visa, one which allowed her to stay up to six months longer, but the conditions stamped on it by the immigration officials were still the same, "No work permitted while you are in this country."

"This is wonderful," Lili said. "*Mahalo.*" She could see that he did not understand. "That means 'thank you' in Hawaiian. But the stamp on the visa still says I can't work."

"Don't worry," the inspector said. "I won't tell anyone, if you don't."

Before she could respond to that notion, the inspector had his back to her and was heading for his car. Lili smiled as she noticed how much he had to scrunch down to fit his body into the tiny, milk carton of a police car. A Nissan.

Inspector Williams waved to her out the window but failed to look at her as they sped away. Instead he spoke with his companion, who drove the car. She started the long walk back to the hotel, struggling to sort through conflicting feelings of fear, want, need and confusion. Butterflies fluttered in her stomach.

* * *

During the ensuing week the inspector never called. Yet Lili's interest in him grew. But she entertained only the most paranoid of conclusions—became certain he was not interested in her romantically, or, worse yet, had a wife and six children. She could picture him mowing the lawn or playing cricket with his sons and gradually slipped back into the depths of melancholy. She longed for her son, Christian, despised the man, Charlie Owens, who had wrecked her life and feared she would not complete her investigation in time to free the frozen assets necessary to rescue her brother's house from foreclosure.

Then there was the matter of her reputation or what was left of it after her criminal trial. She had come to Barbados in an effort to restore it but, so far, there was no material progress.

A short robust woman, smartly dressed, always made up perfectly, who wore a straw hat, had arrived at the hotel a few days earlier on a cruise ship and managed to navigate through Lili's defenses and befriend her. This woman wore long black gloves, similar to ones Lili had a recollection of seeing on her mother as a child.

It was only as a result of Eliza's persistent door knocking and prodding that Lili engaged in conversation with her. The two of them sat at the table before the rest of the brigade returned from the day's activities at the beach and in Bridgetown to take their seats at the table. The Applebys had just left for Martinique's black sandy beaches for a few days before returning to France. Lili found herself saddened by their departure. They seemed to be not only an intriguing couple but a pair with genuine affection for one another. They gave every indication of enjoying the latter years of their lives together talking about their children while taking long postponed vacation days for travel and companionship. They had shown Lili the pictures they carried of their grandchildren so many times that she felt as though she knew them all and could certainly identify them by name. She envied their blissful state. "Do you have children?" Lili asked the new guest. Eliza tried to get her to sip some tea but all Lili would accept was a tall glass of ice water with lemon peel in it.

"Yes, as a matter of fact I do. I have two grown sons," Eliza said. "Both are in the British navy. One is down in the Falklands where they had that skirmish with the Argentineans and the other is in Antarctica on a scientific expedition. I don't get to see them as often as I'd like and I miss them something frightful."

Lili put her hand on top of Eliza's. "I miss my son, too," she said, as she gazed off into the distance toward the choppy, restless sea. Eliza continued to talk but Lili didn't hear her. She pictured her son making sand castles on the beach, knocking them down with his dump truck and giving her a big hug, his curly hair dangling in ringlets. He laughed without care. Then she saw his arms reaching out but she couldn't touch him. He became more and more unhappy and begged for his mother's help but she was powerless.

Eliza took Lili's hand into her palms. "Tell me about him."

"What?" Lili said, startled out of her stupor.

"Tell me about him—your son . . . That is if you feel like it."

Lili spoke as if she were in a trance. "His skin was always fair and soft. He grew weak and pale but his curls never lost their bounce—not even at the end."

Eliza did not speak so as not to obstruct the flow of words which had lessened to a trickle.

Lili's voice trailed in again, like a train struggling to climb a steep hill. "His skin was as fair as milk, and his eyes . . . His father was a *haole*."

Eliza looked puzzled.

"He was a white man," Lili explained. "That's what we call them in Hawaii."

"Where is your son? Is he here in Barbados?"

"He's dead," Lili said. "He's buried in the Kekaho Cemetery overlooking the Pacific on the island of Kaua'i."

"Kaua'i? How beautiful! Oh, but I'm so sorry to hear about your son." Eliza reached over and gave Lili a tug at the shoulders and pressed her head lightly with her forehead. Her touch drew out Lili's feelings like a salve lifting a splinter from its host. She wept and then her sadness gradually turned into anger.

"Christian was cursed from the start." Lili wiped her eyes with a napkin. "He was doomed. My little boy, my darling little boy never had a chance." Her voice echoed the emptiness that had been her constant companion since the day her son died.

Eliza took Lili's hands and lifted her from her chair. She led her over to the porch swing where she could put her arm around her while they spoke.

"How did it happen? What happened to your son, Christian? Christian, was that his name?"

Lili nodded. "It was awful. It took months for him to die. I kept going to the hospital whenever I was allowed. I sat with him during every waking moment but it was no use. I couldn't— "

The porch swing creaked in mourning, as the two women swung slowly from the almost imperceptible nudge of Eliza's foot. A light breeze softened the oppressive heat of midday. "I was told by the doctors he had an allergy to dogs, and he did—but he also had cystic fibrosis."

Eliza shuddered.

"It was an awful death. His lungs became more and more clogged and he couldn't breathe. There was nothing I could do to help him except to hold his hand and watch him slip away." Lili's voice trailed off to a tiny whisper. She cast her eyes to the cement floor of the patio. "Slipped away from me all the while," she said in a voice that was so faint Eliza had to sit up and lean forward to hear her.

Eliza handed Lili another napkin and she dried her eyes. It chafed her raw skin. "All I could do was sit beside him and hold his hand and brush his hair out of his eyes and watch it happen. I felt helpless and now I feel so empty I could die."

Just as Lili said this Eliza Terwilliger's husband and two boarders appeared, chattering like grackles as they climbed the steps to the porch and sat on their chairs at the big round table only casually aware of Lili and Eliza. Lili seized the opportunity provided by the air of confusion to retreat to her room.

As she left Sea Cat appeared with Jack on his shoulder. The monkey jumped onto the latticework of the porch and stared quietly from his perch. He shelled a nut and popped it into his mouth by tossing it into the air with his foot.

* * *

By the time Lili reported for work on the Tuesday after the annual Crop Over Festival she had furthered her notions about the inspector to the effect that he must not only be a married man but have at least two or three mistresses on the side.

At the visceral level she longed for a new relationship with its hopes and dreams and yet she feared it. She craved intimacy but was well aware of the cutting edge of its pinions. One thing she understood all too well was that her judgment, always suspect where men were concerned, reached its lowest ebb in times of need, stress or trauma.

Lili's new boss at the bank, Miss Cumberbatch in bookkeeping, seemed confrontational right from the start. "You get fifteen minutes in the morning and you get fifteen minutes in the afternoon for a coffee break and that's what you get, girl. Don't let me catch you sitting on the toilet for another fifteen minutes. If you've got the runs you'll just have to give up your coffee. It's up to you, girl. That's all I can say. If you want to keep this job you must follow bank policy at all times."

Lili felt like a piece of government certified beef. All that was missing was an official stamp like the one on her passport and visa. The bank itself, however, was as clean and tidy as any place on the island. And she did enjoy her desk by the window. She could occasionally glance out at the passersby busily going about their day-to-day business or shopping at one of the crowded shops on one of the narrow, congested streets in the bustling center of Bridgetown. There was no air conditioning, which suited her all the more, because she could raise the small window slightly to let in a fresh tropical breeze and hear the buses and cars honking and droning through town. Occasionally the smell of partially burned gasoline and diesel fuel would annoy her and she had to close the window. At such times she found the heat stifling.

As a condition of issuing a favorable opinion letter allowing the merger with the Grand Barbadian Bank to go forward the auditors employed by the Central Bank of Barbados had issued a requirement to the Bank of Barbados. It insisted they improve their internal audit controls, especially on foreign transactions, and find someone within the bank to cross-check randomly selected transaction detail between 1990 and 1994 to see that each of them would have passed scrutiny, had the new standards been in effect at that time.

They wanted to be sure there were no hidden partnerships, joint ventures or transactions the bank was not disclosing on its financial statements.

As a result reams of computer runs and bales of "chits" were delivered to Lili's desk. Then when her desk overflowed, they were set on the floor beside her. Some of the chits were so old that the paper had become brittle and begun to turn yellow. Many had faded to the point where they were illegible.

What a drudge. They must not have checked the answers to that math test they gave me on the day I was hired. Undaunted, she dug in. If there were a better opportunity to find laundered money she couldn't imagine what it might be. In many ways it seemed a godsend. In others, when she stood back and looked at the reams of paper stacked precariously in all directions, it seemed as if she were at the brink of an avalanche. But unlike snow, the paper wouldn't melt. The work was tedious and in some respects incomprehensible but she set her mind to doing it, no matter what. All she had to do to stay motivated was to visualize her brother, Mimo, and his family's home being sold on the courthouse steps. She saw the court appointed commissioner for the bank placing his furniture on the street.

Her problems were compounded by the fact that through the little bit of accounting she had had to learn to discharge her duties as mayor of Kaua'i she had learned that debits were a good thing and credits were charges against your account. Here at the bank everything was the exact opposite. It seemed like everything was backwards in this country—debits were reversed from the credits and the cars were all driven on the wrong side of the road.

Lili's frustration was in contrast to her co-workers who composed a collage of cheerful faces flurrying around the office chittering and chattering to one another like blackbirds. To hear them one might have assumed they actually enjoyed working for the bank. Lili later discovered it was not her skill and facility with numbers but her lack of it that made her the perfect candidate for the job. This was ironic because the auditors directed that the bank was to select its most proficient accountant for the task. That was an express condition of the parliamentary resolution which approved the merger.

A young mulatto man came by from time to time to see how she was doing. He usually wore blue jeans and a tie-dyed shirt with a scarf knotted around his neck. His name was Ephraim Whitney. Ephraim had impeccably manicured nails, perfectly groomed dreadlocks but never allowed them to spill out from under his neat and bobbie-pinned yarn cap that he seldom took off. He was a flaming, banner carrying homosexual with a voracious appetite for generously endowed and precocious looking men. His voice was approximately two octaves higher than Lili's and very shrill.

When she asked him about her friend, the inspector, he said, "Now, Sugar, that man is hung, I'll tell you that. You can just tell from the way he carries himself. Why his bamboo and coconuts are so big, he has to walk bowlegged." It made Lili uncomfortable to be having this discussion with a man, any man, so she tried to change the subject.

"He's been very kind to me. Helped me find this job."

"Hung, sister. I tell you the man is hung. Don't tell me you haven't noticed."

I noticed, but that doesn't mean I want to discuss it. The notion of being intimate with the inspector aroused her but she forced herself to keep a nonchalant expression.

Ephraim was considerate of Lili. Her difficulties and whatever skill she lacked in accounting, he more than made up for. He hadn't been assigned to help her and was scolded whenever Miss Cumberbatch noticed he was neglecting his own duties in favor of assisting her. He gave her some idea as to the implications of the task and how to approach it. Until then no one really had. Miss Cumberbatch had barely said anything more than, "Here, Miss Kaleo. Make sure these transactions are in order."

Lili and Ephraim often had lunch together at a little restaurant on the boardwalk near their work, called The Waterfront Café. They shared fish cakes and critiqued the attire of the many tourists who passed by their table or walked across the nearby swing bridge or on the boardwalk on the other side of the Constitution River, which wasn't a river at all, but a narrow channel emerging from the ocean. Lili found it a safe arrangement. Men who saw them together usually assumed they were a couple and left her alone which was just how she wanted things to remain, except, perhaps, for the inspector. She couldn't get him out of her mind.

"Why did you come here?" Ephraim asked at lunch one day. "What in the world are you doing working for this institution? There are a lot better opportunities on this island for an intelligent, attractive woman like you."

Lili said, "I need the money. It was the only job I could find. Besides I don't have a proper work visa and they just seemed to overlook it."

Ephraim looked at her askance. "Don't be naïve, Sugar. Nothing ever happens by chance at the Bank of Barbados."

* * *

After many unfulfilling days at work with her piles of paper Lili looked forward to returning to The Tower each evening and joining the conversation at the big round table. The subject often drifted to sex, especially when the guests were intoxicated, and the talk turned bawdy. When it did Lili excused herself and went back to her room in the main building. But this night she was in a lighthearted mood. She had just gotten her first fifty-cent-an-hour (twenty five cents—U.S.) raise and was giddy over it. It made her feel as though her math dragons had been slain.

When Lili sat down Billy Bob Arnold, a truck driver from Tennessee, was just finishing his rendition of the funniest sexual escapade he had ever witnessed.

"Well, there's this old fart with his pants off, out in the corn field with his mistress, tryin' to outrun her husband's blazin' shotgun, and what happens when he gets to the edge of the field and tries to escape in his car? He sees his wife drivin' off with his pants wavin' like a flag from the antenna."

The guests roared.

"And he's still picking buckshot out of his ass!"

More laughter.

Lili thought this was more sad than funny. She kept thinking about how the man's poor wife must've felt. But she liked Billie Bob and his wife, Sarah Mae, who had also shared more pleasing reflections, such as hiking through the Smoky Mountains with damp fall leaves and crackling branches underfoot, in a way that made Lili long to see them. So she decided to stay. Yet her thoughts drifted as Billie Bob rehashed the story for a third time before yielding the floor to someone else.

By now Lili's thoughts were on her own humorous, sexual experience—although she hadn't seen it as such on the night after her trial. She had invited her lawyer, Izzy Kawamoto, over to have a glass of Sake with the expectation that when the meal was over, dessert would be served in the bedroom. Her desire for him wasn't lustful— as it had been the first time she was with Charlie Owens, the man she had married in such haste. Instead it was a relationship that had stood the test of time and been building, first as a friendship, then with a hint of romance and fomented for many years.

In searching for love, loyalty and companionship Lili had looked everywhere it seemed but right by her side. Izzy had been a lifelong champion of her causes and, if there were a kinder, more considerate, truer friend in the world, she hadn't met him. One thing she was sure of— Izzy deserved the best she had to offer.

She set about lighting candles and incense while Izzy got undressed. By the time he returned their scent permeated the room while the flames flickered against the tapestry that adorned her bedroom. Fondly and with tender affection, she slipped her naked body between a pair of ivory satin sheets she had hurriedly purchased at Liberty House at The Kukui Grove Shopping Center on her way home from the trial just for this occasion.

Izzy returned in his Hapi jacket and by looking beneath its hem she could see at a glance that he was indeed happy. She felt herself becoming eager at the prospect of their togetherness and lifted the sheet for him. Izzy removed his jacket, folded it and lay it on a nearby chair—so Izzy-like. "This has been a long time coming," he said.

"Let's not rush it," she replied. "I want to enjoy every minute of this."

They shared a tender kiss.

Is this the man of my dreams? The very man who's been at my side all along? It's hard to believe.

She lay beside him and stroked his face with her fingertips, brushing his hair out of his eyes. He hesitantly put his hand on her breast and she clasped her hand over his to let him know it was all right. Izzy talked about the trial and she changed the subject. It seemed too much like business and they had shared enough of that over the past several months.

After an extended period of talking and caressing she pulled him on top of her and kissed him with a passion that said she intended to purge, once and for all, the sisterly way in which she had previously viewed him. He inched closer and lunged toward her. He missed.

She laughed and reached down to guide him. But just as she located his protrusion the phone rang.

She shook her head "no" and tugged for him to continue.

Instead he raised himself to his knees.

"Izzy, don't be silly. I'm not going to answer it."

"You have to," he said.

She fondled him; tried to take his mind off the phone. "Why on earth do I have to answer it? I've said everything to the reporters I'm going to say—for today anyhow."

"But, you have to," Izzy repeated. In spite of her touch he had lost his intensity.

If this isn't just like him.

"What if it's about Christian?" He said. Lili had left him in the care of her sister-in-law, Ruth, and her brother, Mimo.

She reached for the phone but just as her fingertips touched the cradle it stopped ringing.

They looked at it and then at one another. They laughed. She arched her back and eagerly pulled him towards her.

The phone rang again.

This time Izzy reached over and grabbed it. He held his hand over the mouthpiece and looked at her for instruction.

"All right. All right. . . . And then I'm taking it off the hook." She said.

"Maybe it's the governor calling to congratulate you," he joked, as he handed her the phone.

She took it, said "aloha," then listened. "Here. It's for you. It's your sister." She handed him back the phone.

His sister, her best friend, Suzie, spoke with such animation that Lili could hear her voice while Izzy held the phone away from his ear.

"Izzy, Izzy, I got the strangest call tonight. It was from Kiku. She said to tell you she's returning from Japan."

"What? Did she forget something? I shipped her the rest of her grandmother's china two days ago. That should be the last of her belongings."

"She said she needs you and wants you. She said she misses you. She even said that she's been stupid and immature and she's going to catch the next eastbound flight out of Tokyo."

Izzy didn't answer. "Izzy, Izzy, did you hear what I just—" He slowly put the phone back on the hook while his sister was still talking.

As he turned to his friend and prospective lover, Lili's face drooped with the realization that their lovemaking was over.

Of course he would graciously accept his wife's return as though she had never left. To do otherwise would be a disgrace—not just to him, but to the entire Kawamoto family. True, Kiku had returned to Japan, but only to "visit her parents to have a few last moments together before settling in America." That was the official version they told their public. But between the two of them it was "a trial separation—to see how we really feel about one another." Lili had known the verdict this time with no need to poll the jury.

She excused herself from the big round table and retreated to her room. A tear slid silently down her cheek.

Chapter Three

The next day at work when Lili took her lunch break, Inspector Williams was waiting for her at the bottom of the stairs.

"Inspector, to what do I owe the pleasure of your company? Am I under arrest?" He looked so striking in his freshly pressed uniform that she had a hard time not staring at him.

"Only if you don't agree to have lunch with me," he said. His voice reverberated, even against the street traffic.

She held out her wrists. "Then you'd better put the cuffs on me."

"A little S & M?"

"Don't flatter yourself, Inspector. I'm real fussy about whom I get kinky with but I did think you might call me. I mean about the money laundering and all."

"I'm sorry. I haven't had time. I wanted to get together with you socially, as well. But I've been working on an investigation that's been keeping me busy day and night."

"And out of trouble?" she asked.

"I'm always looking to stay out of trouble, Miss Kaleo." He looked pleased with himself and adjusted his sunglasses.

The weather was sunny and warm with a light breeze, as it had been every day for the past several weeks. Cars were honking at one another and frantically jockeying for position to get that one free parking spot on the street that everyone was after.

Next to him, she glided up the street toward The Nelson Arms, on the second floor of the Galleria Mall, far removed from the bustle of tourists, matching his lengthy stride step for step. When they entered through the jewelry store below Lili could tell that all eyes were on her and then the inspector and then the inspector and then her—looks alternating between frowns and raised eyebrows for her, broad, alluring smiles and glances for her companion.

"Hi, Lance," one woman said with a voice as syrupy as a whorehouse madam.

"Hello, Inspector," said another from behind her cache of golden rings and bracelets.

"Do you want to come over here and see what I've got?" said another, brandishing an array of gold watches and emerald bracelets, as well as a tight fitting lung-revealing bodice.

They were like piranha feeding off a chunk of beef.

"No, I'll have to see what you've got another time, Deirdre," the inspector said, just before they opened the door which lead to the stairs and the restaurant.

As they entered the Nelson Arms, Inspector Williams looked at an elderly woman holding a tray of dishes near the entry way and said, "You're lookin' real sweet today, Gladys."

The woman blushed.

He leaned over and put his hand on her shoulder and spoke into her ear in a firm steady tone, "You're gettin' *real tight* in your skin!"

The woman's arms shook so hard Lili thought she was going to drop her serving tray.

"Inspector Williams, you're surely nasty—teasin' an ole, worn-out woman like me!"

Without asking Lili what she wanted, the inspector said, "Still got de pepperpot dey? Ain't it jus' ready now? You busy this Friday?"

The woman nodded and said, "You get outta here, Inspector. Go work your charms on some of those young ladies downstairs. They'd know what to do with you. You quit teasin' an ole woman, like me."

After that the two of them spoke so fast that Lili could no longer follow the conversation. The inspector explained that it was Bajan Dialect—a language incomprehensible to Lili, even after a lifelong exposure to Pidgin back in Hawaii. Hawaiian Pidgin was based on English—and while the inspector made the same claim about their local parlance—she failed to detect enough similarity between the two to believe they shared a common dictionary. An impression that wasn't helped by the speed of their conversation.

Soon they had before them—at a counter on a cute little porch facing and overlooking the street below—a stew, laden with various meats and spices. After one bite Lili fell into a coughing fit, then inhaled half a glass of water. When she finished the water, she resumed coughing and the inspector slapped her on the back. "Are you all right, Lili? Are you okay?"

"Don't hit me," she yelled. She slapped him on the chest with her open hands. "Don't you ever hit me."

The inspector held up his arms to protect his body. "Whoa," he said. "I'm sorry. I'm sorry. Are you okay?"

Lili said, "I'm the one who should be sorry. I reacted without thinking. I do that occasionally. It has to do with . . ." she paused. "It has to do with my childhood. I'd rather not talk about it."

The inspector tried to make light of the situation although it was obvious that he could see there was much more underlying her reaction than she was willing to discuss. "I should have warned you about the stew. It's real spicy. That's why we call it 'pepperpot.' It's an old Arawak recipe. Lovely, huh?"

"Did you say lovely or lively? I think it's on fire! The Arawaks must have had stainless steel throats."

"No, I think they were porcelain," the inspector said. "Stainless steel hadn't been invented when the Arawaks were around."

They watched the street traffic and bustling tourists below as they spoke. Lili had noticed that most of the locals shopped on a parallel street about a block away. The traffic was bumper to bumper in every direction. Gas fumes. Honking. Sidewalks crowded with pedestrians.

"Did that woman downstairs call you 'Lance?' Is that a pet name or something?"

"Actually it's a name I got in secondary school. Most people in Barbados don't use their proper names.

They're nicknamed, usually for some event that happened in their childhood and it sticks with 'em for life."

"How did you get yours? Were you a gladiator?"

"I was a promising young cricketer at one time. If I had ever been a really great cricket player, then I might have been knighted. The kids nicknamed me "Sir Lancelot." Over time they dropped the 'Sir' and the 'lot,' and now I'm just plain old 'Lance.'"

"Were you really that good?"

Lili did her best to keep up with Lance's devouring of his pepperpot but it was hopeless. His was almost gone already and she was only able to pick at hers and then had to chase down each bite with a full glass of water. The waitress had a hard time keeping her glass full and finally left the pitcher of water on the table.

Lance replied, "There have been three great cricket players in Barbados whose names start with the letter W—Everton Weekes, Clyde Walcott, and Frank Worrell. I was supposed to be the fourth "W" —Austin Clyde 'Lance' Williams."

"What happened? Do you still play?" As Lili asked this she didn't look directly at Lance. She looked at the crowd below—tourists, workers on lunch break, a few beggars. A couple asking for directions.

"I got hit in the head," he answered.

At first she thought he must be kidding. She laughed. Then she could see the severity of his expression and regretted she had made light of it. "Oops! I'm sorry. I didn't know—"

"The doctors said I shouldn't play anymore. I was playing in my first professional game and after my first time at the wicket I had over two tons of runs— "

"Four thousand?"

Lance laughed. "No, two-hundred-fourteen to be exact. In cricket we refer to a hundred as a ton."

"Huh?"

"I know it sounds weird, but that's how we count our runs—a ton actually means a hundred."

"Is that good?"

"Let me put it this way. Sir Garfield Sobers got three-hundred-sixty-five in one match and that record stood for years. I had one more turn at the wicket and everyone could sense I was on top of my game that day—my first professional match!"

"Did you get the record?"

"No, I was usually a bowler— "

"A what?"

"That's the guy who throws the ball to the batsman. I think you call him a pitcher."

Lili smiled nervously. "Yes. I know what a pitcher is." She picked at her food.

"But they didn't want me to get too tired because I was a fast bowler."

"I'm lost," Lili said as she lifted one of the many bones from the pepperpot and nibbled around the edges. She was eager to hear all the details but didn't want to let Lance know how interested she really was. She wanted to downplay his celebrity. "I don't understand. Why is it you can't play anymore?"

"I got hit by the ball. I was playing at short leg and my teammates and I were so excited that I had gotten all those runs. They never did get me out. I was in after the other ten men were out and that meant I couldn't bat anymore.

"My teammates and I celebrated so hard that night that when it was time for us to take the field the next day I couldn't find my helmet and I had no time to look for it. So I just figured the way things were going I'd be okay."

"And . . . "

"And second ball, I got hit in the head."

"But lots of people get hit in the head in baseball and they keep playing."

"Well the ball is extremely hard and comes at a fantastic rate. I was out cold for about thirty minutes and they had to carry me off the field and I woke up in Queen Elizabeth Hospital being prepped for a brain scan. The doctor said I could keep playing and never have a problem, or . . . " Lance stopped talking.

"Or?"

"Or I could get hit in the head again, even with my helmet on, and a ball that might just hurt someone else could kill me. I get dizzy sometimes, often for no reason and that makes me leery of heights. The doctor said I could black out but I never have, and other than that I don't have any symptoms."

Lili refrained from making light of it this time. She could see Lance was suffering just by telling the story.

He continued, "I would have done it . . . Kept on playing, I mean cricket was my life. But the doctor recommended and the team and the league insisted that I quit."

"Just like that and it was over?"

"Just like that. One day you're a hero in your prime with an incredible future and the next day it's over."

Lili said, "I know that story. Believe me, I know that one all right."

The waitress brought some pone. Lili was hesitant to take a bite at first, especially because it was so warm. She snipped a little bit off the edge and tasted how sweet and moist it was. *Yum! Now this is something I could develop a taste for.*

Inspector Williams took a sip of his tea and said, "Have you learned anything, since you've been at the bank?"

"You mean about money laundering?"

Lance stuffed a napkin into his collar and leaned over his plate so as not to get any of the creamy rum sauce on his uniform. He nodded in agreement.

Lili said, "Are you kidding? When I can understand the dialect in the office, which isn't often, it's usually about someone getting married, someone's child being sick or someone getting one of those seven-sided coins with the fish on it stuck in the coffee machine. But not much about money laundering—in fact, nothing at all."

Lance commented on the sauce. "Mmm! Mmm! Just like my mummy used to make."

"Do you mean your mother?" Lili asked.

Lance nodded. "Yes, that's how we say it in Barbados, 'Mummy.'"

"What is your Mummy like? Tell me about your family."

Lance abruptly stopped his teacup halfway between the counter and his lips, put it down, grabbed the check and got up. He continued to speak as he headed toward the cash register near the front entrance. He looked back at her over his shoulder. "I'd like to, but I've got to be getting back to the station. I just got paged. I hate to run out on you like this."

"Don't worry. I'm used to it," Lili mumbled in a voice too soft for anyone to hear.

The inspector came back after paying the check, leaned over behind her and whispered in her ear, "In about a week you're going to be called into Miss Cumberbatch's office. She's going to offer you a job in the executive suite in the big blue building at the end of Broad Street as personal assistant to Winston Baker. He's in charge of international banking. If there's any chicanery going on at the Bank of Barbados, he knows about it. You can bet on that. Whether or not he's involved, if there is any, is anyone's guess."

"How did you—"

Lili turned around to speak but the inspector was gone. She might have wanted to delay the promotion. She thought she had found some discrepancies in the accounts that she had planned to ask Ephraim to check out for her. But then again she was sure they would turn out to be nothing. It would be a relief to get away from those mountains of paper. She had intended to discuss this with the inspector but now he was gone.

A few seconds later Lili saw him speed past on the street below in a squad car with the emergency lights flashing and sirens blaring, once again being driven by one of his aides.

As she passed the cashier the elderly Bajan woman Lance had teased on the way in said, "How do you know Inspector Williams?" The woman looked at her like a camera panning slowly from the top of her head to the tip of her toes and then back again.

"He's a friend," Lili replied and continued towards the door.

"You're lucky," the elderly woman said.

Lili turned back towards the woman. "Why's that?"

"There's lots of women who would like to be *his* friend."

* * *

If she hadn't known ahead of time Lili would have thought she was being fired when her supervisor, Miss Cumberbatch, called her into her office. As it was the stern look on Miss Cumberbatch's face was foreboding enough to make her wonder if her information from Lance was correct.

Miss Cumberbatch said, "I have no idea who's pulling strings for you around here, Miss Kaleo. If I had my way you'd be fired. You've been working here for nearly three months and haven't brought a single discrepancy of any consequence to my attention—only minor mathematical and transposition errors. With the volume of records you were supposed to check we'd expect you to find at least two or three entries per week that required correction."

Only two or three? There could have been fifty and I would never have known the difference.

"If they'd listened to me you'd have been long gone weeks ago. Instead, starting Monday, you'll be working on the fifth floor in the executive suite with Mr. Baker," Miss Cumberbatch said without making eye contact. "Mrs. Musgrave will be showing you your duties. Her husband works for the British Embassy and is being called to a new post. You'll be Mr. Baker's new executive secretary. Why they chose you I have no idea."

Thanks for the vote of confidence.

Chapter Four

In theory at least Lili had sufficient income now to afford her own apartment but she chose to stay on at The Tower because she needed to funnel money to her brother, Mimo, to forestall the foreclosure proceedings on his home. Aunty Fay could not help him out, as she had once or twice in the past, because she was also in dire financial straits and was very much in need of a stipend to keep her afloat. After giving up that new dress she'd wanted for the third straight month and rallying to those two causes, Lili was left, with not enough funds to meet her basic living expenses. It couldn't go on like this forever. She was accumulating more and more credit card debt and in time she knew she would inevitably sink into its insidious grip.

But she wasn't sad about having to stay on at the hotel because once she overcame her initial reluctance she enjoyed the people she came to meet. She especially liked Sea Cat and Jack, the "minkee," and looked forward to conversation with the boarders—usually merchant marines, gold and emerald prospectors from South America, computer consultants or tourists. She was free to interact with them at whatever level she chose with no long-term consequences. With some she shared her deepest and most intimate secrets. With others she chose to keep her distance and exchange only the pleasantries *du jour*.

One Sunday afternoon she was sitting on her front porch by herself. It faced the swimming pool to the front and the parking lot to the side. She stitched quilt panels, an undertaking that lifted her spirits and, in a sense, returned her to happy memories of time she had spent as a teenager with Aunty Fay. Every time she jabbed herself with the needle she thought of Aunty Fay's thick calloused fingers and the loving touch of her firm, strong fingertips across her cheek.

The day was balmy and bright. There had been a few brief morning squalls but now sunshine was out in abundance. There had been a prior task that had taken her away from The Tower. Having finished it at no small exertion, she had a sense of accomplishment and celebrated by stopping at the old St. Mary's Church in Bridgetown and strolling through the cemetery. For some reason, maybe it was the loss of many of her own family members before their time, she found solace and comfort in observing the names and dates on the gravestones.

After she returned to The Tower she heard the revving of an engine and looked over the wooden railing on her front porch. Down the cement steps at the curb was a man sitting in a yellow Porsche—a man with a broad smile on his face, and a pair of mirror reflective sunglasses over his nose—a handsome-looking African Bajan man—the inspector.

She put down her quilting and leaned over the railing. "Is that you, Inspector?" she called.

He revved the engine. She was a sucker for fancy, powerful cars and the men who drove them.

"It's me all right," he yelled above the noise of his engine. "Grab your things. I'm taking you on a picnic."

She tried to suppress her desire to go with him. "Oh no you don't. I don't think I should mix business with pleasure again." She stepped back and touched her French door as if she were about to close it.

"Purely platonic," he yelled.

She thought she would feel relief at such a remark but it depressed her.

"C'mon," he said. "I won't bite." He reached onto the back seat and lifted a picnic basket to show her. "C'mon. It'll do you good to forget about your worries for an afternoon."

"Oh, all right," she said at last. "Wait 'til I grab my things."

On the way down the stairs from her room—carrying her light green sweater and her purse, she saw Sea Cat. He stepped in front of her to block her passage. "I know where you're going," he said. "The inspector already has more hens in his flock than he can preen, if you know what I mean. Let them have him, Lili. He's going to bring you nothing but pain. I don't want to see you hurt."

She sidestepped him, as well as the issue. "I can't help it," she said as she flung open the screen door on the way to Lance's convertible. "He says I'm special."

The engine cried out as they tooled up the Spring Garden Highway toward Holetown and cut across country toward Cherry Tree Hill. Lili knew where they were going from the signs and from the general direction in which they were traveling but she had never seen this part of the island. Aside from the chattel houses, the roaring buses and pedestrians walking along the side of the road, it reminded her in many ways of her native Kaua'i.

"I wish I'd brought a scarf," she hollered above the roar of the engine as the inspector sped up a hill and around a curve.

He seemed interested in her comment but didn't appear to be able to hear her.

She yelled louder. "I don't suppose you're afraid of being stopped for a traffic violation?"

He stretched his arms against the steering wheel, looked at her, shook his head and smiled. He downshifted and the car slowed. "If I get stopped there's an even 'chonce' it'll be by one of my cousins and if it isn't, there'll be an even greater 'chonce' I'll outrank him."

She loved the way he articulated the word "chance." She assumed it was a centuries old brew, resulting from the mingling of Bajan and British accents, rather than a peculiarity of Lance's. *There's something so dignified and proper about the way Lance talks. He could tell me I just stepped in horseshit and it would sound like clover.*

She wondered why this man spellbound her, often in the face of her better judgment. She longed for his touch. She considered his self-assuredness, his roughly hewn features, the safe, protected feeling she had when she sat in the car next to his agile, trim, muscular body. Then there was the reality that he was black. She had never been on what you might call a date with a black man before. She wondered where the road and the day would lead.

Suddenly the chattel houses stopped crowding the tiny lane and vast fields of sugarcane came into view on both sides of the car. Lance, who she already thought was driving much too fast, shifted gears, worked the clutch and sped up.

The sugarcane made her feel at home. They drove on, often at what she considered breakneck speeds, winding and turning over ever smaller roads—so patched and so bumpy that it was hard to believe there had once been a smooth section of pavement beneath them.

The car slowed to a crawl on a narrow country lane in the middle of nowhere with nothing to commend it but a few scrawny trees, nearby cane fields and the Atlantic Ocean in the distance. *I wonder why he's stopping.* She flashed on an experience she had once had of a man putting his hand on her teenage knee and remembered outrunning him and hiding in the sugarcane, like Br'er Rabbit. *I'll just tell him "no." I can handle this.* At a deeper level she had conflicting feelings that she might welcome such an advance.

The car stopped. Her palms grew sweaty. He downshifted into neutral, set the parking brake and got out of the car.

Here it comes.

"C'mon," he said. "It's time to get out."

"What for?" she said with a chord of reluctance.

"C'mon. I told you this would be platonic. Now get out of the car. We'll have some fun."

There went her mood again—from resentful hesitation to disappointment. She did as he said.

"Do you know what obeah is?" Lance asked.

"I don't have the faintest idea."

"Haven't you read about it in school or in a magazine?"

"Nope, never heard of it."

"It's sort of like voodoo, like they have in Haiti."

"Yes, I've heard of that. I've heard of voodoo."

They were standing behind the car on a steep incline. "Stand over there, off the road underneath the tree."

"What's wrong with staying here?"

"Do you want the car to roll backwards and hit you? I'm going to release the parking brake."

What an idiot. Too bad, too. "That's a fine piece of machinery—as my old friend Izzy used to say, but if—. "

He leaned over the side of the convertible and released the parking brake. Lili expected the car to coast rapidly downhill and could picture the two of them chasing after it, looking like a couple of idiots. Instead it moved very slowly, not downhill, but uphill. Her chin dropped. Not only did it move up the hill but it began to gather speed.

He stood behind the car. "Abra ka dabra; ala kazaam." He waved his arms and fluttered his long fingers as he spoke, as if he were casting a spell. She enjoyed watching the grace and motion of his large hands. *I'll bet Lance can palm a basketball. . . ., maybe even a medicine ball.* "Climb the hill oh, mighty magic car—shazaam, shazaam." There was no way to explain the ascent of the car. Lili was dumbfounded.

"Ala Kazaam," he said. Then just as the car was reaching the top of the knoll he clapped his hands and yelled. "Halt!" The car stopped.

"'C'mon," he said and waved his arm for Lili to follow.

They ran to the car and jumped in without opening the doors. He turned the key, ignited the smooth, purring sound of his Porsche 356 C, steadily accelerated and they sped away towards Bathsheba.

"How did you do that?" She asked.

Lance grinned. "You may think it's the words," he said, "but it's all in the fingertips." He took his hands off the steering wheel and rubbed the tips of his fingers with his thumbs.

Lili shook her head in amazement.

* * *

By the time they got to the ocean Lili was ready for lunch. She had skipped breakfast as a sort of Sunday morning ritual. She wasn't sure it brought her any closer to her Creator, but it helped her get in touch with her more spiritual side—the side that didn't depend on bread for sustenance. Exhilarating. Yet it left her hungry.

And while the mystery of the climbing car left her feeling unsettled she was finding herself drawn more and more under the spell of the man she was with, be it obeah, voodoo or simply his charm and politeness. For a man of his agility and strength he seemed remarkably gentle.

And to her vexation he seemed to be a man of his word. When they stopped near Bathsheba they got out of the car and walked along a path under a spreading canopy of sea grapes to a circular cement bench. It was perfectly cylindrical and looked like an upside down mushroom perched high above the rugged coastline overlooking the choppy waters below. They sampled the contents of the picnic basket—flaky, melt in your mouth fried chicken with a hint of garlic, delectable biscuits so tender and buttery she thought she must allow them to remain stuck to the roof of her mouth forever. Tamarind. Salted fish cakes. Fresh grapefruit and orange slices. And best of all, more of that delicious pone with rum sauce for dessert.

"Did you fix any of this yourself?" She asked.

"I did it all myself," he said. "My Mummy always said a man was good for nothing who didn't at least know *how* to cook."

Lili reflected for a moment on how this philosophy, extended broadly, might have changed the course of world history.

"C'mon, you didn't prepare this yourself. Who did?"

"Shite, girl. I did,*"* he insisted. "I can handle myself good in de kitchen you know."

It was delicious and Lili ate everything but the bones. She didn't realize how ravenous she was.

Afterwards they drove beside a stretch of beach that went unbroken for many miles. On the other side of the road she saw what she thought were goats—but Lance said they were really black belly sheep—wandering among funny shaped rocks that had eroded centuries ago when the ocean had reached that level. They looked more like toadstools or mushrooms.

Lili's hair waved carelessly in the wind. They pulled off the road and parked in a tiny spot, just large enough for the Porsche. After they got out of the car he took her by the hand and they walked a short distance to a rivulet which meandered from the nearby hillsides towards the ocean.

He turned his back after she pulled her swimsuit out of her purse and changed into it in the car. She felt at ease with him but experienced a subliminal tension. She longed for intimacy but feared it as well. *This is a good man. Or is that just what I want to believe?*

Their conversation was smooth and flowing. No hesitation. No painful pauses. No loss for words. They talked about Lili's banking career which had gone nowhere, about Miss Cumberbatch, who was obviously going nowhere, and about Lili's pay raise and Lance's car and how much he enjoyed it. About Barbados and how beautiful it was, how calm and peaceful were its inhabitants and how much they both enjoyed reggae and calypso and couldn't agree on which was better.

"Jazz," he said. "Now that's my favorite. And Arturo Tappin's Java album—an ascension to heaven."

The waves crashed against the nearby shoreline as they spoke. The pool they were swimming in was cold but it was a hot day and the contrast made Lili feel exhilarated. When the waves hit the nearby rocks they sprayed into the sky, higher and higher, as if they had been shot from a geyser—similar to the black lava blowholes in Hawaii. She wondered if these islands were coral or volcanic.

Lance told her that while all of the other Caribbean islands were volcanic this particular one was coral. "That's why the roads are so rough," he said. "Once the pavement wears off you get down to that crumbling rock."

Lili said, "Tell me about your family." She expected him to evade the question again.

"Well, I already told you my father was a legendary traffic cop and my brother, at the age of forty-two, is already a deputy superintendent. One of my great great- . . . grandparents was a corporal in the West India Regiment. I come from a family of eleven children. My father is retired and he and my mother live down by the Morgan Lewis Mill. They grow peppers and make hot sauce for extra income. Dad collects his police pension and he and Mummy rock on the porch most days—nothing exciting going on there. My father thinks he's going to get rich with the hot pepper sauce he makes. It's a secret recipe—the closest thing we have to spice—or jet fuel for that matter—here in Barbados."

"Hotter than the pepperpot we ate at The Nelson Arms?"

Lance didn't answer in words. He flared his nostrils so that Lili could picture the fire snorting out of his nose. "It's good, too, and not many people make it anymore. One of those lost arts that dies out with so called 'progress.'"

"And the rest of your family?"

"Most of my brothers and sisters still live on the island although I had one brother move to Jamaica, one sister to Canada and another brother went all the way to England. From what I understand he does something for the queen. We keep joking that he's just a glorified butler but he insists there's a lot more to it than that. If any of us had the money or inclination, I guess we'd go find out for ourselves.

"One of my sisters is married to a minister, two others work at hotels—one at The Paradise, just down the lane from you. Another is married to an auto repairman. Are you keeping track of all this?"

Lili shook her head, "No." She felt hopelessly lost in the details.

"Well, you get the drift. Nothing out of the ordinary except for me and my brother, Wendell. His precinct is in St. Peter, more specifically Speightstown. I have about fifteen cousins who work for the force but it's only me and my brother in uniform out of our immediate family."

Lili continued, "And what about you? Do you have a family of your own or just a trail of broken hearted sweethearts?"

Lance looked at her and said, "C'mon, let's go see for ourselves." He held out his hand to help her out of the shallow pool.

"What?" she said.

"You heard me. I'm going to take you to meet my family."

Lili suddenly felt queasy. Her knees were unsteady. *Is he married? Does he have a house full of children?* A part of her wanted no part of him if he did and another part couldn't resist the invitation. He'd been honorable all day so she followed his lead—not without hesitation, but with an abundance of curiosity.

Before they returned to the car he dried her with a towel. He patted her slowly and gently, barely touching the edges of her breasts, and then handed the towel to her. She had decided it would be okay if the patting strayed a bit, but it didn't. She finished drying herself then pulled her shift down over her head and slipped the bathing suit top and bottom out from underneath. She had a sudden urge to make love right there on the beach behind the bushes. But before she had time to give any cues to that effect Lance was on his way to the car.

* * *

He drove the Porsche—ah, how sweet the sound of the softly purring engine—what seemed like forever, further up the cliffs. Lance drove slowly around the curves and through the hills so they could enjoy the view.

He said, "When do you start in your new position?"

"Monday."

"How do you think you'll like it?"

"I don't know," she said. "Ask me on Tuesday."

There was a brisk, salty breeze blowing off the coast. They drove with the top down. Lili's thoughts returned to the need to solve the money laundering puzzle in spite of her resolve to take a day off.

Whenever Miss Cumberbatch would come over to check a discrepancy, no matter how small, she carried a handwritten ledger book and thumbed through it until she found the number. Once she did she copied down all the particulars, thanked Lili, told her not to worry about it because it didn't amount to anything and walked off, invariably taking the ledger with her.

When she mentioned this to Ephraim he asked her to make a list of all such transactions and show it to no one but him. Then the preceding Friday, after everyone else had left for the weekend, the two of them stayed late and he went over the list with her and looked up every such transaction.

Lance intruded into her thoughts, "Have you discovered anything yet?"

"Discovered anything?"

"I mean in the books at the bank. Have you found any   discrepancies?"

"I don't think so." Ephraim had stayed even later than Lili. She had to pick up something before one of the merchants closed. Before she left they looked in the spot where Lili thought Miss Cumberbatch hid the key to the locked cabinet. Sure enough it fit and he got access to the ledgers.

"What do you mean you don't *think* so?" Lance said.

"There were a few things Ephraim was going to check out in the computer runs over the weekend. If they amounted to anything he said he'd call me."

"Did he?"

"Why no, er . . ."

He had in fact called her when she returned from her errand and said, "Lili, I think I've found it. The account numbers are coded. . . . I'll tell you about it when I see you."

In spite of her infatuation with Lance Lili was hesitant to confide in him. Besides, she had the distinct impression that he wasn't sharing all he knew with her and that perhaps he had some doubts of his own about her agenda.

"What sorts of things did you ask him to check?" Lance asked.

"What are you, a policeman or something? Can't we just enjoy the ride?"

"I'm only asking because that's why you came here to Barbados—to find the source of laundered funds—and I'd like to help you."

"No, I haven't found anything. Well, I don't think so anyway."

Lance glanced over at her. She knew she had already said too much to stop now.

Lili tried to read his expression as she spoke. "Well, in checking the computer runs against the vouchers I never found anything out of the ordinary. Sometimes I found the vouchers and sometimes I didn't. Anything I found matched. But Ephraim suggested it would be more effective if I checked the vouchers against the computer runs to see if I could find entries for all of the vouchers. Boy, now that was a mess."

Lance said, "And . . .?"

"And believe it or not, I began to make sense of it and there were some accounts I had to ask him about. Sometimes I could find the listing for a given voucher on the computer run and sometimes I couldn't. It reminded me of my brother, Kuha'o, when he used to collect stamps—piles here, piles there, piles everywhere. It was just like that. It was just like Kuha'o sorting his stamps."

"And?"

"And I finally gave up trying to find all of them. I could have looked for years and never had a day off but I did find a few that Ephraim found interesting."

Lance pulled over to show her a vista. It was a wonderful view of the coastline with mountains and rocks and waves splashing against them and producing miles of white, sudsy water. "Tell me about them."

Lance seemed agitated.

She wanted to trust him, feel close, share the power of his mana. "I found that there were some accounts that had more than one account number. You know, like Tropical Shipping—one of the banks' oldest and most

valued customers—had any number of transactions that I
could find and some I couldn't.

"Does that sound strange to you?   Or am I just
crazy?   There were times in my life when people said I
must be crazy."

"And what did you do about it?" Lance asked.

"About being crazy?"

"No, . . . about the bookkeeping entries."

"Well I showed them to Ephraim and he said he
would go over them and see if he could make any sense of
them.   People can say what they want about Ephraim being
gay but it's amazing what a whiz the guy was . . ., I mean is
with numbers.   He has a gift.   I've told him before that if
they hadn't invented computers he could have been one."

Lance turned to face her.   "Is he working with you
on this?"

Lili hesitated,   "Well, I don't know if I should be
telling this to a policeman."

"Lili, I'm your friend."   He reached over and held
her by the shoulders.   She felt herself tremble at his touch.
He looked into her eyes.   "You can trust me."

*Daddy used to say that when someone says, "You
can trust me, it means you can't."*

"Well, I noticed a long time ago that whenever I
thought I had found a mistake, I'd show Miss
Cumberbatch.   Those were my instructions."

Lance nodded.

"And then she would take her keys and go to a
cabinet at the far end of the accounting department and get
out some ledgers—"

"Did you ever get a chance to see them?"

"Well, yes and no.   I mean she would bring them to
my desk and compare them with what I was doing but I
never got to look inside them.

"Did Ephraim?"

"How did you know?" she asked without thinking
and then, recognizing her mistake, went on.   "Well, no, I
don't think he did."

She tried to catch a glimpse of Lance's face to see
whether or not he had caught her slip of the tongue but
there was no change in his expression.

"And, what do you think might have been in there .
. . if you or Ephraim had had a chance to look?"

Lili felt so vulnerable at her slip up that she decided
it best to try to curtail the conversation.   "That's it.   Just

something about the account numbers, but he never really figured it out. At least I don't think he did. If he did he never explained it to me."

In fact Ephraim had gone on to say, "Lili, I've found it. I know how to identify the questionable accounts—the ones that are more than just everyday banking transactions." But she did not disclose this or the following to the inspector.

When Lili had asked Ephraim "How?" He said, "It has to do with the account numbers. Four columns in every affected account match Lord Nelson and the Battle of Trafalgar."

Lili had no idea what he was talking about and expressed her confusion.

"Don't worry about it. I've got it all figured out. I'll tell you about it when I see you. I'm just now leaving the bank."

Lance zigged and zagged through the countryside, up and down hills, over little lanes and around corners until Lili had no idea what direction they were headed. It seemed to her like they had been traveling in circles. Then they went past St. Nicholas Abbey and Lili felt at home because it was followed by a tree tunnel very much like the one on her home island of Kaua'i When they emerged from the tunnel she saw the most spectacular view she had seen in all of Barbados—a gorgeous panoramic view of the coast with mountains and ridges in the foreground, sudsy waves in the distance. There was a light powdering of snow on the mountaintops.

Lili kept wondering whether or not she had blown it by divulging too much. On the one hand she regretted it. On the other she hoped she and the inspector might form an alliance. She was staunchly independent and resourceful. Yet she longed for an unknown ingredient, an X-factor, she had always thought could be supplied by the right man. *Protection? Nurturing? Wealth? Power?* The definition as to what it was she was looking for had been as elusive as the identity of its purveyor. *Could this be him?*

No sooner did she get a glorious rush from the view than Lance made a sharp left-hand turn into the overhanging limbs of a mahogany tree. The tree was so dense that it formed a cavern—with no way to see in or out, except the way they had entered.

Lance got a strange look on his face but didn't say anything. She felt like a teenager out on a date when the guy pulls over and parks. She felt her reason wane, her instincts and passions take over.

"I was thinking maybe I should frisk you to see if I could find any evidence that might help with the investigation," he said.

She had to laugh at that. "You've got a vivid imagination, Inspector. Where do you think I might be hiding something?"

He reached over and evaluated a few possibilities and coaxed her with his hand to do likewise.

"I see you've brought your nightstick," Lili crooned.

"A Bajan police officer always carries his weapon. It's one of the rules."

She felt the rising tide of a sweeping passion. "Well, you'd be a naughty boy if you broke the rules." She brushed a kiss across his lips with her fingers. She felt weak in the knees and overcome with desire.

He grabbed her hand and held onto it while he touched her breasts. He could feel them through the thin fabric of her shift. Her nipples hardened as the last of her resistance waned.

He reached up under her dress and the contact between her body and the warmth of his hand reminded her that she hadn't put her underwear back on after she took off her bathing suit. Still, being in the Porsche was awkward so they got out and she leaned back against the fender, facing him, while he loosened his belt and dropped his pants. She touched him through his underwear for a moment and then pulled them down around his ankles. He entered her from the front.

Just as she was beginning to feel the glory of their togetherness she heard a car coming up the hill and was afraid they might pull in under the tree. Lance continued to make love to her as though he wasn't aware of a thing.

She wanted to stop and she didn't. If the car turned in they would see Lance standing before her, naked from the waist down. The occupants would know what was going on in an instant.

The car slowed as it chugged up the hill. It seemed to take forever. He moistened his fingers and massaged her nipples, this time directly on her skin. She thought about how embarrassing it would be to get caught.

"Lance, stop! Stop it, please. There's a car coming." But he came instead of stopping. And she did, too. He groaned. She shrieked. And the car they had feared continued sauntering up the road and motored on into the tree tunnel.

* * *

On the way to his house Lance pulled into a gas station. This surprised Lili because she noticed his tank was nearly full. But she didn't say anything because she welcomed the opportunity to reassemble herself into a more ladylike appearance. She was ecstatic and yet remorseful at what they had done. She felt a glow in her cheeks, a rich dampness between her legs and a sense of closeness to Lance that she relished. Yet she had misgivings about it. Had she surrendered too quickly and easily? Was this love or the resurfacing of an affliction born in childhood?

Or did her body thirst all the more because she was getting to the point where she might not be able to have any more children? Healthy ones with all their fingers and toes. As she exited the ladies' room, she noticed that Lance was just getting off the phone.

"Warning your wife and six kids we're coming?"

"Police business," Lance said. "I just remembered something I forgot to follow up on last week. That's one of the problems with police work. You never really get a day off."

"Well, I hope you feel as though you've gotten off today," she snickered.

"I can't argue with that," Lance said with a broad grin. He shifted gears, sped out of the Texaco station and accelerated. In a few short yards, he turned away from the coast into the jagged hills. She continued to wonder whether or not she had done the right thing. She knew that abuse victims routinely became either promiscuous or frigid. She just wanted to be able to view herself as beginning a normal, healthy relationship for a change. She longed for this to be the case.

When she least expected it he turned the car sharply down a narrow lane and under low hanging trees and vines. They reminded her of Polihale before they cleared the foliage for the tourists. At the end of the lane was a cute little gingerbread house.

"Daddy, Daddy," several of the children shouted as the car slowed for its ascent up the narrow driveway. Lili fussed with her hair. The children didn't wait for the car to stop. Three of them jumped inside and the little girl hugged him around the neck from the jump seat in the back before he could get the key out of the ignition.

As the car came to a whirring stop another band of little black children came out to greet them. There were so many children she couldn't count them all at first. By using one as a marker and trying several times she concluded there were four boys and a girl, who had run out of the house and up towards the car. Numerous other children ran in other directions, presumably towards their own homes.

Lili felt stunned. *Well, the joke's on me. This man is taken!* Yet Lance was so at ease with the situation that she didn't find herself getting tense. She kept noticing how dark the children were, even more so than Lance. One of the boys pointed to her and said, "Is this your new girlfriend, Daddy? Is this the lady you've been telling us about?"

Lili felt like sliding beneath the dashboard so they couldn't see her.

Lance looked over at her, shrugged apologetically, and said, "Kids! . . . I tried to tell you but—"

Lili was struck by the humor of the situation and laughed. "I always thought you might have a wife and six kids at home. What a relief to find you've only got five."

"Four," he said. "Two of these are my nephews, Desmond and Grafton. My sister sent them over to baby sit. They look after the smaller kids when I'm not here, or they're not all over at my sister's house. I have another daughter inside—a little one. Now you boys go in and look after Emma."

As Lance lifted the bigger children Lili turned to the remaining little boy, William—one whom she was sure had called him "Daddy—" and said, "Where's your mother?"

William cast his eyes downward. "Mummy's dade," he said. "She died a year ago. She drownded."

Lili wished she could take back the question. She flashed on the deaths of her family members. Death was so final, so irreversible, so cold. She felt guilty for resurrecting it in the mind of the little boy.

Lance closed his car door. "I tried to tell you about them but I didn't know where to start."

"Oh, no. This is perfect. I get the picture. Just telling me about them wouldn't have been the same," Lili replied.

Lili had previously decided it would be a mistake to get involved with a man with children. No instant families for her. But she couldn't help liking them. They were super polite and the older ones spoke perfect, proper English with a Bajan—nearly British—accent. It turned out to be a fun filled afternoon.

Lili loved sports and finally managed to set aside her investigation for a few precious hours. The children took her away to where there was pavement. They carried a plywood standard in the shape of a Ping-Pong net, only slightly larger, and they taught her to play road tennis. It took Lili a while to catch on, but once she did, she was very good at it and everyone wanted to play against her. She wanted to include as many children as possible so they played doubles.

While Lance fixed dinner nine-year-old Idalia took Lili into her room to show her her dolls and get Idalia's hair brushed. The room was lavender with daisies and dancing fairies on the wallpaper. Lili recalled the ragged fairy poster she and her sister, Leilani, had shared in their pitiful little room when they were children. Idalia opened the lid of a smooth wooden box and said, "See these. These are from my best friend, Michelle." There was any number of tiny pastel notes folded and tucked neatly into the box. Lili could smell a faint odor of perfume on them. "Do *you* have a best friend?"

"Yes," Lili said. "My best friend's name is Suzie. She lives all the way off in Hawaii and I miss her very much."

"Where is Hawaii? Is it in America?"

"Yes," Lili said. "Hawaii is part of America but it hardly seems like it. There's a movement to make Hawaii its own country all by itself. Once it was a kingdom all its own."

"I'd like to live in a kingdom." Idalia's face lit up. ". . . with princes and castles and knights. I'd be a princess first and later on I'd marry a prince and become his queen. Did you ever think of marrying a prince?"

Lili stroked the girl's hair as Idalia slid the wooden box back under her bed. "Many times," Lili said. "But that's not who I chose. I was married once but he was hardly a prince."

"What happened to your husband? Did he die like Mummy?"

"No," Lili said.   "He went to prison and when it became obvious we were never going to live together again, we got a divorce."

"Ouch!" the little girl said. "That hurt." The brush got stuck.

"I'm sorry, sweetie, I'm not used to hair that's so . . ."

"Kinky. It's okay for you to say. I know my hair is different from a white person's."

Lili said, "It *is* difficult to brush, especially when it's tangled. I'll try not to hurt you." *It would be wonderful to have a daughter someday.*

"What's that? What's a divorce?" Idalia asked. She brushed the hair on one of her dolls with a small plastic brush, while Lili brushed hers.

Before Lili had a chance to give her answer the little girl put the doll down and ran to the other side of the room. "I'll show you a picture of Mummy."   She had a dresser which fit perfectly into the corner of the room.   She rummaged through the drawers and held out a small black and white photo with little black photo corners still on it, as though it had been taken out of an album.

The picture reminded Lili of one that her friend, Maria, had shown her, back when Lili had her first job, as a housekeeper, at the age of thirteen. The photo was tiny but it was plain to see that her mother had been a handsome and dignified woman. She sat on a chair, looking to one side, with her hands clasped on her knee. The woman was dark, much darker than Lance, but she had a tiny, almost European looking nose. She smiled faintly, but alluringly, and had on a dress made of white lace. Lili concluded it must have been her wedding dress.   Her hand shook as she looked at the picture. *Get hold of yourself, Kalili'i Kaleo. You've already decided you don't want to marry a man who has children.*

Lili slipped the picture back into the drawer and closed it. "Thank you for sharing your picture with me. You should be proud to be the daughter of such a beautiful lady."

Idalia blushed and curtsied. "Thank you, Mum."

Lili continued, "C'mon, we'd better get back to your daddy. I'll bet he's got dinner ready by now. Does your daddy fix a good dinner?"

"He sure does, Mum.   Daddy's a fantastic cook. He's an even better cook than Mummy was."

The prospect of a tasty meal lifted Lili's spirits.
"Shhh!" Idalia said. She took Lili's hand. "First,
let's go see my baby sister."

The house had only a few rooms—Lance's room, a
boys' room, a girls' room, a kitchen and a small bathroom
with a porcelain tub that stood on four brass feet.   She
thought she had already seen the entire house and couldn't
imagine where the little sister might be.

"Shhh!" Idalia repeated. "We don't want to awaken
her up."

Lili looked around and saw no clue as to her
whereabouts. They tiptoed down the narrow hallway and
when they got near the end Idalia pushed on a bookcase
and it revolved.   When it turned it revealed a tiny little
cubby.   Other than the revolving bookcase it had no
entrance.   "Daddy says we'll use this room for storage
when Emma's old enough to share my room with me."

The room was light and airy. There were two little
framed windows with lace curtains blocking the diffused
light that came in through glass blocks, the kind you might
find in an art deco setting, which this wasn't.   Hand in
hand Idalia and Lili crept up and peeked over the edge of
the baby bed.

Emma, just waking up, sat on the mattress, rubbing
her eyes.   She was a much paler brown than the other
children, even lighter than Lili—but with her tightly curled
dark brown hair, clearly of African descent.   Lili was
mesmerized by what she perceived to be—even at this
tender age—a remarkable and striking beauty. In sharp
contrast to the tone of her skin, Emma had two of the most
shimmering green eyes Lili had ever seen. They were so
striking, they seemed to glow in the dim light—not an
iridescent green, like cats' eyes, but a bright shining, almost
metallic shade of green. At first these gorgeous little eyes
saw only Idalia and smiled. Then noticed Lili and the child
began to wail.

Idalia struggled to pull Emma over the railing of her
bed but she had difficulty clearing the edge.   Emma
continued to wail. Lili tried to lend a helping hand. Emma
wailed all the louder. She kicked and screamed. Lili had in
mind to ask about the child's lineage with her being so light
and all, but the screaming prevented the discourse.

Suddenly Lance came into the room.   "What's
going on here, Idalia? I thought I told you to stay out of
here while Emma was sleeping."

"But she wasn't sleeping, Daddy. She was ready to get up."

Lance looked at Lili. She nodded in agreement. Meanwhile tears of terror rolled down Emma's face. She kept her eyes riveted on Lili all the while. Lance scooped her up with one arm. "It's okay little lady. Daddy's got you." He put her on his hip and the sobbing ended almost that very instant. The child gasped to recoup her breath. "I've got to get back to the souffle."

Soufflé? Did the man say soufflé?

Lili took Idalia's hand and together they walked the short distance back down the hall to the kitchen where the boys were finishing setting the table. Someone had put a vase of red ginger lilies in the center, next to a big pitcher of pink lemonade. The late afternoon sun glistening through the kitchen curtains still bore heat and the cool pitcher dripped with beads of sweat.

Lance yelled, "I thought I told you boys to keep an eye on the pans while I was gone. Now look. The damned sauce is burnt." He frantically stirred and shook the remaining pans in an effort to salvage what he could.

"We wanted to save the sauce, Uncle Lance, but you told us not to play on the stove."

"So I did," Lance said, as he relit and readjusted the flame on the gas burners. One had gone out and the sweet perfume in the natural gas pervaded the kitchen.

If she hadn't seen it Lili wouldn't have believed it. With the young girl still on his hip, Lance threw out the burnt sauce, cracked several eggs one-handed, dropped the yolks unbroken into the pan and disposed of the shells under the sink, all without removing Emma from his hip. "How about *crème brulee* instead?"

I might have to give this man another look. But with four kids! I don't know about that.

Lance asked Lili to supervise the pans, excused himself and went to change Emma and freshen up for dinner. When he came back they all sat down, and Lance insisted they offer a prayer before anyone touched their food.

Theo said, "Heavenly Father, we thank you for bringing us together so that we may have fellowship. We thank you for our family and friends and that Miss Kaleo could come here and be with us today. We ask that you bless the hands that prepared this meal and that you bless it to our bodies.

" . . . In Jesus' name we pray."

Everyone, including Lili, said "Amen."

Lili thought the prayer was sweet, especially the part about how the little boy was grateful to have her as their guest. It made her feel special. *It sure wasn't like this at my house.* Lili noticed how it changed the mood from one of raucous noise and confrontation among the children to one of tranquility.

They politely passed the corned beef and sweet potatoes, cucumbers in a pickle sauce and stewed guavas. It was a meal that Lili wasn't sure would measure up to one of Aunty Fay's, but it was close. Salt pork, Lili thought. That's what would make this perfect—a huge platter of salt pork, some garlic potatoes and poi.

During the meal Lili's attention was repeatedly drawn to Emma, who didn't seem entirely healthy, so it was difficult to gauge her age. As nearly as Lili could tell, she guessed she was about four or five years old. The child contented herself eating soda crackers. Lili could see out of the corner of her eye that the little girl was staring at her whenever she wasn't looking and Lili tried to connect with her. But each time she looked at the child directly, Emma looked away. When Lili had done this with her own son, Christian, the two of them had turned it into a game of peek-a-boo and laughed. But this darling little girl was taking the situation altogether too seriously for that. She looked as if her life depended upon keeping Lili in sight without making eye contact.

Lili noticed that while the child seemed more than old enough to talk, in fact much older than she would have expected to find in a baby bed taking a nap, she didn't say anything. And while she wasn't wearing a diaper, Lili noticed that she had on pull-ups that Lance had taken her to change. Emma became fussy and Lance, as he was gathering up the dishes, said, "Help Emma down, boys. She needs to burn off some energy. Take her outside to play."

Two of the bigger boys led her away, each holding one of her hands so she could keep her balance and walk. It was then that Lili noticed the little girl appeared to be limping and on closer inspection she could see that one of her legs looked shorter and smaller than the other. Just when she was about to ask Lance about it the phone rang and he went to answer it.

When he got back he looked at the children who were still inside and said, "I'm afraid I've got to be getting Miss Lili back to her hotel."

One of the older boys said, "Daddy, what about dessert?" The younger one said, "And we wanted to show Miss Lili the caves."

"The caves will have to wait. I've got to get to a crime scene. There's been a murder. I'll be gone until late. You'll have to put yourselves to bed tonight. Now go get out my uniform."

"Oh, no," Lili said. "Anyone I know?"

"I doubt it," Lance said. "You know hardly anyone on this island. Besides they didn't say. Sounded like a hate crime."

Hate crime. I wonder who hates who. How can you hate someone in paradise? Maybe someone killed a tourist.

There wasn't time to finish cooking the brulee so Lili gave the children the glazed sugar and blackberries and let them lick the sweet cream off the spoons.

Before she left Lili hugged each of the children, as did their father, and she thanked each one individually for sharing a wonderful day.

On the way back to the hotel Lili rested her head on Lance's well pressed uniform. She had tasted the force of his passion earlier but now basked in the glow of a man devoted to his children. He said, "Lili, I'd have gotten back to you right away. Um, well, err . . . after that first night we danced together but I was afraid for my children. I have to be careful who I get involved with because everything I do affects them."

"How did I do?"

"What?" Lance asked. "How did you do at what? The games?"

"Did I pass?" Lili felt as if she had been on trial again—this time with Lance's children as the jury. She knew the feeling of being in the docket.

"Pass? Of course you passed. Not that you were being tested. I just wanted to be with you *and* my kids today and the only way I could do that was to get you all together. They loved you, especially the girls. Couldn't you tell?"

"I noticed that Emma stared at me a lot. She hardly ever took her eyes off me."

"Don't worry, if she hadn't liked you she would have kept right on wailing or gone and hidden in her room and we couldn't have gotten her out for anything. Once I hired a couple of men to help paint the house and she refused to come out of her room for days—long after they'd left."

It was on Lili's mind to ask what had happened to her. *Why is she crippled?* It was so sad; so pitiful to see this beautiful creature so awkward. *And why doesn't she talk? She's certainly old enough.* But Lili concluded there had been enough sharing for one day. She was exhausted and could tell that Lance was preoccupied with the matters that were taking him to the scene of a murder on a Sunday evening. She decided to just enjoy the ride. There was no more talk during their trek across the island. She listened to the whirring of the engine propelling the car against the opposing wind. At times, she thought she could hear the beating of Lance's heart. *This is a decent man. Not at all like Charlie or Daddy.* She wore a present he had just given her—a yellow and maroon scarf. Although he had just run and retrieved it from the closet and Lili guessed it had probably once belonged to his wife it was still her first present from him. She wore it snugly around her ears. He tucked her head closely to his chest to duck the wind. He put the palm of his hand over her head and kneaded her hair under her scarf with the tips of his fingers.

When they got back to the hotel she thought about inviting him in—in fact wanted to—but knew his attention and duty lay elsewhere. He pulled into the parking lot and backed up to turn around.

She leaned over and gave him a kiss on the cheek before she got out of the car.

Before driving off he said, "It was an illusion."

"Illusion?" she yelled. "I can't hear you. Are you telling me all those children were an illusion?"

"No," he said. "The car rolling uphill. It's a trick we pull on the tourists. It's an optical illusion."

Chapter Five

The next morning when Lili reported to the executive offices of the Bank of Barbados for her new position, everyone she encountered—from the elevator operator to Mr. Baker's receptionist—seemed tense. *Why are these people so uptight?   I hope it's not like this everyday.*

She sat in the reception area while Shirley Bangerter, a gaunt, gangly looking woman, answered the phones. *I can tell this floor is for the top brass.   They either have no sense of time or no regard for me.*

At long last a middle-aged woman, whose tight fitting skirt impaired her mobility came waddling toward her.

Tuck in those buns and tighten those abs. Lili had begun working out to burn off her frustration and recoup some of the strength she had lost during the sedate period of caring and grieving for her son, Christian.

The woman was dressed formally in a gray suede suit.

Lili quickly realized she had underdressed for her new position.

"I'm Mrs. Musgrave," the woman said.   She wore her hair in a bun that was as tight as her skirt.   "I'm here to

show you your duties." She held out her hand and Lili
shook it. Her hand seemed tiny and bony for a stout
woman.

"Mr. Baker is out of his office this morning.
There's been an emergency in the accounting department."
*How can there possibly be emergency in
accounting? Maybe they got their debits and credits mixed
up.* Lili didn't ask about the "emergency" in case she
might be accused of having had a hand in it.

They went in to Mr. Baker's office, one of the
neatest and tidiest places she had ever seen, and sat on
opposite sides of his desk. Lili looked up at the wall and
asked about the colorful flags that adorned it. "What are
those?" she asked.

Mrs. Musgrave replied, "Those are signal flags,
Miss Kaleo. . . . like they use on a ship."

"What do they signal?"

"They say, 'The Bank of Barbados expects that
every man will do his duty.'"

"What about women?" She asked. "Does it apply to
us, too?"

"The masculine includes the feminine," Mrs.
Musgrave replied, ". . . unless otherwise specified.

"It's from the Battle of Trafalgar. You know, like
the statue that adorns the little park beside our building.
Mr. Baker is an aficionado of the battle."

Lili was familiar with the statue of Lord Nelson in
what was formerly known as "Trafalgar Square," now
called "Heroes' Square." She was also aware of the fact
that the taxpayers had recently paid several hundred
thousand dollars to have Lord Nelson turned so that he no
longer faced "Mother England," given the nation's 1966
independence. She was confused by the term "heroes,"
though, in that the only statue she could remember seeing
there was of Lord Nelson. Yet she was told it was
dedicated to all the heroes of Barbados. *Maybe there's
something I missed.*

Lili said, "Mr. Baker must be happy about the
outcome. I understand the British won, although I
remember from my world history class that it was a bad
day for Lord Nelson."

Mrs. Musgrave looked at Lili as though she must be
an imbecile. "It's a good thing you brought this up," she
said. "Mr. Baker is from England but his mother was
French—a direct descendant of Admiral Rosily in fact."

Who in the hell was Admiral Rosily? "You don't say," Lili replied.

"Yes, in case you don't know who Admiral Rosily was, he was supposed to lead the French and Spanish at the Battle of Trafalgar, but Admiral Pierre de Villeneuve disregarded his orders from Napoleon and maintained his command after it was ordered relinquished. Mr. Baker says that if Admiral Villeneuve had followed orders and the Spanish captains under him had followed their lines of command there would no doubt be a statute of his great great grandfather standing out there in Heroes' Square instead of Lord Nelson's."

"You don't say," Lili replied.

Mrs. Musgrave gave her a scornful look. "Yes, and Mr. Baker is also very tidy. He comes from a long line of military figures and believes firmly that cleanliness is close to godliness."

Probably one of those jerks who bounces a coin off the bed to see whether or not it's made properly.

Mrs. Musgrave continued, "This would be a good place for us to start, Miss Kaleo. Mr. Baker is a stickler for sound management and has prepared an organizational chart for our department." She got a key from her desk, came back and opened the file cabinet under the flags. She thumbed through it and pulled out the organizational chart in question.

It was pretty easy to follow since there weren't a large variety of names on the chart. "Who's FG?" Lili asked.

"Why FG is Frank Greenleaf," she replied. "Mr. Baker says you should never let the enemy know who your top man is. Why if Lord Nelson hadn't worn all those medals and ribbons and promenaded around the deck on the day of the battle he probably wouldn't have gotten himself shot. Mr. Baker says he'd still be alive today."

That's a stretch. "What would that make him now, Mrs. Musgrave, about a hundred-and-fifty?"

"I was just kidding, Miss Kaleo. You'll find that Mr. Baker has a wonderful sense of humor."

Lili reviewed the organizational chart. In charge of International Banking was none other than Winston Baker (W.B.), who was also in charge of Multi-National Credit Card Transactions. Under Vice-President for Public Relations for the bank it said, "Winston Baker." Mr. Baker's name and/or initials appeared in about six different

places on the chart. There were only a few names other
than his. Miss "Breidenstein's" name was crossed out and
"Kaleo" marked in place of it at the very bottom of the
chart.

Mrs. Musgrave pointed at various aspects of the
chart, as she continued. "This chart only has to do with our
department although Mr. Baker insists that it be updated
every time a personnel change takes place. 'That's the only
way you can keep the lines of command clear and
unequivocal,' as he is fond of saying." Mrs. Musgrave
took the chart, put it back into the file cabinet and locked it
back up. "If the French had had this Mr. Baker says they
would have won."

*If the French had had that they would have killed
themselves.*

Next Lili was shown Mr. Baker's appointment book
and together they went over his schedule for the week.
"Now," Mrs. Musgrave said, "if you're scheduling him to
be at Sunbury Plantation for a one-hour meeting at two
o'clock you can't schedule him back here for a meeting on
the hour. You've got to allow driving time. It's nearly an
hour to Six Cross Roads and you've got to factor that in.
And what if he can't find parking or has to buy
petroleum?"

Lili kept thinking, What do you take me for, an
imbecile? Nobody is that stupid. But she refrained from
saying what she was thinking and tried to be congenial and
seem interested in the most detailed and boring of
explanations.

Her mind drifted to her forthcoming luncheon with
Ephraim Whitney. *It will be good to see a normal human
being. Ephraim can be so fun. I wonder what he has to tell
me.*

Finally Mrs. Musgrave showed Lili her new office.
It included a tiny glimpse of the Careenage. If Lili stood
on her tiptoes and looked over the partition she could
occasionally detect the white sails of a pleasure yacht going
out the Constitution River. Mr. Baker, of course, had a
panoramic view of the river from the wharf to the swing
bridge. Her office was adjacent to his and opposite the
conference room.

Mrs. Musgrave's next remark surprised her. "You
must remember that Mr. Baker is a married man. Please
keep the proper decorum and maintain a dignified and
comfortable distance at all times."

What's that about?   I hope he's not a heinie pincher.

When Mrs. Musgrave left Lili realized she had twenty minutes to kill before she would be free to leave for lunch. She couldn't wait for the noon hour to arrive. The minute hand seemed to drag its way to the twelve on the big Vienna wall clock in Mr. Baker's office. Since this was her first day in a new position she didn't dare leave early. To break the monotony she decided to call Ephraim to find out where they were going for lunch. He had mentioned Brown Sugar or Josef's Restaurant and she wondered whether or not she needed to make reservations or call a taxicab.

To call him she had to go through the bank switchboard. By now she knew Elayne Headley, the bank switchboard operator, pretty well. They went to the same gym, the Garrison Fitness Center, and often chatted during and after their workouts. Shirley Bangerter also went there but she usually kept to herself and did the strangest exercise routine, sort of a tai chi. Membership in the fitness center was one of the few perks provided by the bank. They felt it helped cut down on absenteeism.

"Extension please," Elayne said.

"I don't know the number but I'd like to speak to Ephraim Whitney."

"Ephraim Whitney? Who is this?"

"Hi, Elayne, this is Lili Kaleo."

"Sorry, Lili. I thought I recognized your voice, but you've changed extensions."

"Yes, I got promoted. I'm working for Mr. Baker now."

"That's impressive. You've only been here, what—"

"Elayne, I'm in a hurry. Can you put me through to Ephraim?"

There was silence. Then Elayne said, "Lili, haven't you heard? Ephraim Whitney is dead."

Lili gasped. She tried to speak. Her lips moved but no sound came out.

Elayne continued, "He was killed over the weekend. The police think he was murdered. Mr. Baker's been over here all morning helping with the investigation. That boyfriend of yours, the police inspector, he's been here, too. I'm surprised no one told you."

Lili wanted to ask about the circumstances but was in a state of shock and upset, not just by Ephraim's death, but also because Lance had not called to tell her.

* * *

After a lonely lunch with an empty chair at the Waterfront Café and an afternoon of listening to Mrs. Musgrave drone on about Mr. Baker's laundry and dry cleaning schedule, Lili couldn't wait to confront Lance. She marched straight to the Central Police Station after work but he had already left. Then she worked her way through complicated bus routings to find her way to his house. With all the stops, starts and circuitous routing, it took her more than two hours to get there. She thought about renting a car but she had never gotten around to getting the requisite international driver's license, and processing the paperwork then getting the car would have taken longer than the bus ride.

All through the ride she kept thinking about Ephraim—about the fun she had had with him, about the shopping trips they used to take together to the Rainbow Boutique to pick out clothes. He especially liked shopping for lingerie. About their giggling over fat women who tried to wiggle into the tiniest of garments. About how sizes were more and more prone to being misnumbered to accommodate women who were unwilling to buy larger sizes but who could no longer fit into the smaller ones. *Who would want to kill him?*

Then she thought about the investigation. *Had he been killed because he discovered something? Or did it have to do with that new lover he was planning to meet for the weekend? Maybe they had a fight.*

Her thoughts turned back to the inspector. She got more and more angry because Lance hadn't called to tell her about it. He just let her find out on her own in a casual conversation with the bank's leading gossip.

When she got to his house there was no one there. She walked almost a quarter of a kilometer to the nearest neighbor's. They said they hadn't seen anyone at his house all day. "Maybe Inspector Williams is over at his parents' place."

"Where's that?"

"Well, you go on up this road and turn left. Then you go down to the end of the lane and turn right—then go about an eighth of a kilometer, past the Morgan Lewis Mill . . . Do you know where that is?"

With only a vague understanding of the general direction of Lance's parents' house, Lili took off on foot. It reminded her of her teenage years, walking nine miles each direction to the Martins' to work as a housekeeper.

When she finally got there, Lance was on the front porch "slammin' doms," (playing dominoes) with a man who looked old enough and resembled him enough to be his father, while the children were running rampant and playing tag around a bearded fig tree, the icon after which Barbados was named.

She walked up to him and when he stood up to greet her, she began hitting him about the arms and chest. "Why didn't you tell me? Why didn't you tell me it was Ephraim? You knew he and I worked together. You knew he was my friend."

"Whoa! Whoa! I didn't know it was Ephraim until I got to the crime scene. This is official police business and I have to keep it confidential. Besides, he signed in under an assumed name and didn't have any identification on him when—"

Lili continued, "I know you knew him, too. He kept talking about how he was attracted to you, because you were so so well, er uh, endowed."

Just then Lili stopped to notice a person she thought must be Lance's mother standing beside them, her mouth open, a frying pan in her hand—listening.

The older gentleman, frail with short gray hair combed neatly in wavy rows, who was now standing next to her, said to Lance, "Eggs don't go at big rock dance."

Lance didn't respond to this suggestion that the woman in his company was above his station in life. "Lili, I'd like you to meet my parents."

Shit! Shit! Shit! I've done it this time.

"This is Clyde Williams—and this fine woman here . . ." He put his hand on the small of the elderly lady's back and pulled her towards him. "This is my mother."

"Umm, well, I'm pleased to meet you Mr. Williams." She shook his hand. "I'm pleased to meet you too, Mrs. Williams."

Each of Lance's parents returned a firm and cordial handshake. Mrs. Williams managed a faint smile but they both seemed bewildered.

"Yep, this is the woman who taught me to cook. We call her Mummy—Mummy Williams."

"You've done a wonderful job teaching your son . . . I mean he's so well mannered."

At this the elderly woman smiled.

Lance interrupted. "Mummy, Miss Kaleo is here to see me on police business. Might we have some privacy?"

Mummy shook her head, took Clyde's arm and led him back inside. On his way in, he looked back at Lance and said, "Don't hang your hat higher than you can reach it!"

Instead of reacting to his father's innuendo that this woman was out of Lance's league, all Lance said was, "Yeah, Daddy, I hear you."

The screen door slammed shut behind them.

Lili said—in a much softer voice, "Don't tell me you didn't know I knew him."

"Lili, what was I supposed to do? Call you up and say I have this police investigation in progress and I want you to know, before we even call the magistrate, that it was a friend of yours, Ephraim Whitney, and give you all of the particulars. Is that what you expected?"

"No, but you didn't have to let me go to work and find out from Elayne Headley. And she said you'd been there all morning investigating. Couldn't you have taken a moment to call and let me know?"

"Lili, I don't know who we can trust at the bank and neither do you."

Lili hated it when someone she was arguing with made a point that made perfect sense.

"Think about it, Lili. Isn't it better that Mr. Baker and his friends don't know you even know me? . . . I mean if there's anything they didn't already figure out from the strings I had to pull to get you that job. Let's keep them guessing as much as we can."

Lili asked, "Do you know who killed him?"

"It was either a hate crime or made to look like one," Lance said.

"A hate crime? Who could possibly hate Ephraim? He was such a sweet young man."

"Sweet or swish, whatever you want to call it. He was gay, wasn't he?"

"I don't know all the details but I think that's safe to assume. Do you have any suspects?"

"I was hoping that perhaps you could tell me. You were on his calendar for lunch."

* * *

The next day at the bank was just as bizarre as the day before, only for different reasons. When Lili got to the headquarters building, one of the few concrete and glass high rises in Bridgetown, it was surrounded by pickets carrying Soviet flags—the hammer and sickle against a bright red background. There were hundreds of them. When she tried to pass, they called her "a capitalist pig."

She didn't dare ask anyone in the international banking group what the demonstration was about. It didn't seem to have anything to do with Ephraim. She didn't get it. She thought the Soviet Union had ended—was Russia again—and they were just as much capitalists as anyone in Barbados.

Later on Lance explained to her that the common people of the island felt as though the banks were working against them. The banker took their deposits—billions of dollars—and then turned around and used their money to buy off the local politicians and support big business to the exclusion of the little guy. They favored a law that forbade local merchants from selling anything on the beach, which in reality meant that the big hotel conglomerates could operate and control all of the surfing and fishing and recreational businesses along the coastline to the exclusion of smaller competitors. The hotel proprietors warned the tourists against speaking to the local populace or even saying "Hi!" or "Good morning," allegedly on security grounds, but really because that might serve as an interlude to solicit business.

And the biggest problem—the issue that brought things to a head—was that the Bank of Barbados was about to merge with the Grand Barbadian Bank, and that would lead to countless job cuts. It would strike hard and deep into the workforce as well as the overall economy of the island. Of course none of the officers or directors would be left without a job or a handsome severance bonus and pension.

It's the same everywhere. The little guy always loses.

Mrs. Musgrave had the day off to pack for her upcoming move. People came and went from Mr. Baker's office and it was obvious that he had been expecting each of them. She thought it was a part of her job to schedule and monitor his appointments. Yet she barely had anything to do. *Did they bring me here to get me out of accounting?* She sat at her desk and fumbled with the few papers she found there, left by its last tenant. She shuffled and reshuffled them until her fingers grew tired.

From her desk, she could easily see into the conference room through its clear glass wall and while she couldn't hear what was being said, she could see the visitors who came and went.

The guests were varied and animated. One was the Minister of Social Transformation—a distinguished looking man of African descent with lots of gold jewelry, including a Rolex. Another shook his finger furiously at Mr. Baker—about an inch from his nose. He had no hair, although Lili couldn't tell if this was because he was bald or had shaved his head. He wore an expensive suit—a smooth, shiny iridescent shade of gray, and alternately puffed on a cigarillo and sat back in his chair, while Mr. Baker did his best to calm him down. It reminded Lili of something her father used to say. "You can always tell who is top dog, just by watching people. You don't even have to hear what they're saying."

At around four p.m., just before Lili was about to wrap things up for the day and go home, Mr. Baker called her into his office.

"Kuh-lee-lee-uh-lee-lee Kaleo, —"

"Kalili'i," she corrected him.

"Kay lily-lee-ee-ee—" He tried again.

"Please, just call me Lili."

He cleared his throat. "Lili, Miss Kaleo, I regret that your tenure with me has involved so little instruction. I'm afraid we only found out a few days ago that Mrs. Musgrave was to be transferred and we had to act quickly. Frankly I expected personnel to send me someone with a little more experience—I mean with the bank, that is—not to imply that you're inexperienced or anything."

"That's okay, Mr. Baker. Mrs. Musgrave did a good job of orienting me yesterday, and—"

"Sounds like Musgrave, Mrs. M., we call her around here. Anyway, call me Winston. . . . Now, Miss Kaleo, my good woman, Mrs. Musgrave is leaving tomorrow with her husband for that post in Surinam. We're all sad about it but that's just the way it is. Stiff upper lip and all, you know."

"Yes," Lili replied, although she couldn't imagine who might miss her, except for Mr. Baker. There were only a few others working in this suite besides the two of them and Shirley Bangerter, the receptionist. *Maybe she has additional responsibilities elsewhere in the bank.*

"I'm sure Mrs. M. has done her best—an amazing woman—but there's a lot more to learn than she'll be able to teach you tomorrow," he said. "I trust you'll join me for dinner this evening so that I might have a chance to orient you . . ."

"Orient me?" *I wonder what that means.*

"Orient you as to our procedures before you get swamped."

With what—that little stack of papers? How could I possibly get swamped?

Lili thought about Mrs. Musgrave's remark about keeping her distance from him. Her palms grew sweaty. She looked at her watch. Three-twenty-five and counting. Just five more minutes and she could escape.

"I'd love to, Mr. Baker, and it's awfully kind of you—"

"Winston. Please call me Winston." He scowled.

"Winston—"

He grinned, disclosing a wide gap between his huge front teeth.

She much preferred an evening with her friends on the porch at The Tower. "Winston, I have a group I meet with every Tuesday night . . ., a prospector from French Guyana and there are two diplomats who work for the state department in Brazil, and—"

"I'm sure they won't miss you for just one night."

She was sorry she hadn't thought of a more compelling excuse. She felt trapped.

"Again, I apologize, Miss Kaylillee-ee, Lili, whatever your name is, but I must insist . . ." He turned a picture of his wife that was obstructing his view of her face down and scowled while he awaited her response.

Lili looked at her watch and said, "Do I have time to go home and change?"

"No, what you have on . . ." He raised himself from his chair, leaned over and glanced at her backside, "what you have on will do quite *nicely.*" He smirked.

When he said the word "nicely," Lili felt as though she was being undressed.

"Where are we going?" She asked. After all, she did like to eat. Perhaps she could make the best of it.

"My apartment," he replied. "My wife has gone on a gambling junket to Aruba with some of her friends. We'll have the whole place to ourselves."

* * *

For dinner at Mr. Baker's house Lili and her boss shared a skillet of flying fish and a delightful cold pumpkin and ginger soup, prepared and served by his housekeeper, Dorothy Eels.

When the unwanted advances didn't materialize early on, Lili began to wonder. *Am I losing my sex appeal?* Not that she had the faintest interest in a romantic relationship with Mr. Baker.

But unpleasantries did come in another form once the housekeeper retired for the evening. "Did Mr. Whitney confide in you?" Mr. Baker asked.

"Why would he? We were just casual friends."

"Casual?"

"We usually talked about fashion and dress, the weather maybe, nothing more."

"Fashion?"

"Yes, Mr. Whitney was as interested in fashion as any of the women in our office."

"Miss Kaleo, I didn't—"

Lili recognized his quizzical expression. "Mr. Baker, Mr. Whitney was gay."

"Oh, yes, umhmm, yes, of course."

She could tell this aspect of Ephraim's lifestyle made him uncomfortable.

Mr. Baker lit up a smelly cigar, inhaled and produced a large cloud of blue smoke. Lili couldn't keep from coughing and struggled to stop. He poured them each a glass of twelve-year-old Mount Gay rum straight up in a clear glass that resembled a small brandy snifter, with an emblem of the bank etched into its side. He handed her this along with a water glass full of ice.

"Now, Miss Kaleo, I understand you've been helping us by checking our books for flaws and errors before the auditors at the Central Bank of Barbados will allow us to merge with the Grand Barbadian Bank. Did you find anything unusual? I mean did you see anything in them that you feel I should know about?"

As if I'd tell you. "Why, no, nothing, Winston. I'm not very good at math—"

"Yes, Miss Kaleo, but you did spend long hours going over those ledgers and you did work with Mr. Whitney on them, didn't you?"

"Yes, but— "

"Miss Kaleo, what do you know about the death of Ephraim Whitney?"

"Not much," Lili said. "Hardly anything. I was just as shocked and surprised by it as everyone else."

"Miss Kaleo, you can confide in me. I work for one of the oldest, most respected banks in the Caribbean." He exhaled another broadband of cigar smoke and took another sip of rum.

She coughed.

"And you'll find by verifying the lines of command at the bank that I'm its official liaison for internal affairs. I mean if there's any chicanery at the bank, I'm the one to know about it."

Yes, I know. "Mrs. Musgrave showed me the organizational chart. I could see you were in charge of many different things."

"Yes, good hand that Mrs. M. Always eager to do her duty, I might add."

And what is that? Mrs. M.'s name was much more obscure on the chart and her duties much less clear.

"Miss Kaleo, you can trust me. If you can't trust me, who can you trust?"

Lili said, "It's not really a trust issue—" She sipped her rum. It tasted like lighter fluid. She figured it would take hair off the inside of her throat—if she had any—or the wax off the floor—if she spilled it.

"Nonsense, I know you're good friends with Lance Williams, the police inspector in charge of the investigation. Some of our people—err, you've been seen with him from time to time around the island—even went to meet his parents from what I understand." He studied her expression.

Lili laughed. "That was quite by accident." *How does he know about that?*

"Nothing happens by accident on this island, Miss Kaleo."

Then he led her into his study.

Here comes the pass. How am I going to handle him? But by the time they got into Mr. Baker's study she could sense that her fears were unfounded. The walls were covered with portraits and drawings of old ships and cannons blazing and billowing white sails and old ship's captains, presumably from the Battle of Trafalgar. There were ship models around the room, some in bottles, some looking as though they were made of brass or copper.

Lili realized she had her mouth open and closed it.

"Are you familiar with the Battle, Miss Kaleo?"

"Not exactly," she replied.

"Yes, yes," he said. "Well, let me explain it to you. Come right over here." He took her to an area of the room with little model ships placed on a thin layer of blue sand. They were carved out of three different colors of soap— white, orange and tan. "The tan ones are French and the orange ones are Spanish," he said. "And the white ones . . . Well, let's just say they belonged to the red coats."

Mr. Baker continued, "Now in all previous naval battles, Miss Kaleo, there was always a frontal attack and since the French and Spanish far outnumbered the British in both men and ships, they would have easily won a direct encounter." He looked at her again then moved several of the models to show their courses, had the attack been frontal. "Do you grasp it, Miss Kaleo? Do you grasp the concept?"

"Yes, I believe I do, Mr. Baker. I think I get it."

He came close to her, reached his hand near her backside, made a lunge, grabbed a pointer and moved away.

"Very well, then. In this particular battle, Lord Horatio Viscount Nelson, God rest the old bastard's soul, decided he would attack in two columns from the side, along with his compatriot, Admiral Collingwood, who attacked in a parallel column, like this, you see." He pointed to various ships as he spoke.

Lili nodded half-heartedly. "I'm not sure I grasp it," she replied, obviously annoyed at the protracted description.

"The point is, Miss Kaleo . . ." He looked directly into her eyes. "The point is that you've always got to be watching your flank. And . . . "

Lili forced herself to look up at him.

He continued, "And you've got to be certain that your lines of command are in place and well understood by everyone in your charge."

Lili felt uncomfortable. She gulped a toot of lighter fluid. It stung her throat.

Mr. Baker added, "Miss Kaleo, I'll be frank. I don't think you're being forthright with me. Accordingly I must conclude our meeting and ask that you depart at once." He took a big swig of rum from his glass and looked at his watch. His cigar had been neglected and was turning to ash which spilled onto the coffee table.

Mr. Baker noticed it and hurriedly grabbed a dust pan from the closet and swept it up. "Mustn't be untidy," he proclaimed.

Lili was surprised and relieved, not necessarily in that order, that the evening had ended so abruptly. Winston saw her to the door.

"I expect you to be in by six a.m. tomorrow morning," he said. "We have a lot of ground to cover. It will be Mrs. M.'s last day, as you know. In the meantime I expect you to come up with better answers to my inquiries. I insist on a full report—on both the ledgers and Mr. Whitney—on my desk by Friday morning."

Lili was relieved to be leaving. At this point she didn't care what he wanted by Friday. That seemed such a long way off.

As she got into the cab that had been called for her she caught a glimpse of a familiar figure turning the corner and ascending Mr. Baker's steps but she couldn't for the life of her think of who it was. Then just as her cab pulled up to The Tower it came to her—Miss Cumberbatch. She wasn't sure about the rest of her body but the sagging rear end in her trademark navy blue polyester slacks unmistakably belonged to Miss Cumberbatch.

* * *

The next day, when Lili returned to work at six a.m. sharp, she was surprised to find that Mrs. M. had already arrived and was in Mr. Baker's office straightening up and looking after his personal effects. Mrs. M. took a look at the picture of his wife and stuck it in a bottom drawer. She appeared sad, much sadder than one might expect for someone about to be liberated from the Bank of Barbados.

"Can I help?" Lili asked.

"No, I'll tend to Mr. Baker's things myself. I heard you had dinner with him last night . . . in his apartment." Mrs. M. didn't make eye contact. She continued to fumble with the things on Mr. Baker's desk. It was obvious she was upset.

"Well, I just had dinner. We talked. It was nothing more, nor less than that." Lili found herself explaining for no apparent reason. "Nothing happened."

Mrs. M. looked comforted but not convinced. "Mr. Baker is a very capable and desirable man," she muttered.

"What, uh, yes, I guess," Lili replied. *Who'd want that flabby old fart?*

"He requires the utmost of personal attention to keep him *on track* and *up to speed* with the many demands and requirements of his position."

Lili said, "I understand your husband has an important position with the British Foreign Service."

Mrs. M. stopped straightening and looked at her as though she had just said something pathetic.

Lili continued, "Do you think you'll like Surinam? Have you found a place to live yet?"

Mrs. Musgrave fell into tears and ran out of the room.

* * *

Later that day, when it was getting close to time for Mrs. M.'s farewell remarks to her fellow employees, she accidentally knocked over a vase in the conference room and stooped to pick it up. Mr. Baker came over to assist her. This was visible through the glass and Lili would have missed it, except that she happened to look up at just the right time. She had been working on a conference program, wherein Mr. Baker was to be the keynote speaker for the Banker's Federation of the Eastern Caribbean States (BFECS) in St. Lucia a week from Thursday.

Mrs. M. had apparently gotten something stuck in her eye when she was brushing the carpet with her hand. Lili noticed that ever so subtly Mr. Baker's hand came to rest on her backside while he probed her eye for the loose particle. Lili thought it seemed too much at home there to be a stranger. It wasn't a blatant overture, just the tiniest variance from propriety. And the confirming observation—Mrs. M. didn't seem to notice it was there.

The rest of the day proved uneventful until the tea in honor of Mrs. M. started in mid-afternoon. Her husband came, and while he looked dignified and proper in his lounge suit and bow tie, the couple seemed detached. He barely said more than two words to his wife, while Mrs. M. appeared to be inseparable from Mr. Baker.

Mr. Musgrave came over and visited with Lili for a few minutes. He seemed to already know a remarkable number of things about her, and even after the conversation had ended, he never seemed to be able to refrain from staring at her over the tops of his glasses.

Miss Cumberbatch arrived, as did Elayne Headley and Shirley Bangerter. Most of Lili's friends and former associates from the accounting department—Trevor Reardon, Leon Alexander, Glendine Bateman and Muriel Montgomery were there along with employees from other parts of the bank. It did seem odd to Lili, however, that she was asked by several of her coworkers on many occasions to point out the guest of honor.

Chapter Six

After the bus ride to Lance's house Lili didn't hear from him again for more than a week. Everything she was able to learn about Ephraim's death she found out from *The Daily Nation.* That's what she put in her report to Mr. Baker.

From what she read it was indeed a hate crime. The words "Gay Shame" and "Faggot" were written in blood across the walls of the Pomegranate Suite of the Peach n Quiet Resort in Inch Marlow. Ephraim's body was found by Mrs. Loveridge, the proprietor, facedown in the swimming pool, slit from his throat to his navel. Lili couldn't help but think of the pigs her father used to hunt and skin and the looks of horror on their slain faces. It made her sad to think a comparable fate had befallen her friend, Ephraim—a friend she couldn't conceive of anyone hating, let alone wanting to kill.

A computer consultant from San Jose, California, who had arrived at The Tower the preceding Wednesday, said, "They have all sorts of gay pride demonstrations back where I come from and I think it just aggravates and mobilizes the gay bashers all the more. There's bound to be a backlash."

Lili said, "Ephraim wasn't the type to flaunt his . . ." Then she stopped and realized he had been just that— proud and open about his sexual orientation. His voice, nail polish and mannerisms marked him, as well.

A vacationing state department worker from Brazil said, "We have lots of gays in our country. They show up at Carnival all dressed up in women's undergarments and strut their stuff and everyone gets drunk and has fun, but no one takes them seriously. When the celebration is over they disappear back into the crowd and no one gives them a second thought."

Lili felt unsettled about the explanation in the paper. She had no hard facts to rely on but she didn't believe the newspaper version.

* * *

Lili had better luck getting news from Elayne Headley one evening after work when they exercised on adjacent treadmills at the Garrison Fitness Center—an elaborate work-out facility near the racetrack. From where they were walking in place they could see Shirley Bangerter acting out a chilling array of hand, arm and body movements in a sort of a *tai chi* motif. Her body looked to be a skeleton with only a thin, taut cover of skin. Yet she moved with an uncanny grace and a gaunt fierceness to her eye.

Elayne said, "I don't think it was a hate crime at all. This is on the hush-hush you understand but I think someone decided to shut him up, and what's more, I think your boyfriend thinks so, too."

Lili was about to object to Lance being referred to as her boyfriend, especially after he hadn't called her in over a week, but for some reason she let the remark settle in and liked the feeling it gave her. "Why do you say that?"

"It's not what the inspector said. It's what he didn't say that convinces me."

"What do you mean?"

"He asked me questions about Ephraim's phone calls that week and didn't seem surprised or ask any follow up questions when I told him there had been no abusive callers I could think of calling Ephraim—not only that week, not ever. In fact the only phone call for Ephraim that I could remember all week was the one from you and that was after he had been killed."

The masseuse came to summon Elayne for a rubdown.

As Elayne toweled off, Lili leaned over the front of her treadmill and said, "What makes you think the inspector is my boyfriend?"

"That man's got it bad for you," she answered. "You can tell that just by the way he lights up when someone says your name."

Lili tried to look nonchalant but picked up her exercise level, as evidenced by the spike in her heart rate monitor.

* * *

The following morning, when Lili arrived, the accounting ledgers that Miss Cumberbatch had kept locked up were laid out across the conference room table. She recognized them immediately.

"Good morning, Miss Kaleo," Mr. Baker said, obviously trying to make up for some of the impatience he had displayed at his apartment. "I'll go over these with you. I just want you to show me where you and Mr. Whitney left off and what sorts of discrepancies you found. I thought if you could see the ledgers, it would refresh your recollection."

"I've never seen these before, Mr. Baker. Well, I've seen Miss Cumberbatch refer to them, but that's it. I've never looked inside them."

"Yes, yes. Well, we'll just have to look and see what we can find, won't we?"

Lili did her best to make sense of them but the numbers danced around in her head like so many clowns in a circus. She did, however, recognize one of the ledgers as being different from the others. It was bound in blue leather but the silver leaf emblem of the Bank of Barbados was different than the rest. The leopard in the drawing had unusual looking spots. When she opened it, the pages didn't look as old, or uniform. It contained accounts and transactions, receipts and disbursements, just like all the ledgers—but by number only. There were no names in the book at all. She wanted to see if she could figure out what Ephraim meant by four columns telling the story but she didn't want to dwell on any particular page to give Mr. Baker a clue as to what she might be looking for.

There was also a foldout in the back of the book—a page that looked like it had been pasted in the book after it had been bound. *A key to the account numbers?* She fumbled with the page but instinct told her not to unfold it in front of Mr. Baker. Instead she held it between her thumb and forefinger for a second, trying to appear nonchalant, and then returned to the body of the book.

Then, right there in the middle of page one-hundred-thirty-four, she saw something that startled her. The entry said, "$ 2,469,735.00 Bds., which meant little or nothing to her, but in the margin beside it was the notation "$ 1,234,867.50 US." She was as familiar with that number as if it had been tattooed on her hand. It echoed the testimony of Mr. Arnold Chan, the Kaua'i County Auditor at her bribery trial. She tried not to let on that anything was out of the ordinary.

And look at the handwriting. It's so flowery.

Lili could feel the heat in her cheeks and tried not to disclose her reaction. She quickly picked up another ledger, thumbed through it, and said, "This looks familiar. Here's a number that looks odd." She pointed. "See how the black ink has been erased and it's been written over in blue."

"Yes," Mr. Baker said. "And what does that mean? It appears to match the balancing entry beside it."

"I don't know. It just looks suspicious." She put down the ledger.   "Mr. Baker, I really can't tell you anything without my notes and I turned them all in to Miss Cumberbatch when I moved over to your department."

"Are you certain, Miss Kaleo?" He looked at her sternly,   "That's all you've seen that seems out of place— just this one erasure?"

She looked back into his eyes and tried not to flinch. "Yes, that's it!"

"Very well then, Miss Kaleo. Very well," he said, as he piled back up the ledgers, put the books under his arm and walked from the room in a huff.

She was relieved when their encounter was over but she was left with the nagging feeling that he had observed her reaction to the notations in the margin.

* * *

That evening, as Lili was leaving the bank on her way to the bus stop, a taxicab pulled up beside her. "Get in," a voice said from inside the cab.

Lili leaned over and looked inside. *Aha!* There was a man sitting in the backseat in a navy blue business suit. He wore a beard and a mustache but she knew by his build and the sound of his voice it was Lance Williams. She turned away and jumped back up onto the curb.

"Get in," the voice insisted.

She turned around and cast a look of defiance. He had had sex with her and then hadn't called! That was Lili's quota for free love. *The man could at least show some interest.* Lance flashed his badge. "I'm not asking you. I'm telling you," he said. "Get in this cab right this instant."

She lifted her chin and continued on her way.

"Your life may depend on it," he said in a deep and commanding voice.

Those last words, along with their tone, got her attention and she climbed into the cab. Still, she looked askance.

"That's right. Your life may be in danger," Lance said.

Lili scowled and looked out the window, appearing not to care about what he was saying.

Lance continued, "We're afraid they may be watching you or having you tailed. We've only got a few minutes to talk and then we've got to get you back to your hotel." The car sped up an alley, around a corner and into a long, narrow street with tall buildings on either side, with barely enough room for their car. It stopped. Once the driver was certain there was no one behind them he sped through the rest of Dromedary Lane and out onto Broad Street.

"I think your friend, Ephraim, was killed because he knew too much. I don't think it was a gay bashing at all," Lance said.

"I know," Lili replied.

"You know? How do you know?"

"Well, first there were those questions we had about the books and then Elayne Headley confirmed it for me."

"Elayne Headley, the receptionist?" he asked.

"Yes, is there another Elayne Headley?"

"No, but Elayne Headley may not be the person you think she is. We're running a check on her identity. You need to be careful what you say to her. Have you said anything to her that might be confidential?" Lance asked. "Has she asked you any questions?"

Lili tried to go over her words in the recent conversations they had had. "What makes you think—"

"We have our methods. We have an undercover department, just like you do in the States. Now listen and listen carefully. We think the bank has become involved in drug trafficking or emerald and gold smuggling—and I know this sounds preposterous—but we can't figure out which. You'd better watch your backside. We think someone at the bank is a hit man and it may be Elayne Headley."

At this Lili laughed—a deep belly laugh. "Are we talking about the same Elayne Headley, the switchboard operator who does her nails twice a week while she talks on the phone and feeds on gossip like a sea cucumber?"

"Let me ask you, Lili. Does she look Bajan to you?"

"Well, no, she said she was from Harrow—"

"And does her accent sound upscale British?"

"No. But, how would I—"

"We think she's from Brazil. Don't say a word to her that you wouldn't want published in *The Barbados Advocate.*"

As the cab sped around a roundabout Lili was momentarily thrown into the inspector's lap. She pushed herself away. "You didn't have to tell me that, Mr. Police Inspector. There are some things we ladies can figure out on our own." They both straightened their clothing after sharing a momentary spark that could have ignited a stone. She didn't know whether or not she bought his explanations as to why he hadn't called her—important business, a case he was working on. She didn't want to get burned—not again, not like she had been with Charlie Owens. The sharing of information about the case seemed to be flowing in only one direction, his.

Suddenly the cab screeched to a halt in the parking lot beside The Tower and Lili got out without looking back and did her best to blend in without anyone noticing her arrival. It wasn't too difficult because everyone's attention was on Jack. Sea Cat had choreographed a routine and taught him to ride a tiny bicycle on a wire stretched across the porch. The monkey was dressed in a red, yellow and blue outfit with a matching cap and a chinstrap. Jack not only displayed perfect balance and aplomb but had come to enjoy the limelight almost as much as the oranges and bananas tossed to him at the conclusion of each performance.

Through this bit of chaos it was easy enough for Lili to tiptoe past the other guests and up to her room unnoticed—or so she thought. Later on Sea Cat commented that he saw her pull up in a small white cab and asked her where she had been. When she admitted she had been with the inspector he dealt her a scornful look and then resumed his duties.

* * *

The next day the entrance to the bank was surrounded and Lili once again had to fight her way through the pickets. There was talk in the newspapers and around the table that violence was possible. Agitators were getting worked up and organizing at the University of the West Indies. They intended to make an example of the Bank of Barbados—as one that had no regard for the common man, saddled them to near extinction with high interest credit card debt and used its influence and prestige only to further the interests of big business. Not all of that legitimate.

And to top things off, the Bank of Barbados' merger with the Grand Barbadian Bank would eliminate, directly or indirectly, hundreds of island jobs.

Lili still had not seen much in the way of added responsibilities in spite of the pep talk she had received prior to dinner at Mr. Baker's house. However, she was now in charge of his day-to-day schedule. She wasn't sure she had his full schedule, though. She came to associate the name Mark Fitzsimmons, with whom he was meeting at the moment, with the baldheaded man in the silver-gray suit. Aside from this Lili was convinced there were many things on Mr. Baker's schedule that weren't in his appointment book.

She suspected that Mr. Fitzsimmons and he were talking about her, judging from the way they looked over at her from time to time. She tried to appear not to notice. That problem was solved at about three in the afternoon when a group of workers came and put curtains in the conference room over the glass walls—curtains that after that day, remained closed at all times.

* * *

Over the next few weeks the crowds of demonstrators outside the bank grew larger and more disruptive, while the people inside treated Lili as though she didn't exist. She wondered whether or not Mr. Baker

or Miss Cumberbatch in accounting had had the same
problem with the picketers.

There were new guests at The Tower but Lili didn't
enjoy them as much as those she had met earlier. Perhaps
the novelty of meeting new people all the time had worn
off. Current guests included an artist from Belgium, two
ornithologists—a married couple from the Netherlands on
their way to the Amazon to photograph the scarlet macaw.
Mr. Hans Jenkins, the merchant marine with the nasty
looking burn mark on his cheek, had returned and she had
come to like him, even though he was brash and intrusive at
times. One afternoon he rescued an injured emerald-
throated-Antillean-crested hummingbird, not much bigger
than a bee, and kept it in a shoebox with twigs and leaves
and fed it sugar water out of an eyedropper until he could
turn it over to the ornithologists that evening.

Lili had substantially withdrawn from the nightly
gatherings and spent most of her free time conversing with
Sea Cat on the little sun porch adjacent to her room,
whenever he had a spare moment from his responsibilities
to the hotel and its guests. They had become such good
friends that he occasionally took her out on his cousin's
fishing boat up the Atlantic Coast out of Skeete's Bay.

"She's not bahd," Sea Cat would say each morning
as he returned from one or another of the cruise ships—
meant as a compliment for his latest liaison. "She's not
bahd."

*Not bahd? Is that the standard for sex around
here? I wonder if that's what the inspector has told his
friends about me—that I'm "not bahd?"*

Sea Cat spoke well of the inspector in terms of his
professional accomplishments. "He's done a good job of
keeping down the crime rate. And he's quite well liked as
policemen go. I'll give him credit for that but I wouldn't
want him marrying *my* daughter—if you know what I
mean."

Lili didn't—at least not exactly but she also wasn't
sure her heart wanted to know what her ears were hearing.
She dropped the subject.

* * *

Then one afternoon a courier came to the office at
the bank. He handed her a plain business envelope—size
ten. She expected to see it addressed to Mr. Baker. Instead
it simply said "Lili" on the front. When she opened it, it
read, "Meet me at The People's Cathedral—Sunday

services, 7:30 a.m. Sit at the end of the pew by the door nearest the overflow assembly."

It wasn't signed but there were two initials at the bottom— "L. W."

* * *

Lili wondered whether or not Lance would bring his children with him to church. She especially liked the little one, Emma. Maybe it was because she felt sorry for her because of her handicap or maybe it was because of the fact that she was somewhat of an outcast, living on the perimeter of the family circle. She wondered what the full story on her was. Her complexion certainly didn't match the other children—and her being crippled like that—what had happened to her? It tugged at Lili's heart all the more because she was so cute and had an engaging smile and cheerful expression in spite of her hardships. And even though she made pleasing and melodic sounds but didn't speak, Lili felt a connection and warmth when she had taken her hand and pulled her close to say goodbye the last time she had seen her.

What to wear? What to wear? She wondered, as she prepared for her first church attendance since arriving in Barbados nearly seven months earlier. She hadn't felt that she had been absorbed into the culture but today she was feeling like trying out a new identity. She asked Elayne to use her connections to get her into the boutique of the Nordic Princess, which was normally closed when it was in port. She bought a rust and black colored sarong with the large print of African children playing in the savannah and riding on elephants. She was assured it would be "perfect for the occasion." It was silk and shear until she wrapped it around her and overlapped it before pinning it from underneath with a large safety pin.

She thought it would be hot but the layers seemed to shelter her from the heat. The humidity was another matter.

She piled her hair on top of her head and held it in place with a smoothly carved wooden stick almost as long as a pencil. She was too nervous to eat, even if she hadn't been in the habit of fasting on Sunday mornings. *I've already decided I'm done with him. Why am I putting so much energy into this?*

Pride in hand and purse in tow, she asked Sea Cat to call a taxicab. She wanted to be as fresh as possible when she got there and left nearly forty-five minutes early so as not to be late. Through a renewed conditioning regimen she had gradually rebuilt her strength and stamina and approached her usual bronze color and vitality. She circled the block a couple of times with nervous anticipation and plucked a frangipani—which she would have called a plumeria in her native Hawaii—from a bush in a circular planter in the middle of the driveway in front of the rectory. It smelled rich and sweet. She pinned it in her hair and bided her time until the faithful began to arrive.

To her astonishment the parishioners came in flocks and quickly filled not only the parking lot but the hillside nearest the church, the grassy traffic island across the road and all of the narrow lanes and roadways in the vicinity. They were dressed to the hilt. Little girls in bright yellow taffeta. Stately ladies with handbags and fashionable hats of every description. The undulating brims on one hat reminded her of the walls of The Guggenheim Museum in New York as Lili had seen it depicted in a magazine.

One thing she noticed that disturbed her was that almost no one dressed as though they were of African descent. She later discovered that three hundred plus years of separation from the continent had left its descendants with considerable insouciance toward their ancestral heritage. Too bad, she thought. It's a beautiful culture.

As she had expected the people sitting close enough for her to see were all black, except for a couple of mulattos and one white woman, who must have been married to or dating a black man. No, it was married she later decided, because they had several children seated between them who seemed an assortment of the various permutations and combinations of shades of white, brown and black that such a union might produce.

The boys wore suits with suspenders, and the girls had on smooth silk blouses with long lacy skirts and matching sequined gloves that reached almost to their elbows. Lili surmised that they were really an older woman's gloves and they looked long on the little girls' hands because they were way too big. One of the things Lili had enjoyed the few times Aunty Fay had taken her to church as a child, was the opportunity to dress up, although she never owned anything proper to wear. Aunty Fay would somehow magically make an outfit appear, which had to be kept especially nice and "changed out of and back into play clothes" immediately following the service.

Once she was made fun of—accused of wearing a dress that Stephanie Goodman, a wealthy childhood acquaintance, had recently "outgrowed."

Although she sat in a pew towards the back Lili could see the choir assemble along with the musicians in the front looking back towards her. There was a drummer, an electric guitar player, a number of trumpeters, a flautist and even a few woodwinds. The hymns began in earnest as she awaited the commencement of the services. It wasn't long until she became aware of two or three voices in the chorus that heralded above the rest. The spirit and vitality with which the choir sang made her feel lighthearted and raised her spirits.

They sang of a train bound for glory with a Calypso beat and a strong and unwavering female voice predominated. It was so soft, soothing and uplifting that Lili was ready to board well before the train left the station. She saw Lance, in the navy blue suit he had worn in the taxicab, standing in the back row of choristers. She was surprised that the members of the choir did not wear robes. She had been certain they would and anticipated festive colors. *It must be to save money or make everyone feel as though they're part of the choir.*

And then there was the preacher. He had a strong, reverberating voice, much like Lance's, only it was deeper and less raspy, like a Reverend Jackson's she had once met on a mayoral trip to Dayton, Ohio. He mesmerized the congregation—first with a call to order, then a call to the Holy Ghost and then a call to Jesus, which he pronounced "Geezus."

"There are those," he said, "who put material gain ahead of Geezus. There are those who put liquor and fast women and idol worship ahead of Geezus.

"There are some who put hatred and racism and unforgiveness ahead of Geezus. And others who put Mohammed ahead of Geezus, . . . those who put their jobs ahead of Geezus, and cricket ahead of Geezus and even reading the Sunday morning newspaper ahead of Geezus."

As Lili sat and thought about it, it seemed there was an awful lot in Barbados that was being put ahead of Jesus, and like everyone else in attendance, she felt terrible about it.

Sweat dripped from the minister's brow, which he blotted with a folded white handkerchief, and his finger shook as he quivered in a shrill demonstrative tone, ". . .

and those who put hanging out in rum shops and fornication ahead of Geezus."

Lili was not certain where all this would lead, but, by now, the congregation seemed truly concerned at the community's lack of emphasis on Jesus.

"And, if you agree with this say, 'Amen.'"

And everyone in the congregation said, "Amen."

"Hebrews Chapter twelve, verse two." Everyone took out his or her Bible to follow along. Someone handed one to Lili, open to the proper page. "Looking unto Jesus, the author and finisher of our faith; who for the joy that was set before Him endured the cross, despising the same, and is set down at the right hand of the throne of God."

"And if you believe this, say, 'Amen.'"

"Amen," said the congregation.

"Praise Geezus," said the minister.

"Praise Jesus," murmured the congregation.

"Praise the Lord, Geezus."

"Praise the Lord, Jesus" they all replied.

"Praise the Lord, Geezus. Hallelujah!"

"Hallelujah! Hallelujah!" they all said. The responses were so rhythmic that the blend of the preacher's voice and the replies from the congregation seemed more of a blended chant than a response.

Then several of the choristers came forward, Lance among them, and stood in front of the rest of the choir. She recognized the tall, slender woman in a long, chocolate brown, flowing chiffon dress that just barely hugged her hips as it dropped to the floor, as the person with the honeysuckle voice in the first song. She also noticed a chemistry between her and Lance. It was not as overt as Mr. Baker's hand on Mrs. Musgrave's rump but it was just as decisive—a glance, the slightest eye contact, a smirk. She wasn't able to identify the telltale gesture but it was there. She was sure of it.

They sang about the joys they would feel singing together in heaven once they got there. After the first verse the entire congregation joined in and swayed to the music from foot to foot and raised their voices and their hands to heaven. Three or four hundred voices rang out in perfect harmony to the ceiling, out the doors, past the parked cars and to the distant corners of Barbados—with Lance's and the other three lead singers' voices higher and deeper than the rest. The experience made Lili feel at peace, as though she belonged on this glorious journey, headed for the wondrous presence of Jesus.

By the time the preacher spoke again they were all transfixed. He said, "My that was beautiful. I'm hereby calling upon the choir auxiliary to see that that number is set to dance for the Easter service in six weeks' time." Oohs and Aahs filled the church with as much fervor as if he'd just handed each person in attendance the keys to a shiny new car.

Then the preacher concluded his message to the congregation by assuring them that none of them were capable of living their lives without assistance from a higher power. "God has a plan and a path in mind for each of you, which you must discover and follow. If you do not you will be hopelessly lost to the ways of the world, which are arbitrary and chaotic. He admonished them to pray to Geezus and Geezus would inevitably assist them and intercede to their Heavenly Father for them, provided they came in faith. But he also instructed them not to come to Him empty handed.

"You must first be baptized and cleansed of your sins to come before Geezus with a pure heart. And if you have already been baptized and later sinned, as we all have, then you must seek forgiveness, praise Geezus and your prayers will be answered. You must entrust your heart and soul to Him and Him alone."

Then the ushers came along in their red coats and skirts and started marking off pews for the assembly to make an orderly ascent to the altar to receive communion. Lili alternated between decisions of going and not going and ended up finding herself drawn to the front to have a small piece of bread slipped into a little basket she made with her palm by mimicking the people around her. This was followed by a small plastic cup of grape juice which she found exceedingly sweet. The experience left her with a calm spirit and a peaceful mood.

As she arrived back at her pew one of the ushers handed her a note. She unfolded it and it read, "When the service is over meet me in the Garden of Prayer. -L.W.-"

* * *

After the rest of the congregation had filed out of the church and the throngs of cars leaving the parking lot competed with those arriving for the ten a.m. worship service Lili circled the grounds to find The Garden. On her way she saw a mural of Jesus with three little children. She noticed He was white, whereas the children with Him were black, brown and white, respectively. *If only it were just that simple . . .*

She walked around the church and came to a door that had the words stenciled in red block letters, "Garden of Prayer." She didn't know whether to knock or enter so she turned the doorknob and slowly opened the door. A familiar voice said, "Come in and close the door behind you."

Much to her surprise the door opened to a beautiful garden with all sorts of exotic plants—fern pines, jackfruit, frangipani, gooseberry, orange-jasmine, ti plants, mast trees and orchids. She couldn't understand how there could be such a large garden within the church grounds—and inside the atrium of the church building at that. But there it was and there was Inspector Lance Williams, looking sharp in his navy blue suit. It was hot and he took off his jacket.

"Why did you ask me to come here?" she asked, hoping at some level that it had a romantic theme and at another that it didn't.

"I want to ask you some questions about the bank."

"And what if I don't feel like answering them?"

"Why wouldn't you? You know I'm on your side, don't you?"

Birds were chirping in the sweet smelling limonia (orange-jasmine) plants next to them. She could hear the choir in the distance singing an opening hymn for the next service.

"That's something I've been trying to figure out."

Lance looked around. "At least you don't have to worry about these walls."

That part was true. It was difficult to see the walls through the banks of tall, red poinsettia hedges, interlaced with delicate tiny white flowers on long, elegant green stems. It was an inspirational spot where one would not expect to find even a scintilla of evil lurking.

"What is it you want to know?"

"I want to know what you know, Lili—about the books, the bank, Ephraim Whitney, everything. Remember, your life may be in jeopardy. You need to be forthright about everything down to the smallest, seemingly simplest detail, even if you think it may not be important. Tell me . . . everything this time . . .everything you know. I think you're holding out on me."

"And I know you've been holding out on me. Why is it that I should be so frank and open with you?"

"Lili, we're on your side."

"You mean to serve, protect and reassure?"

"That's our motto! Do you have any idea, any idea whatsoever, what it was that Ephraim may have discovered that could have made someone want to kill him?"

They sat on a park bench, provided for meditation. The rich, heavy scent of the jasmine wafted into the air. Tree frogs chirped, which was unusual during the day unless it had been raining, but it hadn't. The place seemed magical. A nearby reflecting pool shimmered with gorgeous white crocuses and dark blue and red water lilies.

"You already asked me all that the day Ephraim died, the day we had that picnic together near Bathsheba. Remember?" She paused a moment. There was something about that sequence of events that suddenly struck her, the discussion, the inspector's impromptu phone call, the murder.

Lili asked, "When was Ephraim murdered?"

"What do you mean when? Just when you said— the Sunday we had that picnic."

"No, I mean, what time of day was he murdered?"

Lance replied, "Why do you want to know that?"

"Just curious," Lili said. "I just wondered."

"Well, we don't know. The autopsy was inconclusive on that point, given the length of time from the murder to the discovery of his body. He'd been floating with the hot tub on high for so long he looked like a prune. The coroner said he couldn't get an accurate core body temperature. Sometime on Sunday, the twenty-fifth— perhaps while we were on our picnic."

Lance continued, "So how about those books of account? You told me about a code, some ledgers and computer runs, accounting errors. Could you go over that for me one more time?"

Lili decided not to bring up what had happened between them after their previous discussion on this subject. Perhaps that was all over for him. It had obscured her vision and her judgment, not to mention made her feel cheap for several days afterwards, especially when he didn't call.

"No," she said. "I already told you everything I know. I have nothing to add."

"You said he found a pattern among the numbers. Was it a code, do you think?"

" I don't remember him ever saying anything to me about a code."

"Look at me, Lili. Did Ephraim Whitney have access to those special ledgers you told me about? Did he ever see them?"

Lili still hadn't decided how much she should confide in the inspector. And, she realized, the guy you've been casually bonking doesn't necessarily make the best ally. She looked directly into his eyes and did her best to conceal her thoughts. "No, I don't think so."

"Lili, you've got to tell me. If you know anything about those books, you've got to tell me right now."

She looked away from him. "Why is it so urgent all of a sudden?"

"Do you remember when I said I thought your friends at the bank were smuggling emeralds or gold or engaging in drug trafficking?"

Lili nodded.

"Well, we think they're doing all of it."

"How do you know that?"

"We're working in cooperation with British Intelligence (MI-5) and we also have our own undercover agents."

Lance continued, "We think they're making legitimate investments in emeralds and precious metals as a decoy. Bajan law allows banks to invest a certain percentage of their assets in commodities, such as gold or emeralds, as a means of securing the currency and hedging against inflation. They overpay for these and smuggle others in. Then they mix the emeralds and gold from the various sources, sort of a shell game, and sell them at a huge profit. They make so much money on this they don't know what to do with it so they've 'diversified' into the drug trade. That in turn leads to gun running."

Lili was overwhelmed. "Sounds like a tidy little enterprise. I'll bet it involves a lot of people, if it's true."

"One thing we're sure of by working with MI-5 is that their government's desire for a more thorough investigation is one of the reasons Mr. Musgrave has been transferred so suddenly."

Lili didn't see the connection but he assured her there was one and that she must keep quiet about it. "Who am I going to tell?"

"Our sources tell us there are several ledgers with a certain amount of information but there's one master ledger that contains a summary of all transactions and a detailed history of the larger, more significant ones. If we can get our hands on that book we can break whatever code it's in, trace the funds to their source and find out who's involved."

Lili thought aloud. "That would solve your case and give me the information I need to return home and clear my name. Do you think it's one of the books Miss Cumberbatch keeps locked in her office?"

"It's possible that it was among them, perhaps for a time. But on the whole we believe a book so important, like that one, would usually be kept by someone higher up in the organization."

He let go of her shoulders and let one hand slip down onto her arm. "Lili, we believe this is a worldwide operation."

"And what else do you know about this book?" Lili asked.

Lance replied, "We understand that it's blue—"

"With silver leaf and an emblem that has two spotted panthers hissing at one another on the cover?"

Lance's voice quickened. "How did you know?"

"I've seen it."

"Where?"

"First in Miss Cumberbatch's cabinet and then in Mr. Baker's office. He showed it to me not more than a few days ago."

Lance became animated. "Where do you think he put it? Where does he keep it?"

"I don't know. I've seen it in both places. I'm not sure where it is now. I think I may have seen him leave with it a day or so ago."

"Just as we suspected," Lance said. "We think it's gotten too hot to leave in any one spot for too long and it's about to be transported out of the country."

"Doesn't he have copies of it? Don't you just have to find a copy?"

"These people are too smart for that," Lance said. "You don't keep copies of something like this."

Lili reflected for a moment. "Do you want me to see if I can slip into Mr. Baker's office and find the book?"

"It's generous of you to offer but that would involve an unnecessary danger to you and we're not sure the book's there anyway."

"Where is it then?"

Lance hesitated. He looked at her as if to say, "I trust you; why can't you learn to trust me." He said, "We don't know where it is now but we believe it will soon arrive at one of the old abandoned buildings adjacent to the lighthouse at Ragged Point."

"Ragged Point?"

"Yes, there's almost nightly smuggling activity out of Conset Bay. Mostly marijuana and other recreational drugs out of Jamaica. We think they're so fearful of this book being intercepted that they're going to use unconventional means to get it off island. Normally they'd probably entrust it to someone with diplomatic immunity but they know we might choose to stop and search some diplomats and risk the adverse international publicity. Within a week, or two at the most, we suspect it will be gone."

Lili said, "Gone? Gone where?"

"We think they're going to move it to the lighthouse complex and then ship it out shortly after midnight. That's what our sources tell us anyway. We're hoping we'll be able to confirm that with some real time intelligence but that won't give us much time to act."

Lili asked, "Why don't you just stake out the place, get a search warrant and go in and get it when you're sure it's there?"

"For one thing we'll never be positive it's there and if we turn out to be wrong we'll have tipped them off. For another the banks are so well connected that the judge or one of his clerks might tell them what we're up to. So we can't use normal legal channels."

"Then why not get a large group of law enforcement together and storm them and take what you want?"

"Lili, we're much too civilized here in Barbados for that. Besides, if we send someone in without a search warrant and they get caught, it will end a lot of careers, mine included. Also, if they heard or saw us coming, they might destroy the book. I'd do the job myself if it weren't for my risk of passing out. I'm thinking of getting some of my cousins together and asking them."

Lili knew the area. She and Sea Cat had passed by on several occasions on the weekends when he took her out on his relatives' fishing boat. It was rugged and picturesque and stood out from the rest of the coastline. It had a long sloping beach to the north and sheer cliffs to the south.

"But if your cousins do it, won't that implicate you if any of them get caught? After all, you said your extended family was all tied up with the force. And if there are several of them, doesn't that increase the risk?"

"Lili, someone has to do it or we'll just have to sit by and watch our best evidence slip out of the country."

"Then I'll do it," Lili replied.

"Don't be preposterous. What makes you think you could or that I would let you even if you could?"

"During the summers while I was going to the University of Hawaii I conducted cliff-climbing tours for wealthy American businessmen and women along the Na Pali Coast. I've climbed much higher cliffs than any I've seen around here."

Lance listened. In the distance they could hear the sermon and call to Geezus by the Reverend Le Roy Downings.

Lance said, "But were they sheer, like these cliffs? And do you have any experience with mountain climbing equipment?"

"No, but I'm strong enough and I'm sure I can easily adapt to using equipment, since I did quite well without any."

"Lili, I can't let you do it." At that moment, just for an instant, Lance sounded to Lili like her father.

"Let me? Now I'm sure I'm going to do it," she said. "You have no choice."

"Those cliffs are sheer. You'd have to have the proper climbing equipment and know how to use it."

Lili replied, "You can help me or not. It's up to you. I'm going to get those books. I have as much interest in finding out what's in them as you do."

Lance looked at his watch and began to unbutton his shirt. "I'm due over at Government House in less than fifteen minutes. Do you mind if I change here?"

Lili looked over at the door and then back at Lance. "It's okay with me." *As long as no one comes in.*

He took off his shirt. "Okay, all right, I have to rely on someone. But you won't be able to climb those cliffs without ropes, carabiners, clog stops, anchors and pulleys. Do you know how to use those? Do you know how to tie a clove hitch on a carabiner?"

"No. But if I can climb hundreds of feet up rocky cliffs without them, I'm sure I can climb those to the south of the lighthouse. I've already seen them."

"Well, I'll have to show you how to use the equipment. These cliffs are sheer."

She was struck by how muscular he remained years after his days as a cricketer. Sweat rolled across the smooth, taught muscles on his chest and down his sternum.

"How do you know so much about climbing? I haven't seen much since I've been here that I would even call a cliff as compared to Na Pali."

"Remember when my kids talked about the caves? We rappel into those."

"I thought you were afraid of heights."

"I am. But the caves are dark and I try not to think about it. Somehow going down into a dark place is not as bad as going up a high cliff in broad daylight and then once I'm in there, I have to climb out. Besides, if I get dizzy, it usually passes in a few minutes. With the ropes and anchors the worst that can happen is that I'll be left dangling, but I can't take that risk with a place that may be patrolled."

She put her hand on his chest. "I'd hate to see you left dangling," she said.

They both heard a creak at the door and stopped to listen. Lance walked over, opened the door a crack and bent over to peek out. She wanted him and now.

But on further reflection that seemed sacrilegious, not to mention she'd just heard what the Reverend Downings had to say about putting fornication ahead of Geezus. She suppressed her desires.

Lance finished dressing. They went out the door and headed for his police cruiser. When they got there he put his suit into the trunk and took off his white hat with the silver spike on top and carefully placed that into the trunk, as well.

She leaned against the car in much the same manner as when they had made love near the tree tunnel. In fact she tried to adopt the same, exact pose to see how he would react. "When are you going to teach me?" She tried to look innocent and vulnerable.

Lance looked at her, got a snicker on his face, paused, took a deep breath and exhaled slowly. "Lili, I can train you, map it out and supply you with the latest equipment. There should be no alarms. At least we don't know of any systems being ordered from local contractors. I'll get you in and out of there as fast as possible. We'll try to find out exactly where they're keeping the book within the complex. But don't be surprised if I change my mind. I'm not entirely sold on you doing this you know."

Lance got into his cruiser and prepared to drive off. "I'd take you back to the hotel but I've got to get right over to Government House."

"That's okay," Lili said. "I can take the bus."

"Oh, I almost forgot to tell you."

"Yes," Lili replied.

"There may be some violence at the bank."

"You mean because they're onto me?"

"No, it's unrelated to what we've been talking about. The demonstrators are getting more and more agitated and our intelligence reports tell us they may be about to attack. Unfortunately we don't know what means they're likely to use."

"Thanks for the heads up. I'll try to keep an eye out for them as well."

Lance rolled up the windows on his police cruiser as it began to rain. He drove off, while Lili was left to walk up the street to the bus stop with nothing more than her church program to cover her head.

Chapter Seven

Once the curtains were up in the conference room—
a cheerful light taffeta with green and white checks—the
traffic to see Mr. Baker increased profusely. This was a
surprise because the demonstrators had become much
bolder and more belligerent. Even from the fifth floor
everyone could hear stones and bottles crashing against the
concrete end of the bank building facing the Careenage and
Lili decided it wasn't worth it to go out for lunch.
Normally the police would have dispersed an unruly crowd
like this but the government feared that if they didn't allow
it more people would support them and make matters
worse. A policy of "containment," rather than "dispersal"
was adopted.

Lili ate from a brown bag she brought, containing
apples, bananas, figs and other treats that she mused would
appeal to Jack. She felt she was the one on a high wire
now. She tried to be congenial and dutiful in discharging
what few responsibilities she had, but she didn't hold out
much hope that she was ever going to climb the ladder of
success in Barbadian banking.

Her meeting with Lance had gotten her thinking,
thinking about a lot of things. One of them was the timing
of the murder and whether or not he could have had a hand

in it by tipping someone off that Ephraim had found something important. Then on the other hand she remembered that Ephraim had said he was going to the hotel, long before she had informed Lance of their progress.

Another thing she had been thinking about were the particular accounts in which she had repeatedly found discrepancies. One was an old established business, Da Costa Manning's, and another was Tropical Shipping. Since she didn't have a lot to do and Mr. Baker was in the conference room with another of his associates she decided to sneak a peek at his private files and see if anything might shed more light. He had just told her to stay out of his personal file cabinet which made her all the more curious.

She didn't know how much time she had so she acted quickly. She immediately found one titled "Transcarribean Shipping," which had a number of shipping and receiving schedules. One of the ships that kept showing up was the Tropic Carib. That was Han's ship. *I wonder what they could possibly be carrying that has anything to do with the bank.*

Then she heard someone coming. She slipped the file back into the drawer and slammed it shut just before Shirley Bangerter's head appeared around the corner. Shirley said, "It's Miss Cumberbatch on line three for you, Miss Kaleo." Lili cringed. She thought about picking up the phone on Mr. Baker's desk. The light on line three was blinking but he might finish his meeting and discover she was there. She went back to her desk and took the call.

Miss Cumberbatch said, "Miss Kaleo, we need you down in the credit card department immediately."

A number of people, fearful of the rising hostility, hadn't showed up for work and Lili was asked to answer irate phone calls from customers who felt they had been unfairly charged by the bank on their invoices.

"But I pay my bill as soon as it arrives. I shouldn't be asked to pay a late charge," an irate woman from St. Philip Parish complained.

Lili was flabbergasted. "Let me check into that and call you back."

"I've already been told that three times," the woman said. "I'm coming down to join the protest."

* * *

Later on that evening, back at the hotel, there was a
knock at Lili's door. It was Sea Cat with a message from
the hotel operator. "It's him," Sea Cat said.

The Tower didn't have phones in the rooms so Lili
had to go down the hall to take the call.

"Lance, who?" she said jokingly after she picked up
the phone. ". . . Yes, I'll meet you. Where do you want to
meet?"

"Lili, I couldn't help but overhear you," Sea Cat
said after she had hung up and was heading back to her
room to gather her things.

"I know you don't want to hear this," he said. "But
you should be careful of that man."

"Sea Cat, what on earth do I have to fear from
him?" she said, recalling that he had only once ever laid a
hand on her and that was with her consent. "He's the
police," she said.

"He may have a good reputation as a police
officer," Sea Cat said, "but there are rumors that he killed
his wife."

"You're kidding. That's not possible." *It couldn't
be.*

Sea Cat said, "No, I'm not kidding. I wanted to tell
you before but you never seemed to want to listen.
Inspector Williams took his wife out for a boat ride one
Sunday afternoon off the Atlantic coast of St. Lucy, where
he lives. But he's the only one who came back. There
were storm warnings but they went out anyway—in a little
skiff. Lili, don't go with him alone. Don't go with him at
all. I have bad feelings about it."

"I appreciate what you're saying, Sea Cat, but I'm
going, so kindly get out of my way," she said, as she
entered her room and began getting her things together.

Sea Cat pleaded, "But, Sugar . . ."

She paused and looked at him. "I'll be okay." She
sighed. "The man sings in the choir for heaven's sake."

* * *

Lili was picked up early the next morning by a
young police officer in plain clothes, driving a taxicab. He
didn't come to The Tower. She had to walk down the hill
to The Paradise, blend in with the crowd, take taxi number
seventy-six and wait while he dropped off other passengers.

She recognized the terrain as they turned to head
across country. As the broken limestone flying from the
roadbed pinged against the underside of the cab she kept

coming back to Sea Cat's assertion that Lance may have murdered his wife. Each time she denied that it was possible. The plainclothes driver motored her to an outcropping of small cliffs along the Atlantic Coast near Cuckold Point. Lance was there waiting when she arrived.

This man can't be a murderer she assured herself as she watched him sort out the ropes, anchors and pitons for a test climb. It was Errol Barrow Day in memory of the man who led Barbados to independence from Great Britain and the bank was closed.

Lili was impressed with Lance's knowledge of and confidence in what he was doing. She couldn't help but compare this experience with a similar one many years before with her friends Suzie and Izzy Kawamoto. Only this time the gear was all the best and her ally much more formidable, physically at least—especially strong and—she thought—quite handsome.

"Where do we start?" Lili asked.

First Lance taught her to set the anchors and pitons. He gave her a little hammer and showed her how to pick a hole in the cliff and insert them. The cliffs were coral and easily chipped away.

Then he taught her how to thread her rope through the carabiners and rig a belay. At first she got her rope tangled. But by patiently concentrating on what she was doing and not the whole climb at once, she was able to get the hang of it. She enjoyed the feeling of Lance's strong, masculine arms around her as he taught her how to grip and use the rope to maximum advantage.

Then he told her, "It's time. Let's see how you do."

The cliffs were only about fifty meters high and had a fair slope to them, so they were not impossible for her to climb. But it was still a struggle. Lance had to boost her up from behind to negotiate even the lower levels of the cliff, and once she had gone ten or fifteen meters, she just hung there—tired and exhausted. Along the Na Pali Coast she recalled, the cliffs were more gradual and she was able to climb, using mainly the strength in her legs. Learning to lash the ropes and carabiners was a lot like learning to sail. She believed that if she could just get her gear working efficiently she was athletic enough to do it.

Once Lili learned to keep her ropes untangled and plan ahead, the ascenders and other climbing mechanisms worked miraculously. She was able to make—at first—a little progress and then greater strides.

"It's a good thing I've been working out." She sighed.

Lance ran his fingers along her biceps. She got a tingly feeling. "It's along in here where you've got to build up your muscle," he said. "Next time you go to the gym, spend a little more time on the rowing machine. Even a few days of targeted work will help some."

I'll show him, she thought. Without any help from Lance she set three more anchors, threaded the ropes and climbed onward and upward.

Lance said, "Very good. The only trouble is, you've left yourself in a difficult situation to climb any further. See how that rock is hanging out over your head?"

"Yes." She nodded.

"Don't you think it would have been better to go over this way?" He pointed to her left. "See how it goes straight up with little obstruction."

She had the urge to hit him again. But now she was once again dangling helplessly from the ropes and anchors. She didn't any more know how to climb higher than she knew how to get down. On a more gradual slope to his right Lance climbed past her, got above her, set a toprope with doubled biners and offered her a way up. With her teeth gritted and muscles aching, she struggled to the top.

"Try another?" Lance said.

Lili was exhausted, even on this short climb. "Are you kidding? I think you're right. I need to work on my biceps."

"Always think about how to route your climb," Lance said. "If you're going to be lead rope you have to plan ahead."

She took the fact that Lance didn't argue with her as an affirmation of his feelings about her condition. As they gathered the anchors and pulleys and stowed them in a large blue nylon bag Lance had brought, she asked, "Did your wife used to climb with you?"

"Only down into the caves. She was afraid of the ocean."

"But I thought that's where she—"

Lance appeared to realize where Lili's thoughts were headed and said, "What do you know about Rebecca's death?"

"Only that it was an accident," Lili replied. "A boating accident. If she didn't like the ocean, what were you doing—"

"There are those who don't think it was an accident at all. Has anyone told you that?"

She paused. "Why no. No one has ever said anything like that. I'd never even heard a thing about *the accident* until—" She wanted to ask and yet she didn't. "Why would they say that sort of thing anyway?"

"It *was* an *accident, Lili.* We went out for a Sunday afternoon cruise along the coast and a sudden, unexpected storm came up." Lance pointed. "It happened right out there. I'll admit we'd been arguing and I thought it would calm us down and give us a chance to talk without being interrupted by the kids."

Lili looked at the sea. *You could've done that on the beach.*

Lance continued, "I had been to the rum shop that morning and tipped a few too many. I wasn't at my best sailing in the bad weather and all and the boat capsized. I couldn't save her." Lance's expression drooped and he glanced at the ground.

"I found her underneath the boat and tried to grab her and pull her out from under it and towards the shore. But she panicked and fought me off. When I tried again, she grabbed me, pulled me under." There was a fierce look in Lance's eyes as he spoke.

"I fought back and when I got to the surface, took a few quick breaths and went back under to try again but she was gone. I choked and struggled and searched as long as I could in spite of the giant waves. Eventually I ran out of breath, got weak and numb." Lance looked dejected.

"Finally I had to swim away or there would have been two drownings that day instead of one. The sea was so rough that I barely made it to shore and collapsed on the beach. It was another twenty minutes before I gathered the strength to get up and go look for help.

"No one saw us so there was talk that I may have killed her. But I didn't. It was just bad luck except that I shouldn't have been drinking."

Lili wanted to hug him in consolation and hold him close but didn't want to interfere with his grieving. "Why would anyone think you'd want to kill her? I mean, you have those beautiful children and they worship you and they must have worshipped your wife, too."

"Lili, I don't know how to say this so I'll just come right out with it. Emma's not Rebecca's child."

"What? Did you adopt her?" She thought she understood right away but she didn't want to.

"Lili, Emma is mine. She's just not Rebecca's."

Lili's jaw dropped. "But I don't understand." She hoped she was wrong. "The older children are both of yours aren't they?"

"Yes, of course."

"And you were still man and wife. I mean you were married when Emma was—"

"Lili, I strayed! That's the reason I started going to church. I promised Rebecca I'd go—I mean after I had to tell her about Emma. She said she'd leave me if I didn't. I've gone every Sunday since—even sing in the choir. You saw me."

"Then whose child is she? I mean besides yours?" Lili couldn't decide whether she should be shocked, angry or sad. Lance had become sullen and remorseful.

"Lili, I didn't stray often. And I never stopped loving her. Rebecca always came first."

That's what they all say. "Did you have a relationship with the mother?"

"Not really. I mean I used to sing with a band that went onto the cruise ships when they came into port and I would occasionally find myself attracted to someone—you know—the music, the liquor—the party atmosphere. Occasionally I would—no I mean rarely, but on occasion, you know—get carried away." Then he shifted from a tone of remorse to one of blame. "The women were like cats in heat. They wouldn't leave us alone."

"But you didn't have to say 'yes.'"

"I don't know what you'll think of this next part, Lili."

"Try me," she said.

"I have this thing— "

"Yes, I know." Lili laughed.

"No, seriously . . . about women. It's a problem I've had my whole life."

"Tell me about it. I'd like to hear."

"This may surprise you."

I doubt it.

"But sometimes I have an overwhelming desire to 'have' a woman. You know make love to her for the first time." He paused and caught his breath and looked at her for a reaction, which she hid. "And, then, once we've done it, you know—had sex once or twice, I seem to lose interest."

"You don't say."

"I do say. And that's the way it was with Emma's mother—just once and that was it. I lost interest."

You rotten bastard!

Lance continued, "After we did it, I never had any desire to see her again, if you know what I mean."

"Yes, I think I get the picture, but why are you telling me all this?"

"I don't want you to think I'm a rotten bastard. I'm really a *family* man . . ."

Lili said, "If you weren't a family man, we wouldn't even be standing here having this conversation." Lili thought of the happy brigade waiting for him at the end of the narrow lane.

"And now I go to church and try to live the gospel."

Or, so you say.

"And I like you."

Lili looked away.

"And I want us to be friends."

Lili turned her back to him. He put his hand on her shoulder and turned her around and kissed her—not a peck on the cheek, but a long, lingering, firmly placed kiss on the lips. Then he stopped and it went no further. They got back into the Porsche and he drove her home.

She felt angry, frustrated and confused.

* * *

Lili remained confused. On their outing she had gotten a kiss and a climbing lesson, but that was it. She returned to work in the credit card department the following day, hoping to have a chance to think things over—to evaluate her relationship with the policeman—but there was too much of a frenzy.

She also wanted to get back into Mr. Baker's office to have another look at his files but the phones rang incessantly.

A new policy had gone into effect for all who had credit card balances with the bank. Anyone discovered to be in arrears on any other loan with any creditor—whether as debtor, or even just a guarantor, was charged a delinquency fee as well as a higher interest rate on their remaining balance at the bank. Lili was ashamed to represent these scoundrels and flinched whenever she had to pick up the phone. Those in charge had no shame.

One lady had co-signed on her son's car loan and claimed she didn't know his loan had been in arrears. "It was with the Bank of Barbados," she said. "If you'd called me, I would've come down and made my son's payment for him."

"Too bad," Miss Cumberbatch said to Lili. "She should have known better."

Known better than what?   Signing for her son or dealing with the bank in the first place?

By the end of the day Lili was exhausted and took her favorite seat at the big round table to unwind. It was to be a delightful evening because Sea Cat had announced that Jack had learned to do four somersaults in midair, and—like the world-class acrobatic monkey that he was—would perform this incredible feat before a live audience for the first time ever this very evening. He posted flyers around the neighborhood with a picture of Jack doing a somersault off the trapeze.

The Applebys were back from the south of France for another vacation and Mrs. Appleby had always been a favorite of Lili's. It was hot and humid that day but well worth enduring. The lingering glow of the rust colored sun was extinguished by the calm, light turquoise waters of the nearby shipping lane.

Before the performance Sea Cat let Jack visit with the Applebys. Mr. Appleby held the "minkee" on his shoulder and stroked his hair and commented on what a "fine, furry little minkee" he was indeed. Jack knew right where to look in Mrs. Appleby's purse, even after all this time, and ferreted out the banana embedded with more fruit she had hidden there for him.

When darkness came Tiki torches were lit all around the porch and two trapezes were set up—farther apart than ever before in the history of green monkey performances on the island of Barbados, let alone a baby one. Sea Cat proudly introduced him over a microphone he had rented for the occasion from Carter's General Store and Jack came out and took a bow in the spotlight. He had on his red, yellow and blue outfit with the matching cap and chinstrap.

"Bravo! Bravo!" shouted the crowd. The monkey strutted across the stage—full of pride and vitality—shoulders back, high stepping, like a drum major.

Sea Cat played a drum roll on his tape player. Jack nodded to the audience and took another bow. Then he climbed onto the trapeze and swung it back and forth. With each swing it got faster and faster. Sea Cat used a stick to get the other trapeze swinging at a perfectly synchronized pace. Cheering onlookers lined the perimeter of the porch.

Finally Jack came zooming off the first trapeze, did four full somersaults with perfect timing and grabbed the second trapeze. To celebrate, he flipped over two additional times while the audience went wild with cheers, hoots and howls, lead by Mr. Appleby.

"Bravo! Bravo!" Followed by a torrent of applause.

Jack climbed back down from the platform and ran across the table in front of Lili to take a bow and receive his spoils. The crowd tossed him a bevy of fruits and nuts. He reached up to remove his hat, bent over, stumbled and fell off the table onto the porch.

Everyone laughed. Mr. Appleby led the chorus, "There he goes again, hamming it up—that clever little 'minkee,' to get more treats. Ornery one that minkee!"

But the "minkee" never reappeared. Laughter turned to silence and the crowd's edginess grew sharp, at the delay.

The group at the big table stood up and Mr. Appleby appointed himself to crawl beneath the table to see what that pesky little minkee was up to.

Sea Cat turned on the porch lights and a ripple of murmurs permeated the crowd. Mr. Appleby shrieked from beneath the table and got up off his hands and knees, noticeably shaken. Teardrops dampened his bright red cheeks.

"The little minkee," he said. "The poor little minkee is dead!"

Mrs. Appleby fainted.

By the time the police and the ambulance arrived—for Mrs. Appleby—the crowd from around the perimeter of the porch had dissipated in a whirlwind of conjecture. Sea Cat was noticeably shaken and had to be taken to his room and given a tranquilizer.

Lili insisted on staying with him until he was "resting comfortably."

When she returned to the porch she was surprised to find her police inspector friend, along with the St. Michael District Coroner examining the deceased. Sea Cat had been so upset that he insisted that someone call the police. It was the inspector's idea in turn to call the coroner.

When Lance saw her, he said, "Miss Kaleo, may I speak with you privately?"

He took her by the arm and they went over by the railing. Lili found herself trembling—partly because of the incident, and partly because the inspector was touching her.

He said, "Do you remember when I told you that you may be in danger?"

She looked into his deep brown, concerned eyes and nodded. He had on street clothes.

He went over and knelt by the monkey and motioned for her to join him. "Come over and look at this."

He lifted the stiffened arm of the deceased monkey. Stuck into his side, just below his armpit, was a thin little piece of stick. It had a tiny quill near its end.

"Do you know what this is?" he asked.

Lili shook her head. "No."

"This is a curare war dart. It will kill a cheetah in less than a minute."

She lifted her hand to cover her mouth. "Oh, that poor little monkey."

"It's not the monkey I'm concerned about."

Lili was perplexed.

Lance said, "Where were you when the monkey fell?"

"Why, right in front of him—over there—watching the show."

"That's what I thought. I think this dart was intended for you."

Lili shrieked.

Lance put his finger on the end of the dart and flicked it. Its shrill twang made them shudder.

* * *

Lili returned to work the next day, as usual. There was talk between her and Lance that it might be wiser for her not to go but she wasn't one to shy away from danger. Besides even the police inspector had to admit it wasn't likely that her adversaries would attempt to strike a blow in their own backyard. And there was no proof that the attack on the monkey was anything other than a cruel joke by someone who had gotten tired of hearing Sea Cat rave about his precocious pet.

The uproar of the crowd outside the bank and the barrage of calls soon took Lili's mind off the assault. The crowd poured coconut water on as many of the employees as they could douse on the way in and it was only through

Lili's speed and agility that she made it inside without being soaked. Several of the employees had to stop in the bathroom and accept a change of clothes, supplied by the bank, after their own had been stained.

A co-worker said, "Shhh! Lili, I'll tell you something. That woman who called about making her payment when the bill arrived . . ."

"Yes."

"Well, she was probably telling the truth. We hold the bills until the last possible minute to send them out because it increases the percentage of delinquencies and that increases the late charges and terminates promotional interest rates."

"You're kidding," Lili said.

"No. I'm not. I wish I were. And even if they do send their payments on time who, besides the bank, is to say when we receive them?"

Lili was furious. The Bank of Aloha used to delay posting for days, whenever she made Mimo's mortgage payment for him, until she started sending her payment with a proof of delivery. Even then it took awhile for the bank to realize it wouldn't be wise to continue to tack late charges onto this account. They changed their practices only when her lawyer threatened a class action lawsuit.

Lili may have been disgusted but she still had to field the calls and put on the appearance of dutifully representing the bank. After all every call was "monitored or recorded," and even though recordings of calls that weren't favorable to the bank's position were routinely erased Lili didn't want her handling of these situations to make her stand out any more in the eyes of her supervisors than she already did.

* * *

That evening Lili didn't return to the hotel. Instead she took a series of bus rides—each time taking steps to be certain she wasn't being followed. Finally she ended up at an old bathhouse near the rocks at Bathsheba. No one appeared to have used it in years and signs of salt air erosion were advanced. It begged for a coat of paint.

Lance, who was waiting for her when she arrived, helped her into a dark, form-fitting outfit that resembled a wet suit, although it was made of thinner material and was much more supple, a dry suit. It fit her curves perfectly. She kept wondering if Lance's touch would wander beyond helping her on with the suit, but it didn't.

They went over the ropes, carabiners and pre-planning again as he had taught her last time on the smaller cliffs near his home.

Lili looked around their new location and said, "I don't see any cliffs. I thought you said this would be much tougher than last time."

"Today we're going to climb these rocks." He pointed.

In the waves near the shoreline were a number of rocks that could have come from another planet. They were odd shapes and many of them looked as if they were eroding from the bottom up.

Lili said, "They don't look very high."

"If you can climb these," Lance said, "you'll have no trouble with the cliffs. You use the same principles to climb the last twenty meters as the first. "Trust me," he said. "These will be challenge enough. Once you learn to climb these you'll be ready."

He was right. The rocks were an incredible challenge, much more difficult than the previous cliffs because of their shape. It was like having to climb across a ceiling to get to a roof.

When it was his turn to be lead rope Lance climbed like a spider. It soon became obvious that he could climb any of the rocks in only a few minutes with little or no apparent exertion. Of course they were low to the ground, so the risk was minimal if he passed out. Lili stayed on the ground, watched and served as belayer, while he quickly placed his ropes and carabiners, then "zipped" to the top. It looked so easy. Then it was her turn.

The crashing waves beneath the rocks were distracting and Lili acknowledged this. But Lance said, "It'll simulate what you'll experience on the night of the assault. You'll be hearing crashing waves—only you won't be able to see them. We want to make this as close to the actual experience as we can. Any apprehension you might have about the waves is something you'll have to get over. You've got to learn to ignore them."

Lili remembered most of what he had taught her the time before and in the meantime had read a few books on the subject by the famous rock climber, John Long. The Garrison Fitness Center had installed a wall with pegs that she used to strengthen her upper body and sharpen her agility for climbing.

"I did those rowing exercises you told me to do."

He ran his fingers along her back and arms. She wanted him to stop and kiss her, but he didn't. Instead, he said, "Good work," and patted her on the back.

She wasn't sure his endorsement was sincere. This time she managed not to get the rope tangled and chose the easiest route she could fathom to challenge the rock. Yet its upward angle made it extremely difficult. Through sheer determination she struggled around the curvature of the rock. Once she had gotten that far it was an easy matter to use the finger holds Lance had taught her and climb to the top. When she got there she stood and celebrated. Lance watched from the ground. He was lashed to her and served as her anchor.

She held up her arm and made a fist.

"Bravo! Bravo!" Lance said.

At that moment Lili knew for an instant how Jack must have felt in the spotlight just before his demise. *A bad omen?* It was exhilarating and getting down was easy until she got to the bend in the rock. This time, however, she decided not to climb back under but slid straight down the rope instead. Her hands slipped and were it not for her gloves she would likely have gotten a nasty rope burn.

"Try another?" Lance said.

This time Lili said, "Yes." And each time she climbed another rock she found it easier and became more confident than on the last.

At the conclusion of the exercise Lance ran his hands over her muscles. "A little more work there . . . . Some stretching there. I wish you had time to pump iron and develop more strength in those biceps but just do the best you can."

It was unnerving. *How can he touch me and then stop?*

"Another good workout or two and I think you'll be ready," he concluded.

He took her to a "To City" bus stop and she caught the last bus back to St. Michael's Parish. No kiss. No romance. Only "business" and none of it "monkey . . . ."

* * *

The little patio at The Tower, where Lili and Sea Cat met after work the next day, did not face the ocean. It faced the trees and the up-sloping hillside to the east, and if not for those trees and that hillside one could have seen the road to Speightstown and the bus stop. Yet, it was pleasant and quaint and became shaded shortly after lunchtime.

Lili said, "What makes you think the inspector killed his wife?"

"Lili, the child was illegitimate. Everyone knew his wife detested him for the indiscretion and he probably got tired of her taking it out on him and the child. I heard she was really hard on the little girl. The kid still doesn't talk from what I understand."

"That's preposterous," she said. "It's ridiculous to think he would harm anyone who didn't have it coming."

"All right then, how do you know the inspector wasn't involved in Ephraim's death? He may have thought that Ephraim was a rival."

"Now you're being ridiculous, Sea Cat. Everyone knew that Ephraim was gay."

"Are you sure of that? He used to come here with women. I've checked them in and carried their bags."

"They must have just been friends. I don't know."

"Well for all the time they spent in their room, skulking around the hallways, smirking at one another, I'd say they were more than just friends."

Then something occurred to Lili. "Are you sure they weren't transvestites?"

"That I couldn't say," Sea Cat admitted. "But that doesn't mean the inspector's not on the take?"

"How can you possibly think he is? I've seen where he lives. If he's on the take he's not exactly living in the lap of luxury."

"All right then," Sea Cat said. "Where did he get the money to buy the Porsche?"

Chapter Eight

When the day came for the assault on the lighthouse, as was frequently the case on the east coast, it was raining. There was discussion of waiting for better weather but the inspector said, "We think this is it. We think the book came in this afternoon and is on its way out tonight. And this is our last, best chance to get it."

Lili flashed back on the comments that Sea Cat had made—the warnings, the counsel toward caution. But she desperately wanted to believe in the inspector. She thought of seeing him in church, how sincere he seemed singing in front of the congregation and—the acid test—when she saw him with his children—how loving and responsive they were to his arrival. *So he won't give me the time of day as a lover, that doesn't mean he's not good at his job.*

Nightfall arrived and Lili was emotionally prepared as soon as it got dark. They met at a rum shop near Lance's house and waited. The rain intermittently gave way to a bright moonlit night, so she prayed for clouds.

"I wish we didn't have to contend with the moonlight but it's now or never," Lance said.

Lili refused any rum but Lance tipped a few, "just to be social."

Déjà vu, she mused.

Along about ten p.m. they got into the Porsche and drove over to Conset Bay. Lili was so frightened as they went down the narrow road to the bay that she nearly asked Lance to turn around. The lane was barely wide enough for the Porsche and she was sure another car couldn't pass in the other direction. She felt the risk of being trapped was high but she didn't express this and hoped Lance knew what he was doing.

"There's a lot of drug traffic here—almost every night," he said. "Marijuana and guns from Jamaica and St. Vincent."

That's a comfort.

Lance continued, "We don't want to call attention to ourselves or make anyone think this is a bust."

They got into a small boat with two small windows in the front and an outboard motor. Lili wondered whether this was "the skiff" from which his wife had died but she thought it best not to ask. There was no dock. The boat was lashed to a large rock.

As they proceeded out of the bay they heard other boats and rowdy, drunken voices but she couldn't see anyone. Clouds had crept in and blocked the moonlight.

"You'd be unlikely to see them even if there were no clouds," Lance said. "They turn off their running lights once they get within ten kilometers of the shore. That way our coast guard is less likely to spot them. Every once in awhile they have a collision and we all laugh about that."

Lili had seen the coast guard ships, but had never known one to leave port. As they proceeded out the bay in what she assumed was a southerly direction she felt queasy. The boat listing from side to side, and pitching bow to stern, nauseated her. With little or no control she leaned over the side and vomited and continued to throw up until her stomach was empty.

"Empty stomach; clear mind," Lance said with no apparent concern.

"Good. I barf my guts out and that's all you've got to say!"

Lance said. "You're just a little nervous. I'm sure you'll do just fine."

Lili knew enough about sports psychology to wonder whether he really meant that or was just trying to facilitate positive thinking for the task at hand. What she really wanted him to say was, "This is too hard. And stupid. Let's turn around." But he didn't.

He was right, though. Once she had vomited she did feel considerably better and could think more clearly.

The climb up the face of the cliff was remarkably easy except that the rock was much more dense than any she had encountered on her practice climbs and she had a hard time getting her anchors and pitons in. Once she did though, things went much more smoothly than expected.

The rain clouds stayed out to sea and as she neared the top she climbed into the brightly lit night of a full moon. It was eerie. They had not driven by the lighthouse because Lance said there was only one road in and out and he didn't want to alert the occupants that they were being observed. Instead he had some aerial photographs taken and together they had studied those.

Lili agreed the best approach would be from the south. If one were to expect an invasion it would most likely come from the north, where an assault could easily be launched from the beach. A few hundred meters of hills to climb and there you'd be right at the auxiliary buildings. Whatever patrols they might have would most likely be stationed there and along the road that approached the lighthouse.

The final reconnaissance had placed the book at the top of the lighthouse tower for added security so Lili had to gather and take her rack from the cliffs—the ropes, the carabiners, the ascenders, the works. Lance stayed behind and waited in the boat a short distance offshore, which was their plan. The lighthouse was about sixty meters in height, slightly shorter than the cliffs themselves, so Lili thought it would be easier to climb. She snuck along the coast and cut the barbed wire placed there by a nearby farmer to corral his sheep. She had a hard time walking in her rock shoes and stumbled into a pear cactus. The spines penetrated her dry suit. She cut her palm trying to extricate herself and it hurt like hell. She could hear dogs howling in the distance and hoped beyond hope they weren't guarding the lighthouse. If they were she had no chance.

When she got to the compound she could smell sawdust, a byproduct of construction when the occupants took over the grounds. The sawdust was mixed with the smell of fresh salt air and she could feel a breeze off the coast. In the distance she could see dark cloud formations and dense rain showers against the silhouette of the moon. She wondered whether or not they had reached Lance, the boat and the cliffs.

As she lashed her rope to the exposed beam of an adjacent building and began her ascent she had just the opposite problem as she had on the cliffs. The old concrete was weak and crumbly so she had to pound deeper and deeper to secure her anchors. She hoped the hollow pinging sound wouldn't alert anyone. Often she would end up with just a handful of mortar or old brick dust and was developing serious doubts as to whether the anchors would hold. She alternated them with pitons.

She had to use a frog step and with nothing to anchor her rope but a beam. She knew that if there were a misstep she might just be left dangling until morning, when she would be caught. But the anchors and pitons held and she slowly and methodically made her way to the top. The training had paid off. The climb was arduous but straightforward and uneventful.

There were glass pull-up windows all around the tower, which she'd expected from the photographs. Some of them were broken, but not enough for her to slip inside, so she had to lift one.

When she did so an alarm went off and floodlights came on all over the compound. By instinct she slid down the coiled rope she held for her descent. She tried not to tumble. It was the fastest elevator ride she'd ever had. When she hit the roof of one of the outbuildings she bounced against a vent. She hit her tailbone and it ached. She forsook the ropes, grabbed a rain gutter and swung down the outside.

She saw headlights coming up the driveway so she ran directly toward the sea. The clouds were sweeping ashore and brought more heavy winds with them. She slipped and fell, hit her knee on a rock. It ached. She had no idea how rough the terrain was in that area so she headed inland and back towards where she thought the farm was. She jumped rocks and banged her shins.

But the dogs were silent.

She could hear men talking and then she heard gunshots. *Thank God my suit is black.* She couldn't see the coastline for the dense rain but she could see inland. She bolted at top speed. Wham! She hit another pear cactus. This time she took it full on and hard. One needle hammered her forehead and another barely slid by her eye. She could feel it scratch her cheek. She suppressed the urge to yell and whimpered instead.

The, she heard more gunfire and heard helicopters behind her. She recognized the whirring of their blades. Now she ran for the coast—to where she thought the coastline was anyway—and directly into the rain and heavy winds. When she finally heard the waves roaring in the distance she thought she must be close. She couldn't see the edge of the cliffs. Bullets rang off the nearby rocks and coral. She could see their sparks, even in the downpour.

She ran further towards the coast. She didn't know how much ground she had covered but the sirens were growing faint. She was nearly out of breath yet she ran ahead with all the speed she could muster and knew she was near the cliffs she had just climbed. She had no equipment for the descent. It was dangling from the lighthouse.

She could hear the waves, more loudly, crashing against the rocks. She felt the sea spray. She stopped, sensed she was near the edge. She heard the helicopters overhead and saw the diffusion of their shining beams trying to find her.

She got a running start and bolted off the cliff—by a marker rock she had identified on the way in. It was the longest sixty meters she had ever experienced in her life. She held her nose. Weightless, terrified, she fell.

She hit the water feet first, plunged downward for what seemed like an eternity. The water had knocked her hand loose, Water filled and hurt her nose. She held her breath as best she could. Nothing broken, she hoped. *As long as I don't hit a rock.* Deeper and deeper she went.

Gradually she felt herself ascend—ascend effortlessly. *I'm alive!* Then as if in slow motion, she felt the water coming through the cactus pricks in her dry suit, the cold icy water against her skin. *This thing will fill with water and I'll drown.*

She broke the surface, gasped, screamed, "Help! Help! Lance . . ." She gagged on the salty water that filled her nose and mouth.

A few yards away she thought she saw a beam of light and the red and green colors of running lights but there was no answer. "Lance, Lance! Where are you? Help me! Help me, please!"

She bobbed in the water, felt the suit filling up. Each time she sank she sensed she wasn't returning to the level she had made before. "Help! Help!"

All of a sudden she felt Lance's strong arms around her. She knew they were his without being able to see him. "Why didn't you answer me?" she asked.

Still he did not answer. She pounded at him, first in anger and then tried to grab him in fright. He pushed her away. She felt him slip something over her shoulders, hands and arms. *Is this what he did to his wife?* She tried to fight him off.

She sank more deeply. He was gone. She struggled but she could no longer reach the surface. She struggled again. She knew she was losing the battle.

You bastard!

Then she felt the tug of the rope—its strength, its will. Gradually and steadily she was pulled, first to the surface and then to the edge of the boat. A firm, quiet hand pulled her onboard.

Once she regained strength and composure she hit Lance and yelled, "You son of a bitch! You bastard! Why didn't you answer? Why did you push me away?"

As the boat rocked and listed in the storm she could see that he had retreated and lay collapsed against the side of the boat. He, too, gasped for air. She could barely hear his voice through the darkness of night as he spoke. "I tried to grab her," he said. "I tried to save Rebecca. I used my last breath to reassure her. And that breath—the one breath I didn't have in reserve—may have made the difference between her life and death."

* * *

The next morning before work Lance argued with Lili on the phone. "Our intelligence tells us that the attack by the demonstrators is likely to happen within the next few days. I don't think you should go back to work this morning."

"I have to," she said. "It may be my last chance to get a look at those shipping records in Mr. Baker's office. I've got to figure out a way to get up there to see them."

Once again Lili returned to work. She had caked on her makeup to try to hide the cacti scrapes on her face but she knew it wouldn't take a very close look to notice the gashes. Her body ached from the night before.

She was happy to learn her assignment had been moved out of the credit card department. Things had become so bad there that the bank had stopped answering their phones. Over the weekend the final installation of a telephone answering system took place that would leave the caller in a position whereby they could not reach a fellow human being, no matter what they dialed or which number or symbol they punched. Miss Cumberbatch heralded this as the greatest invention since the light bulb and sent Lili back to international banking.

Lili assumed this would mean alternately watching people come and go from Mr. Baker's office and the slowly creeping second hand on the office clock. It didn't happen that way.

Lili noticed immediately the mood of her coworkers had changed. She felt as if she were on display—in a fish bowl. She was sure they were staring at her gashes and snickering behind her back. Everyone who came to the conference room, they stopped and gawked at her—especially Mr. Fitzsimmons, the baldheaded gentleman in the metallic silver suit. This time she got a close enough look to see that his head was indeed shaved and that he had a blood red birthmark on his neck in the shape of a spider.

What surprised her was that she appeared to have been given Mr. Baker's real schedule to work on. *Why is this?* Defense ministers throughout the Caribbean, heads of state, the CEO's of large, influential corporations, labor leaders, celebrities, even criminals and reputed gun brokers. She recognized many of the names from *The Daily Nation. Why are they trusting me with this?*

But when she tried to call the inspector to arrange to meet with him to share the details she found the phone didn't work.

"Miss Bangerter, why aren't the phones working?"

"It's got something to do with the new system they installed down in the credit card department. I think they're doing ours next."

Lili said, "But I thought I just saw Mr. Baker using his telephone not five minutes ago."

"It's those idiot workmen from the phone company," Shirley Bangerter said. "They get all uppity when you ask them questions. Act like they own the place. I haven't seen a man yet who wouldn't make better company with his balls cut off." Shirley lifted her letter opener and pantomimed the excision.

Lili shuddered down her spine.

By about three in the afternoon she noticed that everyone had left—everyone except Miss Bangerter, who had just gone out, presumably to the restroom. She decided it was her chance to see if she could get another look at the shipping records in Mr. Baker's office. She looked around. Not a soul in sight. She crept into his office.

The file cabinet was locked. She hurried to finish before Miss Bangerter got back.

She rifled through Mr. Baker's top desk drawer to find a key. Instead she came across a letter opener. She went back and tried to jimmy the lock. No luck.

Then she decided to go through the rest of his drawers but they were locked as well. *I wonder if Mrs. M. left her key.* She went to her empty desk, which was in the office next to his. She went through her drawers but there was nothing left in them. The only thing left on the desk was a dust-laden picture of her husband, Bernie Musgrave.

She laughed, picked it up, blew off the dust and put it into one of the empty drawers. Underneath the picture was a key. It fit the file cabinet.

I hope Shirley wasn't trained by Miss Cumberbatch and takes her time in the toilet.

Lili rummaged through the files. There wasn't much of interest. She heard a noise in the common area and looked up. No one there. *Must be the wind.* She considered closing the window but didn't want to take the time.

She rummaged further until she found the shipping file. She thumbed through it. There must have been twenty-five entries on one page referencing the Tropic Carib—Hans' ship. She heard bottles crashing against the side of the building. She tore out the page and put it into her pocket.

She left Mr. Baker's office and returned to her desk. It was unsettling that no one was there. She thought about going back to see if she could find anything else of interest in the locked file cabinet when a slender woman wearing thong underwear and decorated with red, yellow and black paint all over the rest of her body introduced herself with a blood curdling war cry. Lili bolted for the door to the elevators, but it was locked and she was unable to kick it down.

Then there was a smooth, whirring sound and a dart hit the door. It was a small stick, just like the one that had killed the monkey. The room was filled with desks and tables and lamps, but no people. Zoom! A dart into the chair next to her. *Oh, shit. She's trying to kill me.*

She turned over a desk and crawled under it. Zoom! She could hear a dart whir by her ear into the top of the desk. Lili crawled along on the floor but realized it was just a matter of time. It was like being in a pit with a snake. Sooner or later the odds favored the snake.

From her vantage point Lili could see the long, narrow bamboo blowpipe from which the missiles were being launched. There were tiny gray-green-and-black quills near the ends of the sticks. They looked delicate but Lili never doubted their deadliness. She had witnessed the killing of the monkey as well as the speed of his demise.

Her veins popped out. Everything seemed to unfold in slow motion.

Instinctively Lili decided to try to get to the window. Could she climb down the side of the building? She thought of using the curtains but by the time she could fashion anything she would have more quills in her than a porcupine. One dart and Lili knew her life would be over in seconds. Her palms moistened with sweat.

She crept between two rows of desks. The assailant had lost track of her. Lili saw her reflection in the window and could tell the woman didn't know where she was. Lili saw the woman's nostrils expanding and contracting, as if the woman were trying to locate her scent. Lili realized that if she could see the woman, a glance in the right direction would reveal her just as easily.

Desperate Lili threw a chair through the window. With the distraction she thought maybe she could get the drop on the woman but it didn't work. Her attacker gave a bloodcurdling cry and systematically cut off Lili's escape routes. The distance between them narrowed.

Her assailant raised the blowpipe.

Lili shuddered, "Please. Please don't shoot me. What are they paying you? I'll double it. I'll triple it. Please don't kill me!" At that instant she recognized her. It was Shirley Bangerter. She was sure of it. *The Amazon.*

Shirley leveled the blowpipe. Lili could see it was aimed squarely at her heart. She tried to pick up a piece of furniture to protect herself but she couldn't break anything loose. The bottoms of the chairs were all metal.

One more blow and all would be over. Shirley inched closer. She took a deep breath.

"Bam!" A deafening explosion! The building rocked. Debris fell from the ceiling—plaster, concrete, dust. It was impossible to see. Lili groped her way to the doors again—still locked. She felt like she was in a tomb—a tomb with a snake. Where was the snake?

Now she could see but barely—just enough to make her way through the dust and smoke to the conference room. The sprinkler system had gone off and it was raining torrents of water. Carlon's had installed the fire prevention system about a month ago and she knew she could count on it to douse the fire. It would soon go out, unless the pipes broke. *Where is everyone?* She had to get away. Instinct propelled her; reason in short supply.

Frantically she pulled down the curtains and set about tying them together. The curtains were thin and supple but she wasn't sure they'd hold a knot. They were wet and slipped each time she tested.

She managed to tie four of them together. The rest were hopelessly tangled in the debris. Still not enough to reach the street. She thought maybe she could hang alongside the building and kick out a window below with her feet. She dragged the curtain chain over to the window. Still no sign of her assailant. Hurriedly, she tied the end of one curtain around one of the desks and tossed the cloth chain out the window. The water from the sprinklers continued to pour. Smoke seeped in from below. She heard a moaning followed by a muddled war cry.

Grabbing the wet cloth she went over the side, walking against the wall of the building as though it were the side of a cliff. She remembered her training. She worked her way down, hand-over-hand, foot-over-foot. Painful progress. She tried not to look down.

Then, suddenly, she saw Shirley's head peer out the window above. She had an object in her hands and she scraped and poked it against the cloth. Lili's hands slipped. She worked her way down—four stories, then three. She reached the second story and came to the last knot. She was at the end of her rope.

Shirley reappeared with her blowpipe and resumed blowing darts, downward this time. Their trajectory was altered by the wind, but seemed to have been taken into account by her assailant. Lili dodged them by jockeying from side-to-side. She had to bounce lightly so as not to break the glass

Arms aching, she gently, but firmly, pushed her feet against the side of the building. With one big push away she flew back into it and kicked her way through the window. The credit card department. No one there. She grabbed an armful of paperwork from a basket on top of Miss Cumberbatch's desk. She picked up the confidential files, which were color coded red, went through the usual entrance, down the smoky stairs and was greeted by firefighters coming up the stairs from the outside. They helped her the rest of the way down and out onto the sidewalk. For the first time in weeks there were no demonstrators to confront her.

She saw a number of them being put into handcuffs and paddy wagons. Another explosion rocked the building and this time the upper floors were consumed in fire and smoke. Anyone there must have perished, according to the subsequent conjecture of *The Barbados Advocate*, one of two local newspapers.

Lili was checked and treated for smoke inhalation at Queen Elizabeth Hospital and returned by ambulance to The Tower later that evening. Sea Cat was noticeably shaken and concerned when she arrived and refused to calm down until she was comfortably in bed.

When the inspector called shortly before midnight to question her and protest her returning to the bank "ever again" Lili didn't argue. For a greater sense of security she agreed to move in with him until they could work out other arrangements. This time Sea Cat quietly and quickly gathered her things.

He postponed his nightly rendezvous on The Carnival Spirit to be with her. He had just met a French woman and assured Lili that she was "not bahd at all."

"There's no point in asking me not to go," Lili said.

"You have to go," Sea Cat replied. "Maybe I'm wrong about the inspector. I hope I am."

Lili paused and stared at him.

"Perhaps things will work out for you after all," Sea Cat added.

"I'm not sure there's anything to work out," Lili said. "I'm not sure that looking at a future with the inspector is realistic anyway—I mean, even if he wanted me."

"What do you mean? Why wouldn't he want you?"

"You're a black man, Sea Cat. What kind of life do you think we'd have together? Even here. How would we be looked upon here in Barbados? I mean his father says obnoxious things right in front of me. And I don't think I could persuade him to move to Hawaii. Do you think we'd have a chance? I mean a white woman, or even a brown one like me, with a black man—you know."

"You'd think that in this day and age you wouldn't have to ask that question," Sea Cat said. "But every once in a while we have people, usually tourists, who come down here and act 'funny.' Do you remember that couple from Tennessee?"

"Yes," Lili nodded. "Well, whenever nobody else was around, he made a point of calling me 'boy.'"

"You're kidding," Lili said.

"Unfortunately, I'm not. If there's a way to be cruel and insensitive there's always someone who figures out a way to do it."

Chapter Nine

Even though Lili had spent only one afternoon with them the children were thrilled to find her in the kitchen the following morning. Young William, the first to spot her, peeked at her around the corner without saying a word. He wore only a pair of white jockey shorts.

"Come here, Willie. Would you like to have some breakfast?"

"Where Daddy? Where'd my daddy go?"

"Your daddy had to go to work. Somebody did a mean thing at the bank yesterday and he has to figure out who it was."

"I know. They blowed it up. I heard Daddy talking 'bout it on the phone last night. It was *da people.*"

"What people?"

"Daddy sade *da people* gonna blow up dat bank."

"Yes, I guess 'the people' did it. That's what happened."

Within an hour Idalia and her brother, Theo, were up, while Emma slept in late. "Don't you have to get ready for school?" Lili asked. "You don't want to be late, do you?"

"It's Saturday, Miss Kaleo," Idalia said. "We don't go to school on Saturday."

Lili realized she had lost track of the day. The children told her they'd barely seen their dad since Ephraim had been murdered. It was apparent because the house was in shambles. They spent a lot more time than they were used to at their aunt's house and Desmond and Grafton came over to look after them when they were at home by themselves. "Let's surprise your daddy and clean the house."

So they cleaned and swept until Emma woke up around ten. Lili kept having flashbacks to the bombing but she tried to put them out of her mind. That was one reason she organized the cleaning activity. The mindlessness of it suited the occasion and met her needs for a mental escape.

As Lili dressed Emma, Idalia said, "She was up really early this morning—before Daddy left. Didn't you hear them?"

I wouldn't have heard them if another bomb had gone off.

By noon, the cousins—Grafton and Desmond— were over and the children played like renegades. Lili made them all a big pitcher of pink lemonade and tuna salad sandwiches for lunch. She enjoyed looking after them and envied the simple way they looked at life.

"Are you going to stay with us?" Idalia said. "Are you going to live with us and marry Daddy?" The two of them were setting the table before calling the other children in to eat.

"Did your daddy put you up to this? Did he tell you to ask me that question?" Lili wished he had although she didn't know how she would have answered. She was far from sold on the idea of an instant family. Sex, yes. Romance, yes. Children—his children—she wasn't so sure of that.

Idalia looked at the ground. "No, Miss Kaleo. We just want to know if you're going to stay with us." The girls especially were looking for a mother figure in the home. Lili figured it had been too short of a time for them to be attached to her in particular.

"I don't know," she said. "I don't know. Only time will tell. Please. Please call me Lili—or Sugar, if you like—but don't call me 'Miss Kaleo.'"

"Okay, Sugar. I like that name. I'll call you it from now on." And so she did and so did the others, except for Emma, who could only grunt.

Lance didn't return home until about ten-thirty that evening, long after the last child had been put to bed. Lili had just fallen asleep on the couch and the sound of his tires against the rocks in the driveway woke her up.

"Where are the children?" he asked.

Lili looked at the clock. "I put them to bed about an hour ago. Saturday night baths and all," she continued. "Have you figured out what happened?"

"Didn't you listen to the Voice of Barbados?"

"No, I didn't turn it on. I didn't want to worry the kids."

"At least six people lost their lives. The building imploded. The only thing left standing at the end of Broad Street now is Lord Nelson."

"Well, you can thank God for that! That building was an eyesore. I'm sorry about the people being hurt or killed, though," she said. "I'm glad I didn't listen to the radio. I'd like to forget as much about what happened yesterday as I can."

Lance sat on the couch next to her. His head sank into his hands. "It was awful. A woman on the fourth floor lost both her arms."

Lili massaged his back and tired shoulders. She could feel the tension. "I can move out," she said. "I can find a place of my own."

Lance sighed with relief as the pain of a tense day gradually left his shoulders. "What do you mean move out? Did I say anything about moving out? I've had to deal with this investigation all day. The bank building is destroyed. It will take months to clear the rubble. At least a dozen people were killed or seriously injured. Hundreds of others will lose their jobs. I need someone to stay here and look after the kids. You may as well stay here."

Now that's a commitment.

Without pursuing the conversation further, Lance got up, walked down the hallway and collapsed on his bed with his clothes on. Lili picked up two cushions off the sofa, went in the other direction and slept on the floor in the cubby, next to Emma, just as she had slept the night before in Idalia's room.

* * *

By Monday Lili had the children back into their normal routine of doing their homework and going to school. She spent the days, while the other children were in school, alone with Emma. She tidied up the house and fixed the meals and mended the clothes and made the beds and swept the floors and waited for Lance to come home in the evening. Even though she'd had plenty of experience at housekeeping as a teenager, being domestic had become almost as foreign to her as the land she was in. She wasn't sure that's what she wanted for herself long term but for now, it was a welcome respite.

She viewed her days as pleasant, even though she slept on the floor in Emma's room. For the first time in over a year she could feel her maternal juices flowing. She greeted these feelings with a mix of welcome and sadness because they renewed her grief over her son, Christian. But in most ways she found joy, like plants that flourish after a fire in the forest. At times she would see Emma peering at her over the rail of her bed in the dim glow of her nightlight. Emma didn't speak in words. She used hand gestures and grunted or made rhythmic, nonsensical sounds. Lili felt a growing bond. Lance had told her there was no medical reason why Emma couldn't speak and her humming portended a honeysuckle voice. It's just that the melodic sounds were not fashioned into words. Anyone who knew anything about life or the human condition could see at a glance that this child was ecstatic over the presence of her new companion.

The other children would go and play but Emma seldom wandered more than two feet from Lili. The two of them held hands on the porch steps and looked out at the tiny ships on the horizon or swung in the tire swing that Lili put up on a tree in the backyard. She had gotten the tire from one of Lance's brothers. It reminded her of the swing she used to swing in with her daddy over the Hanapēpē River in Kaua'i and the memories were bittersweet. One of the few truly happy reflections of her childhood.

She played games with the older children and helped them with their homework—except math—and made sure their hair was groomed and their clothes and their bodies were clean. She scolded them when they used bad language, or were unkind to one another. She told them how lucky they were to have one another and that they should be kind to each other, "because you never know how long you might have a brother or a sister and you do love them, whether or not you know it. Your friends will come and go but your brothers and sisters will always be your brothers and sisters."

They played road tennis in a nearby lane and she enjoyed it immensely. She was learning how to put spin on the ball and make the children jump out of their shoes trying to hit it back. They became fast friends and one could easily see that the children admired her athletic ability and keen sense of competitiveness. She tried to draw on her experience with volleyball to help them develop healthy attitudes—win or lose.

One day, she decided it would be safe to go to the Animal Flower Cave. It was a short distance away and they took the bus.

"Please don't tell your father we did this," she said. "I wouldn't do anything to harm him or you guys but I don't want to worry him." *I've got to get out of the house.*

Theo said, "You don't have to worry about us, Sugar. We know how to keep a secret."

William said, "Yeah, we're in a secret club with Desmond and Grafton and we all swore in blood to keep one another's secrets."

Theo smacked him up the side of the head. "Willie, you idiot, you're not even supposed to tell that. You're not supposed to tell we have a secret club."

Lili, who was sitting on the seat behind the boys, said, "Now boys. You stop that. I'm not going to ask anymore about your secret club and I'm certainly not going to tell anyone about it." It was the second time she had scolded them in an hour, which reminded her that there were both joys and challenges to a mother's role.

Idalia sat on the seat next to her and Emma snuggled in on the other side as the bus bounced over the rocky pavement going from stop to stop before reaching the caves.

They had a delightful time at the caves and Lili felt less and less guilty all the time for taking them. Theo must have asked fifty questions about sea anemones. "Why do they live here and not further out in the ocean? What do they eat? Why are they all different colors? What's a hermit crab? Why don't they grow their own shells?"

They walked around the perimeter of the inlet in which the cave was formed. It was difficult to walk because the terrain was bumpy with rocks. They looked over the edge at the crashing waves and Lili told them not to get too close. Sugar noticed the really big waves were splashing on the other side so she took them over there so they could see them better. Now they were facing the sun.

She miscalculated how close to allow them to stand. Between the blaring sun and the strong winds near the coast and the size of the waves they lost their margin of safety. A giant wave came flying over the edge and before they could run far enough away it covered them and they all were drenched. Sugar could taste the salt water in her mouth.

The children laughed and at first Emma started to cry and then, when she could see the other children were laughing, she began to laugh as well. Now they were all laughing and the boys wanted to do that again, but Lili said "No." The girls were relieved and they all went into the tiny shop that sold tickets to get into the cave.

Lili had in mind to buy them each something but the goods looked so tacky that she decided it was a waste of money.

A pair of middle-aged British women were in the shop. She noticed one of them, the fatter one, staring at her and the children most of the time. She tried to ignore them but it was such a small place that it was difficult.

The children were good about accepting the proposition that it was not a good place to buy things. "It's all junk. We'd get more for our money somewhere else."

Sugar made her way to the cash register to buy a postcard for Aunty Fay. The children stayed and played with the rubber starfish and clear plastic paperweights that snowed when you shook them.

The fat woman said, "Are those *your* children?"

Lili looked over her shoulder and back at the children.

The woman continued, "Is *that* sort of thing acceptable here?"

"No, I'm just looking after them," she said. Then she hated herself for appeasing the woman.

"You mean to tell me that *you're* the nanny and *those* are your master's children?"

Later on the same two ladies stood in the parking lot and pointed at Lili as she and the children walked up the lane to catch the bus.

* * *

After nearly two weeks of coming home after ten p.m. and leaving before six in the morning Lance finally took a day off and slept the entire day, except for about two hours. Lili longed for him to wake up and spend time with her but it never happened. When he finally did get up they shared a light meal with the children.

"Lili, you've been doing a lot of work around here and taken on a role that I never expected. I appreciate what you're doing but I feel guilty about it. It's way beyond what I had any right to expect. I'm sorry I haven't been much help to you. Can I get someone to come in and help with the chores?"

"It's no bother," she assured him. "The kids help out a lot." *I'm glad you finally noticed I'm here.*

* * *

The investigation into the death of Ephraim Whitney had fallen into obscurity. The inspector admitted as much whenever Lili and he had a chance to have adult conversation away from the children. "Find that book," he said, "and we'll have our killer. I'll bet it's all connected, and I'll bet it's all related to that book."

"Yes, and now we've got exactly no chance of getting our hands on it," Lili said. "Do you think they shipped it out that night?"

"I do. Or at least put it someplace where we'll never see it again. But you've seen it. What do you remember about it? Maybe you can remember something that would help."

"Only that number from my trial. I've gone over it in my head a thousand times and that's all I can remember—just those account numbers and that entry off to the side in US dollars. It was in handwriting that was distinctive—flowery and frilly." Lili still didn't feel it was safe to tell him about the comment Ephraim had made about Lord Nelson.

"Miss Cumberbatch?"

"No, it wasn't her handwriting. I would have recognized it. But it was distinctively like the handwriting of a woman."

"Or a man who writes like a woman," Lance said.

"What do you mean?" Lili asked.

"I don't know," Lance said. "Just something that popped into my head."

* * *

After nearly three weeks Lance got his first weekend off. Prior to that Lili had become more and more involved with his children—even his parents—who were still generally cool towards her, although there had been one tender moment. One afternoon, when she had brought the kids over for a visit, Mummy Williams had given her some of Clyde Williams' hot sauce to take home with her to splash on Lance' omelet. Then, just as she had the children in tow and was walking out the door, Mrs. Williams went to a small tree in a pot on her porch and took off a leaf.

"Here," she said. "It's a bay leaf. It's the only true spice that grows in usable quantities here in Barbados. There may be a little nutmeg and there's one clove tree over in Welchman Gulley, but you better hadn't let anyone catch you messing with it. Try a bay leaf in your stew. It adds a nice flavor."

Lili took this as a peace offering.

But she and Lance may as well have been strangers passing to and fro with hardly more than a "hello" or "good-bye." Lance did spend time each evening reading to his children, no matter how tired he was, and seeing that they always said their nighttime prayers, if he was home early enough.

Whenever she overheard them, she was touched with remarks, like ". . . please bless Daddy and Sugar and let them get married and be happy forever with us. Thank you, Jesus. Amen."

She was sure Lance heard these entreaties but he never commented on them. He seemed impervious to the concept of a romantic relationship. He did express his gratitude to her with a warm hug and a kind gesture from time to time. And there would seem to be a spark every now and then. She could feel it—eye contact when neither of them expected it—or the brush of a hand or bumping into one another in the hallway. But it went no further and Lili remained true to her resolve that she wasn't going to start anything, largely because she wanted to know where things stood. She wanted to get back to the investigation but she would wake up at night, sometimes screaming with memories of the bank bombing and her confrontation with Shirley Bangerter. She needed more time to recover.

On Lance's first Saturday off they played games and had a picnic on the beach. First they played cricket. Even though Lili had a difficult time understanding the rules and conventions it was obvious in fairly short order that she was an excellent fielder. It came to her instinctively to catch the tennis ball, no matter how hard or where it was hit.

"That's amazing, Sugar. Where did you learn to field like that?" Lance asked.

"I didn't. Well, I used to play baseball with my classmates at The Waimea Girl's School but that was with a glove on. It just sort of came to me."

"One of these days I'll have to take you to a game. Trinidad is playing a match against Barbados in the West Indies League, here, beginning next Friday. I think you'd like it."

"Can we go, too?" The children asked, almost in unison.

"We want to see where you used to play, Daddy," Theo said.

"I don't know," Lance said. "We'll have to see, kids. For one thing we have to wait until it's safe for Miss Kaleo to venture out."

"I'd risk almost anything to get out of the house," Lili said. She quickly looked around at the children and was relieved that no one mentioned their earlier excursion. Theo winked at her.

After playing cricket for an hour or so they obliged her by playing volleyball. Lili was in her element and the children marveled at her spikes and sets. Lili was such a dominant force in the game that they quickly lost interest and decided it would be fun to hike or swim and engage in less competitive activities. Throughout the rest of the afternoon the boys clung to their father, while the girls seemed to gravitate toward Sugar.

On Sunday they all got up early, took baths, got dressed up and went to church. Lili wore a hat with a veil for security purposes. This time the church was much nearer to Lance's home in St. Lucy, just south of Speightstown, and turned out to be a big red and white tent, hardly what she had thought of as a church. They were picked up by Lance's sister, Sharee, who drove them in her Suzuki van. Since Lance's car was so small, she either drove the family places, or they took the bus, which provided transportation to just about every square inch of the island.

Sharee was tall and broad through the shoulders, but not so handsome as Lance. She was missing the chiseled features Lance shared with his father and had more round puffy features like Mrs. Williams, Mummy.

Sharee said, "You seem to be right at home with these children. Do you have children of your own?" Lili was suspect of the apparent kindness in her tone because she had heard that Sharee was not altogether accepting of her. Lance had said that she and Lance's other sisters who still lived on the island hadn't decided whether or not they thought Lili was white. If they did they would consider any close personal relationship with Lance to be a betrayal against the sisterhood. If she were brown they tended to be less critical. Although if they sensed that Lili viewed herself as white that would be enough to make them think she was unsuitable for romance, love, sex, marriage or even a close personal friendship with their brother.

Lili resented both the complexity and inconsistency of their views. Lance's youngest sister had married a doctor from Toronto, a white man, and they thought that was just fine, "Love conquers all and romance triumphs over all lesser issues, such as race!" They viewed her as a heroine. *Go figure.* But she didn't see Lance's sister all that much, so she tried to be nice to her no matter what.

"I had a son once," Lili replied.

Idalia said, "You didn't tell us you had a son! Where is he? What's he like?"

Lance said, "Idalia, Lili's son is dead. Maybe she doesn't want to talk about him just now."

"It's okay," Lili said. "He had an awful disease. It's called cystic fibrosis."

Theo asked, "What does cystic fibrosis do to you? How does it kill you?"

Sugar looked at Lance and he nodded for her to continue. "His lungs filled with mucus and he couldn't breathe. He suffocated." Lili had tried to tone down the portrayal but couldn't think of just the right words and could see she had failed.

William started to cry. "Daddy, Daddy, I have mucus. There's mucus in my chest. Am I going to die?"

Theo said, "You will, Willie. You will die—and it's all because you hog the bathroom. You sit on the toilet for hours and you won't let me ride your scooter."

Willie wailed that much louder.

"Nonsense," Lance said. "Back off, Theo. See what you've done."

"No, you won't die, Willie," Lili said. "The disease is hereditary."

"What is hereditatary?" Idalia asked.

"'*Hereditary*' means you inherit something," Lili said. "You get it from your parents."

Idalia said, "I inherited this necklace from my mother." She stuck her finger through her silver chain and lifted the floating heart for Lili to see. It had one tiny diamond embedded in the heart. "Daddy gave it to me after Mummy died. It was their love necklace—the first present Daddy ever gave her."

Lili thought of the scarf she had been given on their first night together. She caught herself being jealous. That's what "Lili" meant in Hawaiian.

* * *

Nearly three weeks after the bombing and over a year since Lili had been in Barbados; she finally got to see her first cricket match. Lance decided and Lili agreed that no one would be expecting her to show up in public and—given the element of surprise—it would probably be safe.

As for her it was wonderful just to get out of the house—into the traffic, the bright sunlight, the hustle and bustle of Bridgetown on a Friday afternoon. Lance worked in the morning and came to pick her up by mid-afternoon. He had taken sick leave as was the custom among many in the police department when a cricket match was in town. Usually they stayed home and watched it on TV but Lance felt he had a pretty good excuse—looking after a material witness— should he ever be challenged.

He told her he normally sat in the Kensington Stand in Kensington Oval when he went to a cricket match, but due to added security considerations, and the fact that he wanted to impress Lili they went to the Garfield Sobers Stand. When he approached the ticket taker the man said, "Lance, Lance Williams! My eyes deceiving me? Dat's you fuh true?"

"That's right, skipper!" Lance replied.

"You doesn't come here too regular," the ticket taker replied.

"Well, I'm here today and I'm afraid you're going to have to put up with me."

The man looked at Lili.

"She's with me. She's a consultant on a case I'm working on."

"Right, mahn. Right—whatever you say, Lance." The man winked at him and nudged him with his elbow. He jockeyed back and forth on his feet like he had to pee.

Lance reached for his wallet.

"Hey, you money ain't *no* good here, mahn," the ticket taker said and nudged him again. "You two are on me."

Lance continued to pull a few bills out of his wallet. "No, skipper," Lance said. "I can't let you do that. I'm a policeman now and people might think you're bribing me."

Even the sound of that word gave Lili a chill up her spine.

The man held up his hand to prevent the transfer of money but Lance kept pushing it towards him until he finally took it. Lili thought she might have seen Lance's expression change, as if to say, "This time I'll pay you," but the clues were too vague for such a conclusion.

They climbed a narrow wooden stairway with only bare wood for a view. She could hear the crowd roaring as the match had started nearly five hours earlier. "There's no point in arriving before they've had their tea," Lance said. "The game won't really be going until afternoon tea has been served."

Lili said, "You're kidding, aren't you? They have tea in the middle of a game?"

"That's the tradition," Lance replied. "The players aren't at their best until they've had their tea and sandwiches."

Lili laughed. Actually she was feeling impatient. She couldn't wait to get there because she loved sports in general and baseball in particular.

The stairs led to a bar with a number of patrons in various stages of repose, sitting around and drinking beer or rum. Upon seeing them and upon their seeing Lance he left her to share the tidings of the day. She seized this opportunity to take a good look around.

There were plaques on the wall and photographs of what she perceived must have been old and venerable cricket teams. She couldn't help but notice that all of the players in the bygone era were white. To confirm her suspicions she took a quick look outside at the field. Sure enough all the players on the field were black. As she looked around the stands, however, there was a mixture of races. There were in fact a greater proportion of white people than she had seen at church.

The stand was full. "That's because they're playing Trinidad," Lance said. "They're our number one rival. Every time someone in Barbados invents something or develops a product or gets a great idea it takes about a week for someone in Trinidad to steal it and make a cheap imitation." He went on to say, "Look there, see all those signs?"

Lili looked around but had no idea what he was talking about.

"Down there," he pointed down the aisle between the rows of chairs. "See, there on the field. It's stamped 'Busta.' Hell, Busta's not even a Bajan soft drink. It's from Trinidad and they've got it plastered all over our stadium. We owe it to them to give them a good beating."

Lili could relate. She remembered drinking Kauaʻi coffee, when she could have had Kona for less.

"C'mon, let's go find a seat."

Lili couldn't imagine where they would sit. The stand was completely full. *Maybe some people will leave soon and we can take their seats.*

As they walked towards the padded chairs someone in the crowd said, "Hey, look! Lance Williams!" He stood to shake Lance's hand.

Soon others were saying, "Lance, Lance Williams. I can't believe it's you, mahn. Where da hell you been, mahn?" All eagerly shook his hand.

There was a man with his wife or girlfriend in the front row. He was white and spoke with a British accent. He was yelling at the umpire and shaking his fist, "You crazy oaf! Are yuh bloody blind or what?"

It brought a smile to Lili's face to see someone so animated at the game, especially from so far out into the grassy area of the field. The people sitting next to him were tapping him on the shoulder and Lili thought they were trying to get him to sit down but if they were, it wasn't doing any good. He wasn't about to have his appeal of a bad call go unheard. At the end of his plea he tapped his girlfriend on the shoulder and pointed towards Lance. She looked irritated as her boyfriend tugged at her to move.

They got up and made their way to the center aisle where Lance and Lili were standing and Lance was signing someone's program. "Hey, mahn, hey, Lance!" The man shook his hand. "I'm sorry I didn't know it was you, mahn. Your seats are right over there." The man pointed to where they had been sitting. "Those are your seats now, mahn."

Lance said, "Don't be ridiculous. We'll just sit here in the aisle until something opens up. We can see just fine."

The man's companion said, "Great! Now can we go back and sit down?"

Instead the man said, "No, me and the wife gotta get going. My son's gettin' married on Saturday—to a Grenadian and we're hostin' the reception."

The woman looked at him with poison dagger eyes at which time he swatted her on the bum and said, "Let's be going now." The woman left without risking further confrontation.

Lili felt awful and said, "I don't think we should sit there. The way that man treated his wife—and in front of us. It was awful!"

"Don't worry," Lance said. "If he weren't actin' like that in front of us he'd be doing it somewhere else. We've had to run him in for public drunkenness and wife beating a few times over the years."

Reluctantly Lili took her seat in the front row next to Lance. It was obvious the crowd wasn't about to settle for anything less.

About that time one of the fielders made a diving catch to dismiss one of the batsmen after one-hundred-forty-three runs. The crowd roared, followed by a healthy round of applause.

"I thought he was on the other team." Lili said.

"He's hit over a ton of runs," Lance replied. "The crowd is showing their appreciation."

Lili wondered what sort of applause Lance had once gotten for over two tons. From the reception he had received on the way in, Lili suspected it was substantial.

Lili looked at the scoreboard. "How can it be three-hundred-fifteen to nothing and your team hasn't even had a chance to bat? It looks like they may as well give up and go home."

Lance said, "See there, where it says seventy-nine overs with eleven overs remaining?"

Lili nodded.

"Well, when ninety overs are gone the day's play will end. Then we'll all go home. The other team will bat after ten men are out. It's a four-day game."

Lili had lost him. *There are too many numbers in this game for me.*

They watched for the rest of the afternoon until about five-thirty. Lili asked a question here and there, usually about the fielding, and enjoyed the crowd reactions and the pageantry and seeing the bowler come running in from the outfield every time he came to the wicket to bowl. But she really didn't 'get it.' On balance, she felt as though she had just watched the paint dry by the time the first day of the match was over and the fans all filed from the stands.

After the day's play and they had left the stand, they went to the Sand Dollar Restaurant at Bagshot House in St. Lawrence for dinner, where they shared lobster thermidor. They were seated by Wendy, who had on a full-length tropical shift and wore her trademark long-curved-fresh-painted-burgundy nails. Donna, whose deep blue bedroom eyes caused Lili to do her best to distract Lance whenever she was near the table, served them. The food tasted exquisite, especially while sitting near the crashing waves with such a handsome and well-respected man. Chris, a popular tenor on the island, sang *Lady in Red* at the piano in the background. All in all it was a delightful evening. Going from being housebound to that night out together may have been a small step for Lance but it was a big leap for Lili.

* * *

After they got home Lili and Lance stayed up and talked, long after the children had gone to bed. Lili said, "I can't remember when I've felt so much at home. Your children are great and they treat me like— "

"One of the family?"

"Well, I suppose they do. Of course I'll never be their mother— "

"They like you, Lili, and I want you to know how much I appreciate your looking after them. I don't know what I would have done—"

He had brought her some pink ginger and heliconia blooms and they talked while she arranged them.

"It was nothing. You would have just taken them to your sister's or your parents' or had Grafton and Desmond come over to watch them, just like you did before I came along. I'm sure they would have managed just fine."

"It's not the same as being in their own home, sleeping in their own beds. I've been out so late they couldn't have stayed here, even with their cousins."

Following the usual routine Lance retired to his bedroom, while Lili went to sleep with Emma. A little over an hour later she felt a tug at her shoulder.

Lance said, "I can't sleep."

Lily was groggy. "Huh?"

"Lili, I'm feeling guilty about you sleeping on the floor, down here with Emma. You can sleep in my bed and I'll sleep on the couch."

"It's okay," Lili said. "Don't worry about it." *What's with him getting a pang of conscience at this hour?* She wanted to get back to sleep.

Emma started to stir. Lili didn't want to wake her so she tiptoed into the hallway with Lance.

Lance argued, "No, you sleep in the bedroom. The couch will be fine for me. I shouldn't have let you sleep in there in the first place. It's just that I've been so tired . . . Had so much on my mind with this investigation and all."

It was dark. There was no light and the floorboards creaked.

"I know," Lili whispered. "It's been a long three weeks since the bombing."

"Has it been that long? If you had asked me I would have said it happened last week sometime."

She took her things into Lance's bedroom. He said, "Let me just get my toothbrush and clothes for morning and I'll be out of your way."

"You can stay," she said.

"What?"

"You heard me. You can stay if you want to. Don't expect me to say it again."

Lili watched in the dim glow of a nightlight while he took off his robe. *Should I be doing this? Will I regret it?* The bed was a cute antique British four-poster—barely a double, with a ruffled white canopy—and she was sure Rebecca must have chosen it. She tried not to think about that.

Out of the corner of her eye she could see the shimmering glow of his dark skin against the moonlight. She craved his body and longed for his gentle touch. Yet she felt inhibited by feelings of uncertainty and doubt. *Will he just love me and leave me?*

She rolled over onto her side and faced away from him. His hand tugged at her waist.

"It's okay," he whispered. "We belong together. It's been all I could do to keep my hands off you. You must know that."

Whether it was his touch or his sweet words or their tone that reduced her resistance to rubble, she soon felt his weight on top of her. The urge to have him inside her became so compelling that she couldn't imagine why she had been so hesitant. She felt his penetration and basked in the resplendence of their togetherness.

They made love woke up an hour or so later and did the same thing all over again. She realized it wasn't the sex she had craved. It was the closeness of his body and the gentleness of his touch. That's what she had missed most during their long period of abstinence.

In the morning he told her, "It was my boss, Superintendent Wilson, who told me not to lay a hand on you. He said if I had "relations" with you while you were living with me he'd have me back handing out parking tickets.

Lili laughed. "I'll never tell." She winked at him and he patted her on the bum.

Disheveled and without any breakfast but with a smile on his face for the first time in weeks, Lance hurried out to his Porsche in the rain with his freshly pressed uniform in a cellophane laundry bag under his arm. He scurried off to work—thirty-five minutes late for the first and last time in his career.

Lili had to scramble to get the children up and dressed and on their way to school.

"Why didn't you sleep with Emma last night?" Idalia asked. "I came down to find you when I got up to go to the bathroom and you weren't there. I went to Daddy's room and the door was locked."

Lili scrambled for an explanation. She looked away from Idalia then back at her and said, "The floor got hard after all those nights and I slept in there with him."

"Are you getting married?" she asked. "Are you going to marry Daddy?"

Lili gasped. *How wise is this kid?* "Don't be silly, Idalia. Why did you ask me that?"

"If he asks you, will you marry him?" Idalia persisted.

"I don't know," she said. "Now go get your teeth brushed and be on your way to school."

Chapter Ten

That night Lili had dinner ready when Lance arrived. He brought her a small box with a smooth green ribbon on it.

Oh, shit, she thought. *This is it!*

"Shall I open it now, or wait until after dinner?"

"It's up to you," he said.

She looked at him and kept expecting him to get down on one knee but he looked perfectly calm. "Let's open it after dinner," she said. "We'll save it until after the kids go to bed." She smiled and gave him a hug.

She had finally found an excellent supply of salt pork from a nearby Jordan's Market and fixed a Hawaiian meal, complete with poi that Aunty Fay had sent her in a C.A.R.E. package. It reminded her of home. In spite of sharing the table with four children they had a quiet, upbeat dinner amidst an occasional flirtatious glance. It seemed like forever until bedtime arrived.

When it finally did she was exhausted. She'd had a chance to think over her answer and was leaning toward saying "yes," but would probably ask for time to think it over. She thought that would be a more proper response. She wanted the memory to be perfect.

She had misgivings about the possible skin colors of their prospective offspring but consoled herself with the fact that as a Caribbean man of African descent he would be very unlikely to be a carrier of cystic fibrosis, as Christian's father had been.

She sat on the bed beside him and opened the box while he lay next to her smiling. "I hope you like it," he said. The night was warm but a gentle breeze came in through the window slats, along with altogether too many mosquitoes.

After she removed the cotton she could see it was an eighteen-karat gold brooch with emeralds in it. It was gorgeous—not too flashy, but elegant, of obvious value and quality. He pinned it to her nightshirt. As he did so she said "My answer is 'yes!'" and kissed him.

"Yes?" he said.

Lili regained her composure, "Yes! Why yes, I'll keep it. A girl has to think it over before she agrees to keep an expensive present like this."

By then Lance was busy removing her bra and panties as well as the nightshirt that housed them. Both disappointed and relieved she once again went with the tide.

And it went on like that for days and the days turned into weeks. Thoughts of the Bank of Barbados and the blue book with silver-leaf etchings and the Amazon woman began to fade, except on the few days when Lili was called in for questioning or to authenticate the paperwork she had taken from the credit department and given to the police.

It turned out that Lili had grabbed some excellent records to make a case against the bank. Files showed logs of payments received days before they were credited, late charges made that weren't due, phone calls not returned when customers asked for information regarding how and where to make a payment. They weren't big infractions taken one at a time but as a group they were highly damning of the individuals involved if they could get someone to cop a plea and cooperate with the prosecution.

As Lili recovered from the trauma of the bombing she began to worry more and more about what must be happening to Aunty Fay and Mimo and her civil lawsuit. She wished she had taken action earlier on their behalf, no matter how she felt. *But what to do next? Where to turn? What steps to take?*

One of these days she would have to call Izzy to see if he could help her figure things out. But making an international phone call would be a major undertaking and the Barbados Cable and Wireless Company would cut them off after eleven minutes, whether or not they had completed their conversation. She didn't want to find herself debating an important legal issue over the phone, only to find herself listening to a dial tone after a stern recorded lecture that she had exceeded her credit limit. Instinct told her not to use Lance's phone and it was on the tip of her tongue many times to ask him for help, but she sensed that his mind was deep into the investigation in areas where he might view her inquiries as an intrusion. He never came right out and said that but that was the feeling she had. She had the distinct feeling that he had never been completely candid with her about what he knew and where he got the information.

One day she got a letter from Izzy that had been sent to The Tower and rerouted to her by the police. He had written to say that her case had worked its way up on the court's calendar and that the discovery, whatever that was, was about to begin and that she would need to make herself available. She had been unable to pay Mimo's mortgage for him in months. She hoped that Aunty Fay would come to his rescue.

But all too often these practical thoughts seemed to get lost in the heat of passion. She felt not only guilty about that but as though she were searching for something unattainable, something she could never clearly define. As sick as it sounded to her in many ways she thought it might have to do with something that had been missing in her relationship with her father.

At some level she wondered whether or not she would be spending the rest of her life in Barbados—perhaps in this house—and whether or not she could forge a permanent relationship with this African Bajan man and his four children. Although his extended family was kindly toward her she knew full well by now they talked about her behind her back because the children began to ask her questions in words that didn't fit their vernacular, "Are black people and white people supposed to live together as man and wife?"

"Can they possibly cleave together as one?" Theo asked.

Lili could only imagine where they had heard such things.

The worst of the remarks was, "Are you a white whore woman?"

"No, of course not," Lili said. "Where did you hear that?"

"Sammy Johnson said it at school," Willie answered.

Idalia asked, "Sugar, what's a whore woman? Are you a whore?"

At that point Lili felt compelled to reassess the situation and spent her waking moments trying to reconcile her present circumstances with what she had been taught.

Lili was at Aunty Fay's Quonset hut one day when she overheard her tell a friend of hers, "Das okay you go have your t'ing wit da Pōpolo [local slang for black] guy, but you no like have kids wit him because den da kids fo'evah mahked dey whole life. Dey skin going be pāpa'a [burnt black] and dat buggah no can wash off, you know. Not even in salt watah."

Daddy, as usual, had professed profound thoughts on the subject. "Coloreds are black," he said. "And they're always looking for a handout or a favor or some special consideration." This was interesting to her because that seemed to be just what Daddy was trying to accomplish by getting tribal status recognition for Hawaiians so he and Uncle Max could open a gaming facility.

Max Martin, who employed people of all races on his sugar plantation in Hawaii, had said, "If we just don't call them black or African Americans or anything special that will solve the problem and we can all be treated alike." Lili thought that sounded nice on the surface and many of its proponents thought of themselves as beyond reproach but it was probably the most subtle and deadly form of discrimination. It ignored reality and left them with little hope for a hand up the ladder to equal status and opportunity. In a sense she thought of Uncle Max as the modern day slave master and of herself as having been one of his slaves.

Sugar had never known any black people who lived on Kaua'i, and the few she had known at the University of Hawaii pretty much stuck to themselves. *And what about raising these children who aren't mine? I know there'll be problems and I could never be their mother. And while I was caring for them I'd always be wishing it were Christian instead.*

She thought about the mixed racial family she had seen at church. *Do I want to bring another black child into the world, just so he can be looked down on by people like those ladies at the Animal Flower Cave?*

These were things she thought and fretted about during the day but at night, once Lance came home, they all faded. They enjoyed quiet, peaceful dinners—together with his children. For the next several weeks bedtime arrived earlier and earlier, and Lance and Lili began to think and feel as one. The ebb and tide of their lovemaking—in sync with the passion of their rapidly beating hearts—blended into a blissful harmony.

And then there were the nagging feelings of guilt at not facing the investigation and not wanting to risk her tranquility with Lance by bringing it up.

* * *

"Bombers arrested," read the headlines of *The Daily Nation.* "Three individuals suspected in the bombing of the headquarters building of the Bank of Barbados were arrested this morning when they tried to make their escape through Grantley Adams International Airport."

"We had the airport staked out," Lance said to the news media. "Figured it was just a matter of time until they turned up. We had pretty good pictures of them from the bank's surveillance cameras and they were easy enough to spot, even in their disguises. We figured they had to come through there sooner or later."

Lili listened on the radio and enjoyed hearing about Lance's accomplishment and the well-spoken, confident manner in which he described it for the press.

"Two of them are from Kingston," Lance said. "And so far they're claiming it was an act of war and that sometimes there will be collateral damage."

"Will they ever get out of prison?" The moderator asked.

"Not unless they break out. We put them in Glendairy and, while I realize there have been a few successful breakouts in recent years, you can rest assured that security will be extra tight for these three."

When Lance came home Lili said, "I know they're criminals but I still feel sorry for them."

Lance replied, "Really? I feel sorry for the people they maimed and killed."

"I do, too. It's just that they had a point. It's too bad they didn't know how to express it constructively. And what about Shirley Bangerter? Did you ever find any trace of her?"

"Not a clue," Lance said. "We've searched the rubble over and over, with heat detectors and then dogs, but no luck. It's like she just vanished into thin air."

"And escaped?" Lili asked.

"More likely, *incinerated*," Lance responded.

* * *

About six weeks after the bombing Lili was spending a quiet morning with Emma while the other children were in school. Lili was bored and wanted to do something special with her. Then she got what she thought was a wonderful idea. She would teach her to do the hula.

At first she couldn't think of where to get the music. She could clap her hands and that would work. But then she realized she might need her hands to guide her movements. The radio? No. You couldn't repeat the music for practice. A cassette player? She wasn't sure they had one and if they did, calypso or jazz just wasn't going to work.

Then it came to her. Idalia had a music box. It played *I Left My Heart in San Francisco* but that would do.

Emma was a remarkably good student and laughed and smiled throughout the lesson. Within an hour she had made amazingly rhythmic hip and arm movements. They couldn't talk so Lili praised her with hugs and kisses.

If only those cultural elitist bigots in Hawaii could see us now. Lili could never understand how "the insiders," as the self anointed pontificators of Hawaiian cultural standards called themselves, could take something so beautiful and be so arrogant and mean about sharing it. She had found no inkling of any such attitude on the part of local residents regarding Bajan culture. The people here were open and eager to share information and insights into their history, dance, music and art.

Lili cooed, "Emma, Emma. You look so cute. You're adorable." She had fashioned a makeshift grass skirt for her out of banana tree leaves.

"Sh-Sh-Shoogah!" Emma replied in the joy of approval. And then, "Shoogah!" just as plain as day.

Sugar threw her arms around her and hugged her. Lili had come to learn that, like her, Emma had been the victim of abuse—not sexual abuse and not at the hands of her father but at the hands of her mother's husband, once he

found out about the pregnancy and deduced that the child
could not possibly be his.

He used to beat his wife while she was pregnant and
one day knocked her down the stairs. He refused her
proper medical treatment and the baby's improperly
developed and crippled leg was the result. The woman was
told to leave the house, have the child and return without it.
That's how Lance happened to have custody. There was
never any custody dispute. The stork landed in Barbados
and Lance agreed to raise her over his own wife's
objections. It was the only decent thing to do.

The crippling of the child's self esteem came later.
According to Idalia and Theo and even Willie, who was too
young at the time to remember much on his own, "Mummy
didn't like Emma. She used to leave her in her bedroom
for hours and let her cry."

"That's why she don't talk," Willie said. "It wasn't
doing her no good to talk to Mummy. Mummy didn't
want no one to see her anyway. Dats why she hide her in
dat room by herself."

Idalia said, "I used to sneak in and pick her up and
hold her or she never would have been held. Mummy
wouldn't even let Daddy go in and pick her up, no matter
how hard she cried." Daddy would sneak in, but if
Mummy caught him there, they would scream and shout at
one another and I would go over to Desmond and Grafton's
to play.

They all said their Mummy and Daddy used to
"fight all the time after Emma came—right up until
Mummy died."

Willie said, "It just got worser and worser."

"Did your Daddy ever hit her?" Lili asked Idalia.

Idalia didn't look at her as she answered. "No, I
don't think he hit her. But she said he did sometimes and a
few times she had bruises. But Daddy always told me that
every time she bumped into something she blamed him."

This renewed doubts in Lili's mind about the
circumstances surrounding Rebecca's death. She decided
she had better get to a doctor and obtain some means of
birth control. They'd long since discarded using condoms.

Lili had just put Emma to bed and thought she'd do
some light housework and then sit on the porch for a while
and ponder. She thought that maybe she should move out
because things were beginning to seem less clear during the
day, although they continued to be ever so compelling at

night. They couldn't wait to clear the dinner dishes and get the children read to, comforted and settled down for bedtime so they could pick up where they had left off the night before. A few times Lili thought about refraining but it was no use. No rationality; no condoms, no hesitation—just peaceful and delicious surrender.

However, Lili kept coming back to the same proposition. *I've got to get away from here, or I'll never get things sorted out.*

She heard rattling sounds in the hallway. *It's too early for the kids to be home.* She was just about to open the revolving bookcase when she became certain that she'd heard someone cough—not a child's cough that she would have recognized, but an adult's cough that she did not. *It can't be Lance. He said he was working late tonight.*

Emma was restless but still sleeping. Lili took a stool from beside her bed and slowly and quietly crept over to the bookcase. Then she got up on the stool—ascending gradually and trying not to make a sound. The floor creaked and the coughing stopped—right beside the bookcase. Lili held her breath. Her muscles tightened. She flashed back on the darts; instant death whirring by her ear.

Once she got on her tiptoes she could see—not over the top of the case, where there was some space between it and the ceiling, but through a crack beside it that had developed from being neglected over the years. The crack opened down into the wall.

There were at least two men. She couldn't see their faces. She didn't recognize one of them, but the other—the one in a silver gray running outfit—had a spider-like, blood red birthmark on the back of his baldheaded neck. *Mr. Fitzsimmons?* She thought she saw the reflection of a knife blade in his hand.

Lili didn't dare make a sound as the men roamed the small house. *Certainly they don't think I would have been stupid enough to bring those files here. They must be looking for me.* The children were due any minute and Lili prayed they would not return home on time. Emma rustled. She had heard Sugar climbing down off the chair and woke up. Sugar tiptoed over to her baby bed and gestured, "Shhh!" Emma grunted, rolled over and got up on her knees, ready to pull herself up on the railing. She smiled at Lili. Lili held her back with one hand.

"Sh-Sh-Shoogah!" Emma said. "Shoogah!"

Lili tried to quiet her—then a loud bang. Lili gasped. It sounded as though the sound had come from outside.

Quietly and carefully Lili picked Emma up. The child held Lili's neck tightly and Lili tried to quiet her—get her to stop making sounds and even breathing. Cautiously she crept forward. Emma said, "Shoogah!" Startled, Lili jerked to a halt.

Then she heard the sound of ground coral on the driveway. She crept out of the room and into the living room prepared to fight—to give her life for Emma, if necessary, but there was no one to be seen. She went first to the door and then peeked through the curtains. A bright orange Suzuki van with a huge, black harp painted on the side, sped down her driveway. She caught enough of a glimpse to see that the baldheaded man was at the wheel.

* * *

When the children got home Lili decided there wasn't a second to lose. "Sugar's going to have to leave for awhile," she explained.

The cousins, Desmond and Grafton, were there, too.

The children were noticeably shaken not only by Sugar's agitation, but by the disheveled house, as well. They cried, "No, Sugar. Please don't go! We need you. Sugar, you're the best." And then the one that really got her, "We love you, Sugar!"

Emma just looked on. Sugar wasn't sure she even understood what was happening. She just stood there and grimaced. Not being able to tell Emma what was going on hurt her the most. Even Desmond and Grafton begged her not to go.

"It's just for awhile," Lili assured them. "Just for a little while."

Idalia wrapped her arms around Sugar's leg. "You can't leave us. You're our Mummy now. Daddy told me you were going to be our Mummy."

He could have consulted me about that. "I have to go," she said. "I don't want to, but I have to. There are some bad men after me." She gave each of them a good long hug in succession, including Desmond and Grafton. Then she hugged them all at once and they hugged her back.

"Bad men?" Theo said. "My daddy will get them. That's what Daddy does. He catches the bad men."

"Daddy will eventually get them," Lili said. "I'm sure of it, but they might hurt me first—or worse than that—you guys. As long as I'm here you're all in danger. I've got to go and I've got to go now, before those men come back.

Idalia said, "Where are you going, Sugar? Where can we find you?"

"I don't know. I don't know where I'm going. I just know I need to get out of here."

Theo said, "Why not call Daddy? He'll protect you!"

Sugar hesitated for a moment. *If I do that I'll never get things sorted out.*

"I know where you can go," Desmond said. "We'll take you to the caves and no one will be able to find you there."

Yes, the caves. That would be perfect. "I can't go anywhere until I make sure you children are safe."

She looked at Desmond and Grafton. "Grafton, you take these children over to your house and I mean now. Do you understand? There are some bad men after me and you've got to get them to safety."

Grafton replied, "What about Desmond, Sugar? Isn't he coming, too?"

"Yes, he'll be coming but he's going to help me gather my things."

"To go to the caves?" Idalia asked.

"No, to help me get to the bus stop," Lili answered. "I have a plan."

She knew they would easily accept this explanation since the vast majority of miles traveled in Barbados were by bus.

Lili gave them all another warm hug. She hugged Emma first so she could also hug her last and not make anyone else feel shorted. Tears rolled steadily down her cheeks. "Go on, now. You all get out of here, and now! I'm not sure when those men might be back."

"Do you know a safe way to your house so you won't be seen?" she asked Grafton.

"You can count on me. Follow me you guys," he said, as they reluctantly bolted out the door.

They got about halfway down the driveway and Idalia had to turn around and run back to grab Emma, who was running back towards the house.

* * *

Desmond, who was the oldest at fourteen, said, "I don't know why you need me to help you get to the bus stop. Do you want me to help carry your things?"

"No. Get the climbing gear," Lili said. "We don't have a moment to lose.

"Climbing gear? What do you need that for? I thought you said you weren't going to the caves."

"I couldn't tell them," Lili said. "They would have wanted to come along. You won't tell them will you? You won't tell anyone?"

"Not if I promise not to."

She grabbed him by the shoulders. "Desmond, promise me. I need a place to hide. I'm desperate. Those bad men want to kill me and I need a place to hide for a few days while I decide what I'm going to do. Please promise you won't tell anyone, will you?"

"I promise. I won't tell," he said.

"Not even Grafton?"

He hesitated.

"Promise me you won't even tell Grafton." She shook him by the shoulders as she spoke.

"Not even Grafton," he replied. "I promise I won't tell Grafton."

"Do you know the way?" Lili asked.

He nodded. "Sure I know the way. We all do."

"And will you bring me food and water while I'm there?"

"I'll bring you food and water and you can stay there as long as you like." He had the broad smile of a knight about to rescue the damsel in distress.

Desmond quickly gathered his uncle's climbing equipment out of the shed at the end of the carport, while Lili gathered her clothes and part of her belongings. She purposely left a few things, such as her hairdryer. It made her feel as though she were still connected to the family and would have to come back sooner or later to retrieve them. She took her brooch, her passport, her credit cards and the list of account numbers she had been trying to decipher. In haste, she rummaged through both her drawers and Lance's. She inadvertently opened one that he normally kept locked. She needed some socks and when she reached down to grab a pair of his, she felt something hard. After pulling away a thin layer of socks and handkerchiefs, she found it was full of gold coins—Canadian Maple Leaves, and jewelry, not just a few necklaces like the one Lance wore to the Paradise Hotel the day she met him, but tens, if not hundreds of them. All appeared to be made of gold. There were rings and bracelets as well. Some for men, others feminine in appearance. She thought about taking a handful. *No. That would be stealing.* She thought about just pushing the drawer back in, laying the socks over the trove and leaving. *What if that's what they're looking for?*

Being careful not to be seen by Desmond, she put the drawer across the arms of an office chair that Lance used for doing police paperwork at home and rolled it down to Emma's room. She further loosened the board in the wall through which she had spied on the invaders, scooped and dumped its contents behind it, listened while the gold fell into the hollow space between the walls, and replaced the board to its original configuration.

"What's that?" Desmond yelled from the kitchen.

"I'm just tidying up in Emma's room before I leave. Putting away her toys."

She yelled to Desmond, as she neared the kitchen, asked him to look outside and see if anyone was coming and replaced the chair, the drawer, the socks and handkerchiefs in Lance's room without being seen.

Lili considered waiting until nightfall, or at least until early evening to make her move to minimize the chances they'd be observed but she was afraid the men in the van may have just gone to a neighbor's house to ask about her and they might be right back. It was raining. The sky was dark gray and overcast—not unusual for this side of the island.

Instead of taking the road they donned raingear and crossed fields whenever they could. They soon tired of carrying all the gear as well as Lili's belongings. They stopped and Lili consolidated the supplies while Desmond made a sled out of sticks and brush. He was very adept, especially for a boy who had had little training from his father. His dad had been what they call in Barbados a "visiting dad," who had sewn his seed in so many locations that he had to make the rounds, like a doctor making house calls, to cultivate them.

Lili suddenly remembered she had neglected to bring the small supply of food she had set out to last until Desmond could bring more. She supposed it was because she had become so upset by discovering Lance's treasure trove. "You will come by soon and bring me food, won't you? I left the sandwiches and lemonade on the counter."

"Of course we will," Desmond said.

"No, I mean you, Desmond. You're not to tell anyone. Remember?"

"I remember," Desmond replied, obviously pleased that he was the one upon whom Sugar had decided to bestow her confidence.

As they approached the main road above the cliffs they heard a vehicle rumbling in their direction. There was no place to hide so they dropped the lean-to and ducked behind it as best they could. They heard the vehicle slow as it passed but no one dared to peek. There was a loud bang, just like the one Sugar had heard in the driveway. What she had thought was a gunshot turned out to be the backfiring of an old van. It turned up the narrow road toward Lance's house and gathered speed as it went.

"Come on, Desmond, we'd better hurry. They'll have no trouble tracking us in this mud."

Desmond recalled that he knew there was a way in and out of the cave without the need to rappel but he couldn't remember where the entrance was or how the caves might be interconnected.

"You'll be safer in the main cavern anyway," Desmond said. "No one would expect to find you there." He pointed to a small, round hole in the ground with a short, unpainted wooden picket fence around it, barely big enough for a person to climb through.

"I hope you can remember how to find me. I'm counting on you." The tiny hole overlooked the cliffs. "Are you sure there's a cave in there?" Sugar asked.

"Positive," Desmond said. "Uncle Lance has taken us in there lots of times. It's a long drop but it's really fun once you get inside and start crawling around with the lamp."

"That reminds me, Desmond, you'd better give me the carbide lamp now so I don't forget it."

"Lamp? I thought you brought it."

It must be on the counter next to the food. Lili tried to avoid becoming frazzled. "I'll use this flashlight until you can make it back with the lamp." She tapped the small flashlight she had stuck under her belt—the one she had grabbed off the top of the refrigerator. "You can bring me the lamp tomorrow morning before school, when you bring my food."

Sugar sorted out the rappelling gear. In the distance they could hear vehicles. Lili hoped that one of them would not be the van. There would be no chance of escape. She gave Desmond one last big hug—and then an endless, neither-of-us-wants-to-let-go hug. Once again she heard the vehicle. The sound of the engine was identical to the one they had heard a few minutes before.

"You get going, Sugar. You don't have to worry about me. I'll just hide over there." Desmond pointed to a ravine full of rocks. "They'll never find me in there. And they're certainly not going to be able to track me."

Sugar believed him. "Okay," she said, as she lashed her rope to a nearby rock. "Once I get in there you cut the rope and toss it in after me, you hear? Go straight home and don't tell anyone, especially your uncle, where I am." Desmond nodded. "You can tell him about the men at the house. You should do that. But you took me to the bus stop and waited with me until the next "To City" bus came and I left and then you went straight home. Okay?"

"I'll do it," Desmond said. He gave her a reassuring smile and a wink. "Don't worry. I know a short cut home. It doesn't go anywhere near the road."

With that Lili descended in the harness she had anchored near the hole. It was eerie, like floating into a sea of black ink. She was terrified the rope might break or slip from its anchor, although it felt secure. She had tested it several times when she uncoiled it and checked it carefully for abrasions, wear and incipient chemical damage. It was dark, so dark in the caves that she couldn't see her hands or the rope she was releasing to descend. *Will there be enough oxygen?*

Lili rappelled deeper and deeper into the crevice and still did not reach the bottom, nor could she see or feel its sides. It smelled musty. The air grew cooler as she descended. She heard the wind howling around the hole above, but not a sound below her. She pulled the flashlight from her waistband to see where she was. It slipped from her grasp and plummeted into the dark abyss. A few seconds later she heard it crash. She thought about climbing back out before Desmond cut the rope, but she was tired, scared and didn't want to endanger him any further by delaying his departure. She was committed now—to the deep, dark bowels of the earth.

Chapter Eleven

If rappelling down into the cave seemed like it took an eternity, being there with virtually no light and only the sundries she could stuff into one of the children' backpacks was even more unnerving. At first she crawled around on her hands and knees, trying to find the flashlight, but she was sure she had heard it break. Bits of crumbled rock tore the fabric of her already worn-thin jeans. Her blood stuck to the cloth and her skin smarted whenever she moved. She fought the urge to panic. *I've been through tougher situations than this,* she tried to convince herself. But the realities of her limited mobility soon became evident.

She could still see the dim light of day shining through the tiny hole that now seemed about twenty stories above her. She thought about her girlhood friend, Izzy. He would have dropped a rock down the opening, timed its fall and then known how deep it was. She didn't know how to make the computation and she was in no position to drop a rock.

Lili thought she heard crashing waves faintly in the distance but had no idea whether the sound was coming from connecting passageways or the proximity of the opening high above her to the cliffs.

Suddenly she remembered when she had been on a college volleyball trip and their charter flight was delayed due to mechanical problems. Instead of drinking and gambling with the rest of her teammates Lili decided to go with one of her girlfriends on a historical tour along Highway Forty-Nine to a place called Moaning Cave. She remembered in the old days that people fell into the cave and were usually injured in the fall, which was about thirty feet. Then while they recovered and crawled around looking for an escape, they ended up falling even further into a deeper pit, which was one-hundred-fifty feet more— to an almost certain death below.

Lili decided she had better stay in one place and wait for the food and the lamp.

She slept uneasily and tried to convince herself there would be no creepies or crawlies in the cave. She had long been comforted in her native Kaua'i that there were no poisonous insects or reptiles as one might expect in a tropical climate. But she didn't know about such things in Barbados.

In the night, she heard a drip and didn't know if that might be a spring, or if she was only dreaming. Whether her eyes were open or closed, she could hardly tell the difference. She flowed in and out of sleep, like the disappearance and return of shadows under passing clouds. Then she heard a flapping and a clapping and glimpsed a swarm of creatures vented through the opening. *Bats! A covey of bats.* She covered herself with the extra clothes she had in her backpack and shivered with fright.

When daylight came she awaited Desmond's arrival but no one came. *Will I die here? Will I starve? Did the men in the van get him?* She tried to remain optimistic but there was something about the darkness, the deep and uncertain nature of the cave that troubled her. Once again she thought she could hear crashing waves in the distance. To be so close to the ocean with no means of getting there seemed like a cruel joke. *There must be a way out! I've got to find it!*

Then she began to get hungry and remembered what it had been like to starve as a child. This brought back memories of the day her brother, Mimo, had offered her a piece of rat, fried to a crisp in a cane fire, and how it had tasted like the dark meat of chicken and how she wished he were here now to provide even such a feast. And what if she couldn't get out and get money flowing again to Mimo and Ruth? Izzy had cautioned them that the peace they had made with the Bank of Aloha made it possible for the bank to renew the foreclosure process, rather than starting over, if they missed even a single payment. She hadn't sent any money again this month. She couldn't. *And, what about Aunty Fay? They may have already taken her Quonset hut and she'd be too proud or considerate to tell me.* Then she heard the dripping again. The incessant, annoying, rhythmic dripping.

She decided she'd rather die trying to find her way out than just sitting here thinking about it. So she crawled to the source of the drip, her knees aching all the way. The old scabs broke off and formed new wounds with an even tighter grip on the cloth in her jeans. There was a puddle of water and she drank from it, like a dog, until it was dry. She saw no good options. She was just acting and reacting—no thought, no plan, just an instinctive quest for survival. And then she collapsed into a delirium and slept.

* * *

On the morning of the third day she heard, "Sugar! Sugar!" She wondered if she had been dreaming. She hesitated for a moment in case it were her assailants but she soon realized the child's voice was familiar and did not sound troubled, "Yes, yes. I'm right here."

Desmond stuck his head over the hole. "Sorry I couldn't get here sooner, Sugar. After what happened Uncle Lance told my mother not to let any of us out of her sight. Emma and Idalia and Willie and Theo are all staying at my house just now. They had a police escort to school—with squad cars, guns and everything. It was neat. All the other kids were jealous. Mummy's been keeping a close watch on us, too."

"Did you say anything to anyone about my being here?"

"No, of course not. You can count on me. I haven't even told Grafton."

"Did you bring me any food, Desmond?"

He held up a bag in the light, so she could see it. "Yes ma'am, I did."

"And the lamp. Did you bring me the lamp?"

"I couldn't get a lamp so I brought you another flashlight. I'll sneak over to Uncle Lance's as soon as I can and lift his lamp."

Lili couldn't remember such a welcome sight as the food and the flashlight being lowered down on a thin piece of twine. She no longer felt helpless or hopeless—a little sustenance and she would be ready to explore the cave, find the escape route and consider her next move.

* * *

For the next day or so, Lili was able to get a look at the interior of the cave, albeit in small segments. In general its interior reminded her of an insulation they used to spray inside public buildings in Kaua'i. It didn't help that it was the same color as vomit. All the while she was concerned about the batteries running down and was not altogether certain there wasn't another lower level which she didn't want to find via the express elevator.

She was convinced by now that there were creepies and crawlies in the cave but was unable to spot any with her flashlight. It didn't surprise her that wherever she flashed the light there was nothing but rock. She pictured varmints darting just before the flow of light. She had heard whirring and screeching sounds. A stench in the distance convinced her there must be a roost of bats but she wasn't sure she wanted to spot them hanging. Had she wanted to, she could have followed the smell.

By flashing the light here and there she saw groves of stalactites or stalagmites, which fascinated her but also limited her mobility. They were prickly to the touch and she felt guilty whenever she broke one off. *I don't know how many centuries it may have taken this to form*, she mused. She thought about asking Desmond to tell Lance where she was and to get her out, but Lance was one of the things she had run away from. She had to be certain of him before she returned and she was convinced that once she got her strength and her bearings she could find the passage, which Desmond had reassured her went to the ocean.

While she waited for him to bring her the lamp to give her the best possible chance of escape at the lowest risk, she sat and considered her future. She could have asked him to secure a climbing rope at ground level so she could climb out. She still had the gear intact but it would be difficult and dangerous—especially if she couldn't see. And where would she go if she did get out? She needed a plan. The only true source of nourishment that had come down the rope was an apple and an orange. There were assorted Paradise Plums and Bulls Eyes and sugar cakes and an old ham sandwich that she was afraid to eat—the sort of thing a child might discard from his school lunch bag.

Lili was just about to conclude that she'd just as soon meet up with Mr. Fitzsimmons and his accomplices as spend more time in this cave, when on the next morning, Desmond appeared at first light. This time he hoisted down a pair of rotis from a nearby fast food restaurant, called Chefette—similar to what Mexicans might call a burrito, consisting of curried chicken in a soft tortilla shell, folded into an oblong shape. They were tasty and still warm. Lili was ravenous and devoured them in an instant. This renewed her strength and her will, her capacity to make meaningful plans.

"Has your uncle been asking about me?" Lili asked.

Desmond answered, "He asked just about every one else but me. They all said you took the bus and left. I didn't even have to lie to him."

Good, she thought. Lili had decided that the only safe thing to do would be to get off the island. *But how?* She didn't want to run off without seeing the children again and assuring them that her departure had nothing whatsoever to do with them. *But is that the whole truth? Am I less able to accept them because they're black? If they were white would I be staying here to be their mother?* She couldn't face these questions anymore than she could have faced a bright floodlight at that moment and tried to put them out of her mind.

"How is everyone doing? Are they all okay?"

"Yes," Desmond said.

"Has your Uncle Lance said anything about me?"

"Not to me he hasn't. Whenever someone asks about you, he says, 'Good riddance.' But Idalia says that's because he misses you and he's angry that you left without saying good-bye."

"Did you bring me the lamp, Desmond?"

He started to cry. "I couldn't. I couldn't get you the lamp, Sugar. I haven't been able to get over to Uncle Lance's when he's not home. Everyone is still staying at my house. I'll try again as soon as I can."

Lili's throat was growing hoarse from yelling back and forth and she suspected that Desmond's was, too.

"Desmond, promise me something."

"What is it Sugar? What is it you want me to promise?"

"Promise to come back tomorrow." *If I haven't figured my way out of here by then, I'm going to ask him to tell Lance where I am.*

"I promise, Sugar. I'll come back tomorrow if I can get away. They're watching us pretty close. I'm the only one who is allowed to go anywhere without an adult."

"Desmond, if I'm ever not here, you don't worry about me, okay? I may just have moved my hiding place but I'll be okay."

"But where else would you go?"

"I'd tell you Desmond, because I trust you, but I don't know myself. I may have to find a more secure place where I can do a better job of thinking things through. Now you go straight home. I don't want to be responsible for anything happening to you. Do you understand?"

He said he understood and left.

* * *

In spite of Lili's watching the hole for hours on the following day, Desmond didn't come. By now she missed the other children terribly and missed Lance, too. And while she had convinced herself this was the ideal time to escape and leave the island, she had trouble accepting the separation. She thought of the little kindnesses, first by the children—a tiny hand in hers, an upward glance of joy and approval, and then of Lance—a welcome hug, a quiet smile, a gentle touch—and, as always, unerring politeness. She longed for the sight and feel of his burly chest. The smooth taut muscles on his buttocks that she grabbed when they made love, and finally, the cozy, often disheveled home at the end of the lane—curtains in the windows she had added, and a hot meal on the table. *By escaping from Barbados, will I be escaping the bank, Lance, the children or myself?*

On the morning of what must have been about a week in the cave, Desmond showed up with a carbide lamp. He had remembered to bring matches and it already had fuel in it. She hesitated a moment, thinking the cavern might explode. But she lit it anyway, and when she adjusted the flow of acetylene gas from a mix of carbide and water it offered a bright light and the majesty of the whole cavern shone itself for the first time. It was breathtaking. She was in an area that formed a huge cathedral and the stalactites and stalagmites were profuse. Some of them were almost pure white, while others portrayed the yellowish cast of the ages. There was a rust colored stream in the setting, imperceptibly flowing deeper into the earth.

Somewhere in the recesses of her mind she remembered she had seen a TV program that showed a man playing stalagmites and stalactites as though they were parts of an African balaphon. She searched for an object she could use to strike them. Lili found a little piece of coral rock that had broken off and in a short time she was able to make simple melodies by tapping it against the stalactites. She played the harmony of Emma's sweet little voice and longed for the feel of her arms around her neck. The sound echoing throughout the chamber was eerie, but mesmerizing. And when the lamp was lit—casting a glow upon her gorgeous surroundings—she fantasized she was playing in a grand cathedral, while Lance sang in a husky voice from the choir loft.

* * *

On the next day, Lance's children came to see her— all except for Emma. Desmond had not broken his promise. Grafton had followed him the day before, which convinced her that she would have to escape immediately or risk detection by anyone who had an interest in finding her. Words were few because they had to shout and repeat almost every phrase two or three times. Yet she was elated to see them and they brought her all sorts of food and drink, which was a big improvement over the fouled water that she was confident had been giving her diarrhea.

Idalia said, "Sugar, let us get you out of there and take you home with us."

Lili was tempted but said, "No, I think I can find my own way out and when I leave, I can't come to your house. I have to find somewhere else to hide." She didn't tell them that she had also concluded that she had to get off the island. She decided she would give it another day on her own and if that didn't work she would ask them to go and get help.

By now Lili had explored enough to conclude that the caves were interconnected and that one or more of the passages were linked to other caves that in turn opened towards the ocean. She just had to locate the right passageway.

Willie broke down and cried. "Sugar, we need you. And Emma won't sleep or eat without you. She wants you. And Daddy do, too."

"I'll come and see you as soon as I can. I promise."

Lili also didn't want to find herself back in Lance's bed until she had had a better chance to assess her feelings for him and define her resolve. She had been swept into a bad relationship once before and this time she wanted to be sure this was the right one. She needed to be away from him a while longer.

Ideally she'd like to talk to one of her confidants—Suzie, or Aunty Fay—or someone like her old friend, Maria, the housemaid she had known in her youth. She longed for an opportunity to hear their wisdom.

* * *

Early the next morning she set out following the various tributaries she was convinced had gathered to form this one large cathedral. *Where shall I begin?* She chose the furthest tunnel from where she was standing and decided to work her way around the cavern until she had tried every one. The first several ended in passages so small that nothing larger than a gecko could have made further progress. Most of them were full of water and she faced a serious risk of drowning if she pursued them further. Yet she had felt an occasional breeze and deduced that it could not be from the opening near the top.

After countless dead ends she decided to try the tunnel that had been right next to her. She stood and walked into a crevasse. Then she crouched down until it became very narrow. It seemed to be going deeper into the earth. The lamp went out, signaling the loss of oxygen. Yet she crawled on. She was sick of being an underground prisoner and was determined to find her way out.

She had to leave her lamp and slither. After a short distance she realized she couldn't turn around. There wasn't room. She was committed. She tried not to panic. The passage was too small for her to rise up on her hands and knees. She inched her way along. Finally she came to a place full of water. *A dead end and a dead Lili. No one will find me here.*

She collapsed and fell into a stupor. She wanted to drink but she was sure the water was polluted. *Guano.* For hours she kept waking up and thinking she'd have to move on. But she couldn't. She was stuck. *What will Aunty Fay and Mimo do without me?* Intermittently she thought she heard voices, while she slipped in and out of a dreamlike state.

She remembered Lance saying that once he got into the caves he had no choice but to climb out. She wondered if she had been mistaken about the passageway. And to make matters worse, she had told Desmond not to worry about her if she was gone.

She thought she heard a French accent. *Am I going crazy?*

She thought it was Mr. Appleby. *Totally ridiculous. He couldn't fit through that hole!* Then all of a sudden bright lights flooded into the tunnel from the other end. They blinded her. She had no idea how long she'd been stuck.

"Help!" she cried. "I'm here. I'm over here." It didn't matter who it was now. She had to get out.

"It's okay, Miss Kaleo." She recognized the voice. It belonged to Mr. Appleby. "We're here to help you. We know you're in there."

Then she heard the comforting voice of her friend, Sea Cat. "It's okay, Lili. Mr. Appleby just wants to help you." Sea Cat's voice renewed her strength. She heard more voices.

"Yes, I can see you in there," Mr. Appleby said. To his companions he said, "Go and fetch us a rope."

They tossed her a rope but it fell hopelessly short. Then they tied a rock to it and it landed closer. Still she couldn't reach it. Her hands and fingers were weak. They poked the rock with a pole and poked and poked it. *A few inches, only a few inches more.* She stretched her hand out and couldn't reach it. They gave it another poke. She had it in her hand. Trembling and in agonizing pain from crawling on jagged rock she managed to untie the rock and retie the rope under her arms, around her torso.

Slowly and with immense pain to her they pulled her through the remaining feet of the tunnel. Exhausted and barely conscious she emerged—a physical and emotional wreck.

She gasped as she clutched at Sea Cat's knees. He reached down to comfort her. He flipped her over and poured water over her lips from a canteen. "How did you find me? What are you doing here?"

Sea Cat said, "After Jack was killed Mr. Appleby went to Martinique and hired a detective, the famous Monsieur Le Mot, to find his killer. You were at The Tower the night Jack was shot with the dart. Then you disappeared. The detective figured the two events might be connected. He wanted to ask you some questions."

"But how did you find me?"

A tall, skinny man with a raincoat draped over his shoulders shone a flashlight under his face so she could see him. He had a long and pointy nose protruding from a bony face. He said, "We followed Inspector Williams' children when they came to see you a few days ago. It took us so long because they didn't come but once. We finally figured out that you got your supplies from his nephew, Desmond, and it had never occurred to us to follow him, as well.

"Then we had to figure out how to get to you without alarming you. We didn't know whether or not you were armed. One of our men descended into the large cavern about an hour ago, but you weren't there. We were afraid you'd been captured, killed or arrested."

Lili said, "Arrested?"

"Yes. There's a warrant out for you. It seems they have films of you breaking into the Ragged Point lighthouse and they're trying to implicate you in Ephraim's murder and the bombing."

"Preposterous!"

"They've even got the police inspector after you."

"Inspector Williams? Lance? He knows I didn't have anything to do with any of those things."

"Yes. But, Lili, you're on Barbados. The banks control everything. You know the golden rule, 'He who has the money makes the rules.'"

"I'm sure they put pressure on him," Sea Cat said. "He's been on TV, offering a reward for your capture. That must be why he betrayed you."

Betrayed—the word struck her like one of those curare darts. *No. He wouldn't **betray** me. This man's not like Charlie.* "Lance wouldn't betray me. I know he wouldn't," she said. "He's a good man and a loyal friend. I know it! I just know it! He must have known I'm in danger and he's trying to protect me."

"I wouldn't count on it," Sea Cat said. "He's condemned your actions and said that you may be armed and dangerous. He also said you stole some of his deceased wife's jewelry."

That bastard! What a cheap shot! And how does he think I carried it off? In my purse?

* * *

It felt so good to get back to The Tower and take a bath that Lili thought she was hallucinating. Everyone said she needed medical treatment. Sea Cat said she was as pale as when she had arrived there over a year earlier. But they all also agreed that she should not go to the hospital for fear of apprehension. Monsieur Le Mot used his connections to locate a doctor. Sea Cat secreted her into the servants' locker area, which he locked and told everyone it was closed for maintenance. The doctor said she was dehydrated and put her on an intravenous drip. She convalesced for two or three days with Sea Cat seeing that the fluid bag was changed at proper intervals. Finally the doctor returned and removed the I.V.

"She's free to eat solid food now," the doctor said. "But she should remain quiet and rest for at least a week."

During the afternoon, when the manager took his break, Sea Cat was in charge of the hotel. He found errands for the other workers to get them away from the hotel, while Lili got cleaned and dressed.

After that she had to hide in the attic in a little nook, where Sea Cat had a bed he used when he had to work late or find an impromptu place to entertain one of his lady friends from the cruise ships. It had only a bed, a dresser and a lamp. But it was comfortable. There was no window but it did have a vent facing the ocean, which admitted welcome breezes. The vent was wooden and through the slats, she could see the commercial shipping vessels coming and going from port.

Lili thought about calling Lance and seeking his protection and telling him where to find "his wife's jewelry (a point which she did not share with the others)" but Mr. Appleby, the detective and Sea Cat reminded her that she was wanted. The bank had given a video surveillance tape of her break-in at the lighthouse to several TV news programs, which were running it on a regular basis. Although the burglar wore a mask, it showed the similarity between the build and mannerisms of the intruder with surveillance shots of Lili taking something out of the file cabinet in Mr. Baker's office on the day of the bombing.

They had also discovered a strand of what they believed to be her hair in a book that Ephraim had left in the dining area of the Peach n Quiet Resort, when he went there for a meal.

An indictment had been issued and Lance would be duty bound to arrest her and bring her to justice. *I can't go through another trial.*

But after having spent nearly two weeks in a dark cave she also couldn't stand being isolated. So as soon as she was feeling better and able to get up and walk around she decided that she had to have more company than just Sea Cat. She convinced him to help her work up a disguise so that she could return to the big round table in the evenings and chat with the guests. She also knew she had better make a plan to get off the island.

There was a major construction project at the nearby University of the West Indies that everyone knew about so Sea Cat helped her dress up as a construction worker, complete with a yellow hardhat under which she stuffed her hair. Her fingernails were reduced to stubs after living in the cave so they were no problem. She practiced making her voice sound deeper and more masculine. That was not easy and it made the back of her throat sore.

"Hans Jenkins is returning today on the Tropic Carib so you'll get to test your disguise with him," Sea Cat said. "He won't be expecting you to be here. If you can fool him you'll be able to fool anyone."

That's it! I'll try to fool him and then see whether or not he'll let me sneak onboard as a stowaway. That's my ticket out of here.

She put on loose fitting coveralls so that her breasts were not well defined and sat at the table, drinking a beer, just before the others arrived. At the very last minute she got up from the table, looked carefully into the mirror and then went to tell Sea Cat it wasn't going to work and she would spend the evening in the attic.

"You could've fooled me," Sea Cat said.

"Really?" Lili said. "What about the whiskers? Does it look as if I've shaved lately?" She stoked her chin.

"I guess you've got a point there. Most of my dates from the cruise ships have better mustaches than that. But let's not give up. I think I can help."

He found a full beard used by Faldo, the Magician, during the annual Emancipation Day celebration at the hotel. It was black and nearly matched the texture of her hair. Lili looked in the mirror and this time concluded that she looked so much like a man it was frightful.

Hans accepted the costume and the charade so fully that he asked Dudley—Dudley M. Cronk—Lili's alias, whether or not he would like to have a job repairing shipping crates down on the dock when the construction was over at the university. The other guests drank their fill, tired of the conversation and had long since retired from the table. "You'd be a splendid man to have on our team," were Hans' exact words. "We can always use a good hand."

The adhesive stung when Lili pulled off her beard and mustache. "How about a good woman?" she asked.

Hans' opened his already protruding eyes so wide it looked like they would pop out of their sockets. "Pardon me. I think I've had too many brews. For a second I thought you looked like a woman friend of mine."

Lili's voice changed from hoarse and husky to normal. "Hans, I am a woman friend of yours. It's me, Lili, Lili Kaleo."

He blinked, looked at his hand close up and inspected it. He studied the label on his beer bottle. He looked back at her face and studied it. "By God, that is you. That is you, Lili." He held out his coarse hand and Lili took it and allowed him to examine her features.

They talked well into the wee hours of the morning. In the distance they noticed when the band at The Paradise Beach Hotel had played its last set.

Lili said, "Do you think you could get me on your ship, Hans? Do you think you could sneak me out of here?"

"As a stowaway, you mean?"

"Yes, Hans, as a stowaway."

He downed his last slug of beer and then belched. Lili tried to ignore his bad manners.

"Let me think it over, Mum. Let me think on it until tomorrow. We don't ship out until Wednesday so give me a chance to think about it."

* * *

Lili cooperated with Monsieur Le Mot by telling him everything of significance she could think of that had happened since she had arrived in Barbados, except, of course, for her affair with Lance and his golden stash. She supposed he had either guessed of the romantic entanglement or been told so by Sea Cat. In return he shared his suspicions about emerald and cocaine smuggling from Colombia, gold smuggling from Guyana, Surinam and Northern Brazil as well as the money laundering and the guns it would take to support such an operation. "The smuggling activities are regional but the financial connections are worldwide. The tentacles of this operation stretch over many continents," he assured her. "And someone in the bank is a key player. The police must already know that. It took me less than two weeks to piece that much together and they've had years to work on the case. I wonder if everyone on the police force is on the up and up."

"Or on the take?"

"*Oui*, 'on the take.' That would be one way to put it."

"Monsieur Le Mot," Lili asked. "How do you think the contraband is shipped in and out of the island?"

"You mean what sort of transportation or by whom? What is it you want to know?"

"Just in general, by what mode of transportation?"

Mr. Le Mot replied, "I'm sure some of it comes in and out by fishing boat, probably from Jamaica. That would be the pot and meth-amphetamines. Then some would come by plane, commercial aircraft—the higher end stuff, cocaine and jewelry, that sort of thing—mostly from Colombia and northern Brazil."

"Any of it by freighter?" Lili asked.

"*J'ne sais pas*," he replied and shrugged his shoulders. "I do not know."

Monsieur Le Mot curled the tips of his heavily waxed mustache with his thumb and two forefingers as Lili spoke. "How about the Tropic Carib? Could it be hauling, say guns or gold?"

"Hmm!" Monsieur Le Mot replied. "It sounds perfectly plausible but I have no such information. Do you, Mademoiselle?"

Lili said. "I was just curious. It's something I think I'll ask Hans about."

"I hate to be so grim but I would be careful to whom you ask such questions, Mademoiselle. I do not wish to see you taken out of here feet first, like zee little minkee."

* * *

When Hans returned from his day's activities Sea Cat ushered him to the attic. Lili had already decided to trust him. Sea Cat was upset that she had immediately taken Hans into her confidence but Lili said, "Every once in a while you've got to trust someone. I've always trusted you."

"I've thought it over, Lili," Hans said, as he entered the room squinting. His big protruding eyes were having difficulty adjusting to the light.

Sea Cat sat on her bed and watched the two of them as they talked. The slightest breeze penetrated the wooden slats. Lili looked at Hans in eager anticipation.

"I'm sorry, Lili. It wouldn't work to have you as a stowaway."

Lili's heart sank. "Why not, Hans? I'd be careful and if they caught me— "

"But they would catch you, Lili. They would catch you right away. Every two or three months we take on some special cargo and I've found out from one of my shipmates that we'll be doing it again this time and it will be guarded the whole trip. I might be able to get you into the cargo hold but the guards would be there, too, and sooner or later they'd catch you."

"The cargo, Hans," she looked at Sea Cat, "what do you know about the cargo?"

"Just that every once in a while we have a special shipment out of Barbados that requires some guards. I have no idea what's in it. They don't put it on the regular ship's manifest."

"Have you told this to Monsieur Le Mot? Have you told the authorities?"

"No, Ma'am and I'm not about to tell any of them. I'd lose my job. We—the crew that is—sometimes talk among ourselves but we'd never discuss this with anyone else. In fact I shouldn't have told you." He looked downcast.

Lili said to Sea Cat, "Well, I guess I'll have to find another way."

Hans replied, "I didn't say I couldn't get you onboard the ship. I said I couldn't risk taking you on as a stowaway. We've been looking for a radio operator's apprentice to train for another ship in the line. And since I'm the radio operator on this ship I get to hire him, or in this case her." He reached into his shirt and pulled out a set of documents—an Antiguan passport with no photo, a set of ship's union apprenticeship papers, a credential that she had completed her training at West Indies University and a contract of employment, as yet unsigned. All were made out in the name of Dudley M. Cronk.

"We leave in twenty-four hours," Hans concluded as he handed her the papers.

Lili jumped up and down on the bed as if it were a trampoline. She jumped off and hugged Hans then went over and put her arm around Sea Cat. She finished with the proclamation, "I love you guys!"

* * *

Sea Cat went out to purchase the things she needed to perfect her disguise. He also borrowed a Nikon camera from a professional photographer for the passport photo, had it developed and got it to Hans in time for him to arrange to have it laminated into the passport.

The sailor outfit made her feel gay and lighthearted. It included a broad striped turtleneck shirt and bell-bottomed pants. Lili padded her stomach so it wouldn't seem so incongruous to pad around her breasts. She knew this additional padding would be far too hot to wear onboard ship but it was okay for getting onboard and then she would tape her breasts down. She found out what it would be like to be fat. *Poor Mr. Appleby.*

They told Monsieur Le Mot what they were up to and asked him to evaluate her planned method of escape from the island and propose alternatives.

"Even if you left on a fishing boat they'd insist on seeing your exit visa and the authorities would be watching for you. The same would apply to a yacht. They won't be expecting a fugitive to show up as a normal part of a ship's crew, especially one with an Antiguan passport and a matching photograph."

* * *

At six a.m. on the eighth day after her rescue, Sea Cat awakened Lili and they had a light breakfast of fresh honeydew, papaya and French toast on the sun porch adjacent to her room. "I hate to see you go," he said. "I've grown accustomed to your being so single-minded."

Lili reached over the table and pinched his cheek. "No more single minded than you going off to entertain the ladies every night." After all this time Lili still hadn't reconciled her fondness for Sea Cat with his nocturnal escapades. She viewed them as exploitations, whereas he seemed to revel in them as conquests, much the same as she had feared from Lance.

Sea Cat smiled. "It's my duty as a young Bajan 'mahn' to make lonely foreigners feel welcome."

Sea Cat appeared distressed at the prospect of her leaving and it surprised Lili. When he spoke of his liaisons that were "not bahd," she had often wondered whether or not he was sensitive and caring. But he had come to the

fore, as of late, as her loyal ally and protector and she came
to realize that she had developed a great affection for him.

Then the moment came for another sad experience.
Without fanfare, Sea Cat quickly cut her hair to fit under
the stocking cap Hans had provided to enhance her
disguise. It would be impossible for her to keep her long,
flowing, black hair hidden during the voyage and Lili had
viewed the cutting as inevitable but hung onto her hair as
long as she could.

As Sea Cat snipped with the scissors and shaved
bordering areas with his electric razor Lili thought of all
that had happened since the ends of that hair had broken
through the top of her scalp. Her tears and her hair both
fell in clumps. She comforted herself by thinking that
maybe this would be a turning point.

* * *

Once the taxi was loaded with Lili and Hans and all
their belongings Sea Cat said, "I'll miss you, Lili Kaleo."
The cab was parked in the same parking lot that Lance had
once entered, holding up a picnic basket. It seemed like an
eternity since then. Lili could barely sustain her
composure. She looked up at the porch of The Tower and
visualized the collage of experiences she had had there
from frolicking laughter to the feverish antics of the
adorable "minkee."

"I'll miss you, too," she mouthed through the closed
window as the cab turned and started to pull up the narrow
lane one last time. Lili rolled down the window, stuck her
head out of the cab and turned her face towards him.
"Don't forget to call Lance's children for me!"

"When you're safely away," Sea Cat yelled. "Only
when you're safely away."

It tore at Lili's heart that she was not able to keep
her promise to see Lance's children before she left. She
had tried to call them. She went up the road to the
Convenience Mart and had the phone in her hand when
Detective Le Mot intervened, grabbed her hand and gently,
but persuasively, put the phone back on the hook. She
knew he was right. It was for her safety and theirs.

About a half-mile into the ride, Hans said, "This is
not the way to the ship."

"It is," the cabbie insisted. "They have the road
closed due to construction."

Lili didn't know the way but she could see at a
glance how upset Hans was. She began to consider how

she might escape from the cab. It sped up. She gauged the speed of the car and took a look at the pavement outside. The thought of skinning herself or being hit in the heavy traffic worried her, and she shuddered at the thought of the pain and risk of being seriously injured or killed. The driver frantically circled a roundabout. The padding in her sailor outfit made it unbearably hot, even with the sun barely above the horizon. Sweat dripped from her brow.

Next they were in downtown Bridgetown. *Why would he bring us here?* Even at this early hour the honking and congestion were evident. The cab slowed. They had to stop for the traffic to clear. Ride on or jump? She considered. Before she could make up her mind the driver picked up speed, sped by the cricket stands, through a roundabout, and down towards the wharf.

I'll jump out at the next light. But the cab driver ran the stoplight. He blared with his horn as he sped through. In Barbados it seemed that must be a legitimate alternative to stopping because drivers did it all the time.

After a few more emotionally charged glances between Hans and Lili the cabby screeched to a halt, leaned back over the seat, stared into their eyes and announced that they had arrived at the Tropic Carib and that the fare would be forty-one dollars, Barbados, or twenty-two, U.S. Two sighs of relief.

* * *

"Okay, you men," barked the crew chief, who met them in the loading area near the ship—first in Spanish, next in English and then in what Lili presumed was Chinese or Japanese. "Carry your bags up there and put them down on the deck. They'll all be gone through and returned to you." Damn it! I've got my panties and bras in there, Lili realized.

"Make sure they're all labeled and then report to the bursar's office to get your pay cards and report for duty."

Lili put her duffle bag on her shoulder like everyone else, carried it up the gangplank and placed it down next to the rest. As she did so she pulled off the identification tags. If they ever figured out whose bag this was she knew she was in trouble. Otherwise she was confident she could fool her shipmates about her gender, given her conditioning and size and assuming she didn't have to take a shower with anyone. She was pale after all those days in the cave but she had quickly regained her strength. She wore a stocking cap at all times, even in the intense heat.

In many ways she was fearful of the days to come on the high seas performing a challenging job for which she had no training, although Hans had promised he would cover for her and no one would be any the wiser. Yet she felt exhilarated by the salt air and the adventures that lay ahead. At least she didn't think she had to worry about Messrs. Fitzsimmons or Baker for a while. And she'd be outside breathing fresh salt air and not stuck in a dingy, cold, humid cave.

Sadly and resolutely, as they proceeded out the shipping lane, she looked back and watched The Tower fade into the distance. It was hard to imagine that on so many wondrous and magical evenings she had sat back there on the porch amidst the fun, excitement and pleasant conversation. It was difficult for her to face the fact that she had grown so attached to this tiny country of Barbados and stared in awe of what an important role it had played in her life. Tears seeped out the corners of her eyes and dampened   her   windblown   cheeks.

Part II

Guatemala

1995

Chapter Twelve

As the ship progressed out to sea Lili felt more and more confident she had made the right move. She worked in the radio operator's room, assisting with radio navigation. Although numbers were used she seemed to gain a reasonable grasp of the operation, allowing largely to the spatial relationships involved with triangulation. The drawings fascinated her. However on their second day at sea, just when she thought she was getting acclimated, she got up feeling queasy and couldn't stop vomiting all morning.

Hans said, "You don't look so good, sailor. Don't have your sea legs?"

"I thought I was doing okay but when I looked at myself in the mirror this morning I hardly recognized myself. There was this green looking thing staring back at me."

"You'd better not let the captain or first mate see you. They'll send you to sickbay." "I could use some Dramamine," Lili said, as she felt the ship tilting to and fro in a disgustingly perfect rhythm. She felt numbness around her jaw that extended into her throat and threatened to invade her stomach. She assumed that. when it found its mark, her cookies would come up again.

"Yes, but that quack down there in sickbay is apt to give you a physical to bring your sailing credentials up to date. That should prove interesting. He's blind in one eye and as myopic as Mr. Magoo in the other but even he's not going to overlook a few things missing in your drawers."

Just then a horn sounded, calling for all hands on deck. On the way up the stairs to the main deck Lili dumped what was left of her breakfast over the railing. What didn't get blown against the side of the ship fell into the sea below. She wanted to curl up and die. *Give me back the cave.* Then, as she arrived on the main deck, the cool salt breeze restored her vitality.

The ship was on its way to drop off building supplies, pepper and pharmaceuticals in Guatemala, pick up bananas and coffee along the coast of Central America, pass through the Panama Canal and deliver them along the North American coast, all the way to Vancouver. She had seen the heavily guarded cargo Hans had mentioned as it was being hoisted onboard. She was determined to find a way to steal into the cargo hold to see what she could find out about the contents.

On the whole she was excited about the entire sailing experience. Lili had heard and read about the huge locks in the canal and was anxious to experience the passage from the Atlantic to the Pacific. It was a one-mile climb or drop, she couldn't remember which. She marveled at how large the ship appeared relative to the people onboard but how small it seemed when compared to the open sea.

Even though this was a civilian crew they were trained to stand at what one might loosely define as "attention" —in even and well-defined rows, while the captain addressed them.

The captain spoke in bold, broad brushed tones. "For those of you who got onboard in Barbados, my name is Rolf Andersen. I'm your captain. I expect every one of yous to work hard, do what yer told and mind yer own damn business. You'll be paid well, provided with good eats and I'm expectin' you'll honor yer contracts in return. A little sweat from yer brows every now and then would be a welcome sight."

Next he reviewed their itinerary and told them their first stop would be in Puerto Barrios. "And I want you men to behave yerselves there, ya hear! The last time we was there I had to bail two of your *former* fellow crew members out of jail fer soliciting prostitutes and I'm not doing it again." The crew laughed. "Your horny dicks can rot in their stinking jails!" They laughed all the more. "And the clap can kill ya for all I care."

So much for standing at attention. The men were bent over in deep belly laughs.

"Now I might not have called you together to hear that but for one little nagging detail." Lili felt as though she might faint.

The captain continued, "When we inspected the baggage that was brought on board in Bridgetown we found these." He held up a handful of Lili's panties . . .

It had to be the lavender and pink ones. Damn it!

. . . and her bra. The men cheered. It reminded Lili of her trial when Aunty Fay had done something similar.

"I'm sure the offending party realizes we can't tell whose these are because there were no tags on the bags but I will say this. 'There's going to be no lascivious behaviors and no perversions on my ship, God help me! Do you hear me one and all?'"

The men nodded in agreement and clamored amongst themselves.

"Aye, Aye, sir," said one of the deck hands standing near the front of the brigade. It was a scruffy looking bunch—not what you'd call clean cut and when the wind shifted at least a few of them projected the stench of stable animals.

"Aye, Aye? Well, ya damn well better pay attention to what I'm sayin', because, if there's any funny business goin' on on this ship yer gonna be scrubbin' floors and polishin' brass 'til you've got no elbows." He walked off, repeating his resolve under his breath to the first mate.

"Is he really as tough as he sounds?" Lili whispered to Hans as the men "fell out."

He nodded "yes" and ran his finger across his Adams apple in a throat slitting gesture. Lili felt her knees buckle. She grabbed the railing to keep from keeling over.

One of the sailors in a navy blue coat with a matching stocking cap said, "Never fails. There's a fancy pants in every crew."

The other said, "Well, he'd better stay at least fifty yards from my ass. If he needs a bonk, I'll bonk him with this." He lifted and shook a sparring pin.

Rather than go back to the radio shack Hans convinced Lili they should go to the galley and have lunch. On the one hand she thought the last thing she wanted to see right now was food. Ironically, on the other, she was starving. She ate runny eggs and deep fried potatoes. *I guess this ain't The Sand Dollar,* she thought as she spread her toast from the largest jar of margarine she had ever seen. *Will I be able to keep this down?*

She missed Lance a lot more than she had expected and couldn't believe he would betray her. *He might graze in another flock or even be on the take. But he would never betray me. I'm sure of it.* And those children, those precious little children. She could never seem to get them out of her mind. She kept thinking of how much they would enjoy being onboard ship and how many questions the boys would be asking about the engines and navigation equipment and how everything worked and how much they would want to be at the helm and steer the ship. Her heart ached at not having had a chance to see them and share one more hug or try to explain things before she departed.

* * *

The days passed routinely except that Lili continued to be sick, usually first thing in the morning. She had the misfortune of throwing up on the feet of the first mate, who had stopped into the radio room to find out their ship's exact position, in view of an impending storm. He insisted that she report to sickbay immediately. He didn't want anyone else to catch whatever dread disease she might have. Lili figured her charade was over.

She had faced near exposure a few days earlier when she was using the community shower. Lili couldn't stand the fetid odor that followed a few of the men around and decided that that wasn't going to be her plight, nor the plight of those around her—no matter what. But she obviously couldn't shower when everyone else did. So she decided to bathe at around two a.m. and set her alarm for one-thirty.

She kept a towel nearby just in case and thought she was alone when she heard a noise in the changing room adjacent to the shower. It sounded like metal banging. *Something must have fallen over. I wonder if someone is out there.* She grabbed her towel and turned off the shower. If she were to wrap the towel around her it wouldn't have covered all of her vital statistics so she had to settle for continuing to disguise her front, leaving her bottom exposed. Fortunately she hadn't shaved her legs since she was in the cave and her leg hair was thick and dark.

As she bent over to pick up the soap she had dropped she heard a raspy voice. "Nice ass, sailor! I know who you are. If you know what's good for you, you'll meet me outside cabin forty-one in thirty minutes."

Of course she had no intention of meeting him. His voice gave her the shivers. *Did he see more than just my bum and my legs? Does he really know who I am?*

Right now she had no choice but to meet Dr. Magoo. She and Hans took the first aid kit into the restroom and taped down her breasts as flat as they could with adhesive tape. It hurt something fierce. "I'll bet the sailors would be drooling over these," Hans said, as he wiped saliva from his lips with the back of his hand.

Lili looked askance.

"Sorry, Mum," he said. "But I *am* human."

Lili smiled. "Where is this doctor who can't see? I hope you're right about his eyesight."

There was a map of the ship on the wall and Hans showed her directions. To get there Lili had to slip by the captain's cabin as well as "cabin forty-one." She did so without incident but not without curiosity as to who the occupant of cabin forty-one might be—but not enough curiosity to "inquire within."

She wanted to detour into the cargo hold and see what she could figure out about whatever it was that was important enough to guard, but right now she was committed to seeing the doctor. She had seen the huge crates and containers, some of them covered with tarps, when she first arrived on deck. But she was so busy pulling off her nametags that she didn't get a good look at it or its guards.

Lili felt claustrophobic. She couldn't get over how narrow the hallways were or how low the ceilings and doorjambs. Finally she came to a door marked "Doctor Sam Nielsen."

"Come on in, sailor. What seems to be ailing you?" The ship rocked.

Instinctively Lili took off her cap. She had been planning to leave it on—as a bargaining chip over how much clothing she would take off—allowing that to be the first and only item. However it didn't seem polite to leave it on so she found it in her hand seconds after she had entered the clinic. *So much for bargaining.* The room smelled of medication with an overriding hint of iodine.

"Dr. Nielsen at yer service." He held out his hand for her to shake. He had on a monocle attached to a long silver chain that seemed to blend with his silver white hair. Lili stared at it with an open mouth—the worst, but most productive kind of staring, according to Aunty Fay.

"What's wrong? Never seen a monocle before?"

"Why, yes. Of course. Of course, I've seen a monocle before." She couldn't remember ever seeing one, except maybe on television. "It's just that it's so thick."

He allowed the monocle to drop and bounce when it reached the end of its tether. He held onto the hand he had just shaken and began to rub Lili's palm. "Good grief," he said. "We must have you polishing silverware. I don't feel any calluses."

Lili felt defensive. "I've done my share of hard work in my time. It's just that they've got me working as an apprentice in the radio room—not my choice. That's just where they put me."

The doctor walked over, opened a tiny circular portal and appeared to gaze out. She couldn't imagine what he might be seeing. *Maybe he's taking in some salt air. It is stuffy in here.*

"There, there, sailor. I didn't mean to challenge your, umm, 'virility.' Now what seems to be the problem?"

"I've been sick almost from the very day I got onto this ship. It gets better through the course of the day and I actually have a pretty good appetite but I can't seem to hold down my food, especially in the morning."

"Hmm!" Doctor Nielsen shook down a thermometer and stuck it under her tongue. He used a light with a bright narrow beam to check her eyes. "Interesting," he said. "Deep brown eyes, but you have a little fleck in your iris. Did anyone ever tell you that?"

"My son and my father had one, but nobody ever told me that I—"

"It's very faint, but it's there all right. It's hereditary, just like a fingerprint."

Lili liked the old man right off. He seemed kindly.

"Okay, unbutton your shirt. In fact you'd better take it off. Have you ever had motion sickness—cars, airplanes, anything like that?"

Lili flashed upon an airsickness incident she once had with her friend Suzie on their way to a Bikers' Faire on the Big Island. She also remembered getting sick once in awhile on the winding road through Koke'e Park on Kaua'i in the back of her daddy's pickup truck.

"Yes. As a matter of fact, I have been motion sick." She reluctantly took off her shirt.

The doctor put his monocle back in and inspected her chest from a distance. He flicked the adhesive tape with his fingers. "Injury?"

Lili gave him the huskiest theatrical voice she could muster. "Yes. How did you know? . . . Bar fight back in Barbados."

"Really? You'd better watch those. Captain hates 'em."

He took her pulse and then listened to her heartbeat in a bare area between the bandages. "Umm. Hmm," he said. "Yer ticker sounds fine. Let's take that temperature again. It's reading a little high. I'm not sure I shook it all the way down." He stuck the thermometer back under her tongue.

*I think I've fooled the old geezer. He **must** be blind.*

"Have you ever considered you might be pregnant?" He asked.

Lili blew the thermometer out of her mouth, like a pea through a straw. It flew several feet across the room and broke on the floor. The mercury beaded. She coughed and gasped for air.

"I'd have to be blind not to notice," he continued. "I could tell from the shape of your hips the minute you walked in. And those mounds under your bandages—who did you think you were going to fool? I'm not that blind! And you'd better take off the bandages and let your skin breath. Otherwise you're going to end up with a terrible rash."

Lili didn't know whether to laugh or cry so she did both.

"Please, please don't turn me in," she pleaded. "Please don't report me to the captain."

The doctor just looked at her. He lifted his monocle, put it in place and stared. "Why don't you tell me about it while we take those bandages off? If we don't, they're gonna adhere to you so hard I'll hear ya yellin' all the way from the sailors' quarters."

She told him enough—just enough between screeches during the bandage removal—to gain his sympathy. Not the part about the bombing but the part about the inspector and his children and the apparent betrayal *du coeur.*

"Okay," he said. "I'll be retiring in six months so I don't much care what they do to me. But you, as for you, you'll have to be getting off this ship before the men figure this out and I'd be a bit surprised if some of them haven't already. They won't be able to keep their hands off you."

The doctor removed his monocle and looked over the top of it. "Has anyone approached you? . . . I mean, you know . . . made advances?"

Lili thought about the nocturnal intruder but she didn't answer.

"I thought so," the doctor said. "The only way I'll go along with this is if you get off in Puerto Barrios—our first stop. And if anyone confronts or bothers you in the meantime I don't know a thing about this."

"Thank you Dr. Nielsen. Thank you so much." She got up and hugged him. "What do you think, doctor? Do you think I'm pregnant?"

"I can't say for sure. The symptoms you have could be either from an inner ear imbalance, more commonly known as motion sickness, or you could be pregnant. A simple drugstore test would tell you for sure but I don't have any here. I can't remember the last time one of my sailors got pregnant."

They laughed and then she cried tears of despair at the fear of pregnancy. Can't I learn one damn thing in life? She asked herself.

* * *

For the next several days the ship's progress was delayed by a terrible storm. It listed from side to side and pitched from front to back. Lili occupied her time by trying to remember what her science teachers had said about the center of gravity. The closer she could get to it, she reasoned, the less the boat would be moving relative to her. She didn't have much freedom of movement, but with what little she had, she moved closer to the center of gravity. Now she vomited incessantly—both day and night.

Lili still had to attend to her navigational duties and they were even more significant because every fraction of a degree relative to the course would mean an earlier arrival in Puerto Barrios. Even Hans looked haggard and seemed to be suffering, although he wouldn't admit it. "Just give me my coffee in a cup that won't tip over and I'll survive." He drank from a huge red cup, glued to a matching oversized saucer.

Only the hardiest of men, or the most stubborn, didn't report to sickbay at one time or another as the salty gusts blew across the main deck. In spite of this everyone inside the ship, including the cook, the ship's engineer, the bursar, came to the main deck to breathe the fresh air whenever they could. Lili was miserable. The doctor only prescribed half the normal amount of Dramamine in case she was pregnant. And in the midst of her misery, when she would hold onto a railing or a spar or a beam or a column—anything to give her stability—she decided it was the perfect time to go down into the cargo hold to see what was there. She had seen the guards pass the radio shack on their way to the main deck.

She didn't conspire with Hans because she didn't want to implicate him any more than he was already, if she got caught. She did refer to the ship's map he had shown her and from a careful study of it she knew which way to go. She told Hans she'd had all she could take and had to go see the doctor again.

The ship tossed and turned unmercifully as she made her way down the stairs. She had already thrown up so much there was nothing left but dry heaves. She bounced back and forth from wall to wall against the palms of her extended hands. She found an empty container, held it and tried to heave into it but couldn't.

It was dark in this part of the ship because the lights had gone out. Emergency lanterns flickered in the act of producing what dim light there was. She was surprised to find the door to the cargo hold open. *I guess they're not worried about intruders.*

She carried a pocket flashlight—something she had resolved never to be without after leaving the cave. She squeezed it and shed a beam of green light across the blackness. The ship lurched in the water.

After a few minutes of bounding around in the cargo area she located the two large pallets she had seen brought onboard by the crane. The ones that had always had the guards at their side. They had padded tarps around them, secured by white synthetic banding tape. She had no knife and could barely see anything in the hold. She pulled frantically at the tape, trying to get a look at the contents, but it was too secure.

Then she noticed there was a rip at the bottom near the floor. When she reached down to pull it up she jabbed herself with a rusty nail sticking out of the pallet. Her hand bled on the tarp and onto the floor. Carefully, she lifted the small torn covering. There were even stacks of black bars. *Ingots.*

She and Suzie had watched *The Maltese Falcon* many times at Suzie's house when they were children, and she remembered what Sydney Greenstreet had done when he got custody of the black bird and had a chance to examine it. She pulled out the rusty nail and scraped it across one of the ingots. Unlike the Maltese Falcon, this was gold bullion. She ran her fingers across one of them. It felt smooth and glorious to the touch. *I wonder what one of these bars is worth.*

She dropped the torn fragment of tarp and noticed a bill of lading in a plastic pouch. She fumbled and hurriedly tried to pull it out. She caught just a glimpse of part of it, *Secretaría de Relaciones Exter--*, before the lights suddenly went on. She quickly slipped it back into the plastic.

A man entered talking to his rowdy companions, "Wow, what a ride. I haven't weathered a storm like this in years. I hope the ship holds together."

Another said, "One more wave across the bow and we'd have capsized."

Lili slipped into an empty shipping container.

The first one put his hand on top of the tarp which covered the bullion, "It's a good thing it didn't or we'd have lost all of this."

Another said, "I wouldn't want to have to explain that to the boss."

"Yeah, we might as well go down with the ship as tell him that."

Lili made herself as small and unobtrusive as she could in the back of the container. The sawdust on the floor made her sneeze.

"Did you hear that?" one of the men said.

"I didn't hear nothin' but the boards creakin'." The ship was still listing and yawing, tossing and turning in the waves. Every board ached. Every stomach longed for shore.

"Say," one of the men said, "Have you gotten a look at that new radio operator?"

"Yeah, he looks like a pansy ass if you ask me. Do you think he's the faggot the captain is looking for?"

"Better yet," the more boisterous of the men said. "I think that he may be a she. I seen him or her or it, whichever it is, in the shower the other night when I got my break from the watch. Whoever it was had a nicer ass than I've ever seen on a man."

"Well, you'd certainly be the expert on that," the other said.

That was followed by a brief scuffle that ended when the violence of the ship's lurching and yawing returned.

Lili perched there quietly for at least an hour, her back aching, her stomach convulsed. She thought about Lance and his family and the children and how she missed them. She thought of her son, Christian, wherever he might be. How she longed to be with him to give him the nurturing she had been unable to provide during her long, arduous trial when he needed it most.

Must I go on? For the second time in her life the answer was "yes." Not for me—but for whatever soul I may be carrying deep inside me. The prospect of the glory and burden of motherhood once again lay at her doorstep. She worried about what color the baby might be. Explaining the birth of a child out of wedlock would be one thing. Explaining why he or she was black would involve another dimension she preferred to avoid.

An hour or so later the storm lessened its fury. The men all fell asleep at the first sign of relief and she quickly and quietly snuck back out of the cargo hold and up to the radio shack. Hans was waiting there for her.

"Damn it, Lili, I was worried about you. I would've told the captain you were missing but I didn't want him to get suspicious and ask questions. Where were you?"

"I snuck into the cargo hold and couldn't get out. The guards came back and I had to wait for them to fall asleep."

"Find anything?"

"I found that we've taken on considerably more ballast than I might have expected."

* * *

In the remaining days at sea Lili avoided contact with her shipmates. Hans brought her food in her room. That was one of the perks of this job in that radio personnel had to be on twenty-four hour standby and her room was right next to the shack. In spite of the pitching and yawing of the ship she gradually seemed to grow her sea legs—an immunity to the vomiting or lack of fluid to expel—she wasn't sure which. Then—just as in her native Hawaii— the waves calmed and the sun appeared as though it had always been there just waiting to be seen and appreciated. The flashing beam of a lighthouse on a Belize atoll winked at them as they passed.

The day the ship entered Puerto Barrios was glorious in many respects—light, variable winds, bright and sunny. The Antiguan flag on the stern barely rippled and the trees waved politely in the distance. It was, however, oppressively hot and humid. The passing storm might have cooled things off for a brief period but that period was past. Speaking of periods Lili had still not had hers and nearly two months had elapsed since the last one. She felt like a worrisome teenager who had taken her first lover.

She was on the verge of panic because all through the storm and the seasickness and the fears of detection she had not had a chance to make a plan. The day before they landed Hans had told her, during a torrential downpour and shellacking waves, that he had received and destroyed a cablegram. It was from the commissioner of police in Barbados advising the captain that "one Lili Kaleo—a prime suspect in a terrorist incident as well as a murder may be onboard the Tropic Carib as a stowaway." It went on to say that "if discovered, her belongings should be confiscated and she should be apprehended and detained with the tightest of security measures to prevent her escape."

Hans agreed to help her, notwithstanding the cablegram. But in less than twenty-four hours the ship was to leave port and she knew he would be on it and she wouldn't. *Where am I to go? What will I do?* Before she left the ship she drew her pay—a check made out to Dudley M. Cronk, her alias. *Will this do me any good? I can't ask the purser to cash it. He'll ask too many questions.*

She decided not to confess her deception and claim her belongings, even though she desperately wanted her clothes and cosmetics. Lili didn't want to call attention to herself, even though she no longer cared about anyone's impression.

"Thank you. Thank you, Hans," she said.

"C'mon, Lili. Don't mention it. Sea Cat told me you was a good man, er- woman, well you know what I mean, and that I should look after you. They don't come no better 'n Sea Cat."

Chapter Thirteen

They scurried down the gangplank and were the first ones off. Lili grabbed Hans' hand and led him between two large warehouses that lined the pier. She hurriedly took off her beard and discarded it along with her disguise in a trash bin so that no one from the ship would recognize her if she were seen. She peered out from between the buildings, while asking Hans to stay well back.

Hans asked, "What are we doing here? What's the all fired hurry?"

"Shh! I don't want anyone to hear us. I want to see if they unload the special cargo."

Sure enough, the ingots, covered by the same tarp that hid them on their embarkation, were hoisted off the ship and onto a flat bed truck which in turn pulled into one of the nearby warehouses.

"Of course they unloaded it," Hans said. "You could've just asked me. It happens like that every two or three months, just like clockwork."

"Hans, I think you'd better get another job. Sooner or later this ship's due for a visit from law enforcement."

"You don't have to convince me of that, Lili. After that last storm I think I'll get a job on one of them cruise ships. I understand they have special weighting and gyroscopic stabilization that makes for a much smoother ride. I'm getting too old for that creaky old tub. It's just like being in jail. Only if yer in jail you don't have to worry about sinking."

They crept between the buildings then tried to blend back in with the crowd. They walked along the shoreline to the tiny shops that greet tourists who arrive by ship. It was amazing to Lili that the shops had the audacity to be so vibrant with cheerful tapestries, hand carved Mayan warriors and bright, colorful clothing when she felt so glum.

"Pardon my asking, Miss, but what are we gonna do now?" Hans asked.

"I've been trying to figure that out ever since we left the ship."

"I noticed you was distracted."

"First we've got to figure out how to cash my paycheck. It's made out to Dudley M. Cronk and the ship's security people are holding his passport for me until I get back."

"I guess the captain don't want nobody jumping ship," Hans mused as they walked.

"I need to find a friend of mine. Her name is Maria. I used to work with her. She'll know who I can trust around here to tell about the cargo and get me safely out of this country." One of the things Lili had learned in Barbados was not to go running into the police station to ask for help. She felt she had been lucky the first time in Barbados and didn't want to press her luck.

To see Maria would be a godsend. They had been close allies when they once worked as domestic servants together when Lili was very young. She loved her friend and sensed that Maria felt the same. *But how in the world might I find her?*

Hans asked, "Do you remember her last name?"

"I've been thinking about that. I've been thinking about it a lot." Lili felt stifled from the heat. "I keep thinking 'Fernandez,' but I don't know if that's her name or just a name I associate with her—you know, like some people might refer to all Hispanic men as José—no matter what their real names are. Isn't that awful?"

Lili had regained her vitality and Hans had trouble keeping up with her as she strode down the street—long, quick strides with an uncertain destination.

Hans said, "This is no time to worry about being politically correct. It *is* time to be thinking about what you're going to do after I leave this evening. Do you want me to quit right now and stay here with you?"

Lili stopped walking and faced her companion. "Hans, don't be ridiculous. The two of us traveling together would be just that much easier to spot. You'd have an impossible time getting another job if you quit without notice. And if they ever figured out you destroyed that cablegram—"

Hans replied, "I'll have a hard time leaving you here all alone by yerself, Mum."

"You're going back to the ship—tonight by eleven, in fact ten-thirty. It wouldn't hurt you to be there early for a change. If you decide to quit there are lots of better places than Guatemala for you to get off. Plus they still have your passport, your pay and all of your belongings. Unlike you, I have no choice."

"And what shall I do if I get another cablegram?"

"You'll give it to the captain, just like you should've given him the last one. You're a dear friend, Hans, but there's no sense in you putting yourself in danger over me."

"But, Mum— "

"Silence," she said. "Or should I say *¡silencio!*?" She put her finger to his lips.

A few minutes later she asked, "Do you think we can get some advice and directions?"

Hans said, "I don't know, Mum. My Spanish is none too good. How's yours?"

"I took a semester of it in high school," Lili said, "but I didn't learn much. I just ended every other word with "-o." You know. Like, 'Let's-o all go-o to the movie-o' and we all laughed about it and I did well enough on the final to pass. Do you want to know the truth, though?"

Hans shrugged, "Sure."

"I don't think the teacher understood it very well either. She was French and her French class was super but I'm not sure she knew enough Spanish to order a taco. I don't know where to start."

Hans said, "Why-o don't we take yer paycheck-o to one of these lovely bar-oes and see whether or not we can get it cash-oed?"

Lili said, "Oh, no, Hans! What was I thinking when I dumped my disguise back on the pier? I can't go anywhere where I might stand out to anyone who might remember me in case someone comes along later trying to track me. And I have no I.D. that says I'm Dudley M. Cronk. Could you cash it for me? I'll wait for you here—in the cemetery." Lili had been lured inside its gates by the Hindu mausoleums with elephant sculptures. For some reason she always felt at peace in a cemetery. She was surprised to find so many gravestones with surnames like La Pointe, Lelouche and Devereaux. And there were graves surrounded by clusters of geraniums, petunias and pansies, in spite of the wilting sun. Some of the oldest graves were Mayan.

"I'll wait here." It wasn't her nature to delegate such an important task. She had intended to negotiate with the moneychangers on the docks but was disappointed to discover there were none in attendance because of the parades and festivities attendant to the celebration of *Semana Santa,* known elsewhere as Holy Week. She was consoled only by the beautiful painted sawdust and floral murals that adorned the streets and sidewalks. She trusted Hans and figured he'd have a better chance of passing himself off as Dudley M. Cronk than she would and besides, she was exhausted. In spite of premonitions about being followed, she sat down on a bench.

"And you don't think you'll have any problems with strangers if I leave you here alone? What's to make you think you wouldn't be better off with me?"

"Hans, I'm tired. I'm dirty. I didn't dare take a shower for the last four nights we were out to sea. I vomited at least a dozen times. I probably smell. They'll think I'm dead and waiting to be buried."

Hans lent credibility to her hypothesis by not arguing with her and saying, "Okay, I'll go in the *Casa de Los Gatos* and have an ale. I'll try to cash your check-o."

"*Bien,*" Lili said. She waved goodbye to Hans and continued to watch him until he zigzagged to dodge an old pickup truck on his way across the distant street.

For the first time in days Lili didn't feel queasy or ill. As she surrendered to her fatigue she consoled herself by thinking that her assailants might want to put her in the cemetery, but it's not a place where they would likely look for her—*not yet, anyway.* She was so exhausted that she fell asleep in broad daylight. While the wind blew and the breeze caressed her she dreamed she was back in Barbados, rocking Emma on her lap on the front porch, resting up for a romantic evening with Lance—alone at home without the children—an eventuality that never arose, not even once.

* * *

Almost two hours later Hans showed up with beer on his breath and a few coins jingling in his pocket. He had to shake Lili's foot several times to wake her and when he was finally able to do so she was groggy and complained of a headache.

Lili asked, "What time is it? What took you so long? Were you able to cash the check?"

Hans reported that the answer to the last question was "*si*," but he wasn't sure he'd gotten a fair price for it since he didn't have any identification. And, at that, he had to sit and drink and converse in broken English with the bartender until they felt comfortable with one another. "I told him it was for another sailor who was still aboard ship and wanted me to bring him his money. Then he asked me, 'If you're leaving tonight then why does he want his money in quetzales?"

"That was a tough one," Hans continued. He scratched the burn mark on his cheek and sat down next to Lili while she sat up, stretched and yawned. "I said, 'He asked me to buy something for his wife and bring back the change. And the bartender said, 'Then why don't you just give the shop the check?' 'That's easy. They don't take checks,' I said—but by then I don't think he believed me. I could've gone to another bar and started over but I'd already spent two hours building up rapport at that one."

"That's okay," Lili said. "I'm glad you didn't decide to 'build rapport' at another bar and leave me out here roasting in the hot sun for another two hours. How much did you get?"

"I don't know," Hans said. He reached into his pocket and pulled out a wad of green and grimy notes, called *billetes*, and some *centavos* of various sizes. He dropped several of the coins on the sidewalk and had to pick them up.

Lili was angry—not about the length of time he had taken to cash the check—but about the paltry sum she'd ended up with for her days at sea. She tried not to show it and risk losing his further help. *Besides, what difference does it make now? There's nothing I can do about it.*

Lili said, "So what time is it now?"

"Around three," Hans replied.

Lili said, "That leaves us what—eight hours, no seven-and-a-half—to find my friend Maria so you can be on your way?"

For the next two-and-one-half hours they wandered around Puerto Barrios while Lili alternated between looking at every woman she saw for a familiar face and looking over her shoulder to make sure they weren't being followed.

"Am I being paranoid?" she asked.

"Perhaps," he said. "But just because you're paranoid doesn't mean you're not being followed."

Lili enjoyed Hans. She found him bright, resourceful and witty. As she surveyed the women, she thought, *It's been ten or fifteen years at least, since that day Maria left in the cab with Alfonso in front of the Martin's house. It's hard to believe it's been that long. I hope she remembers me and what good friends we were.*

Lili lamented that she hadn't written to Maria, even though she had planned to. She'd received any number of letters from her, talking about how happy Maria had been to return to her daughter, Roseangela. Lili had been happy to get the letters but was so busy she didn't have time to write back. Lili thought, *If only I'd written, maybe I could've remembered her last name and the city—what was the city?*

They looked in the local phone book under Fernandez. There was page after page of Fernandezes listed. Of course, there was nothing under "Maria Fernandez" or "M Fernandez" either—almost no women's names listed at all. And besides she may have remarried.

They were drawn to a street vendor who sold them churros and marzipan. He had roasted meat dripping from a spit. Lili watched it rotate and wanted desperately to have some but she thought it might make her sick and she hated to think about it being about the size and shape of a dog. The oils and grease from the animal sizzled and sparked whenever they dripped through the grill into the charcoal below. Under normal circumstances Lili couldn't imagine liking it. But for some reason she had a craving for it.

Finally she succumbed and gorged herself with the meat. It tasted sweet and chewy and slid down as easily as the desserts.

Then, it dawned on her—not Maria's city, but a clue. "Maria used to talk about how—no matter how poor she was—she would always give alms for the poor. She described how the poor would gather on the steps of a big Catholic Church—a cathedral perhaps—and beg. And there was something special about it—something I can hear her saying. She loved the Blessed Virgin. That's it! She lived near a great cathedral with a statue of the Blessed Virgin."

Hans said, "Now you're onto something, Mum. I'll go over to that bar across the street and ask around. I'll bet they can tell me the town."

"Oh no you don't," Lili said. "There's a church right down the block." She flipped her fingers in a "move along" gesture. "We can ask the gardener."

The gardener summoned the priest who spoke almost no English.

"Church, *si*," he said. "There are many churches in Guatemala, including *Catedrales*.   And they all have statutes of the Blessed Virgin."

Then it came to Lili.   *"¡Virgen del Socorro!"* That's what Maria used to say. "I pray to the *Virgen del Socorro* to intercede whenever I'm in despair. There's a beautiful statue of her near my home by the great cathedral."

"Catedral," the priest said at once. It ees *Catedral Metropolitana. Metropolitana Catedral."*

Hans said, *"Si, padre.* Where is the Metropolitan Cathedral?"

The priest looked around him—down toward the port in the distance, over his shoulder at the verdant mountains, up at the blistering sun and then he pointed. "It ees that way," he said at last. "Guatemala City. *Catedral ees in Guatemala City."* He pointed towards the rising hills.

Lili said, "Is it near here? Can we walk?"

"No," Hans said. "It's in another city." He gestured by spreading his hands various distances apart and holding his palms face up as he asked. "How far is Guatemala City, Padre?"

The priest stroked his chin, looked toward the port again, the lush, green mountains in the distance, up at the bright mid-afternoon sky and said, "About two-hundred-and-fifty kilometers."

Lili looked at Hans. "Around one-hundred-fifty miles," Hans said. "You'll have to take a bus."

"Or a taxi," the priest said as though he had just gotten the gift of tongues. "You can take a taxi. Most of the men here are out of work so you can hire a taxicab at a very reasonable price." After that he did not again speak two consecutive words of proper English.

Lili thought about all the transfers she had had to make just to get from Bridgetown to Lance's house and how that took nearly two hours on a small island. She also thought, *More people would see me on a bus.* "I think I'll take a cab." But the consideration that really persuaded her was that she wanted to be able to relax for one night before it was time to continue the hunt for Maria—by herself—the following morning. "*Si*, a taxi."

Within minutes Lili found herself saying a fond good-bye to Hans. She thanked him for all he had done, gave him a hug, warned him to quit the Tropic Carib as soon as he could and got into a cab. The taxi driver assured her that the amount of money she had in her pocket was "just right amount for trip to Guatemala City. . . . I take you tonight."

Lili hesitated for a moment and thought again about taking the bus. Then she decided, I have my credit cards. She waved for the taxi driver to drive on. Lili had not wanted to use those credit cards for lots of reasons. For one thing she saw credit card debt as the shackles of big business. Secondly she figured they'd sell her whereabouts for twenty-five cents. She would avoid using the cards as long as she could, but knew she had them available if she got desperate. She had made arrangements to have minimum payments deducted from her checking account automatically, if she weren't in a position to make them herself, so she knew they would be honored.

Soon she was sweeping across the countryside in a taxicab with a stranger who drove like a maniac, while listening to blaring music on the radio in a tongue she did not understand. Meanwhile she feared that Hans was probably back in a tavern, and for the price of an ale, loosening his tongue to whomever might be within earshot.

* * *

Seconds turned into minutes which turned into hours as the cabbie sped across a countryside Lili could only imagine. It was so hot—even at night, that he had all four windows rolled down to allow a warm breeze. If he had an air conditioner he didn't use it. From time to time she would see lights in the distance and presume they were homes. She wondered about the inhabitants and what sort of lives they might be living and how they might compare with hers. The road itself seemed relatively flat.

As they drove on it came to her that Maria lived in the capital city of Guatemala and she had had a cousin who was a high ranking public official or had worked for a high ranking public official or knew someone who had once worked for one. She wasn't sure which. It occurred to her that if she could find Maria, maybe she could inform the right person about the gold bullion and perhaps even get a reward that might in turn help her to solve some of her other problems.

From time to time she dozed off. She didn't have to worry about the cab driver taking her money for all she had was the agreed-upon fare. She had heard about banditry but what could they gain by robbing her? Everything she had of any value now belonged to the cab driver except for her passport, her credit cards, the now tattered list of questionable account numbers and the brooch Lance had given her. She had kept these items on her person at all times, whether in the cave or on the ship.

Every once in awhile they would hit a pothole and the cab would shimmy and the cabbie would shout, *"¡Ay Carajo!"*

Lili would wake up, turn on her side and do her best to catch whatever sleep she could. After about the twelfth time of having her sleep interrupted by that annoying word, *"¡Carajo!"* Lili asked the taxi driver what it meant.

"Hmm!" He said. "Come to think of it, I have no idea. I'm not sure anyone does. I'll try to be more quiet."

It was about three-thirty or quarter-to-four in the morning when the taxi driver said, "Here eet is— Guatemala City. Where to now, *Señorita*?"

Lili looked around and the lights had become an unending sea on all sides—blurring into stores and buildings on the boulevard they were on. Lili was struck by the narrowness of the streets and bustling activity, even at this wee hour. She would later discover that the reason for this had to do with the much-anticipated mid-day heat.

"The *Catedral*," Lili said. "Take me to the *Catedral Metropolitana*."

"*Señorita*, the *Catedral* ees closed. They won't have the first Mass until six-thirty. That's almost three hours. The beggars won't even be there yet."

Lili couldn't face the idea of being put out on the street in the middle of the night in a strange place with people who didn't speak her language, with no luggage, no money and no one to share the risk. "Let's drive near the Cathedral and see if I can spot a place to stay."

Lili picked the most broken down hovel she saw, the Hotel Bristol, thinking it would be the cheapest. And it was cheap but she hadn't counted on double occupancy with cockroaches. Broken down she could take but vermin, bugs and rodents turned her stomach. She was so tired she was in no condition to bargain or weigh her options. She could barely keep her eyes open.

Yet she probably didn't sleep but two or three hours more and at first light woke up and sprang to her feet, checking her body carefully for signs of nocturnal infestation. She was able to take a shower, which felt great, even in this dingy hovel. Her head ached, but for the first time in weeks, the ground didn't seem to be moving up-and-down in a perfect, tortuous rhythm.

She thought about purchasing a change of clothes but risking additional credit card transactions was not something she wanted to do. When she had checked into the hotel the man took the card into another room to ring it up and she hoped he had not sought an authorization. *This place can't be all that expensive. Maybe he won't call it in.*

The day was so bright her eyes ached. She was surprised that the activity she had seen in the middle of the night had tapered off and the heat was unseasonably high for the altitude—stifling.

She thought about going to the police department but remembered Lance's admonition when she had first arrived in Barbados. "What if I'm on the take?" he had said. She didn't have much faith in third world police departments to begin with and figured if the opportunity arose they might sell her out. *And what about the cab driver?* She had an uneasy feeling about him, too.

Where can I turn? I speak almost no Spanish. I don't even know Maria's last name.

Then it dawned on her. *I'll ask the priest.* She went to the Cathedral with the blue domed bell towers and sure enough there were people she presumed to be homeless or blind or both—begging for alms on the steps. *There but for the grace of God go I.*

She circumnavigated the marble fence, which surrounded the church, went up the walk toward the huge wooden doors of the Archbishop's Palace and rang the bell.

The archbishop and his staff, through their aides, summarily refused to see Lili but there was an underling priest who agreed, after half an hour of broken English and hapless Spanish interchanges, to see her for a *"few momentos."* At last, she was escorted into his air-conditioned chambers by a short, squatty housekeeper, who wore a white servant's outfit, much like the one she had remembered Maria wearing when they both worked at the Martins.

The priest seemed distracted. He sat at a desk and toyed with a pencil. He lifted it from the task to which it was employed in a feigned attempt to appear to be listening.   "Padre, I am eager to find my friend—Maria. I think her name is, or at least was, Fernandez and she had a daughter —at least one daughter, probably a lot more than that— called Roseangela."

"*Rosa Angela,*" the priest said.

"What?" Lili asked.

"Your pronunciation of the child's name is its English version. Here we would call her '*Rosa Angela.*'"

"Yes, that's the daughter's name. I'm looking for her mother, Maria."

"María, yes," said the priest. "It has the same pronunciation as in English, but your accent is wrong. Put the emphasis on the second syllable, Ma-*rí*-a."

Lili continued, "*Si*, thank you, Padre. Ma-*rí*-a was very religious. She attended Mass regularly and always gave alms to the poor." As she said this Lili realized how preposterous it must sound that she expected to find her by giving this broad description.

"My child," the priest said, even though Lili surmised they must both have been about the same age, "you have described hundreds, perhaps thousands of women here in Guatemala City and hundreds more across the countryside. How long has it been since you've seen this Ma- *rí*-a?"

Lili thought about it. "At least fifteen years—maybe twenty, I guess."

One of the servants came and offered them coffee. They both accepted and the priest put so much cream in his cup that the black java marbled into a light tan. Looking at it swirl as he stirred made Lili feel nauseated. "Then I guess it would be difficult for you to give us a current description of her. It would be helpful, at least, if you got her last name. Could you call someone else who knew her, back in Hawaii perhaps, and get her name from them?"

Lili thought of the Martins. She felt queasy. *Would they even speak to me? And if I did call them, wouldn't that leave a trail?* "That sounds like a good idea, Padre. But I'm not sure who I could call."

"And why are you so anxious to find this friend of yours?"

"It's just for old times." By now Lili was preoccupied with getting back outside. She was afraid she was about to vomit. Her speech quickened. "She was a dear person and I want to see how she is doing. I want to hear about her children and grandchildren and . . . Do you think you might know her?"

"I might without knowing it," he said. "Unfortunately since we closed the school I don't get to know the parishioners' names like I used to." The priest sipped his coffee like he had no responsibility in life other than to finish it.

Lili got up and moved toward the big wooden doors. "Could you point out some women named María? I'll start by questioning them."

The priest picked up his cup and saucer and followed. "I could. I could point to the congregation and as many as half of them might be named Ma- *rí*-a. Besides, my child, I have to warn you . . . . Are you feeling okay?"

Lili had her hand to her mouth. She bolted to the door, ducked her head out and barely made it to the sidewalk before she threw up.

The priest came to the door and waited for her to finish without offering assistance. He gestured to the gardener to come over and clean up the mess. "I must warn you. We've had a lot of social unrest here in Guatemala and people don't respond well to those who ask a lot of questions." He smiled politely then closed the door behind her.

So it went for Lili for the next several days. Gradually her vomiting subsided. She told herself it was the "dog" meat and she felt better. But the contacts with the residents weren't much more productive than the one had been with the priest. At first she told herself it would be just like campaigning as she followed people from church and tried to strike up conversations. But she was usually greeted with a cool response. And when she wasn't, there was the language problem. Then there was the problem of too many sixty-something year old women being named *María* with thirty-something year old daughters named *Rosa Angela*. There were many "sure sightings" in way off and strangely named places like Chimaltenango, Zaragoza and Quetzalestenango. But Lili thought most of these leads were unwise to pursue, given the dereliction of their purveyors.

Discouraged and after less than a week Lili gave up and decided to go to the airport, use her credit card and return to Hawaii. There she would find her lifelong friend, Izzy. She knew this choice would make her vulnerable to her adversaries and yet she didn't know what else to do. She briefly considered another alternative, calling a very powerful man in Hawaii, who had once promised her a favor in return for one she had unwittingly done for him. Then she decided that he had probably long since forgotten her and his promise by now. She comforted herself with the conclusion that *Izzy will know.*

She was grateful that through everything, she still had her U.S. passport. In thumbing through it, she noticed it was about to expire. I guess I'll have to go home and face the music, she reluctantly concluded.

She cleared her bill at the hotel by signing the credit card voucher and summoned a cab to the airport. She had no money to pay the cab driver but figured she'd think of something once she got there. If not, she would offer to send him a check or pen him an I.O.U. She was able to check the flights because there was an English-speaking assistant at American Airlines who booked her a seat to Los Angeles. Once she got to L.A. Lili figured it would be an easy matter to catch a flight to Hawaii. She didn't want to make getting out of Guatemala any more complicated than it had to be.

Once the cab driver noticed that her Spanish was limited to simple phrases that began with "*Buenos*," the conversation turned to English.

"How did you like our beautiful country?" he asked.

"I don't know. I didn't get to see much of it."

"Why not?" he asked.

"I was busy trying to find an old friend of mine but I couldn't and I've run out of money so I have no choice but to go home."

The driver weaved his cab through the busy intersections, dodging pedestrians, cars and bicycles. Then he went around a traffic circle and got onto an *aveinda* that traveled much more smoothly. Lili assumed it was the Guatemalan equivalent of a thoroughfare.

"Who is this old friend? Maybe I know him."

"I doubt it," Lili said. *"Her* name was María and she had a daughter named *Rosa Angela.* She must be about sixty now and her daughter around thirty-something. Either everyone thinks they know her or no one does. She and I used to work as housekeepers together in Hawaii."

The cab driver pulled over to the side of the road amidst the honking and jeering of passing motorists. He looked at her in his review mirror.

"Cómo te llamas? / What is your name?"

Lili thought about lying, but by now she was on the brink of despair. *What's the difference. As soon as I buy that plane ticket, everyone will know who and where I am.* "Lili Kaleo," she said. "Kalili'i Kaleo."

The driver stared at her in the mirror for a few seconds and then turned and looked at her over the seat. "Don't you recognize me?" he asked. He took off his sunglasses. He looked sixty-something himself and was thin with wrinkled skin and a colorful Mayan print shirt, buttoned at the top, even on this scorching day.

Lili looked at him and he did look somewhat familiar but she had met so many people over the course of her years as mayor of Kaua'i that she didn't want to hazard a guess—at the risk of offending him. He did look a little bit like a member of the trade delegation from Buenos Aires.

"Lili, I'm Alfonso—Alfonso the cab driver from Kaua'i. Don't you remember me?"

Lili practically leapt over the seat. She hugged and kissed him. "Alfonso, Alfonso, the cab driver. Yes. I remember you! You're Alfonso—Alfonso, the bowler!"

* * *

When Lili saw María's house, she marveled. It was within two blocks of the Cathedral. She had been only a few minutes away all along. *And to think I might have left and never found her.*

From the outside María's *casa* blended with everything on the street and Lili was not sure she would even have distinguished it as a house. "Dilapidated" was a word that came to mind—no paint, an earth tone—perhaps not so much by choice as by the will of the hot, arid weather and vagaries of time.

But when Alfonso got out and opened the big wooden gates of the tall adobe fence that blocked any view of the interior the street instantly gave way to a large, beautiful courtyard and a fountain. There were citrus trees laden with oranges and lemons—and green grass galore. Lili had not noticed any birds before but they were fluttering here and there—and bees. She was not surprised to see the bees because there were bunches of beautiful carnations and orchids in patches along the driveway. Lili was dumbfounded.

"Just a second," Alfonso said as he closed the gates. "I'll go see if she's in. On Wednesdays she usually watches the grandkids. . . . And the great-grandkids," he added, just before the door slammed behind him.

Great Grandkids. Imagine that. Well she certainly deserves them!

A few seconds later a beautiful woman appeared on the porch—not a woman whose beauty relied upon youth for resilience. It was a beauty accentuated by the marks of devotion to duty and hard work set in her wrinkles, just as the façade of a great monument is often marred by the traces of wind and rain. Still adjusting to the light the woman crept down the two or three stairs to the courtyard, while Lili rushed towards her with open arms.

"María! María! It's Lili, your friend—your other daughter, Lili Kaleo."

María's quizzical look gradually gave way to a smile. The two of them embraced while Alfonso closed and locked the gates and moved the cab into the carport. They kissed one another on the cheeks and wept as they felt the warmth of one another's grasp and the fullness of one another's spirit—like the return of a ghost ship to the safer, more innocent harbors of youth.

Chapter Fourteen

After swizzle stick pastries, a huge cup of hot chocolate with cinnamon, and introductions to a throng of children, whose names Lili couldn't anymore keep track of than the letters in her soup, Lili, Alfonso and María began to talk. But before the two women had a chance to get caught up on one another's lives, Lili said, "I believe there are men who are after me—men who may want to kill me. Are you sure you want me to stay here?"

María asked, "Why do they want to kill you, Sugar? I can't imagine anyone wanting to kill you."

"I'm not sure," she said. "I think they're afraid I know something about the inner workings of a worldwide drug smuggling and money laundering ring."

Alfonso asked, "Do you?"

Sugar answered, "Not really. I mean, a friend of mine was killed—presumably for what he learned from a ledger that we saw. But as for me, I can't remember seeing anything of particular interest in it, except for an entry that probably had to do with my trial. It was just a jumble of numbers dancing in my head. I made a list of the important ones. I have it here."

She pulled out the crumpled piece of paper. "You're the first ones I've shown this to besides Ephraim Whitney, the man who was killed."

Alfonso said, "It looks just like a bunch of random nine digit numbers to me."

María got up and came back with a pad and pencil and handed them to Lili. "Here, you'd better recopy your list. It's barely legible."

Lili thanked her and began rewriting the numbers. "I did learn where and how they ship huge quantities of gold bullion but I doubt they realize that. And I didn't learn it until after someone had already tried to kill me." She went on to explain about the cargo, its manifest and its intended destination.

Lili continued, "There was a bill of lading on the gold which I believe said it was going to the . . . just a second I wrote it down as soon as I got a chance to . . . Here it is, *Secretaría de Relaciones Exter--.* I didn't get the rest of it."

"It's the *Secretaría de Relaciones Exteriores,"* Alfonso said. "The Ministry of Foreign Affairs."

"The Guatemalan ministry?" María asked.

"Why, yes. I mean I think so. Well, I really couldn't say. When I was looking at it the guards came back and I had to hide."

María said, "Do you know who it was addressed to? I mean at the ministry."

Lili shook her head no.

"It's too bad," María said. "My uncle used to work there."

Alfonso leaned back and clasped his hands together under his chin. "What makes you think they could find you here?" María looked on intently.

Lili responded, "I've made mistakes. I took a taxi here from Puerto Barrios and the driver, well . . . he could identify me. There was something I didn't like about him—a look in his eyes maybe. Then I stayed at the Hotel Bristol and used a credit card. As you know, I made plane reservations to L.A. and then cancelled them. And I talked to the priest at the *Catedral Metropolitana.* He wasn't exactly cordial or helpful. Those are just the mistakes I can think of. There must have been others. Oh yeah, I had a shipmate cash my paycheck, made out to Dudley M. Cronk, at a bar in Puerto Barrios. Now how stupid was that?"

Alfonso replied, "It sounds like you did everything but send up a flare. But since all you had available to tell anyone was María's first name—you weren't sure of the last—and the name of one of her daughters, the trail may very well have dried up once we closed the gates of the courtyard behind us."

"I hope so," Lili said. "I couldn't have done a sloppier job of protecting my identity. You wouldn't think I dated a policeman for several months." Lili was distraught and dabbed her eyes with a tissue.

María asked, "What could happen to her here, Alfonso? What if she stays inside and never goes outside the gates?"

"I think that would be okay," Alfonso said. "As long as you don't make any long distance calls or talk to strangers who might happen by—or the handyman. It seems to me your trail would lead only to Guatemala City and Guatemala City is a big place."

"I don't want to put you in danger," Lili said. "I already put Lance and his children at risk and I feel awful about it."

María looked at Alfonso. He nodded. "I think it would be okay for you to stay with us. What are friends for anyway?"

She and Lili shared another long, comforting hug. Then the gabfest began—a marathon gabfest that lasted not only several days, but several weeks.

During one such session Lili asked, "How is your mother? Did she recover that time when you said she might die?"

"Yes, she's just fine. She's eighty-five now. We lit candles and we poured holy water over her forehead and she made a full and complete recovery. She embroiders linens they sell at the church and the money goes to help the poor. She's starting to lose her eyesight though, and while she says the poking of her fingers with the needles doesn't hurt, she's going to have to take up knitting instead."

They laughed.

María asked, "And, what about your child, Christian? Fanny Martin sent me the clippings of your trial but I was most worried about the child they mentioned. Is he okay?"

A hanging head and a drooped expression told the whole story. The two of them embraced. They didn't speak. And the trauma of the loss of the child was—for a few precious moments—lessened by the comforting hug of a true and dear friend.

Lili asked, "What about Alfonso? How did he get here? Certainly he didn't drive his cab all the way here from Hawaii."

María laughed. "You know how Alfonso likes to bowl. Well, when he first came here he had aspirations of opening a bowling alley and capturing the 'huge' market of everyone who had not yet discovered this wonderful game. But that didn't work out. Fortunately for both of us he was never able to raise the necessary funds and went back to driving his cab."

"Are you? Are the two of you— "

"Married?" María replied.

Lili nodded to confirm the question.

"No, Our Holy Mother, The Church, would not recognize such a marriage. I have another husband somewhere—Eduardo, the father of four of my children, if he's still alive—God help the worthless bastard." She made the sign of the cross. "So we're living in sin."

Lili touched María's hand to console her.

"No remorse necessary," she said. "This way I tell him he must treat me properly or I throw him out on his butt."

Lili laughed. She looked around the house. "Is this . . . Is this beautiful home all yours?" Just the massive mahogany bureaus and dressers alone seemed well beyond whatever means Lili would have ever expected to be María's.

"Yes," María said. "Am I lucky or what? My uncle, the one I mentioned earlier, died and left it to me not long after I returned here from Hawaii. He was a diplomat. And this house is among the spoils. That's the way government works in this country."

So that was the connection.

"He said it was always intended to belong to my father after him and my father had long since passed away by then and my uncle had no children so he left this wonderful place to me. We make good use of it don't we, Alfonso?" She winked at Alfonso as he passed, carrying in groceries he had bought when he was near the market.

He winked back. "Yes we do," he said. "We surely do."

Lili blushed. "Still bowling those extra frames?"

"You bet your ten pins!" María exclaimed.

Lili asked, "And what about the taxes? Do you have property taxes? How do you afford to pay those?"

"Taxes?" María said. "There hasn't been a tax man in here since, what—1926? Lili, here in Guatemala it's much easier to bribe the taxman than it is to pay him. It's all okay. The people expect it."

Lili felt hurt and angry. Here she was facing the repercussions of a bribe she had not agreed to and now she was in a country where it was no big deal—in fact the everyday custom. "I've got to get back to Hawaii and defend myself," she said. Then she quickly reconsidered. "But then again if I do I may just be facing extradition to Barbados."

A lengthy conversation continued with the ultimate resolve being the happy conclusion that Lili must stay put for now and sort things out before doing anything hasty. "You'll be safe here," María assured her. "I will pray to Frances Xavier Cabrini, the patron saint of immigrants." Figuring out a way to contact Izzy without placing a call from María's house seemed like the best course of action.

* * *

Within the next few days Alfonso bought her a pregnancy test which she took by capturing her first water of the morning. She didn't have the composure to look at it without María present. So she put the test tube on the bathroom counter while she got her friend.

"You look at it, María. I want to know, but I don't. *You* look at it."

Just like the surrogate mother María had been during Lili's teenage years she took the opportunity to lecture Lili on the availability of birth control and the irresponsibility of not using it—notwithstanding the Pope's views to the contrary. Lili gave the requisite "yeah, yeah, yeah's," that one might expect from an errant daughter. María said, "All right, I'll go check."

When she returned a few seconds later Lili was both happy and distraught by the news.

* * *

Sugar helped María tend to her grandchildren whenever they were over while she tried to develop a plan. She loved them immediately. It was fun to be an instant aunty.

At times her thoughts wandered back to Barbados where she fantasized about what it would be like to make a home with Lance and care for him and his children—that is if she could ever get her legal problems behind her. She liked the idea of starting and raising a family but the vision was not without blemishes.

"What do you think of the prospect of marrying an African Bajan man?" Lili asked María one day, in the front of her house while they cut red and white carnations for the dinner table.

First Lili explained about the gold she had found in Lance's drawer, which they both concluded was only circumstantial evidence and should not be considered without giving him a chance to explain.

Then María moved closer to Lili so the children playing in the distance wouldn't overhear them. "I had a black lover once," she whispered. "He was the ace of spades."

Lili stood up and laughed. "You're ornery, María. What are you talking about—the ace of spades?"

The remark had sounded right on the edge between derogatory and flattering.

María continued. "He was a banana worker and I'll tell you what! He knew what to do with his banana."

Lili giggled. This was so much like a talk they might have had fifteen or twenty years before while doing dishes at the Martins. A part of her said, "Stop this right now." Another part said, "Go on.".

María continued, "It was no *¡chiquita!* I can tell you that."

Lili burst out laughing. They both laughed and held their stomachs and their sides. Lili could picture María with her dark skinned lover. With anyone else—she probably would have walked away or tried to change the subject but she had a weakness for such talk with María— the experienced mentor. It was like being the younger sister invited to play with the big kids.

María continued, "Right after Eduardo left I needed a man, if you know what I mean." She winked at Lili. "Well I was alone with six kids and at first I just let him come over in the evenings after the kids were in bed." María went back to cutting flowers.

Lili said, "And . . ."

"And, he kept coming over for about a month. And . . ."

"And," Lili repeated.

"And," María looked somber. She held a bouquet of red carnations upside down in one hand and handed them to Lili to put on the cart. She looked into Lili's eyes and her expression changed to a smile. "And I was so tired after entertaining that man for the better part of a month that I finally had to move out and not tell him where I'd gone."

"And, . . ." Lili said, "I have a feeling there's more to it than that. I know you pretty well, María."

María's went on, "*And*, I barely got an ounce of sleep that entire month, if you know what I mean. I had six children to raise and his prospects weren't likely to make mine any the rosier. But we did have a wonderful time together while it lasted.

"After I got to know him better I let him come earlier and play with the children. He was great with the kids and they loved him." María's eyes became teary. "He used to whittle and he played a harp he had carved and strung all by himself. Can you believe that? He played like a virtuoso and sang to them, kept them up late, way into the early morning hours. And they hung onto that man like berries on a vine. Ah . . . , he was handsome—so very handsome."

Lili asked, "If you liked him so much, did you ever think of marrying him? Did you ever think of trying to make a life with him?"

María put a bunch of flowers on the little pushcart she used to tend the garden. "Oh, no," she said with sadness. "It wouldn't have done for us. It wouldn't have worked out." She squinted away the tears.

"Why not?" Lili asked.

"Well, for one thing, my mother would have disowned me. And just then I needed her help in the worst way."

"Did you ever regret it? Did you ever wish you had gotten married?"

María didn't answer. She turned away.

Lili could tell she had struck a nerve. "Do you think I should have gotten involved with that black police inspector. . . . I mean, romantically and all?"

María said, "You mean let him steal your heart? Get tight under your skin? Sweep you off your feet?"

Lili said, "Yes. All of those things."

"Sugar, you of all people should realize that every now and then you've got to have a little spice in your life!"

* * *

Over time Lili played in the courtyard with the children, while María tended to her household chores and

Alfonso drove his cab. In the evenings they met to consider Lili's options but none of them were appealing. The idea of calling Izzy was discarded since they figured his line may be tapped. She was convinced that if she fled she would be captured or attacked. If she stayed she feared she put her friends at risk.

One thing Lili wanted to do, especially if she were stuck in Guatemala City for a while, was to find out more about the gold shipments. "María, do you really still know anyone at the Ministry of Foreign Affairs?"

María said, "Who were you thinking of? Some of my uncle's friends may still be there."

Lili said. "Anyone you think we could trust who might be able to help us trace the gold or turn in the people responsible for shipping it. I agree with Alfonso's interpretation that the gold was scheduled to go to there. Do you think that's possible?"

Alfonso said, "Anything's possible in this country."

María said, "I could go and ask one of my uncle's friends to look into it, but I'm not sure whether or not any of them are still there. I think they would remember me. I used to go have lunch with him and he introduced me to many of them."

Lili said, "Wouldn't it be better to call?"

Alfonso said, "I don't think there's such a thing as a private call to a diplomat. How much gold do you think there was?"

"At least the two pallets that I know of—maybe four meters high by about six meters on a side filled with bars, cross-stacked in rows," Lili answered.

Alfonso looked as if he were off in a daze. The evening was still. The day had been hot and arid. "Billions. Billions of quetzales," he mused.

María shook her head in amazement. "I'll bet the wrong people would like to get their hands on that."

"Maybe they already have," Lili said.

Alfonso said, "This may sound crazy but I think the two of you should go to the ministry together. Lili, you can hide in the back of my cab. No one will see you. If you find the right person perhaps they will agree to hide and protect you, or perhaps help you escape from Guatemala altogether."

"Yes," Lili said. "It would be good for me to get away from here."

María said, "I think I'll be able to find someone. I just need to get a good look at the building directory."

Alfonso said, "Yes and you may only get one chance at it. Once you've been there too many people will know and it wouldn't be safe to go back."

Lili said, "If you'll just give me the names of your Uncle's friends I'd be happy to go alone. I could wear a disguise."

María replied, "You're not going alone. That much is for sure."

After a lengthy debate it was decided that Lili and María would descend upon the Ministry of Foreign Affairs late the following afternoon, where María would scan the directory for familiar names. If there was at least one she was comfortable with and he was in they would approach him. If not they would leave and formulate a new plan.

Lili asked, "Do you think there's any chance your government might give us a reward?"

Alfonso broke out in laughter. "Now that's a knee slapper."

María continued, "I know a few men we can trust if they're still there. We can sound them out by dancing around the edges at first. Then if it doesn't feel just right to us we'll tell him we just wanted to see whether or not my uncle had any back pay or retirement benefits that he never collected. We'll leave and regroup."

"Agreed," Lili said.

"*De acuerdo,*" Alfonso and María repeated in unison. They agreed, as well.

* * *

The next day Alfonso drove them past the *Torre del Reformador.* The tall steel structure looked a lot like the Eiffel Tower except that it had a bell in the top which Alfonso said was rung once a year on June thirtieth to celebrate the Liberal victory of President Barrios in the 1871 Revolution. They proceeded down the *Avenida La Reforma,* lined with lavender flowering *jacaranda* trees, until they passed the *Politecnica* which looked like a classic military fort out of a child's toy box.

Finally they came to the Ministry of Foreign Affairs. Alfonso let them out at the curb and said he would circle the block at fifteen-minute intervals starting in thirty minutes to see if they were ready to go. Traffic was heavy and he warned that if he was late not to give up on him.

Lili and María got out and walked across the wide sidewalk towards the building. It was modern looking with a heavy use of tinted green glass and steel. It was windy and dust blew as a blustery precursor to a nasty storm. They walked with their heads down to keep the dust out of their eyes. Lili kept a scarf drawn tightly over her hair and held it wrapped partially around her face to hide it. She bumped into a man in a similar posture who was heading in the opposite direction on the way out. She momentarily let go of the scarf and it blew across the sidewalk. The man ran and retrieved it for her. They looked at each other briefly and continued on their way.

A few seconds later, as the man was approaching the curb, he turned and yelled, "Lili Kaleo! Is that you?"

When she turned around, he added, "I thought I recognized you."

As she walked towards him, it took her a moment to figure out who he was. "Mr. Musgrave, what are you doing in Guatemala?" It started to rain so they all stepped inside the lobby. There was a mural of Justo Rufino Barrios on the wall.

"I'm on a diplomatic mission," he replied. He looked at María.

Lili was at a loss as to what to say. "This is a friend of mine," she said at last. "María, this is the husband of a colleague of mine who used to work at the Bank of Barbados. How is Mrs. M.?"

"Mrs. M.? You mean Bonnie?"

Lili nodded.

"Oh, she's fine."

He looked back at María as though he were studying her face.

This made Lili uncomfortable, "María's uncle was a diplomat," she finally said to break the silence.

"Really," Mr. Musgrave said. "What's his name? Perhaps I know him."

"He died a few years ago," María said. "His name was José Alejandro del Río de la Vega."

"Ah yes, Joe Vega?"

María nodded.

Mr. Musgrave continued, "I knew him. I met him when I just started working in the British Embassy as a young attaché many years ago. I'm so sorry to hear he died. He used to have Bonnie and me over for dinner at his house, poor chap. Lovely place. Over by the *Catedral Metropolitana*. Whatever happened to the house?"

Lili and María looked at one another. María failed to read Lili's cue not to answer. "It's still in the family," María said.

Lili spoke up before she could continue. "We've got to be going. I just remembered that I forgot to put money into the parking meter."

"I'll walk out with you," Mr. Musgrave said. "Where is your car parked?"

Lili took a step or two forward and then rubbed her eye. "Darn! I must've gotten some dust in my eye from the wind. I'd better run into the restroom before we go. C'mon, María, you can help me. I'm glad we ran into each other, Mr. Musgrave . . . . Good luck to you and Mrs. M. — I mean Bonnie."

From a distance Mr. Musgrave yelled, "Bradley. Call me Bradley. It was great fortune . . . , I mean very enjoyable running into you as well."

When they were confident Mr. Musgrave had left, María checked the building directory and read it over several times. "I was afraid of that," she said. "It's been too long. I don't recognize a soul."

When Alfonso picked them up on one of his drive bys they told him what had happened. He said, "Don't worry. It was just a chance meeting. He's probably already forgotten about it."

* * *

Lili noticed that in every group she always had a favorite child—often one with a handicap or disadvantage. Maybe this was because she had always felt she had been disadvantaged or put into this world to love and assist the disadvantaged—Mimo, Christian, the church day care centers she tended and the ones she established as mayor, little Emma in Barbados. In this group that child was Antonio. He had a learning disability but was a gifted athlete and teaching him to play cricket—right here in Guatemala, right here in the courtyard—was an activity greeted with jubilation by both. He was María's grandchild, the son of her third daughter. He had dark curly hair but fair skin and freckles on his nose. María joked, "Freckles just like their mailman's," and scratched her chin with a smile.

In a way Lili wished she had turned out to be pregnant and that the child would look exactly like Lance.

But in most other ways she was relieved not to be with child. If she had been pregnant her course of action would have been clearer—to be a responsible mother and raise the child. Now she felt as though she had been thrown back out to sea. This time without a compass.

She rolled a tennis ball past the little boy toward the wicket and laughed while he ran to pick it up. It reminded her of watching Christian chase his beach ball across the sand at Salt Pond Park. She snipped off a baby carnation with her fingernails, nails which had begun to grow back after the rigors of keeping her balance and investigating the cargo onboard ship. The flower emanated the rich, sweet fragrance of cloves.

Then she heard the roar of cars outside the gate followed by short bursts of loud cracking noises— *gunshots!* A spray of bullets hit the fence. She screamed at Antonio to take cover. He was hit. His blood splattered on the wall as he collapsed to the ground. She dove behind the fountain and began crawling towards him. She could hear the boy moan. Bullets whistled through the plants and pinged on nearby rocks.

María came outside, dropped a huge pot she had been carrying and ducked back inside, screaming. Ping . . . ping . . . ping. Bullets every which way.

Grapefruits splattered and dripped their over-ripe contents to the ground. The gunfire continued for several minutes until the sound of sirens began in the distance, first faintly and then more and more loudly. The gate and adobe walls crumbled and broke away, disclosing the street and armed gunmen leaning against their cars to support their weapons. Lili got to the boy and put her finger on his gushing blood. She had to keep her head so close to the ground it was difficult to see what was going on. She held him tightly with one arm—as she had Christian when he was dying—and prayed for their safety. Then as the sirens grew nearer the bullets stopped and were replaced by the squeal of tires. María shrieked as she ran back out onto the porch, stepped over the broken pot and ran towards Antonio. The two women tried to comfort the little boy but he was unconscious.

Soon there were so many vehicles in the courtyard Lili couldn't begin to count them. The red flashing lights of an ambulance whirred in her eyes as the child was fitted with an oxygen mask and loaded for a trip to the hospital. There were *policia.* Many *policia.* They asked lots of questions and looked at Lili's passport, including her visa to Barbados, then took down her name. They didn't seem to notice there was no visa for Guatemala—or if they did, they didn't mention it.

Lili knew she had already stayed too long. She believed the assault must have been related to her chance meeting with Mr. Musgrave. *I must leave immediately.*

Then she decided she had nothing to lose. *Why not try the most powerful man in Hawaii?* Maybe he'd remember her. Maybe he wouldn't. The worst he could do is say "no." Perhaps he would remember and keep his promise. He had told her, "If you're ever in trouble give me a call. Keep me in mind if there's ever anything I can do . . . ." Yes she should contact (pronounced Gay-org) George Santini. And right now, right at this very moment, she felt as though she might be in trouble.

* * *

It was touch and go for twenty-four to thirty-six hours for Antonio while she waited for George to call back. When he finally did he assured her that he remembered her, remained indebted to her and intended to be true to his word. Plans were made.

Lili quickly gathered her things and prepared to leave. *I've got to get a bus schedule.* She didn't have enough money for a taxicab and certainly had no plans to use a credit card or borrow money from her friends. She sat down to write a note to María and Alfonso. "Dear Alfonso and Maria, Look at me," she began. "Look at the curse I have brought upon your home. Trouble just seems to follow me around. I should have known better than to have allowed you to shelter me—"

She heard a noise in the driveway and went to the door. *Not more gunmen!* Lili was relieved to find that María had sent Alfonso home to check on Lili and get some rest from his vigil at the hospital.

"How's Antonio?" Lili asked. "How's María?"

"It's hard to say. He's still in a coma. The doctors refuse to speculate. María's frantic but she'll be okay so long as Antonio survives. The next twenty four hours will be crucial."

Lili fell into tears. "It's not safe for me here—or for you as long as I'm with you. I was just about to leave when you drove up."

Alfonso looked at her things near the doorway. "And just where do you think you might be going?"

"I have a plan. I called a powerful friend in Hawaii who I think may be able to help me. His name is George Santini. He remembered me and said he would help if I could get to his men for safety."

"And just where might that be? If there's somewhere you need to go I'll take you."

Lili touched his hand which was resting on the table. "No, Alfonso. If we've learned a lesson by now, it's that I should not bring danger to my friends."

Alfonso replied, "Here's the lesson I've learned. Look." He pulled back one of the curtains. Lili could see a man with a gun on the roof of the carport and one walking back and forth on the front porch carrying a rifle.

Lili winced. She held her hands to her face.

Alfonso continued, "Those are my friends. They will protect us. Now you can't be going out there in broad daylight. First I must get some sleep and then I will drive you. You'll be safe here until dark and then I'll take you wherever it is that you need to go to meet your friends."

"But— "

"I insist," he retorted.

Lili asked, "What if I just went to the police instead?"

"Lili, it's not like it is in your country. If the police feel like it they can just detain you indefinitely, with or without any charges being filed. You might disappear and we might never see you again or be able to find out anything about what happened to you."

She pressed her finger to his lips and said, "It's settled then. We'll leave tonight at dusk." Then she went back to finish her note to María.

* * *

Sugar wanted desperately to go to the hospital to see the little boy. One bullet had lodged in his knee. The other pierced his chest but missed his heart.

Just before dark one of the guards opened what was left of the gate and Alfonso and Lili slipped first into the cab and then into the night. "I hope your little grandson will be okay," Lili said to Alfonso as he drove eastward on the main highway. Both of them glanced behind them from time to time to be sure they weren't being followed.

"If he isn't it won't be for want of prayers or good wishes," Alfonso said.

Lili thought, *I wish I had my wishing blanket.* She believed in the power of wishes and remembered Aunty Fay's teaching. *I'll bet I could wish him well if I had a blanket and a peaceful place to ponder.*

"Trouble just follows me around," Lili repeated. "I should have known better than to bring it to my friends' doorstep. I'm so, so sorry for all that has happened. I so hope little Antonio will be okay."

"It's not your fault, Sugar. You get that out of your head. Trouble finds everyone. It's how you handle it when it finds you that makes the difference."

Lili barely heard him. She was consumed with grief over the wounds to the darling little boy and once again felt powerless to help a child in mortal danger. He had required four blood transfusions already and was scheduled for an operation in the morning to fix his lung. She felt awful at taking Alfonso away from his bedside.

They turned northward and drove farther and farther across the arid plains until they came to a town that had such a tiny isthmus of land that it was almost an island in the middle of a lake. It was breathtaking in the bright light of a full moon—tranquil and serene. She could see the reflections of the water rippling in the shimmering white glow of moonlight. They got out of the car and sat at a piano bar and shared a few last words together. "Tell María that this time I'll write for sure. I promise. And you have to write and tell me how Antonio is doing as soon as there is any news—any news at all—good or bad! Do you promise, Alfonso? Do you promise me you'll do that?"

"*Te prometo, Lili.* / I promise, Lili. But where will I find you?"

"Through Izzy—Isito Kawamoto, my attorney. He's listed in the Kaua'i phone book. Just tell him. He'll know where I am and how to reach me. While you were sleeping I asked one of the guards to mail him a letter. It's best if you and María don't know my plans." She told him only of their next stop.

As soon as they got back into the cab for the few remaining miles of their journey Lili fell asleep in anticipation of needing energy for the next phase of her challenge. She had also begun to feel queasy. Not from pregnancy but from the travel of the cab up and over one hill, around the next bend, up and down a rise in the road—ever threading its way deeper and deeper into the dense flora of the forest they had gradually crept into during the night. The sleep provided relief from her nausea.

Lili didn't notice when the cab stopped and continued to sleep. When she awoke, she was surprised to find that Alfonso was asleep in a nearby hammock wearing only his boxer shorts. He had parked his car in a tourist lot next to the Mayan Temples at Tikal. She recognized them from postcard pictures she had seen.

Lili got quietly out of the cab, left the door ajar and climbed to the top of the easternmost temple—up the stairs on its face. Roots and rocks impeded her progress but she was persistent and made her way to the top. The sun had still not risen and there was no one there but her. The experience was exhilarating. As the sun crept over the horizon it sprayed glorious pink and blue rays across the forest, which showcased its own early morning drama of mist and fog. Howler monkeys screamed in the distance while toucans played in the updrafts beneath her. Her bare feet felt the ancient limestone of the Temple of the Masks and it made her feel connected to the spirits of those who had built and occupied it in centuries past. She felt as though she were in the presence of a queen. If she could not be with the spirit of her ancestors it felt good to be connected to those that might be sympathetic to her cause.

Lili wondered about the lives of the people who had once lived here and what they might have in common with her people—not the ones who lived in Hawai'i but the ones before them who populated the Marquesas Islands, Tahiti, Indonesia and the Far East. The experience refurbished her spirit to get her through the challenges that lie ahead—the uncertain but sure to be turbulent times to follow. As she stopped on her way down the face of the temple she spotted a sundial and could see there wasn't much time left. She ran back towards the cab and for the first time in months—no years—she felt the glow and joy of hope for the future.

Alfonso jumped out of his hammock, put his pants on over his boxer shorts and ran to the cab where Lili was standing. He opened the trunk and handed her a backpack. "These are some things that María wanted you to have," he said. "She was sad she couldn't give them to you herself, but—here, she wanted you to have these."

Lili knew she didn't have time to investigate the contents but took a quick peek and saw that some of those colorful clothes, like the ones she had seen in the shops in Puerto Barrios were now a part of her wardrobe.

Instinctively and impulsively Lili reached into her pocket and handed Alfonso the emerald and gold brooch that Lance had given her. "Here," she said. "I'm not sure why I'm giving you this but I have a feeling you'll need it more than me."

Alfonso held up his hand to block its transfer. "Lili, I can't take this. It's from your lover."

Even in the early morning heat that word "lover" gave her a chill.

Lili pushed back his hand. "No, you'll need it. Don't ask me why or when. I just have that feeling."

She kissed him on the cheek and slipped the brooch into the pocket of his pants. They walked a short distance to a part of the park that appeared not to have been used for many years.

"It's time," Lili said. "They should be here any minute. I'm going to miss you, Alfonso. Congratulations on becoming a part of such a wonderful family. That's what life is all about, you know!"

Alfonso looked around to see who might be joining them for he had given up on asking who to expect and when. "I know I'm *buenos* luck-o, as you say it."

They embraced and pressed their cheeks together and kissed the air beneath one another's ears, Hawaiian style. "You had better write," he said.

"I already promised," Lili said. "This time I swear it on my mother's grave. And you will tell me how Antonio does—and the rest of my Guatemalan family?"

Alfonso nodded in agreement. "*¡Acuerdo!*"

And then right on schedule there appeared—first as a tiny dot on the horizon and then in full view, flaps down, sharp descent—the pure white body and silver wings of a Gulfstream III (G-3), like an angel of mercy sent directly from heaven. No more did it touch down than it sped past them bobbing on the grass-filled cracks in the runway that had lain fallow for so long. Its engines whistled and screeched in a shrill tone, rising many decibels above their range of hearing.

One last embrace and the stairs of the plane descended for Lili's boarding. She grabbed the backpack and ran. The stairs were sleek—in sharp contrast to the gangplank of the Tropic Carib. Written across the fuselage in rainbow colors were the words "World Peace" with tropical flowers interspersed among the letters. There wasn't time for stopping the engines because the national park police patrolled the area. The runway was officially out of service—in fear of drug trafficking. The stairs were barely retracted from Lili's boarding when it taxied downwind and turned into position for take-off. Then it brought its Rolls Royce engines to full power with the brakes still engaged, released them and began a rapid acceleration under full throttle and full flaps. The small but powerful spec lifted off as gracefully into the wind as a Laysan albatross in a Kiluea updraft.

The plane gathered altitude did a one-hundred-eighty-degree turn with a steep bank. Lili sat comfortably in her soft, yellow leather seat and was handed a *Pina Colada*. She could see there were not just a few Mayan ruins in the center of the complex where she had been, but hundreds, if not thousands of them. Her jaw fell in awe. Then she saw something that startled her—a nest of police cars swarming around Alfonso's cab. She hoped beyond hope they would not "detain" him "indefinitely."

Part III

Hawaii

1995

Chapter Fifteen

After many hours of crossing the sea we broke out of the clouds and I could see the twin peaks of Mauna Loa and Mauna Kea in the distance. I felt the mana of my ancestors and a rush in my heart—a rush similar to the one the golden plover must feel when it first sees Hawaiian shores after traveling so many miles on its annual journey from Alaska.

I had traveled to many countries over the course of the past year and a half—first Switzerland and then Barbados, finally Guatemala. Now I was happy to return to the Kingdom of Hawaii. As the smooth, sleek sailing airship extended its flaps and gear for landing I kept my nose pressed to the Plexiglas window. I hadn't realized how anxious I had been to get home—not just escape my pursuers but get home—until this very moment. I think that at some level I had feared so much that I would never return to Hawaii that I didn't allow myself to fully long for it while I was gone.

And while I hadn't considered the Big Island to be home in the past, it was Hawaii and by now I considered Hawaii—any precious part of it—home. I couldn't wait to kiss the ground in much the same way that I'd once kissed the ground in Kaua'i, when I received a sign that my deceased brother, Kuha'o, had been returned to me after his death in Vietnam. I could see the little Upolu airstrip on the northern tip of the island. As the plane completed its downwind leg, shortly before landing, I could make out the beautiful red, purple and orange bougainvillea that make such a sharp contrast against the pure black lava rock, which distinguishes this island from the others.

When the plane completed taxiing and the engines were shut down I stood impatiently by the exit door, as its sole passenger, waiting for the steward to unbolt it. I could hardly refrain from pushing it open myself. I ran down the steps and across the sun-bleached asphalt runway. I ran to the black rocks that bordered it. I fell to my hands and knees and in spite of the pain of the razor sharp edges of the lava rock, I kissed it. I kissed the soil. I kissed the rock. I kissed the precious *aina*. And I ran and held huge bunches of bougainvillea in my arms—throngs of red and orange and yellow—and I embraced them as well, even though they were stickery and hurt.

I picked up handfuls of that pesky red volcanic dirt that stains your clothes and I poured it down my arms and allowed it to spill onto my blouse and hoped that it would stain me and my clothes forever. I hoped the scent and feel of it would never wash off.

"Kalili'i Kaleo," I said to myself, "you're home now, girl. By God, by Kāne, by the graves of your mother, your brother, your sister and all of your ancestors—you are home now, my friend!"

Then I noticed two black limousines parked near the end of the short taxiway. The men standing near them looked calm, very businesslike, dressed in suits, starched white shirts and aloha ties, with jackets on, even in the warmth of the midday sun. Those men troubled me. There were three or four of them. They held machine guns—not rifles or handguns—which, if I had thought about it, I might have expected to be in the arsenal of the man I had been told was the most powerful man in Hawaii. I thought of all those holes in María's fence and how the adobe wall adjacent to it had been reduced to rubble. I had hoped I was getting away from all that. But this time those guns were not pointed at me. They were pointed at those who might wish to harm me and for that I was grateful.

I was not familiar with this remote northernmost tip of the Big Island but I loved it just the same as if I had spent my whole life there. I reveled in the nearness of my mother and my brother, Kuhaʻo, and my sister, Leilani—of my ancestors and their *mana.*

The terrain was rocky and remote, but the ride was smooth in the long black limousine. We went through Hawi and I saw a cute little yellow shave ice stand. Shave ice! Now, there's something I hadn't seen, nor thought of, all the while I was gone. Yet it made me feel all the more at home to consider choosing a grape or raspberry or cherry shave ice. I tapped on the window behind the driver.

"Yes Ma'am," he said politely as though I might have been a visiting dignitary.

"Can we stop? Can we stop for a shave ice?" I pointed.

The two men in the front seat were obviously surprised and spoke privately to one another. "Sure," the husky one on the right said, as though he must have been in charge. "But, we'll have to get it for you. What flavor?" he asked as the two big, black limousines pulled barely off the road so the remaining traffic could pass.

"Let me see," I said. "I think I'll choose lime if they have it. Otherwise cherry." I thought of Lance and his lime cologne. I wondered if that's why I ordered it.

The next thing I knew the driver put the window down and the husky man, whose name I later discovered was Gerard Dougan, nicknamed "Tiny," stuck his brawny freckled arm over the darkened window pane to hand me a cherry shave ice. He had taken off his coat and rolled up his sleeves. He smiled politely.

Now, this is living. . . . A man in a white shirt and tie going to get me a shave ice. Then I wondered if he had ever killed anybody. I had heard that George had the power to administer life and death but to tell you the truth, even after having been the mayor of Kauaʻi, I had no idea whether or not that was true.

The cherry shave ice was sweet and refreshing. Shortly after I started eating it I realized I had to go to the bathroom, but I decided to hold it until we got wherever we were going. I didn't want to be more trouble or seem more like a child than I already had.

We went past the stained glass mural of a large hawk against a cloudy blue background with his wings outstretched in full flight against the green and brown Hawaii coastline. Then we turned inland, toward the mountains to the south. To this day, I still remember how peaceful and serene the long needled pine trees seemed, as they blew back and forth in a gentle trade wind, along the highway to George's house. They were elegant, swaying in the cool breeze of the higher elevation, and whenever dusk fell along that road, they took on an aura of magic and mystery.

I spotted the green roofs of the Santini compound, lurking what seemed like only an inch or two, above the horizon of the rolling hills.   We turned the corner and checked in at the gate. For all the security precautions I knew this place must possess, I was surprised to find that the gatekeeper's building was almost all glass—small panes of what appeared to be ordinary window glass.

Not so with the limousines.   I figured those windows were so thick they could take a bullet and not be penetrated. When we passed by the guard and he called the next security checkpoint I knew I was safe. Safe at last. Home at last. I couldn't wait to see what adventure lay before me. I looked up and saw several huge windmills— stark white windmills with enormous blades turning gently in the breeze—lazily as though time were standing still.

I had only a vague recollection of George, his wife and their two small children, who must be grown and gone by now. But I remembered he had been very kind to me when I was there. Fed me a delicious meal. Thanked me for supporting his cause in a labor uprising that I didn't even realize I had supported and offered me a favor in return if I ever needed it. Now I needed it. I *needed* a favor and that is why I was here.

I was flattered that George himself came out to the limousine to greet me. In fact he opened the car door.   The last time I came here it was by helicopter to the top of one of the many buttes that dominate the nearby hills and I was whisked through elevators and tunnels into his study and then into his dining room.

But this day here he was—so casual, so cheerful, and I dare say, handsome. I can't imagine that I hadn't noticed his features before—his dark, ruddy skin, clean shaven masculine face with rough-hewn features and deep-set sharply contrasting light blue eyes. His eyelashes were so long they curled until they touched his eyebrows. He wore a frilly cream-colored shirt with ruffles like a tuxedo shirt, an attire I later found he chose because it showcased his Portuguese ancestry.   And even though we were outdoors I could smell his bay rum aftershave.

But what I remember most vividly were those long black eyelashes against his ruddy, tan skin and his smile. His smile, *Mon Dieu!* It was perfectly curved, like a slice of melon, and so broad that it reached almost to his ears. And here he was—the most powerful man in Hawaii, the head of organized labor, surrounded by security forces and servants—politely opening the car door for me.

He patted his palm on the trunk and someone got out my backpack and the few sundries I had gathered on my trip—honey nuts from the seat pocket of the Gulfstream G-3, a few napkins, a magazine, the clothing from María and anything else she might have given me. I still had not had a chance to go through the backpack to see what she had put in there for me. Our departure had been hasty and the steward had put the backpack in the luggage compartment.

"I hope you'll enjoy your stay," George said to me. "And if there's anything I can do to make it more pleasant for you—"

"Oh, you've been too kind already. I mean, a plane ride from Guatemala. That alone is far more than I ever expected."

"Don't mention it," he said. "I was in your debt and I'm merely repaying a favor."

I kept thinking, if this is how you repay your debts I've got to think of more ways to keep you owing me a favor. I had no idea he had really meant it when he had told me years ago that he would one day be happy to return a favor. Otherwise I would have called him much sooner. I thought he would have forgotten me by now. Even though there were rumors—not just rumors but investigations of this man, countless ones—I had to say to myself, "This is a gentleman and a charming one at that."

* * *

Tiny showed me to my suite. Altogether it must have been bigger than Mimo's house. It had a large walk-in closet that was so big Alfonso could have built his bowling alley in it. The bedroom had a queen-sized bed with a canopy. It was ruffled and had floral designs on it, wisteria, as I recall. There was an enormous bathroom with a skylight, a spa and a bidet.

The spa was large enough to allow short laps of swimming and permitted its occupant to traverse under the glass relief on an interior wall and swim directly through a channel into the courtyard pool without ever getting out of

the water. I remember thinking it would have been
expensive to heat except that George later told me the
entire electrical system in the compound relied first on
solar power, then windmills, next diesel generators, and
finally Hawaii Electric Light, should their services ever be
needed.

Tiny said, "This used to be Mrs. Santini' s suite.
The boss, er-, Mr. Santini, says you may as well use it."

I couldn't resist. "Mrs. Santini?" I had a vague
recollection of what she looked like—a reasonably
attractive woman with a child on each knee. "Will she be
returning soon?"

Tiny paused as though he were considering whether
or not to answer my question. "They got divorced.
Actually the boss says it was an annulment but you know
what I mean. Beth . . . Mrs. Santini spent her last night
here about five years ago."

"And the children? I remember there were
children."

"Children is growed. They don't come around
much. Beth . . . Mrs. Santini took the children with her
when she left."

I badly wanted to ask him what had happened to the
marriage but I didn't dare. Besides who owed me an
explanation?

Tiny went over to the armoire and opened the door.
"Towels and linens in here."

There were dozens of them in assorted shades of
pastel. Light green. Pink. Peach. Aqua. All of them huge,
fluffy and spotless.

"Dinner's at six in the main dining room. The boss,
er . . . Mr. Santini don't like to be kept waiting. Feel free to
use anything you find in this here chamber. It's been
stocked for you."

"Thank you, Mr. Dougan," I said. "You've been
very kind and considerate. And thanks again for the shave
ice. I'm sorry to have put you to so much trouble."

"No trouble," he said as he walked to the door. He
still had on his hat which I later realized was because he
didn't like to expose his baldhead, because others made fun
of it. "I like a good cup of shave ice meeself every now
and ag'in. Bubble gum's me favorite."

I couldn't help but laugh—thinking of this big,
burly man enjoying a cup of bubble gum shave ice. After
he left I took a bath—a nice, steamy hot bath in a tub so

large I could have swum in that, too. I made bubbles and the water smelled sweet and fragrant. In fact if Mrs. Santini had been gone for five years you couldn't have told it from anything in the suite. It wasn't the least bit musty.

Through the course of my bath I wondered whether or not I was being watched. I had that same uneasy feeling I had when I was in Puerto Barrios. *Don't be ridiculous.* God, that bath felt good—piping hot. When I was done I wrapped myself in one of the huge bath towels I found in the armoire and powdered myself from the tips of my toes to the nape of my neck.

Before I was able to dress there was a knock at the door. "Yes," I said.

"May I come in, Mum?" A woman asked.

For a moment, from the British accent, I thought I was back in Barbados. "But I'm not dressed," I replied.

"I've brought you some clothes."

Now, this is service. "Yes, of course," I said. When I opened the door she appeared in French clothing—a black and white servant's outfit, predominantly black with a white apron with a ruffle around the edge, a big bow in the back and black nylons on her legs. The nylons had that seam down the back like they used to have in the nineteen forties.

I later discovered there were six such women on the household staff—very efficient and obedient but if they had one brain to share among them it always seemed to be on loan to one of the others. I ended up calling them—not to their faces, of course, or even to George—mostly just in my own mind—the "pixies." Beautiful women to the last—large breasted, curves in the right places—two brunettes, two blondes, a redhead and probably the prettiest of them all, Roxanne, who had jet black hair, blacker even than mine. There were also two older, gray haired women on the staff who did the cooking, heavier cleaning and laundry. There were two chauffeurs when none of "the men" were available for driving, a fixit man, named Paulo Roberts—and Tiny, who seemed to be an "all-arounder" for this place in the same sense as Sea Cat had been at The Tower. This was not counting the security force or the rest of the men who worked outside the main house.

The maid laid out the clothes, turned down the bed and left. I didn't understand why she had turned down the bed. *Does she think I'm going to take a four o'clock nap?*

I whiled away the rest of the afternoon doing my nails, doing my hair. Everything I needed was in the bathroom. And it was well suited to me. In fresh, new containers were the right colors of mascara, the kind I used, the right colors of eye shadow, the kind I used, and so on down to the nail polish I used to wear on occasion to mayoral functions. Even the dress I was brought reminded me of the long flowing gowns with embroidery I used to wear to Kaua'i County functions. On the one hand it was a comfort—no, a luxury. On the other it was unsettling—as if someone knew a little too much about me.

* * *

George was a gracious host. When I came into the dining room he walked over to the entrance and escorted me on his arm across the hardwood floor to my seat. I could feel his strength through his white ruffled shirt, more strength than I would have imagined for a man with silver tipped sideburns.

The room was two-story, like my bedroom suite, with a vaulted ceiling and exposed beams at the top and fans for circulation. There was no air-conditioning anywhere in the house. We sat at the end of a long koa wood table with candle chandeliers at either end. The fans and chandeliers were staggered in such a way that the fans could circulate the air without blowing out the candles. There were also candles floating on water lilies in bowls on the table.

George liked the ambiance of the lit candles and said he didn't like to rely on electricity anymore than he had to, even though windmills and solar panels generated most of their power.

He asked, "How was your day? Did you find everything you needed in your room?"

Room? You call that a room? It's more like a house—a suite at the very least. "Yes, I found everything I needed and then some. Thank you very much. I'm beginning to think someone has been following me around my entire life. I mean, someone seems to know me better than I know myself, right down to my favorite bath soap. How did you find out?"

"I'll congratulate my staff. When we heard you were coming we tried to take a few steps to make sure you felt welcome."

It's unbelievable. Lili smiled but at some level she also found it unnerving. Then tallow dripped on her arm from the chandelier and it smarted.

George apologized, rang the silver bell beside him, stood, walked around the table and peeled the wax off with his fingertips and rubbed the residue gently with a white linen napkin. His hands were coarse and rough, as those who knew work, but his touch was soft and gentle.

"Mrs. McAffe, you'd better see that the candles are replaced. The tallow has just overflowed and burnt our guest.

"Of course," she said as she curtsied, then turned and left. A short time later Paulo arrived with a new set of beeswax candles, climbed a short ladder that he placed next to me and replaced them unobtrusively while we ate. He didn't look at us or join the conversation.

The main course was veal cordon bleu. I shouldn't have been surprised. We were less than thirty minutes from the Parker Ranch, the largest privately owned ranch in the United States. Charlie, my former husband, worked there when we first met. It had hundreds or thousands of head of cattle, enough to feed an entire state.

I had secretly been hoping for Spam and runny eggs all day, reminiscent of my dinners at Izzy's parents, the Kawamotos, when I was a youth. But I have to admit that once I took the first bite I was glad I hadn't expressed that preference. Wild rice, a fruity port from the Douru Valley. Succulent avocado salad with shrimp in thousand island dressing. Why haven't I ever thought of collecting on this favor before? I mused.

"What would you like to do while you're here, Miss Kaleo? How will you spend your days?" George passed me the butter.

I said, "The first thing I have to do is meet with my lawyer, Izzy Kawamoto."

"Yes, Mr. Kawamoto. He's made quite a name for himself since you've been gone. Have you heard?'"

I put down my port to listen. "No," I said. "I'm always glad to hear exciting news about my friends."

"He's started an investigation into the building of the new convention center in Honolulu."

"You mean the big glass one on the Ala Wai?"

"None other," George said. "It seems some of the smaller contractors didn't think they got their fair share of business and some of them who did get business ended up not getting paid, so they got together and hired your friend, Kawamoto, to champion their cause."

"Sounds like Izzy! He's always looking out for the little guy."

"A menace—" George stopped himself and changed course. "Menacing publicity for some. He's been using words like 'Hawaiian Mafia' and 'organized crime.' Even had some nasty things to say about me. Has he mentioned anything like that to you?" George leaned forward.

"No. He and I haven't communicated much but we really must now, so I can see how— "

George relaxed back into his seat. "How the foreclosure proceedings are coming against your brother and his wife?"

"Yes, but how did you know about that?"

"Lili, once you've been in a high profile position you're forever newsworthy for the piranha of the press. I read about it in *The Big Island Gazette*."

"I know what you mean. *Honolulu Magazine* did an article on me right before I left and mislead their readers about the facts. They asked me to confirm something and when I told them I had to check it out they published their false innuendos and claimed I had 'neglected' to call them back. That was after they said they probably weren't going to run the article anyway."

George said, "I don't think your friend, Kawamoto, has any idea what a hornet's nest he's getting himself into."

I sopped up the last bit of cheese sauce from my plate with a crust of sourdough bread one of our servers mentioned had been flown in from San Francisco. By now the main course was long gone. "If anyone can handle it I'm sure it's Izzy."

"I hope so," George said. "I hope he doesn't end up stepping off a cliff."

I looked at George to see whether or not he was joking. I had heard reference to the Hawaiian Mafia most of my life but again—even as mayor of Kaua'i, it was a legend I could neither confirm or deny.

Mrs. Silva served a flaming black cherry soufflé for dessert. My appetite soared although my mood sank. I couldn't help but think of Lance and the fire on his stove and the soufflé he never got to serve me. George made a gesture to Mrs. McAfee and the next thing I knew there was a trio with a guitar, a viola and an accordion at the opposite end of the room, playing fado—a unique blend of Portuguese folk music, opera and blues.

George said, "Well one thing is for sure. We've got to get you out of the house and into some fresh air tomorrow."

His remark lifted my spirits. "How about Hawi? I saw some cute little art shops there when we drove by. Can you have someone take me there?"

"Of course, whatever you say. But tomorrow I was thinking maybe the two of us could go horseback riding. Do you ride?"

I said, "I'm afraid you'll find I'm not a very accomplished rider but I would love to go. The countryside looks beautiful. I'd like to see it close up."

The soufflé was soft and fluffy, the music seductive and the dinner magnificent. After dinner we sat on the veranda and looked up at the stars. It was amazing to me that George could name—or at least convince me he was naming and identifying—six or eight constellations. He had one of his "men" bring us a telescope and together we studied the rings around Saturn. It's remarkable how many stars you can see from this remote part of the Big Island— far from city lights.

* * *

We met outside the stables shortly before sunrise the following morning. It put me in mind of the morning I had been at the Tikal pyramids with the diffusion of multi-colored light. George had on tight fitting blue jeans which defined a remarkable shape for a man in his fifties. Whatever I lacked in riding skill he more than made up for and it was obvious his horse liked him. I figured that was a good sign.

There was a delicacy about him. He wore a paniolo shirt. It was silk with scenes of cowboys roping steers and driving cattle over a precipice. He must have anticipated I'd say yes to a horseback ride because one of the "pixies," the redhead, the one with the humongous breasts, brought me some riding breeches and boots shortly after dinner and they fit perfectly. When she leaned over to put them on my bed I wasn't sure she'd be able to stand back up.

We rode across the rolling green hills of the Kohala Mountains while the sun came up over the horizon to the east. It started out orange but turned yellow as the day and our ride progressed. A hawk flew lazily in the thermals as we cantered across his property toward the ocean. From time to time I would see men, usually in pairs and wearing boots and fatigues, roaming the terrain with rifles under their arms and binoculars around their necks. Some were on horseback; others on foot.

"Hunters?" I asked.

"They're here for your protection," George answered. It was a pleasant thought in some ways but somehow sounded a lot like that "for your protection" statement you get from a banker just before she invades your privacy or takes some aggressive position regarding your account.

George led us to a trail that wound down the cliffs of the eastern seaboard onto the beach below. There was a river that emptied into the ocean and George galloped ahead of me and splashed his mount through the water. The look of accomplishment in his eye and joy on his face was obvious as he returned to my side and encouraged me to do likewise.

"Lazy Susan will love it," he assured me regarding my horse. "She's a stable mount."

I could tell that. His horse seemed considerably more spirited than mine but my horse, a small boned Arabian mare, was just as he said, "stable," and to my relief not the least bit lazy. I remembered all too well the horse I rode one day at Ōpaeka'a Falls Riding Academy on Kaua'i that kept trying to return to the barn from the minute I mounted her until she got her wish.

On our way back from the cliffs George and I passed the butte where I had a vague recollection that I landed in the helicopter years before. "What are they doing over there?" I asked, pointing to the vehicles and men going in and out of an entrance that appeared to be about the size of a double car garage.

"We call that 'the bunker,'" he said and awaited my reaction.

"What is this a war zone?"

"I hope not," he said. "But if it were ever to become one I think you'd find we could hold our own. C'mon, I'll race you."

With that he urged his horse into a lope. I did likewise and then we gathered speed and galloped across the meadow towards the stables.

* * *

On about the second or third night George had a business dinner to which I had been invited provided I didn't interfere with or change the subject whenever the discussions might turn to business affairs. Two men from Mongolia comprised the guest list. They wore traditional clothing—rugged coveralls that must have been blazingly hot in the afternoon sun, along with circular hats. One hat came to a peak. The other ended in a spire. Big furry mucklucks. They were probably about my age but appeared much older—older even than George. They wore the inscription of a hard life on their faces.

They were polite to a fault and considerate. I think they figured that I wasn't thrilled with the primitive food being served—disgustingly odoriferous ancient eggs, although I did like the pork rinds and flaming pupu's we had before dinner. George had gone all out to see that his guests were pampered and well cared for.

I didn't stay for dessert because the conversation had soon become tedious. Besides it was to be lychees with ginger ice cream and neither appealed to my palate. If it had been mango ice cream I might have stayed. One thing I recall that seemed strange to me was all the conversation they had about shipping "buggy whips" to one of George's business locations. At first I couldn't imagine what they were talking about and then I decided it had to be something else. I mean, who uses buggy whips nowadays anyway? And for the few who do I didn't think they would choose to account for them in kilos per month.

* * *

For the next couple of weeks I was content to bathe, use the sauna, read, recuperate, ride the horses—over which he gave me free rein so to speak—dine with Mr. Santini and his guests every evening and stroll the grounds and the gardens at will. In many ways it was idyllic. I was concerned about George's possible criminal activities but he was my protector. I decided not to draw any hasty conclusions.

To entertain myself I worked crossword puzzles and when the Sunday *Honolulu Advertiser* came on the weekends I worked the word jumbles and number puzzles in the entertainment section. Sometimes Tiny would join me and we'd work on them together.

After this brief respite I kept coming back to the notion that I needed to see my lawyer. Whenever I brought it up George always seemed to have something else that needed to be put on our agenda beforehand and told me that his lawyers had checked on Mimo's foreclosure and the county's case against me. There was nothing requiring immediate attention and still plenty of time to attend to both. I hadn't forgotten about the gold shipments into Guatemala but I also hadn't figured out what to do about them. I wasn't ready to confide in George and I desperately wanted to see Izzy.

One night George took me into Waimea and we had dinner at Edelweiss. I know it sounds like a corny name for a restaurant but the food was delicious and the atmosphere charming. The waitresses wore Austrian dresses and the male servants had on *lederhosen*. Their strudel was fantastic and they heaped on plenty of French vanilla ice cream for dessert. After dinner they sang the Austrian national anthem around their piano and gave us tiny red and white flags as souvenirs of our visit.

A few people there recognized me. One was a man of obvious Hawaiian descent and with a *haole* companion. Another man was Japanese. They each came up to our table in turn on their way out. "Lili, Lili Kaleo," the Japanese man said. "Where have you been keeping yourself?"

"I've been trying to stay out of trouble as best I can," I replied.

The Hawaiian man shook my hand by first reaching past it and clasping it in the shape of an 'X.' Then he let his fingers slide and catch his fingertips against mine. Finally he formed a fist as I did and tapped it on top of mine. He smiled broadly. "We were awfully sorry to hear about your son. Is there any chance you're going to be running for governor?"

"Not anytime soon," I replied.

Then he gave me a hug on each side of the face and ended by kissing me on the cheek the latter part being a deviation from the usual custom. It had been over a year since I had been greeted in this fashion and it felt wonderful. It was so good to be home.

I sensed that George felt left out and was in some ways put off by my celebrity. No one appeared to recognize him but he seemed to prefer it that way.

* * *

Another time a helicopter picked us up and we toured the Volcanoes National Park and then ate in the main lodge overlooking the primary crater and its cauldrons. It was an overcast day and the mist dampened the window as we watched mysteriously shaped clouds of steam spew from the vents and cracks below.

Once he even took me to Honolulu which was reminiscent of my days with Max Martin. Only George was much more interested in the environment and culture so we went to places like Hanauma Bay and the Polynesian Cultural Center. On that occasion there were so many people who recognized me and wished me well that George resolved that he should not take me to such public places while I remained in danger.

I told him we had a wonderful botanical garden on Kaua'i and he said he knew. He was familiar with the gardens at Smith's Tropical Luau and promised that one day we would stroll them prior to one of their delicious meals. How I longed to return to Kaua'i and see my Aunty Fay. I had no idea whether or not she knew I was back.

While we were in Honolulu I once again asked to see my friend, Izzy, whom I learned now had offices in Honolulu and Lihue. But George told me that I would be able to attend to my legal concerns soon enough and once I did I would wish I had taken longer before I jumped in. He said, "Sugar, you know I said I'd protect you and I will. That means both your physical well being and your legal problems. Trust me."

Hmm! The "t"-word. Where had I heard that before?

* * *

I can't say that the interlude between arriving in Hawaii and dealing with my legal problems was unpleasant or unwelcome. George treated me like a princess. Over time we had fewer interruptions with business affairs at dinner and during the day he would often find me in the garden, perhaps under the shade of a monkeypod tree. We would walk and talk, often about our common philosophy toward protecting the environment.

One day while we were talking he said, "I've always wanted to be self-sufficient—I mean live in an environment in which I didn't depend on the outside world at all."

I giggled because of the visual image I had in my head. "You mean like a terrarium?"

"Exactly. Exactly like a terrarium," he said. "I came from nothing—the bastard son of a vineyard owner in Portugal," he reminded me for the second or third time since I'd been there. "And now I have all this." He gestured at his estate with his hand and I have to admit it was an impressive spread. "And I have a lot more properties—all over the world. At last, and I'm still only middle aged, I am truly wealthy."

"But what did you have to do to get it?" I blurted out without thinking.

At first I could tell he was upset by my question. I sensed he was not used to being challenged by those around him.

After a brief pause, while his red face returned to tan, he said, "I can be a very kind and gentle person. . . . And I certainly know how to take care of my friends."

"And your enemies?" *Damn, there I went again.*

I saw a fierceness in his eyes—the sort he displayed as he rode the galloping horse through the stream. "And my enemies? Yes, I know how to take care of them as well."

His last remark sent a cold shiver down my arms to the tips of my fingers which were holding a thorny, red velvety rose at the time. I carefully set the rose down, hoping not to be pricked by its thorns.

* * *

One of the things I relished was that I had time to write to my friends. I had considered calling them, and for a while, I considered whether or not it would be rude to call long distance from the *Quinta*, as George called his enormous estate—the *Quinta Da Bela Vista*. I thought about asking him for permission but he had been so evasive about me contacting Izzy that I decided to chance it and make a few calls anyway when no one was around. If he objected I would pay him back—or send him a check after I left.

There was a phone in my suite but when I tried to use it I found a dial-in code was required to access long distance. So I wrote letters instead.

Dear Alfonso and Maria,

I regret that I had to leave Guatemala City in such haste. I regret even more that I brought upon your home such an utterly despicable deed as to result in harm to poor, dear Antonio. I hope and pray that he is well and enjoying a complete and full recovery.

Alfonso, did you make it home from the pyramids okay? As we flew away from the ruins I could see that you were in peril. Have you made good use of the brooch? I know in my heart that there was a reason why you needed it more so than me.

I would call you if I could but my host believes that the less contact I have with the outside world the better my chances are for survival. Please write back to me right away and let me know the fate of your darling grandson. I must know whether or not there's blood on my hands. Even though I haven't seen him for some time your best bet is to send your correspondence to Isito Kawamoto, Esq., either in Lihue or more likely to his impressive new offices on Bishop Street in Honolulu.

With much aloha, hugs and kisses for all, Lili Kaleo

I started many letters just to Lance but I never finished one:

"Dear Lance, I'm sorry I had to leave without saying good-bye. But, then again, I'm not sure whether or not I could trust you—I mean the TV spots, and all . . . ." (I tore this one up.)

"Dear Lance, I remember with fondness all of the good times we had together and regret that things did not work out for us. There were times when I found myself feeling close to you and wondering whether or not you were 'the one.' But you didn't seem to return my affection, at least not in the way that I had hoped and expected. You seemed to waver in your feelings for me. And then there was the problem of . . . ." (I tore that one up, too.)

Finally, I wrote and sent the following: "Dear Lance, Theo, Willie, Idalia and Emma,

We try to plan our lives and live according to that plan, but sometimes there are events over which we have no control that send us in directions we never imagined. This doesn't mean that I never loved you, or you, me. Nor does it mean that I don't long to return to you, even if just for a single day. To play volleyball on the beach, read stories together, swing in the backyard with Emma on my lap or smell the sweet fragrance of frangipani in a vase on the table while we all savor a delicious home-cooked meal together.

"I regret that I was never able to share a proper good-bye with any of you— 'aloha,' as we say in Hawaii. I want each of you to know that it was only concerns for my safety, your safety and the cause I have undertaken that kept me from doing so. It is no reflection on the depth of feelings I have for each of you and the value I place on the warm embrace that you each deserve from me for all you have done to bring joy to my life.

"Perhaps the future will be kinder to us all. You will be in my thoughts, wishes and prayers not just now but for as long as there is a breath of life within me.

"Theo, if you'd just add a little over-spin to your serves (your dad can show you how), you'll win a lot more road tennis games. I could readily see your potential. Your defense is incredible, but then again why shouldn't it be, considering that you are the son of the fourth 'W.'

"Much aloha—that you will be with joy when this finds you and sadness that I am not able to deliver it personally, Lili "Sugar" Kaleo."

I gave the notes to Tiny, and although I trusted George with my life and owed my continued well being to him, I asked Tiny not to discuss them with him before he mailed them. I could see the hesitation on his face.

"Tiny, these are personal, have nothing whatsoever to do with my legal case, and I promise I'll never tell a soul who mailed them or even that they were mailed."

He looked at the letters I had handed him and then he looked at me. I walked around behind him, hugged him and then clasped his hand tighter on the letters. "You'll have to buy some stamps for these. I'll pay you back with a shave ice." I winked at him before I walked over to my dresser and turned my back to him so that he would not see my tears.

I blinked them away and then turned and showed him a broad smile. "Thank you," I said.

"No thanks necessary, Mum. You treat me like I'm worth something and not just a stupid hulk whose only good for knocking heads."

I hoped that meant he would mail the letters and not mention them to George.

* * *

When George and I went through the bunker to get to the helicopter for the flight around the volcano, it gave me a chance to look around. There were racks upon racks of guns of all shapes and sizes and what appeared to be ordinance: grenades, rocket launchers, machine guns, even a bazooka. *This man is armed to the teeth! But he is kind and gentle to me.*

"Why do you have all these weapons?" I asked. ". . . along with the men who appear to be assigned to use them."

"You can bet they know how to use them," he replied. "We have a rifle and pistol range down in the scrub. Perhaps you've heard the rounds when the trades are blowing towards the house."

I had wondered what the situation was with the fireworks since they're only legal in Hawaii on New Year's and the Fourth of July.

George asked, "Did you ever hear about that guy, David Koresh, down in Waco, Texas?"

I agreed I had heard about him and the terrible destruction that accompanied his extermination as well as the embarrassment to the government that seemed to reflect the poor judgment of those in charge.

"Well, there are those who think I'm a wrongdoer," he answered. "But I'm not." He paused to let that sink in. "I've spent my whole life looking after the needs of the working man and what you see around me . . ." he swept his hand to present the property, "are a few of the rewards.

"But, power, freedom and wealth don't come without a price," he continued, "We have a right and a duty to protect ourselves and our interests. That's all we're doing with the weapons."

On the surface that sounded reasonable but I doubted I was hearing the whole story. Aunty Fay always used to say, "When you dunno who fo' believe, make sua you listen to ev'rybody who stay saying some 'ting about, well, what evah it is." In other words, "Keep an open mind and welcome the insights of others."

At that point we boarded the chopper and it was so noisy we were unable to continue the conversation.

Chapter Sixteen

After about a month at the Quinta I decided it was
time to see Izzy whether or not George agreed with me. I
would go to Honolulu, or Kaua'i, if necessary, to find him.
"I'm going to walk right down that driveway past the
security gates and hitchhike if I have to," I said to George.
"But I've got to see my lawyer. It's time. You can try to
stop me, if you want to, but you may have to call in
reinforcements."

He laughed. "That's not necessary. I'll make
arrangements for him to come here on Friday. Does ten
a.m. sound okay with you?"

He couldn't have had a better answer ready for
when I had reached the limits of my tolerance. Every time
I got close to mistrusting him or thinking him heavy handed
George always seemed to come up with a perfectly
plausible explanation and resolve that justified every aspect
of his behavior. Besides—I felt deeply indebted and didn't
want to offend him.

* * *

The day that I issued my ultimatum to George about
meeting with my lawyer, he became the most attentive man
I have ever seen, responding personally to my every whim
and desire.

We went on a long horseback ride. This time we rode down the gradually sloping mountainside to the western seaboard toward Kona and had a picnic in a grove of thorny keawe bushes near the beach. He pointed out some petroglyphs and I got feelings of *déjà vu.* But this man was not Charlie. For one thing he had a job. He was the head of organized labor for the entire state of Hawaii. *The people who elected him and re-elected him time after time must have known what they were doing.*

At first we hobbled our horses and then later on allowed them to wander in the thick gravelly sand of a washout while we had lunch on a lava rock. As we unwrapped the shells for our chicken fajitas—something I requested, because it was the closest thing I could think of to a roti from Chefette—he swept back my hair and kissed me. There was no indecision on his part, no lack of direction or commitment to his objectives. Lance had always seemed so ambivalent towards me.

I felt uncomfortable at first but George had been persuasive and consistent in his declarations of affection. And the man was handsome, rich and powerful—some pretty potent aphrodisiacs, especially for a woman like me who had a hard time differentiating among the good, the bad and the ugly where men were concerned. Whenever I'm hooked on a man I'll admit that a chump element sometimes comes into play because he could have taken me then and there. But he didn't.

Instead I had to wait the nearly two hours it took us to ride back up the mountain to find out what was on his mind. Along the way I relished certain aspects of the idea of being Mr. Santini's woman, even if it didn't involve a long-term commitment. It reminded me of when I used to ride around with "Stingray" Martin in his Corvette and knew that all eyes were upon me. Now, in my late thirties, I knew the opportunity for such a role was quickly passing me by.

* * *

Dinner was scheduled for late that evening and I was disappointed to find that George had invited several of the neighbors over to meet me. There was Frank Beatty who owned a small dairy farm near Waimea, Becky Smith and her husband Ted, retirees from Hawi, and Ralph and Sydney Carter who were on the faculty at Hawaii Community College.

Becky interested me the most because she was in her eighties and recounted much of what she had observed through the better part of the plantation era. But all too often the men turned the conversation to grazing cattle and horses, the weather and the hapless Rainbow Warriors who had just ended their longest football losing streak since anyone could remember. In the wake of it all they fired their coach in spite of his sterling player graduation record, which they had previously told him was paramount.

The last guest left at around eleven and I couldn't wait to get to bed. By now the aches and pains from the ride down and up the mountainside had become all too apparent and I couldn't wait for a hot bath. George had other ideas.

After I went to my suite and began to undress one of the blonde pixies came to summon me to Mr. Santini's chambers. When he beckoned me and I thought it was probably for sex, I was prepared to refuse—out of principle. I mean, a girl likes to be seduced. *He could have come and gotten me instead of ordering me like a pizza.*

His chambers consisted of not just a bedroom but a study, a bathroom with a pool entrance like mine and an exercise area. When I got there he was waiting for me, not in his bedroom, but in the exercise area. He was standing beside a long, black leather table that looked like a folding picnic table and said, "I thought that if I took you out on such a strenuous ride the least I could do would be to give you a rub down."

From the looks of things I surmised he knew his trade. There were oils with various scents, each heated above room temperature so that I wouldn't be startled when they touched my skin.

"Sure," I said, so desirous of the pleasure I had been offered that whatever sense of caution I might have had evaporated. I remembered being massaged once after an important volleyball match at UH by our female trainer. This was to be my first massage by a man.

"Am I supposed to take off my clothes?" I asked, feeling like a fool upon realizing that I had conceded that point prematurely, just as I had with the shipboard doctor.

"Here. You can keep this towel around you." He handed me a towel about the size of a handkerchief.

I lay on my stomach with the towel over my bottom and he began with my neck. He knew right where to root out the tension and snuffed it out with the strength and agility in his thumbs. I once again reflected on the coarseness of his hands in contrast to their soft but firm touch.

From there, he worked his way down my body towards my toes. I could feel the tension in my muscles move towards my feet as surely as if he were sweeping it with a broom.

"May I reach under the towel?" he asked.

"Umm hmm!" I replied.

He leaned over my ear for clarification.

"Yes," I said.

The room was warmer than normal. There were electric coils in the ceiling over the massage table with a built in fan behind them. It heated my body to a warm, comfortable level. When he came to my bottom he rubbed it but not in a sexual way. I groaned, not with passion but with gratitude and relief. I could feel the remnants of every misspent hoof print over that hard lava rock. The pain was whisked away with the circular motion of his fingertips. I felt at peace.

I knew that at some point he would ask me to turn over and I would likely say "yes," without hesitation. But that's not the way it happened. Sometime between the time he rubbed the aches out of my rear end and reached the bottoms of my feet, I fell asleep— pleasurable, carefree sleep. I must have laid there a couple of hours unattended.

Then, as if in a dream, I felt his hands upon me again. Only this time the feelings were different. He had lifted off the little towel before he started. He caressed my back and bottom with his hands, just above my skin, to where they barely touched the hair follicles. I could feel their presence, the warmth of his hands, but the touch itself was so light I could barely feel it. I wanted to feel it. I longed for it. I longed for the pressure of his touch.

Then the feather light touching on my backside ended with me still moving in and out of a stupor. He moved to my feet, the bottoms of my feet. He pressed his thumbs into them. They say that you can send a nerve signal to any area of the body if you know just where to press on someone's foot. And he knew just where to press. He sent waves to my most sensuous regions. I felt awakened, feminine, eager and alive.

When it was time for him to turn me over he didn't ask. He merely tugged at me as an accomplished dancer pushes ever so gently into the small of a woman's back to direct her to turn or twirl. He nudged me and I rolled my naked body over and lay on my back. The heat from the overhead coils was warm and I could hear a fire crackling in the distance.

He kneaded my nipples and my body sprang to attention and anticipated his next advance. Lance had been a good lover but this man was phenomenal.

He slipped his fingers between my legs and put pressure on just the right place to bring my passions toward a crescendo. "I want you. I want you now," I said.

I reached beside me and untied the belt on his white terrycloth bathrobe and pulled it open to see what was in store for me underneath. He widened his arms to slip the robe off his shoulders and let it drop to the floor. He dripped with anticipation and I reached for him with impatience. "Now," I said. "I want you inside me."

He climbed on top of me but delayed his insertion until I begged for it.

"Forget the rubdown," I said. "I've got to have you." Then at what must have been three or four in the morning, I arched my back, spread my legs and we rode the express train to heaven.

* * *

For the next several days we never left his chambers, except to hold hands in the garden and catch our breath. We went naked most of the time and remarkably no one came around. Our meals were brought to our door and he must have anticipated this because he never rang for them nor told anyone what we wanted to eat. The food always came at just the right moment, albeit simpler fare than we normally ate—oranges, apples, fresh pineapple, toast, jam, coffee, ham, sausage, lean bacon and eggs. Eggs prepared every which way.

We made love over and over again, him on top of me, me on top of him, back to front, side to side—like a prospector panning from every angle in search of the richest ore.

The next thing I knew it was eight a.m. on Friday morning. I was so eager to see Izzy that I quickly dressed and showered and rushed up to the sun porch a little after nine a.m. to wait and watch for him. It was raining and I had the staff roll an awning over the porch to keep me dry. I was intoxicated, not from alcohol, but from the taste, smell and warmth of George Santini on my mind, body and lips.

* * *

After the blitz of romantic encounters I was off balance but not so off balance that I wasn't overjoyed to see my friend Izzy arrive at the front gate. I knew that he would arrive in one of George's black limousines and waited and watched until it came. Since it was driven by one of the estate's drivers I knew it would take less than the usual time to pass through security checkpoint one.

At checkpoint two he was dropped off to walk the rest of the way to the main house, even though it was raining. Knowing Izzy as I did I knew he would separate from the convoy at his earliest opportunity. As he exited the vehicle I ran across the veranda, down the stairs, down the hall, past my room, down the spiral staircase—bounding down two steps at a time, out onto the lawn and down the driveway. Gasping for air I yelled, "Izzy! Izzy Kawamoto! Izzy Kawamoto from Kaua'i—my brother, my long lost brother!"

I ran to him and hugged him. I took away his umbrella and tossed it. Then to his surprise I wrestled him to the ground as we had done many times as children. His glasses were thicker than ever and I accidentally knocked them off. He wrestled me back and fortunately we didn't break the glasses.

After we were completely exhausted and his suit thoroughly soiled he got up and straightened it. I handed him his wet, grimy glasses. He pulled out a kerchief and wiped them carefully, so Izzy-like, and put them on in the rain.

I said, "Look at you! You need windshield wipers."

And then we laughed and laughed.

"You haven't changed, Lili Kaleo," he said at last, with little more breath left than I had. I picked up his umbrella but did not hold it over either of us. We walked to the house together, arm in arm, allowing the rain to pour down relentlessly while we basked in the glory of a friendship that had bloomed virtually our entire lives.

* * *

Izzy and I walked in the garden and from there we moved to a nearby hillside and strolled the grounds. He was paranoid about "listening devices" so I obliged him by taking our conversation away from the walls that "might have ears." He had changed into in one of George's pinstriped dress shirts, a pair of my running shorts and some low cut pink tennis shoes one of the pixies had lent to him. Even with his shirttail out and his bony pale legs I still saw him as my knight in shining armor.

He told me about his wife, Kiku, and showed me a picture of their new baby, Mishiki. She was an adorable little girl and I asked him why they hadn't named her after his sister, Suzie. "Kiku and Suzuko don't get along all that well," he said. On his face I could see unspoken words and a world I knew it best not to explore. Oh, I was certain they were polite to one another and that Kiku would make him proud in many ways but I also sensed there was an iciness about her that had always been there, an iciness that would not melt in the tropical sun.

I brought him up to date on my experiences and a filtered version of my love life, that is through the day I drove into the gate at the *Quinta Da Bela Vista*. I did not continue the story to the present moment. I feared he might not approve. But I think he pretty well guessed what was going on.

He said, "For weeks, no months, I was afraid your civil case would go into the toilet and that the county would be awarded summary judgment because I was not able to produce you as a witness nor gain your assistance in preparing a defense. And that's exactly what would have happened, except—"

"Except what?" I asked. "Where does the case stand now? Talking about it makes me tense."

We sat down on some rocks and in the distance I could see the wind whistling through the ironwoods. Further towards the west we beheld the entire Kona coastline. Izzy looked so silly in his ragtag attire. By now it had stopped raining and the sun felt warm and we welcomed it.

He answered, "About four weeks ago, which would be about two weeks after you arrived back in Hawaii from what you've told me, someone filed an *amicus curiae* brief challenging the constitutionality of the Hawaii statute that enabled the litigation which the county brought against you. Now everything is miraculously delayed until the appellate court gets a chance to review it and decide whether or not the case should be allowed to proceed. That could take anywhere from a few months to a few years."

"Do you think it was—?" I nodded my head toward the main house.

"I have no way of knowing," Izzy said. "But if I had to guess, then yes, I think there's a link . . ." Izzy discreetly flicked a finger or two from his clenched hand towards the entrance road. "To these gates."

I felt silly that we weren't finishing our sentences, or completing our thoughts, as though someone were eavesdropping and Izzy felt we had to play a charade.

I said, "It sounds like a clever tactic. No offense to your lawyering, because I know you're the best, but I'm surprised you didn't think of it yourself."

Izzy still looked handsome in spite of the increased thickness of his eyeglasses and his silly attire. He said, "Oh, but I did think of it. It's just that normally you can't test the constitutionality of a statute in the appellate courts until after all such matters, including the verdict, have been adjudicated and final judgment entered at the trial level."

"You're losing me, Izzy. It sounds pretty complicated. I think you're telling me that someone has been unusually clever."

"Or had considerably more influence over the rulings of the appellate court than either you or I might have, or ninety percent of my colleagues in the Hawaii State Bar."

"Or got lucky?" I asked.

"Or got very, very lucky," he replied.

"And what about the foreclosure? Are we too late to save Mimo's house?"

Izzy looked at me and said, "It's 'on hold.' Someone's been making their payments for them."

This time, neither of us had to point.

* * *

Before fixing lunch for Izzy, which I insisted on doing myself, I stole away to read a letter he had handed me shortly after he changed his clothes. It had been in his inside coat pocket so it wasn't terribly wet and the ink was barely smudged. It was postmarked "Guatemala City - - - Guatemala," and read:

"Dear Sugar, I am not as clever or well educated as you so I will only say what is in my heart and hope it all makes sense.

"First of all our dear blessed Antonio is okay and is expected by the doctors to make a complete and full recovery. We prayed over him for days and for a while it looked as though God might take him from us. But the priest came and administered the sacrament of Extreme Unction and my mother and Alfonso lit candles in the Cathedral and kissed the feet of the black Jesus. Two days later he recovered. I know you are doubtful about religion but this was a miracle. I swear it on the cross of Our Savior, Jesus Christ.

"It appears you are to thank for a miracle your ownself. After you left the police arrested Alfonso and took him in for questioning. It looked hopeless but he argued with them that if he could produce something of uncommon value they should let him, a common drug courier (he had to admit this, or be tortured), go. After receiving their word, which one cannot always count on (this is part of the miracle, too), he took them to his car where he had stuck the brooch Señor Williams had given you underneath the dashboard and gave it to them. Alfonso described to me this beautiful piece of golden jewelry with enormous dark green emeralds and I know it was difficult to give up. May the Lord, God bless you for your sacrifice!

"After that they kept their word and let him go with no record being made of the arrest. He says to tell you that he is eternally grateful and will be forever in your debt until he has a chance to return the favor.

"Oh, I almost forgot to tell you. When Antonio woke up he didn't know all the worry he had put us through or trouble to the doctors. For him it was just a long, peaceful nap. He says he enjoyed the game of *policia* and *bandidos* that you two played and he can't wait for you to come back so you can play it again. He wants to know if this time he can be one of the men with guns. Sugar, I would love to see you but if you do come back, you and Antonio will please play all of your games indoors—and there will be no *policia* and *bandidos*, even though I haven't yet had the heart to tell Antonio.

"I've got to run. Alfonso is honking for me in the driveway. One last thing—if you want my honest opinion I think you should marry the black man. It is obvious to me as our many conversations dance in my head that you and Inspector Williams are deeply in love. In time, you will forget the color of his skin. *Buenos dias.* Alfonso honks even louder.

Your loving friend and "other" mother, María Fernandez

With the damp, crumpled letter in my hand and a tear in my eye I hastily fixed a light lunch of tuna sandwiches, oxtail soup and tea for Izzy and me to eat on the sun porch overlooking the estate.

* * *

The breeze on the porch was warm and welcome after the torrential rains of the morning. The servants rolled up the awning and someone on the staff had taken Izzy's suit, shirt, tie and pants to the cleaners and now he was changed back into his lawyer outfit. I must say, however, that I was a bit disappointed. He had looked cute in the shirttails and gym shorts, not to mention the pink shoes belonging to the pixie named Melanie.

I tried to assure him that no one would have taken the trouble to bug the sun porch but he still spoke, for the most part, in cryptic words with noncommittal tones.

He said, "I'm handling some cases against the general contractors in the building of the Honolulu Convention Center. Have you read about it in the papers?"

"No," I said. "But George told me about it."

"It's no wonder," he said. "I have no doubt but that he knows a good deal more about it than you might find in the papers."

"Isn't that just good business? I mean George is the president of the federation of all labor unions in Hawaii and, as such, one would expect— "

"Yes it's good business, I'll grant you that, but our civil discovery to date corroborates . . . . I can't say too much about this because of the attorney-client privilege but let me put it this way. I used to think organized crime in Hawaii was just that— 'in Hawaii.' Now I think it's only part of a much more complicated, far reaching network. Hawaii may even be at the core."

I felt concerned for the citizens of our state.

"I think it encompasses drug trafficking, money laundering, gun running and . . . ."

"Smuggling?"

"How did you know?"

"Gold, emeralds, diamonds?"

"How did you know that, too?"

"Just a wild guess," I joked. "Actually, I know there was gold being smuggled on the ship that took me from Barbados to Guatemala."

"What makes you say that?"

"I snuck into the cargo hold and saw it. In fact I touched it and scraped the bars with a nail. It was gold all right."

"Are you—"

"I'm sure, Izzy. Could you get word to a friend of mine, the police inspector in Bridgetown that I was telling you about earlier, Inspector Lance Williams?"

"Can he be trusted?"

"Let's put it this way. I'd bet my life on it."

"And you may be doing just that," Izzy replied. "What is it that you want me to tell him?"

"Tell him that I believe . . . No, that I know, that gold bullion is being smuggled out of Barbados in bars on a regular basis on the Tropic Carib. Also tell him that I ran into Mr. Musgrave at the state department building in Guatemala City. Tell him that less than a day after I ran into Mr. M. I was attacked. Tell him that if he follows the trail of gold bullion or Mr. Musgrave I think he will find they are one and the same."

Izzy wrote down the most important points I made. "Yes, I remember you telling me something about that before lunch. I'll tell you the worst part about all this, Lili. I think the trail may lead right through that gate." He pointed down our driveway.

I wasn't ready for that part. I couldn't allow the conversation to move in that direction. I asked, "How about your dispute with the bar association, Izzy? How does that stand?"

"They put it on hold until your civil case is resolved but now I'm not sure what they'll do since that may be delayed for another year or two. They can't afford to have a loose cannon like me out there giving a bad name to the legal profession."

"C'mon, Izzy. If you're a loose cannon then the bar needs lots more artillery like you. You're a credit to the profession. You're the best lawyer I've ever met and that's why I hired you."

"It all sounds very nice," Izzy said. "But I doubt they'll see it that way."

"What can I do to help you? I'll do anything. I'd give my life for you, my friend. I know you're fighting against some powerful adversaries—-often adversaries without faces. Are you sure you're not in danger?"

"I know that I am, and . . ." this time Izzy looked like he was looking for a place where a microphone might be hidden. "I've taken precautions. I've taken strong precautions—to see that should anything ever happen to me, all the evidence I have at my disposal will be preserved and immediately turned over to the proper authorities."

"To Mr. Noble, the Kaua'i County D.A.?"

"No, to the Feds. Lili, the only thing that's ever going to stop these shenanigans is the direct involvement of the U.S. government. Do you remember hearing about the Abscam scandal in California or the way the Feds went into Louisiana and straightened out their elections? Well, that's what has to happen here for us to have any chance at government that is responsive to the people."

Izzy went on but I had a hard time concentrating even though I agreed his points were vitally important. My thoughts had drifted to "the black man" in Barbados that María had mentioned in her letter.

*Why hasn't **he** written?*

And the black Jesus. It was funny María should mention that. I remember seeing a long line at the *Catedral Metropolitana* and wondering where it led. And what was really mysterious was that once the people got to the head of the line and did whatever they did there they backed out of the church, never turning away from the statue. It was eerie.

So I stood in line for almost two hours, dancing from foot to foot to keep my knees from giving out. I asked people outside the church about it but the ones I approached only spoke Spanish and by the time I got into the church I didn't feel it was appropriate to disturb their silent prayer.

Later on I learned the statue was a replica of the Black Christ of Esquipulas, unwittingly carved from balsam, a dark wood, and the church had no idea how it would be revered. I got in the long line and got all the way to the front but when I saw it was my turn to kiss the feet of the Black Jesus, I couldn't do it. I couldn't bend down on one knee and kiss its feet.

It wasn't that I didn't feel reverent toward the church, or its parishioners, or even the Black Christ for that matter. It was that I had found the icon to be too powerful and I was scared. I wondered if the statue was a sign that I should marry Lance or that my hesitancy to kiss its feet meant I should not. I became scared and confused and left.

"Oh, Izzy!"

"Yes."

"By the way, when you contact Inspector Williams, please tell him to check inside the wall behind the loose paneling in Emma's room. He'll know what I mean."

* * *

I surmised that whenever George Santini wanted something, he usually got it. Unlike Lance—where the subject of Lili Kaleo was concerned—George appeared to know exactly what he wanted and acted on it. We spent the better part of the next two or three weeks between the smooth black satin sheets of his massive mahogany bed. I was under his spell and overwhelmed that he would use his enormous power to protect me.

He, or someone on his staff, had an artistic touch because there were candles lit throughout the room with some placed in tiers behind the bed, like an altar. When the weather cooled at night we also had a fire in the fireplace and read or caressed one another and bathed. I took to quilting again in the manner that Aunty Fay had taught me many years earlier. This time appropriating quilting fabric and supplies was no problem and I decided to start a quilt for Kuha'o, the newborn child of Mimo and Ruth that Izzy had told me about on his visit.

As the fire reflected off my skin George commented that laying there naked, he would have mistaken me for a goddess next to the fires of Pele. For a brief moment, I thought about Lance's humble abode with his cute little four poster bed, usually piled high with clothes and the sound of children frolicking down the hall.

Otherwise after the meeting with Izzy I didn't give much thought to Lance. My mind was too preoccupied with savoring the attention I was getting from the rich and famous, or some said "infamous," labor leader. Izzy had been so bold as to tell me that he had heard on reliable authority—through one of his colleagues—that the grounds for George's divorce included wife beatings. But when I asked George about it, in as subtle and non threatening a manner as I could, he said there were always malicious rumors about public figures and I certainly could identify with that.

When I asked him why he got divorced, he said, "Beth refused to meet her 'wifely responsibilities.'"

I suspected I knew what that meant and I could see that with his voracious appetite that might be a problem.

And when I asked him if it were true that he had gotten an annulment, he said, "Yes, the Holy See (referring to those in the church hierarchy, who made such decisions), were magnanimous in providing us with an annulment."

I said, "But hadn't you consummated the marriage? I mean you had children together . . . ."

George explained to me. "Sugar, you try your best to persuade people to see things your way and, if they don't, you do your best to help them come around to your point of view. That's all I did. At first, they refused. Then I built them a monastery. As the bricks and mortar were being laid and completion of the project came into doubt they gradually came around to my way of thinking."

Whenever I had a question or concern that George couldn't or chose not to address, he took me into bed and we developed better understandings of one another on the shiny, smooth surface of the black satin sheets. I couldn't eat or sleep. He was all I could think about.

Chapter Seventeen

One day George asked me whether or not I'd like to have children. I said, "Yes, I'd love to have children. I can't think of anything in the world that I'd find more fulfilling than having another child." I especially wanted a daughter. No one could ever replace Christian. So I thought the best place to start one day, when I had a chance, would be with a daughter.

George said, "Not just one. I mean *lots* of children. I'd like to have an heir, several of them in fact, but Beth has poisoned my son and daughter against me. Do you think you would ever like to have children with me?"

This caught me completely off guard. When I left Guatemala Maria had placed six different sizes of diaphragms (since I didn't have a chance to be fitted for one), several dozen condoms, assorted creams and jellies and so forth into my backpack in the same package as the St. Christopher's medal. George knew that I was excusing myself from time to time to put in a diaphragm. So I was surprised when he said this. I had assumed he didn't want children. "Well, yes. One day perhaps, after we get to know one another better, I'd consider having children with you. They certainly wouldn't want for anything."

"Certainly not for a beautiful and courageous mother," he said. He always seemed to know just the right thing to say under every circumstance. "Then we'd better get married at once," he said. "Our biological clocks are ticking."

"That's it?" I replied. "No engagement, no proposal, just 'we'd better get married' because of our clocks?"

He got down on one knee, took my hand and said in '*Ōlelo Hawai'i* / traditional Hawaiian, "*Kalili'i*, meaning the dainty one,"*E hō'ao no 'oe ia'u?* / Will you marry me?"

"Yes," I said without thinking. "Yes. Well, er . . . , I'll have to think about it."

"Which is it, my darling?" He asked. "Yes now, or you'll have to think it over and then say, 'yes.'"

The way he said the word "darling" sounded really sweet. "I mean both. Well, I mean . . . I'm not sure what I mean. I mean, well, er-, yes, George Santini. I'll marry you."

He picked up the phone and called for my engagement ring to be brought from the safe. They must have brought it in a wheelbarrow. The diamond was so big that from that day forward my left hand hung closer to the ground than my right. "This is merely a trinket," he said, as he slipped the ring onto my finger. "Your wedding ring will have to be brought over from my estate in Portugal. It's in a family vault. It once belonged to my beloved mother. It's simple, but sacred to me."

* * *

With barely a month to plan for the wedding and a budget of "whatever you can manage to spend in five weeks," there was a lot to require my attention. The decorations, my dress, the bridesmaids and their dresses, the invitations, the cake, the entertainment, the honeymoon—although George said he would take care of that and surprise me. I was to "pack for a Mediterranean climate." This in turn meant shopping for a whole new wardrobe. There were at least a dozen other things I must be forgetting.

In the midst of this—it came like a dousing with cold water on a hot day—George had an antenuptial agreement prepared as a condition precedent to the marriage. I guess I should have expected something like this from a man of so much wealth and power. But when it came I was shocked. I knew he could trust me and I said,

"If you don't trust me, maybe we shouldn't get married at all."

"You don't have to worry about a divorce," he said. "Beth's walking out on me was a source of great embarrassment and I'm not going to allow it again. Only *death* will do *us* part."

A chill ran down my spine. *Don't be silly. He's only joking.*

"This document is just to establish that I am to manage all of my affairs and assets privately without interference or intervention. When I die all I have will belong to you and our beloved children."

Just when things seemed to be going in the wrong direction the man made perfect sense. But when he asked me to sign the agreement and have it notarized, stating that I had reviewed and discussed it with my attorney, I balked.

Once again he said the perfectly reasonable thing. "By all means go over it with Kawamoto. I have made arrangements for him to receive a copy and trust he has already begun reviewing it on your behalf. You and he should schedule an appointment to go over it."

For a man who had previously shown hesitation at me seeing Izzy he showed a remarkable change of heart and dialed in the code for long distance, got Izzy on the phone and handed it to me.

Izzy said, "No, I haven't seen it yet, but I'm in Kaua'i today. It could have arrived in Honolulu a couple of days ago and I wouldn't know it yet. By the way, congratulations!"

I heard him say "congratulations" but it didn't sound sincere. Of course George had dialed him so he may not have felt free to be himself.

* * *

When Izzy insisted on meeting me for lunch instead of coming to the ranch I had in mind somewhere extra special, such as Huggo's with a beautiful view of Kona Bay. But George impressed upon me that it wasn't a good idea to travel so far. It would be difficult to protect me on the open road. So we went to the Bamboo Restaurant in Hawi, which is a fine restaurant although it doesn't have such a commanding view.

I had hoped Tiny would not go with us but he did. George reminded me that it hadn't been all that long since people had tried to take my life and, even on a simple outing like this, being sensible and taking precautions was a good idea. Tiny joined us in the restaurant but agreed to sit on the opposite side of the room. Still this did not make Izzy feel comfortable so I asked Tiny to go and get us both a shave ice and that it would be my treat.

He said, "Okay, I'll be right back."

I said, "Tiny, my lawyer and I need time to talk . . . alone. Can we have some privacy? I promise I'll be here when you get back and I'll be okay. So take your time, all right?"

Tiny had a tender heart where I was concerned. I knew right off that he enjoyed pleasing me. He did as I asked at what I perceived might be his own peril. I resolved then and there to avoid doing anything that might put him into disfavor with George or get him into any sort of trouble that I could not erase.

With that and an order of chicken saté pot stickers that we shared, Izzy and I got down to business.

"Well, what do you think?" I asked.

"Are you really sure you want to know what I think?"

"Of course," I said. "That's why I'm paying you."

"Lili you haven't paid— "

"Just kidding. If I were paying you—and I will. . . . George said that he would pick up the tab for all the charges on this agreement, including your plane ticket to get here. I have found George to be a man of his word."

Izzy said, "George knows how the game is played. I'll give him credit for that. Lili, if you really want to know what I think, I think you should not only not marry this man but leave here right this minute while your bodyguard—or should I say jailer— is gone. Get as far away from here as you can. That's what I think."

"C'mon," I replied. "Tell me how you really feel. I hate it when you sugar coat things."

Izzy looked at me like a nene. "What?"

"Just kidding, Izzy. Don't you know when I'm joking? Things are perfectly fine between me and George. He's never been anything but a perfect gentlemen."

"Lili, it's not funny. There are about a dozen strike breakers they found mired in cement under Rainbow Stadium who aren't laughing."

"I know. I read about that. How awful. But George says, 'For every event that takes place the authorities have to find a scapegoat and nine times out of ten, when that involves a labor matter, that scapegoat is me.

If I did everything they accused me of I'd have to be as much of a magician as Harry Houdini, the great escape artist.'"

"I wouldn't be so sure of his innocence," Izzy said. "I want to tell you something, even though you'll probably say it's preposterous." He had a look of consternation on his face.

"Go ahead, Izzy. You'll still be my friend no matter what. You know that."

Izzy continued, "In preparing for your trial and making such progress as I could in your absence I took it upon myself to interview the jurors in your criminal case."

"Can you do that? Is it legal?"

"Yes, if they don't object, and I'll have to admit that most of them did object but I managed to talk to four or five of the others."

"And . . . ?"

"And, I made the most startling discovery."

"Which is . . .?"

"You know how we both marveled at the end of the trial about what a great and persuasive lawyer I had been?"

"Yes," I nodded for him to continue. That was true. He had done an incredibly good job.

"You remember the guy with the mustache who wore the shell lei?"

I nodded again.

"Well he told me that on the next to the last ballot the vote was eleven to one in favor of your conviction and that he had been the lone holdout."

"Really? It's amazing that they made a complete turnaround and eventually voted for my acquittal."

"What's even more amazing is that the foreman, Mr. Murphy, told me the jurors were all on the fence. There wasn't one who didn't think you were innocent from the very beginning, except maybe for Mrs. Gonzales, the woman who had worked on the governor's campaign. But they were also mindful that if they didn't do the governor's bidding they would miss out on all the lucrative contracts and deals that might come along on the island over the next five or ten years."

"You're kidding."

"Lili, you know I'm not kidding."

"But they did vote for me. Look at me—I'm free." I held out my arms to show him. "Look, no handcuffs!"

"Are you free?"

"What's that supposed to mean?"

"Are you really free? Can you get up from this table right now and walk out of here of your own free will?"

"Absolutely."

"Then by God, do it. Do it for me. Do it for Suzie. Do it for Aunty Fay and Mimo and Ruth. Do it for everyone who loves you."

"Izzy, I'm only being protected." *Izzy's jealous. That's why he's making all these petty remarks about George.*

"Someone's being protected, but it's not you."

I said, "Izzy, don't be ridiculous. I *am* being protected."

We stared at each other. Neither of us had touched our pot stickers.

Izzy said, "Let me finish the story about the jurors. All of a sudden through the deputy in charge of the jury word came down that you were to be acquitted."

"From heaven? From the stars? What do you mean, 'came down?'"

"You might say 'from on high,' or you might say 'from George Santini.'"

"No," I shook my head.

"Yes," Izzy shook his.

"How do you know?"

He reached for my hand. "You know, Lili. You already know the answer and you're still asking."

"But those are just rumors. That Hawaiian Mafia warning business is just a hoax."

"Okay, try me. Make one guess and we'll see if you're right." He let go of my hand and leaned back in his chair.

"Someone handed them a plumeria, the *make* man's [dead man's] flower, with a fish hook in it, carved out of white bone. Is that what they say happened?"

"That's exactly what happened and once they saw it they knew they'd better change their votes or end up providing underground support for some athletic facility."

"I don't believe it."

"Well, you'd best believe it! After I got this information from Mr. Murphy, I managed to confirm it with three or four other jurors."

"And the rest of the jury?"

"They all say it's preposterous and never happened."

"Let me see if I understand this correctly. The jury voted eight-to-four or seven-to-five—that what you're telling me is preposterous and yet you expect *me* to believe it? I've always had my doubts about Murphy and so have you. If you'd asked me to pick someone out of the jury box who was wacko, it would have been Murphy . . . . That's why we called him Mad Dog in grammar school. Remember?"

"Lili, that's not the point. The point is that his story makes perfect sense and it's been corroborated. You know how things are done in Hawaii. You know the facts of life here in the islands. It's cooperate with the powers that be, no matter what, no matter how much it turns your stomach, or perish. You know it but you're in no frame of mind to hear the truth."

"The truth, yes. Idle conjecture, no. Even if all this were true what could we do about it? Do you honestly believe that you and I could alter the system of perks and balances?"

"Do you remember that night, that first night Suzie went to her piano lesson and you and I met at the Russian fort, as lovers in the moonlight?"

"Yes, and I want to apologize for what happened there, or rather, didn't. I've felt terrible about it for years—"

"I don't care about that. Not now. I'm thinking about the pledges we made to one another that we would each commit ourselves, our lives, to doing something worthwhile. To making a difference. A difference for the better, each in our own way. Has that changed for you?"

"No, of course not. That's what I'm about—now more than ever. And with all the resources I'm about to have available— "

"With all the resources you're going to have available you may as well have been convicted and gone to prison because that's where you're going to be. That's where you are now."

"What would you have me do? I mean if I were to try to change things. What is it you think I should be doing that I haven't done already?"

"I'd ask you to help me instigate a federal investigation. I've had time to consider all this and I've come to the conclusion that the only reason you were acquitted in your criminal trial was because George Santini was afraid that if you were found guilty with the whole world watching there would undoubtedly be a federal investigation. That's what he was trying to prevent—not your going to jail."

I felt a dagger penetrate my heart. I couldn't stand to hear this. I didn't want to deal with it. How could this possibly be true? It couldn't be, not fourteen days before my wedding to the man whose attributes and resources were well beyond my wildest dreams. He had used his powers to protect me. He said he would make me incredibly happy. That was my reality and I didn't need Izzy to disturb this and ruin my happiness before it ever began.

"Right will prevail in the end," I said.

"You mean the end justifies the means?" Izzy replied.

"That's not what I said."

"Being passive doesn't cut it, Lili, and you know it. You've got to be proactive."

"That's not it at all," I said.

"Then what is it?"

"Izzy, if I thought you were right about George being the person you've described, that the press has described, that seems to be the *public* perception, I wouldn't marry him in ten million— "

Izzy opened his mouth to speak but I leaned forward, reached across the table and put my finger to his lips, "*¡Silencio!* Hear me out," I whispered. I leaned back in my seat. "Whatever his public persona there's another side to him. I've seen it. I know it from being close to him. I know it in my heart. George Santini would not harm anyone he didn't see as a threat and he certainly knows how to take good care of his friends."

"I agree with the last point," Izzy said. "But I'm not so sure about the others."

I noticed Tiny had come back and was once again seated over by the window. I don't think he was listening. He had the blue dye from his bubble gum shave ice on his chin and I had an urge to walk over with a napkin and clean it off. I saw him give my cherry shave ice to our waitress and tell her to take it to the kitchen and freeze it until we were finished.

Izzy continued, "Lili, I just don't want to see you get in any deeper."

"Deeper than what?" I replied. "I'm already in love with the man. How can you get in any deeper than that?"

"Do you think he loves you?"

"Of course he does," I said. "Otherwise, why would he want to marry me? And ask me to have his children?"

Izzy looked startled. "You're not preg— "

"Of course not," I said. "What kind of a fool do you think I am? This is the nineties, Izzy." I hadn't told him about the weeks of carelessness with Lance when the subject of birth control had never once crossed my mind.

"Fool enough to walk right into a disaster," Izzy said. "You want to know why he's marrying you?"

"I already know, but you can tell me why *you think* it is."

"He's marrying you because you are a folk hero in these islands and you command a strong political base. He's marrying you because you're of Hawaiian ancestry and that's important to the workers. You're the perfect trophy bride for a man like him. I'll admit you're beautiful, and that may be a part of it, but a more compelling consideration is that he's having a hard time holding his political base together. He almost lost the last election. Tommy 'Boom Boom' Mickelson came within three votes. With you at his side the political balance will change in his favor. That's why."

"I don't want to hear any more of this," I said. "The man loves me and I know it. He puts our relationship way above any political considerations. Women have a way of knowing these things. Let's go over the document he sent you so I can get back to the ranch."

Izzy looked at me but didn't say a word—not with his tongue. His face, however, said, "See, I told you. Listen to what you've just said, 'so I can get back to the ranch.'"

After a long pause, he said, "I'm not sure where to begin. You probably already know what I'm about to say so let's cut to the chase."

"Please," I said. "Please do." I looked at the clock on the wall. It was getting late and Tiny was beginning to look edgy. He was running his palm up and down his arms, sitting up in his chair and glancing over at us with increasing frequency.

"Lili, don't sign this agreement and don't marry this man. That's the best advice I can give you as your friend and as your lawyer."

I said, "Izzy, you've made at least one good point."

He looked up at me, as if to say, "What's that?"

"You've just made me realize that I'm going to sign that document no matter what it says and I'm better off not knowing what's in it. Could you please just sign there where it says you're my attorney and you've advised me about it, explained its terms?"

"Are you sure, Lili? Are you sure that's what you want me to do?"

"Yes, I'm sure. And you know me, once I've made up my mind . . ."

"I do. And that's the only reason I would ever consider signing it. Are you sure that's what you want from me—no explanation, no review, no advice?"

"You've already given me your advice, which is don't marry the man, but I'm not about to miss out on the opportunity of a lifetime, based on idle conjecture and a few skittish jurors."

I could tell Izzy was distraught. I changed my tone and my tack. I leaned forward and put my hand on his arm. "I'm asking you as my friend."

"Lili Kaleo, of all the things you've ever asked of me, this, and this alone, is the most difficult. I'd sooner help you blow up another pipeline."

"Shh!" I said. "You know what you always say about the walls."

Izzy said, "I think the statute of limitations has long since run on that madness."

We laughed.

I said, "C'mon, Izzy. Give me your blessing. I've got to be getting back."

Izzy took a pen out of his jacket pocket and signed the papers. He handed them to me for my signature. "This doesn't mean you have my endorsement of this debacle, Lili Kaleo. I signed these as your friend, not as your lawyer. As a lawyer I would have told you to burn those papers. I would sooner burn with them than sign them."

I took his pen and signed them just above his signature saying he had advised me as to their content. I gave them back for him to forward to George's attorneys. I summoned Tiny over to the table and told him I was ready to go. I took him, my shave ice, my copy of the document and walked towards the door. I turned and looked back just before we went outside.

Izzy said, "Don't worry about the check, I'll get it. Tell George I took a taxi back to the airport."

* * *

For some reason I felt depressed when I got back to the ranch but once again, George had all the right things to say.

He was totally sympathetic. "I understand," he said. "Going over a document like that must have been daunting, even with a bright young lawyer like Kawamoto. And I can see where you'd have doubts about it. It was only with extreme reluctance and the prodding of my own attorneys that I ever considered asking you to sign it. Beth and I had no such document and our parting was ten times worse than it could have been had we had things worked out in advance."

He seemed sincere and compassionate and I must have looked distant and depressed. Strangely we both acknowledged a sexual tension at that moment.

We went into the bedroom and I lifted my dress and held it over my back and he pulled down my panties and entered me from behind. By the time he was doing it for the second or third time I found myself on my hands and knees on the bed. He reached around and massaged my nipples and kissed and nibbled at me on the side of my neck. His thrusting felt magnificent. He shrieked loudly each time he climaxed and by then, I felt strangely at peace with whatever role he might have in mind for me.

Chapter Eighteen

We quickly sent out the wedding invitations, but I didn't know where to send the one for Daddy. George dialed in the code and invited me to call Aunty Fay to find out but even that didn't work. She had no idea where he was. George put his attorneys on it who in turn hired an investigator and the only information they could come up with was that he was last seen preaching the gospel from a small podium he carried with him in front of the International Marketplace in Honolulu.

According to their reconnaissance he would stand on that soapbox on the sidewalk on Kalakaua Street for hours at a time reading scriptures and extolling the virtues of the Bible and of following Jesus to all those who might be passing by. The reports of him when told to experts (George never did anything second class) left them with the impression that he might be suffering from dementia from his years of drinking excessively and that his brain might be permanently damaged as a result. In spite of everything he had ever done to me and my siblings it still hurt to hear this diagnosis and think of the huge, magnificent wedding I was going to have without Daddy there to give me away.

Sometime in early March Daddy abruptly quit going to the marketplace and no one had seen him since.

* * *

At my request there were no showers for me. After
all what would I ever need that George couldn't buy?
However I asked if some of my best women friends and
cherished relatives could come a few days early so we
could visit together prior to the blessed event. George, as
usual, was his same, gracious self. "Certainly," he said to
another of my many requests.

On the Wednesday before my Saturday wedding I
was with George in his chambers. He was getting dressed
when all of a sudden the alarms went off. They were loud
and penetrating. It sounded like one of those civil air patrol
sirens in Honolulu. I couldn't imagine what was
happening.

George said, "Head for the bunker," as he threw on
his fatigues and ran out the door to the front of the house. I
hoped he wasn't being foolish. *Isn't the front the most
vulnerable spot?*

Talk about being foolish I was too curious to go to
the bunker as George had suggested, although I'll admit I
was interested in having another look at whatever was in
there. This day, though, I was even more interested in what
was going on out front.

All the commotion seemed to be at checkpoint one,
the main gate. I always thought those glass windows were
vulnerable. I watched from the front of the house, hidden
behind some oleanders. From between their leaves and in
view of the downhill grade to the gate I could see one of
those big horse-hauling trucks—a white one that seemed to
have the whole road by the rows of ironwoods blocked in
both directions. It was long—two trailers and white. *What
in the world is going on?*

As I watched a group—or should I say company—
of men came running out of the bunker in bulletproof vests
and hard hats—actually more like helmets than hard hats.
They had rifles and streamed in columns from two different
directions. A helicopter that had been just about to land
took off and reversed its direction. Even from the front of
the house and out onto the lawn and the driveway I could
hear the sirens.

Then all of a sudden they stopped. The company of
men double-timed back towards the bunker and George
came sauntering up the driveway. "I guess it can't have
been too important," I said to myself and came out from
behind the bushes. The engines of the big truck with the

horse trailers started to scream and then its twelve or sixteen or however many gears it had started to be run through and it gradually lumbered on past our place and in the direction of the Upolu Airport.

I jumped up and down and ran and hugged George. "You're all right! You're all right! Tell me what happened."

"There's a crazy woman down there who claims to be your aunt. The driver of the truck says he gave her a lift from Hilo, where she was walking alongside the road, and brought her up here to see you. When one of the men thought it sounded preposterous and insisted on frisk—, I mean searching her—you know patting her down for weapons, she got hostile and kicked him in the nuts."

I laughed.

"Then when he bent over wheezing she gave him a rabbit punch in the back of the neck and was just about to hit him over the head with his flashlight when two of the other men grabbed her . . . ."

"Aunty Fay!" I yelled. "It's my Aunty Fay! I hope they didn't hurt her." I ran down the driveway.

"Not likely," George yelled after me. "Not likely they hurt *her*."

When I got there about six men were trying to fit Aunty Fay into a straight jacket. She was kicking or biting whoever came near. Another man was just getting ready to give her a shot.

"Put down that needle! Let go of her!" I yelled. "That's my Aunty Fay. You can't do this!"

The men stopped at the sound of my voice. They looked askance. They let go of her and the one who appeared to be in charge finally said, "Okay, then you try to reason with her. Tell her she can't enter the grounds without being searched."

I ran up and hugged her. "Aunty Fay. Aunty Fay," I said. "She needn't be searched. I'll vouch for her."

The men looked at her and looked at the ground and finally the one who appeared to be the leader nodded his assent.

I said, "You men apologize to her. This is my Aunty Fay." I hugged her.

After what seemed like an eternity one of them stepped forward and said, "Sorry Ma'am but we thought you was an intruder."

"I no 'tink you going have lots a people fo' bottah wit' if you keep ac'ing laddat wit' dem," Aunty Fay quipped. "No one goin' come ovah da way you act."

* * *

I had Aunty Fay to myself for almost an entire day before Suzie came. After the first couple of hours with her I wished I had insisted that everyone come much earlier and spend at least a week. George was very understanding and left us to ourselves.

"Eh, dis place get cats, oh wot?" she asked me shortly after her arrival.

I said, "I think there are a few down in the stable but none in the main house."

"What kine man no like cats?" she asked.

I was at a loss as to what to say. "Well, Aunty Fay, he has a lot of other good qualities."

"Like wot?" she asked. "Go. You tell me da kine good stuff about 'em."

"Well, he's kind and attentive, handsome— "

"I seen dat," Aunty Fay interrupted. "So, go on, 'den."

"He's industrious. He's managed to build all this after starting out life as the bastard son of a vineyard owner."

Aunty Fay said, "You watch dat bastard son-a-magun. Your own faddah, who is my braddah, he one bastard buggah too, and look wea he when en' up."

I thought she had a point but a vague and difficult one to evaluate. From time to time over the past couple of days I had gone over my conversation with Izzy at the Bamboo Restaurant and hoped I hadn't offended him. In the end I decided that his judgment was obscured by his continuing love for me—a love that had brought us to a conjugal bed where it was never consummated. But when Aunty Fay expressed any doubt—any doubt whatsoever I had resolved to listen more carefully.

I went on, "He wants to have children."

"Das a good 'ting, Sugah. You going be one good maddah."

I took that statement as her definitive endorsement of the prospect of matrimony between George Santini and me and was careful not to bring up subsequent points that might reopen and confuse the issue.

She did caution, however, "Das good he know how fo' take kea you, but, das not how love is all about, you know. You can nevah fo'get dis."

We talked about Lance Williams and my experiences in Barbados and I gave her a general idea as to what had gone on with the black police officer.

I was surprised to hear Aunty Fay say, "Maybe you nevah undastand me, or maybe you when change small kine, or some'ting. But, I no remembah saying da Pōpolo guy no good 'cause his skin calah no can wash off, or wot evah."

But all of that was academic now that I had decided to cast my lot with George. I still had feelings for Lance and I knew it—deep down under all the layers of joy and excitement this prospective change in my marital status had brought me. But I figured that was all behind me now—not to mention nearly six thousand miles, two oceans and a continent away.

* * *

Next it was Suzie's turn to arrive. She was still dressed as prim and proper as always—long white linen shorts with a matching blouse under a mottled blue zip up sweater, smooth navy blue leather loafers with oblique toes and light blue socks that rose above her ankles. She also carried her ever-present cotton canvas tote bag.

When she had worked on my mayoral campaign she had been ten years behind in fashion and now that she was still wearing the same thing, it had become nearly twenty. But I loved her just the same as if she were dressed like Miss Hawaii. She arrived on Thursday afternoon with far less fanfare than Aunty Fay.

We spent our time in the garden and in the sauna— the three of us, eating and drinking and being merry. When Aunty Fay seemed to be getting weary of the festivities Suzie and I went horseback riding and left her to work on the quilt I had started for Mimo and Ruth's new baby.

As Suzie and I rode through the rolling hills, I said, "What do you think of all this, Suzie? Can you believe that in only two days it will all be mine?"

"I think it's lovely, Lili—leaves little to be desired and I can't think of anyone more deserving."

"Girl, that's a relief. After what Izzy had to say to me I was afraid— "

"Oh, I'm not saying you should marry this man. I'm only saying that the setting is gorgeous and the amenities exquisite. Very tastefully done."

"Then you don't think I should marry him?"

"I can't say, Lili. I've only just met the man and he is very charming, seems intelligent and handsome . . . Yes, he's *very* handsome."

"What do you think, then? What does your intuition tell you?"

"My gut feeling is that Izzy thinks these men are hoodlums—bums, organized criminals, Mafioso and Izzy is usually right about such things."

"Hmm, well, of course, those would be some things to consider before walking down the aisle and all. But do you think maybe Izzy is biased about all this? I mean, because . . . well, you know, because he and I were almost lovers."

Suzie's horse whinnied and we pulled up alongside one another on a butte overlooking the Kohala Range and the rolling hills and winding road to the north. It was majestic and the warm gentle breeze that had accompanied us on our ride caressed us.

"I won't lie to you, Lili. He was devastated when Kiku called and broke up your romantic evening. And when she came back he was sullen and depressed for weeks. Sometimes men are disappointed when their wives leave them. This time it was his wife returning that ruined his day."

"You can say that again."

Suzie caught my humor and laughed politely. She blushed and said, "He's still got it bad for you, Lili. But you won't say anything to him about it—you won't act on it—I mean for the sake of the children and all? I fear that if you did he would leave his wife and children for you, even now."

"Of course I won't say anything. And I certainly won't act on it. Suzie, I love your brother, just as you do—but as a brother, nothing more. I wouldn't do anything to harm him or his family. You know that."

"That's what I figured. It's the only reason I felt I could tell you."

* * *

Suzie and Aunty Fay and I partied on with Mai Tai's and pupu's and ice cream and sushi and anything that met our whim or fancy. At first we were served by the pixies. I introduced them to Roxanne, the striking beauty with black hair, milky white skin and coal black eyes. Her white skin was stunningly accentuated when it contrasted with her black chambermaid outfit. At first I thought she wore too much red lipstick but on further reflection it made her seem more vivid.

If one of the pixies had half a brain, it was she. The others came and went early on during our visit but gradually became more and more scarce and were entirely replaced by the older women as the wedding drew near.

Aunty Fay, Suzie and I spent most of our time reminiscing or talking about the wedding or more trivial matters than we had when they first arrived. I think we all took it as a given that I was to be married on Saturday at two in the afternoon and adjusted our conversation to things which had not yet been decided.

By Friday morning, Ruth, my sister-in-law, Mimo's wife had arrived, along with Stephanie (Goodman) Dreyfuss, Fanny (Martin) McNicols and Tami Kapika, who was still unmarried. Yes I had a weak moment and broke down and invited Tami. I've always hated to do anything I thought would hurt anyone's feelings and it seemed like a small price to invite her. She was certainly attractive enough to have a husband and the men in the compound drooled over her so I figured she had been inept at hiding those nasty personality traits which we all knew teemed just below the surface. She had obviously subscribed to the wonders of cosmetic surgery and dressed like a whore. She got more than her share of catcalls from "the men."

George greeted each of my guests as they arrived and spent a few minutes entertaining while he escorted them to my suite. He was most charming and tried to accommodate the modest requests any of them had, like showing them where the nearest bathroom was located or taking their wraps or scarves. At around nine p.m. George retired for the evening and said he couldn't wait to see me in the morning. He gave me a little peck on the cheek and left.

We sang and danced and played loud music and carried on like a bunch of teenagers. By the time Elayne Headley, my associate from the Bank of Barbados, arrived around ten p.m., I must have been three sheets to the wind. I had asked George to invite her to the pre-wedding party but I had no idea she would actually come. He had made arrangements to fly her to the Big Island on his G-3 when it was in Bridgetown "to pick up some pharmaceuticals."

"I have to talk to you," she said, as I hugged her on the way in. "I've got to talk to you immediately."

"Sure," I said. "But we've got to wait for the party to wind down." She seemed alarmed and I would have gone off with her right away but I had to wait for the alcohol to wear off. She could have told me anything and I wouldn't have been able to process it the way things were at that moment.

By two a.m. the party ended. We noticed that the pixies had disappeared a little after dinner and after the elderly maids had also retired we had to fend for ourselves. But we had a blast.

Aunty Fay said, "I telling you, Sugah, da pixies is da man's harem. Dey when go entatain da mastah and das when dey when go disappeah."

I was embarrassed at having her think that, let alone mention it in front of my friends, especially Tami. "Nonsense," I said. "I'll admit they're beautiful—"

"And voluptuous!" Tami said.

"But you have to understand George. He loves things of beauty. He wouldn't flirt with the help. I've never seen him flirt with any of them, not even once." That wasn't entirely true but I didn't want to admit it. Besides whatever he had done before we got involved was his business as I saw it. "I'm intending to speak with him while we're on our honeymoon and see if we can place them in other households."

"Eh, dat place gotta be one brothel," Aunty Fay said.

"Aunty Fay, you're too cynical. I know George and I know he wouldn't risk our marriage on the likes of them." I had told myself all along that the reason he kept them around was because they were collectively too stupid to remember and divulge any of his secrets and I was confident I was right about that. But Aunty Fay's comments did get me to thinking.

* * *

It was almost four in the morning before Elayne and I got a chance to sit down and talk. A couple of my friends, two lesbians, teammates of mine from the University of Hawaii volleyball squad, were still howling and carrying on in the garden so we had to go to the sun porch to chat.

I held her hand, barely able to sit up and keep my eyes open. "What is it Elayne? Gee, it's great to have you here.   What's   so   important?"

"I thought you should know. He's still in love with you."

"Who's in love with me?"

"Don't be silly. Barbados' most eligible bachelor, that's who!"

"How do you know?" It didn't seem relevant anymore but I knew I would enjoy hearing the details.

She said, "It's all over the Garrison Fitness Center. That's all they've been talking about since you left—how you, of all people, had the audacity to jilt Lance Williams and how broken hearted he is over it."

"But Elayne, I never jilted him. I had to run for my life."

"He knows that. He's also been very successful in his investigation since you left. They're talking about promoting him to Deputy Superintendent after the bank credit card prosecutions— "

"Credit card prosecutions? At the bank? The Bank of Barbados?"

"Yes, I thought you knew. There was enough information in those files you gave him to send Mr. Baker and Miss Cumberbatch into Glendairy until both of their mustaches are white. I thought you knew!"

I was so tired that I yawned in spite of the good news. "No, I didn't."

"When I found out I was coming here—to your wedding I went to see him."

"Does he know I'm getting mar— "

"If he does he didn't find out from me and he didn't mention it so I don't think so."

Whew! That's good news! I said, "What did he say?

"He said that now that he's got Mr. Baker and Miss Cumberbatch behind bars and several of the other VIP's at the bank he thinks he's very close to solving Ephraim's murder. He's not sure he'll ever get the "knife" or "trigger" man, whatever you want to call him, but he's pretty sure he knows who arranged the hit."

Then he must have decided it wasn't me. I shuddered at the visual image I had seen of the way Ephraim's murder had been carried out by "some sick-o"

—the viciousness, the reveling in his blood and the removal of his unmentionables. It made me sick to think about it.

"Yes, Lili, that's the word he used— 'hit.'" This time it was Elayne's turn to hold my hand. She scooted closer and put her arm around me.

"Did he have anything to say to me? Did he know where you were going?"

"He knows I was coming to see you but he doesn't know exactly where—Hawaii, yes, but the Big Island, no. I don't think he knows one Hawaiian island from another."

There was a bright moon, nearly full, and at that moment it was so bright that it seemed like mid afternoon. I was beginning to feel awake—a burst of adrenaline.

Elayne continued, "He said to tell you that you are in no danger of being prosecuted in Barbados, that was all a smoke screen to confuse the enemy. He said that you may be in more danger now than you realize and that those who you think are your friends may really be your enemies. Watch your backside and give him a call as soon as you can. He said he's tried to reach you several times and is working with an FBI agent in Miami to solicit their cooperation, which he says has already been forthcoming. Here, he gave me the agent's card in case you ever need to get in touch with him."

She handed me a small, white business card which I stuck in my bra.

"Lance said he was about to post a letter to your lawyer with a good deal more information."

"Is that all? Did he say when I would get the letter?"

Elayne said, "No, he just said he was about to send it and that he feared that his own life may be in danger."

I was distraught. "Elayne, why didn't you bring it with you? Why didn't you bring me the letter?"

Currents of nausea ran through my body.

Elayne held my head while I heaved my Mai Tai's and pupu's. She patted me on the back and waited until I was done.

Then she continued, "Lili, the people who 'invited' me here looked like they should have had names like Lenny "the trouble maker" and Guido "the bouncer," if you know what I mean. Lance said, 'I don't want this information getting into the wrong hands. No offense to you but I don't know who else will be on that charter.'"

Once again in my life a man whom I had not expected to do so had made perfect sense.

For a few minutes I grieved. I grieved that he was not the man I was about to meet at the altar. That we would never share that little abode at the end of the lane, the one where I had lived with him in harmony for so many weeks with the children running to and fro. And then I wondered what it would have been like to have been pregnant with his child and returned to him instead of the *Quinta*.

I wondered if it would have been a black child or a white child or somewhere in between? In my stupor I pictured it as a black baby girl, the little girl I had always wanted with bright pink ribbons braided into her cornrows. But I also pictured her being mistreated because of her race. She was good but never good enough for people to look past her appearance and accept her for who she was. And that was a prospect I could not face.

Chapter Nineteen

On the morning of my wedding I woke up with a headache. There were half-empty bottles and cans lying around and the smell of stale champagne, wine and pupu's everywhere. My mind was no less disheveled. My friends were strewn from one end of my suite to the other and drawing straws to determine the order of their showers. There were still no pixies available and the two older ladies were joined by the chauffeurs in helping to prepare and deliver breakfast. Still it was a sparkling, sunny, Hawaiian day. A day for celebration.

George called me into the main library and I hoped beyond hope that he was not expecting sex. I feared he might be and I would definitely have had to refuse him, mostly out of fatigue, but he didn't lay a hand on me. Instead he gave me a peck on the cheek and asked me whether or not I was as joyous as he was at the prospects of our glorious union.

I nodded. To tell the truth I hadn't really had a chance to digest everything I had heard in the last twenty-four hours and the easiest thing to do was just nod my head.

He said, "I've got to admit, Lili Kaleo, that your lawyer, Kawamoto, drives a hard bargain."

"He does?" I asked.

"Yes." He said he had a signed copy of the pre-marital agreement for me but he would only deliver it if I agreed to a few things so I'm here to tell you that all of your demands have been met."

"They have?"

"Yes," he said. "Damn fine negotiator that Kawamoto—a bit of a blood sucker if you ask me but undeniably effective. I admire that in a man."

"Yes," I said. "Izzy is a good friend and a good lawyer."

"Well anyway, we don't have long before the wedding, so here goes."

We sat down at the large table in the dining room under the candle chandeliers. The floating candles with black burnt wicks were still on the table from dinner.

George said, "Here's your brother's mortgage on his house from the Bank of Aloha, marked 'paid in full.' And we started the renovations on your Aunty Fay's Quonset hut as soon as she left to come here. I'm sorry I didn't make the connection between her and the charming lady who protested being searched at the front gate. Has she ever expressed interest in security work?"

I laughed although not everything I was hearing seemed funny. I was so happy for Mimo and so grateful to Izzy that I could barely sit still. I tried not to show my surprise or elation.

George continued, "Here are the educational trusts you insisted on for each of Mimo's children, including unborn children. They can go to the college of their choice, provided they make reasonable progress towards a degree and finish by the age of twenty-five. Satisfactory?" he asked.

"Yes," I nodded. I thought about saying something but I noticed he still had a large stack of papers and things seemed to be going my way so I allowed him to continue.

Then he produced an enormous document. "This is a trust for our children or any child subsequently born to or adopted by either one of us. I wanted it to be only for children of our marriage but Mr. Kawamoto reminded me that I'm considerably older than you are and he felt that it was only fair to provide for any children that either of us might have over the course of a lifetime.

"There's plenty of resources—five million dollars—more or less—committed to this trust so that any such child can not only go to college but study the arts, learn a trade. Anything that the trustee, Bank of Aloha [I cringed at that], deems fitting and proper for the cultural or educational advancement of the child. And it extends to age thirty, instead of just twenty-five, as with your nieces and nephews."

"Satisfactory?" he asked again, just like one might say at the laying down of weapons at an armistice. To me this was no less significant. I had seen Mimo and Ruth want for things. I had seen members of Lance's extended family living on the edge of poverty, as well as Aunty Fay. I had seen my father impoverished for most of his life and now I could rest assured that those days for Mimo, Ruth and Aunty Fay were over forever.

I was getting worn out with excitement and at looking at the Byzantine legal documents I could no more have understood than my bank statement.

The last document was a trust for Daddy. "This one provides for your father's treatment and housing—minimal living expenses but only if he is free of drugs. I refuse to support a bum," he said and I fully agreed and understood.

George went on, "Your lawyer and I agreed that Mimo should be gainfully employed and that he should have the impression he is fending for himself. So what I've agreed to do for him is to arrange for him to find a construction job that meets his skills and interests as nearly as possible. He will receive an offer of employment next week, while we're gone on our honeymoon."

"George, you're wonderful! I love you so much." I was so ecstatic by then that I didn't care whether Mimo's job was with Weathervane Electric & Light or not. I had seen what unemployment had done to his morale, his self-esteem and how his family had suffered. "A job with anyone and reasonable security is all I ever wanted for him."

"Yes, he'll be held to a lower standard than the rest of his crew, but he'll never know it. As long as he makes a sincere effort he'll always have a job and he'll never know why or how, except that someone had heard of his reputation with his last employer.

"Finally," he said. "I can't promise about the outcome of your case with the County of Kaua'i but my attorneys will take over the litigation and I've agreed to indemnify you from any damages. It was that blood suck . . . Ah, umm, Kawamoto's idea. The following part of this agreement will be kept secret. We, and only we, will have the right to determine if and when you testify in any sort of a proceeding whatsoever."

Any hesitation I had had of marrying George had evaporated.

"Oh, by the way, your lawyer is a bit of a chump in at   least   one   respect."

"What's that?" I asked.

"He only asked for ten dollars in legal fees. I would have thought ten or twenty thousand, as a minimum, would have been more appropriate. Is he still sweet on you?"

"He's taken the place of the brother I lost in Vietnam," I replied.

* * *

The ceremony took place at St. Joseph's Catholic Church. It was an ornate old structure that adorned a hillside setting on Kapiolani Street in Hilo. It was pink with a lofty bell tower that supported a silver dome with an eight-day-strike clock on the face. It was the only place we felt would seat a reasonable number of people (sixteen hundred) and we knew the church would be filled. For most of our guests, sadly, we could invite them only to the reception at the ranch for there was not enough room in the church.

Cardinal Carlos Da Silva from Lisbon flew over to marry us and the Catholic Youth Organization (CYO) choir for all of Hawaii was booked to sing the High Mass. As expected—not only was the church filled with our guests and the press, but the steps, the surrounding hills, sidewalks and rooftops were also full. Our guests had to park at nearby Homeland Memorial Park. Driving a car through Hilo that day would not have been a pleasant task.

When I asked George before we left for the church how he had arranged for the Cardinal, when he was divorced (even though, he kept insisting "annulled") and I was not even Catholic, I was not surprised by his answer. "It was easy. The Cardinal is a very practical man. The monastery required chalices, candelabra, marble altars and statues of the saints."

Then he said, "I even had to check and make sure that the justice of the peace at the Hitching Post in Las Vegas, who married you to Charlie Owens, was not affiliated with a Christian religion. Otherwise I would have had to buy you . . . I mean, arrange another annulment for you, as well."

"You're kidding," I said.

"No, that's the way the system works—marriage for life, unless, of course, you can manage to arrange for a 'special dispensation.'"

I wonder what that would have cost him. A convent?

George and I arrived in separate white limousines. He did not want us to see one another after we left the ranch until we stood before the altar. This felt strange and struck me as funny after all the black limos, and only black ones, I had seen since I arrived.

When we got to the church I noticed there were men with musical instrument cases at the top of the church steps, in the garden to the left of the front entrance. "Portuguese music?" I said to the man who was assigned to guard me.

"No," the man said. "They won't be playing at all, unless someone decides to interfere with the wedding."

I later discovered there were snipers on the roofs, as well, and when I asked George about it he casually said, "You can never tell when there might be trouble," and shrugged his shoulders. "It's a fact of life."

Mimo looked gallant in his tuxedo although he and George agreed that none of the men in the wedding party would wear ties. Instead they wore ascots which matched the cheerful yellow dresses of the bridesmaids. The dresses were made of raw silk. Suzie was my maid of honor. I bought the women in the wedding party dresses and accenting garnet jewelry that they would be proud to wear for years to come. I also gave them matching large brimmed hats swathed with veils, purses, diamond earrings, and shoes.

I made sure they weren't just suitable for weddings. I could easily picture them in their outfits dashing down a fashion runway, which is how I had selected them at Christian Dior in the Ala Moana Shopping Mall in Honolulu. I was assured they carried the very same fashion design in Milan, Rome, Athens and Paris. *Suzie will stun them in that outfit. That should keep her looking nice for many years to come.*

Her mother, Mrs. Kawamoto was there, although I was sad to hear that Izzy's father had died while I was in Barbados, during a time when I could not be reached. Suzie jokingly told me later that they had buried him with a pack of cigarettes and his beanbag ashtray. "That's what killed him," she said.

Mrs. Kawamoto wore a black kimono with white embroidery and had a white fan tucked in her cummerbund. She had painted her fingernails white to match the outfit. She looked as dazzling to me that day as she had when I first saw her as a little girl.

María and Alfonso came to the wedding, although María was not able to make it to the bachelorette party the night before, nor could she and Alfonso attend the reception afterwards. She had stayed at Antonio's side right up until the time she left, because his mother worked and she was the only other person who could provide the comfort and sense of security he needed after what had happened. María did not mention anything about contacting the authorities regarding the gold shipments and I did not ask. I figured she had had her mind on her grandson and I did not want to seem insensitive to that. She and Alfonso arrived that morning at the Hilo airport and had to leave right afterwards.

But María wasn't about to miss the opportunity to attend a wedding officiated by a cardinal. I made arrangements for her to meet and talk with him briefly after the wedding.

She was overwhelmed and said, "Lili, most people don't get a chance to visit with a cardinal during their entire lives. I so wish I could come to your reception. Will he be there?"

I assured her he would, but sadly, on further reflection, she insisted she was still unable to stay for it. George had paid for their passage as well as for repairs to her home and Antonio's doctor bills and she and Alfonso offered him many, many thanks in return.

It was fun to see the same men who had earlier tried to put her into a straightjacket ushering Aunty Fay to the front of the church. She made her own private fashion statement by wearing her trademark flowery hat, which was overdone, as always. She added an apple and an orange to it that day in honor of the special occasion. Daddy didn't make it and never showed up for the reception either, although I hadn't expected him. Still I was sad. I think if I had seen him that day I would have told him he was forgiven. Life is too short to bear a grudge and I was so happy.

Mimo, my handsome, tall, burly and well-fed brother, gave me away. I was so proud of my "soon to be employed" brother that day I could have danced up the aisle.

Tiny was George's best man. He said that he had asked his son but even though he was in his late twenties by now, his mother wouldn't permit it. He invited him to the wedding anyway and hoped he would be there or at least come to the reception. But we had not seen him yet.

The only other important person missing at the start of the wedding was Izzy. I couldn't imagine where he was. I hoped he hadn't gotten mad at me and decided not to come. When I asked Suzie about it, she said, "Oh, no, he plans to be here. He and Kiku went shopping this week to buy new outfits for her and the kids just for the occasion."

The wedding was scheduled for two p.m. but I had it delayed for fifteen minutes while we waited for Izzy. I had this awful feeling that something might have happened to him and possibly his wife and children. I knew he had played a high stakes game with George and hoped he hadn't lost it in the end. Yet I was confident George would not harm him if he ever expected to have a meaningful relationship with me.

The cardinal appeared and I must say he looked impressive, with pure white hair creeping out under his bright red zucchetto, cape and vestments. There were probably more oohs and ahs for him than there were for me as the bride.

I wore a simple white crepe wedding dress, sleeveless with a keyhole back and a halter neckline. It had a train but it was very subtle and short. So I required no assistance to manage it.

My hair was still shorter than usual from being cut for the boat trip to Guatemala and I wore it up with a white blue nun orchid in it that María had carefully preserved and brought with her from her garden in Guatemala City so I would have "something blue."

I wore a lei of pinkish white orchids from the Big Island and a carried a bouquet of day lilies that Aunty Fay had gathered from my mother's and my brother's graves at Kekaho cemetery on Kaua'i. I also had on a pair of long, sequined, shimmering white gloves that had once belonged to my mother (something old), and borrowed a silver comb for my hair from one of the guests, just as the organist began playing the processional. I felt that I already had enough new things with the dress, the ring and all that I didn't want to add too much to my attire and cheapen it by detracting from its simplicity.

As a matter of fact—at the last minute—I kicked off my shoes and walked up the aisle barefoot. I was taller than George as it was and enjoyed the humbling nature of the gesture. It also seemed in keeping with the spirit of my ancestors.

After all the singing and gospel reading and kneeling and standing and sitting and bells ringing and incense burning and coughing and babies crying and exchanging of vows and rings, George said he did and I said I did. No one could think of any reason why this union should not be allowed, or if they did, they didn't say. We walked out of the beautiful St. Joseph's Church, arm in arm, as man and wife.

Izzy had still not arrived.

* * *

The principal members of the wedding party—the cardinal, George, me, Suzie and Tiny all rode together in a white stretch limousine back to the ranch. We had a police escort and must have gone eighty miles an hour at times. George wanted to get there in time to prepare to greet the guests. I got nauseated and we had to pull over and stop under a bright orange royal poinciana tree so that I could calm my stomach and avoid regurgitating. George patted me on the back, but said, "C'mon, Sugar, we'll lose our lead time." I gradually felt better and we proceeded.

When we got there we went into the study and the first thing we did was sign the wedding certificate and have it witnessed. I noticed when George signed his name and penned in the date that the letters and numbers were so ornately inscribed that they looked almost like embroidery. I thought this was an interesting paradox for such a powerful man.

The focal point of the reception was in an area near the main house which formed a sort of a bowl in the center of the surrounding hills, except that the path was still downhill from there to the main gate. There were big white tents at the top of the hills. They reminded me in many ways of the church I had been to in Speightstown, only not so colorful. One tent had seafood, another salt pork from George's *imu* and desserts. One had Hawaiian music— some ukulele, old and mellow—alternating with peppier slack key renditions. Another had Portuguese music with dancers in their beautiful native costumes—black dresses for the ladies with intricate red, green and yellow embroidery on their bodices. At the center of it all were the gardens around the main house where George and I greeted our guests.

The cardinal stood next to me near the end of the line, just before George and Tiny. So many people knelt to kiss the cardinal's ring and speak with him in English (of which I suspect he understood very little) and he took so long to respond to their kind remarks in Portuguese (that I know none of us understood at all), that our reception line lasted nearly two hours. And that was with most of our guests giving up at the sight of the line and sharing their good wishes at a later time or date.

We greeted and we smiled and we smiled and we greeted and tried and tried to think of kind and clever things to say to one another. I had no idea how many people the two of us knew and I still have bad dreams about the outstretched hands of throngs of people waiting to shake mine. I had some hesitation at shaking Tami's hand, given the way in which she had treated me as a child. But I was so amused by her behavior that it was almost pathetic. She came on to every one of the men in the line, including the cardinal. By the time she got to George who responded more cordially than I might have hoped, I laughingly said, "The two of you should get a room."

I noticed that Suzie, who was one person closer to the front of the line than the cardinal, was holding up really well, still smiling and greeting people after more than an hour. She had confided in me that she was going to run for the Kaua'i County Council in the next election and I was thrilled for her. She would be an excellent choice for the voters. "You are such a hard worker," I said. "The citizens of Kaua'i don't know how lucky they'll be. Maybe one day you can run for mayor."

"I doubt it," she said. "I don't have your charisma. But I am enthusiastic and willing to work hard to understand the issues."

"You'll be a credit to the county," I said to Suzie. "And in time you'll be surprised how much the people will realize who you really are and what you stand for. Never underestimate the people." In that instant for some reason I flashed on a comment little Willie had made about 'da people,' but the thought dissipated before I could make any real sense of it.

Countless of our guests told me how happy they were to have me back in Hawaii and asked me when I might be running for governor. I could tell that George tired of the adulation of the electorate. In spite of his prominence he appeared to have successfully been able to keep his life much more private.

I had worried about Izzy almost the whole time since we had left the church and right then, toward the very end of the line of guests approaching the receiving line, there he was. I wanted to jump out of line and hug him and revel in the fact that he and his wife and children were all right. Kiku couldn't have looked more beautiful. There was a daintiness about her—a daintiness I never had except perhaps as an infant—even though that was my name. Her soft, alluring, dark eyes accented a muted blue, yellow and white kimono with a bow and a fan tucked in the back. I was envious of her in many respects but wished them every happiness from the bottom of my heart.

When I turned to share with George the joy of Izzy's arrival my husband was gone. *I guess he's still resentful of Izzy after negotiating those trusts for my family.* Izzy seemed serious and withdrawn. "I'm sorry I didn't make it to the wedding. I'll explain in a moment."

When the line broke up and he was able to send Kiku and his children off to the Hawaiian tent with Suzie and Aunty Fay he and I went around to the front of the house and hid behind the oleanders to talk.

"Where were you?" I asked as I straightened his tie—a first in my relationship with Izzy, but a role I enjoyed.

"We landed at the Hilo airport in plenty of time and George's chauffeur came to pick us up right on schedule. I think it was around ten a.m. at the time."

"And . . ."

"The chauffeur had two of George's bone crushers with him and when they pulled out of the airport they turned the south instead of north and took us to the volcano instead of the ranch."

"What? Were they knuckleheads?"

"No they knew exactly what they were doing." Izzy was as animated as I had ever seen him. "It appears George was upset about the concessions he had to make to get your signature on the pre-marital agreement and they wanted me to know how easy it would be for someone to 'take me for a little ride in the country.'"

I was so mad I spit three or four times right there behind the oleanders and was ready to plant my fist on George's chin.

Izzy continued, "Oh, they didn't hurt us. In fact they were very pleasant—most polite to Kiku or I think she would have given them a karate lesson."

That image appealed to me.

Izzy went on, "They took us through the Volcanoes National Park and even drove us down near the ocean so my son could see molten lava flow into the water and form hydrochloric acid. My punishment, I believe, was that I would have to miss the wedding. 'The boss don't want his wedding spoiled by havin' to look at your ugly kisser,' I believe was the exact terminology of the bone crusher."

"Even if they didn't harm you and had no intention of doing so," I said. "I'm going to go have a word with George." I took a couple of steps back towards the party.

"Wait!" Izzy said. "Wait just a minute."

I expected him to say something like, 'Don't, Lili. It's your wedding day. No use getting George upset,' but he didn't. Instead he reached into his coat pocket. He pulled out a letter. As soon as I saw the stamp with a picture of Grantley Adams on the front I knew it was from Lance. It also had "Lance Williams, Chief Inspector, Royal Barbados Police Force, Central Police Station, St. Michael, Barbados, West Indies" in the upper left hand corner of the envelope.

My hand trembled as I took the letter. My first inclination was to open it and read it right then. Then I decided it wouldn't change anything. *I'm already married.* I put it in my purse. Through the course of the day I decided that it would be best kept hidden until some quiet moment on our honeymoon when I could steal away to have a private moment with the words inside that envelope.

Then I went to find my husband but no one had seen him. In looking for him I had the strangest experience. I came upon a man from behind—a man in a gray iridescent suit. I didn't see his face but I saw a birthmark below his right ear. He was talking to several of the men. *Mr. Fitzsimmons?* The birthmark matched but he had a full head of hair. I noticed that he held and puffed his cigarette from his left hand and tried for the life of me to remember whether or not Mr. Fitzsimmons was left handed.

Then, I realized. *This is Hawaii, not Barbados. It couldn't be him.* I thought about circling around to see his face but right then I had to find George. My anger was wearing off and I wanted to catch up with him while I was still upset.

I asked around and finally, out of desperation at having to shake guests off me at every turn, decided to check in the bunker. It was the only place I could imagine he might be unless he had left the ranch altogether.

On the way over one of the men stopped me and said, "The boss is in there. He's checking his weapons before the trip. He don't wanna be disturbed."

I tried to argue with him and go in anyway but he stopped me and a couple of other men headed in our direction. Since I was outnumbered I turned around and rejoined the party. I stood where I could periodically glance at the bunker.

Almost an hour later I saw him heading back towards the party with Tami hanging on one arm, her hair disheveled. Instinctively I ran towards him. I thought the men might try to stop me but they didn't.

"Where have you been?" I asked.

He laughed. "I was checking our weapons before the trip tomorrow. Didn't the guards tell you? Your old high school chum showed an interest so I told her she could come along."

"Georgie's—she had the never, or stupidity to pronounce his name Jorgee, instead of Gay-org. Jorjee's got quite and arsenal in there," she said giddily.

I wanted to scratch her eyes out. She had that same expression on her face just like she had that day she spit bubble gum into my wash water when I was working for Daddy at the gas station. But I tried not to give her the satisfaction of knowing I was upset.

"He showed me his bazooka," she added and tugged playfully at George's arm.

"She's got a couple of nice bazookas herself," George said, looking over at her admiringly. It was clear he had been drinking so I tried to discount his remark by its alcohol content.

"Only her bazookas were bought off the clearance rack and yours wasn't," I replied.

Tami looked furious and stomped off down the driveway towards the front gate.

"Do you want me to have a couple of the men speak with her . . ."

I looked at George quizzically.

". . . about discretion?"

"Tami can shoot off her mouth all she wants and no one would believe her anyway," I replied.

I took my husband by the arm and we went back to the party. Nothing serious could have happened, I tried to convince myself. The man's got better taste than that. Yet, I could smell the mixture of alcohol, bay rum and perfume on George's breath and shirt. *Sometime I'd like to go to a party where the alcohol is kept in the cupboard.*

After that George was perfectly attentive, both to me and our guests. I was still aggravated about the way he had treated Izzy but decided to bring that up later in our conjugal bed.

Chapter Twenty

George surprised me by saying we were going to take a commercial flight for our honeymoon. He said it was such a joyous occasion that he wanted to spend it with lots of people around. I later got out of him that the courier service one of his companies used between Brazil and London had been interrupted and the G-3 was needed to "haul goods."

When I asked about protection, he said, "Don't worry. We're being looked after."

If we were being looked after, it was discreet. I couldn't pick anyone out whom I thought had us under surveillance. Every time I thought I had identified someone they disappeared and later on it would be someone else I would suspect. I didn't ask about it though. I wanted to enjoy this precious time away from the rigors of George's business affairs. He was often so preoccupied.

Fortunately for me he didn't believe in pagers, fax machines, copiers, cell phones and such—at least not for himself, although his men used them freely and I had seen a fax machine in the bunker. We had no such technology in the main house, not even a copier. He stayed away from the phones almost the entire time we were gone and I had him to myself.

As we circled before landing I said, "Oh, there's Lisbon. How beautiful!" I could already see the traffic circles, old churches, the monastery George had built— high on a hill overlooking the city—and it looked gay and colorful, even from the air.

"Leash-boa," he said. "The locals call it 'Leash-boa.'"

"Leash-boa," I repeated. "Isn't it beautiful?"

I snuggled close to him. We were in first class and he sat by the window. "Do you want to change seats?" he offered.

"Oh, yes!" I said and scooted over him for a better look. "What a beautiful city."

* * *

We only spent a couple of days in Leash-boa, seeing the sights, shopping, going to museums and weaving in and out of traffic. George drove a metallic blue Mercedes Convertible like a racecar driver, with the top down. I joked that it was a good thing he normally had a chauffeur.

Then we left by rail for the Douro Valley where George said he owned an estate, complete with vineyards. In fact his mother had once worked on the property as a laborer. George had bought it for her later in her life as a reward for all she had been through to bring him up, when the owner's father had refused to acknowledge him as his son. The vineyards had fallen onto hard times during the regime of Antonio Salazar and buying it from the man's son was George's way of rubbing his half-brother's nose in his misfortune.

In many ways I was disappointed to leave the city but once we got to the valley my attitude changed. We arrived at the train station in Pinhão, where soft blue and white panels of hand-painted Danish-style tiles, called *Azulejos* (pronounced oz-way-lōs), richly depicted the grape harvesting scenes I was about to enjoy. They were so well done that I couldn't imagine that the actual vistas would be any better.

I was not disappointed, however, when I saw the real thing. The way the vineyards were terraced on the hills was like a storybook land. They looked like little patchwork quilts crisscrossing—one row of grapes entwined with another, methodically and intriguingly thatched across the hillsides. I am at a loss to describe their full beauty—idyllic, serene, late summer green with a backdrop of blending autumn colors. Lush hillsides. Splendid lakes. Magnificent gorges and precipices. Brisk cool weather, especially at night.

When we got to his estate I marveled. "You mean you own this, too?"

"Lili, *we* own it—it belongs to you and me. It's ours. Didn't you read the pre-nuptial agreement?"

"I must confess I didn't." I had remembered the many pages of "asset lists" that made it so bulky. It went on page after page and I thought it was tedious and boring. "I did thumb through the asset list. I thought maybe you owned a share of stock in this, a share of stock in that, certainly not the whole thing."

Later on Izzy told me that he had to list all of his assets, or the agreement would not have been valid.

When we arrived at George's estate he said, "Lili, do you remember that black figure on the bottle of port you liked so well?"

"The one that looked like Zorro with the flat, wide-brimmed hat and the black cape?"

"Yes, that one. Well, this is where it's made."

"Is it yours?" I could see George was about to correct me. "Is it ours?" I corrected myself.

"No, many of us in the valley have formed a cooperative and a few of us are authorized to share the black label."

The air was brisk. Fall was setting in. The leaves had begun to change to red, yellow and orange while a few had already crinkled and turned a golden brown. The grapes were being harvested and it was enchanting. Smudge pots kept the last few grapes of the season from freezing on cold nights and the smell and crackling of nearby fires to keep the farm hands warm was delightful.

We got to help pick grapes and had races among those present to see who could do it the fastest. I think George felt intimidated by my athleticism as there were people gathering around me after just about every "heat" congratulating me and saying what an asset I had been to them. It reminded me of the camaraderie on our volleyball team.

Then—well beyond my wildest imagination—a dream came true. We got to crush grapes with our feet. About a dozen of us, many of whom were tourists who had paid high prices to see George's estate, rolled up our pants or held up our skirts and squished our feet in the smooth mush of spent purple and burgundy grapes.

I said, "Mark the bottles wherever these grapes go so I can avoid drinking anything made from them."

George chuckled politely at my humor. "These grapes are filtered so many times and aged before bottling that no one need worry about a little toe jam."

Toe jam? I hadn't heard that expression in years, not since Kuhaʻo used to tease me by sticking his feet in my face as a kid.

Then we got to meet the head taster and master blender—Mr. George (pronounced Jorj) Leite, a distinguished looking blind man with thin white hair. He told us how port was originally blended with brandy to preserve it on boat trips to London and that it was so well received that the tradition continued, even though better methods of preservation came along many years ago. We even got to taste the brandy that was mixed with the wine.

And we saw the boat races—darling little sailboats with big broad grayish white or black sails—which once transported the wine and still did in certain instances. George's company, Bogeyman, was pitted against all the other vineyards in the region. His boat had the black Zorro symbol on the sail and I cheered it on as if it were Lance playing cricket. *Where did that come from?* I still held Lance's letter in my purse but had not yet opened it. Somehow I knew my mood would change whenever I did and I wanted to preserve the fun and frolicking as long as I could.

Then we went to festivals—so many I couldn't count them. It seemed every little village had a festival to celebrate the harvesting of the grapes or some religious holiday. It reminded me of Crop Over in Barbados. But why did I keep coming back to such thoughts?

The tall papier-mâché puppets were hilarious, along with people on stilts, dancers in black costumes with yellow and red and green embroidery, similar to the ones who had danced and sung at my wedding. In the religious parades shrines were carried on people's shoulders like the Ark of the Covenant in the Bible—or an Egyptian Pharaoh. Posters of saints were displayed and heralded, lead by a priest carrying a crucifix or spreading incense before the procession. I think they had All Saints Day / *Todos os Santos* or All Souls Day or both while we were there. We celebrated so many holidays and historical events and watched so many parades and processions that it all became a blur.

The best times I remember in mainland Portugal were cruising the mountain lakes on a riverboat and enjoying quiet moments together. George's voracious appetite for sex seemed to have waned but we did have our intimate moments and when we did, they were quiet, tender moments with an extended afterglow. I would twirl his chest hair around my fingertips or gently pinch and caress his earlobes with my fingers or tongue or lightly stroke his still muscular chest. *Mon Dieu*, that man was handsome— and now he was in his element, dressed so much like the locals that I could barely tell them apart.

Time evaporated like the morning fog and soon it was time to move on for a few days in Algarve on the southern seaboard, near Gibraltar. The weather was sunny and warm during the day, brisk at night. It was our last stop before we left for Madeira, where George had arranged to take me because some of my ancestors were born there.

* * *

When we got to the beaches of Albufeira I was surprised to find that most of the women were topless. But George explained that this was the European way. Nevertheless I didn't feel like flaunting my wares. I had resolved not to ever do that again after that terrible day many years earlier when I had joined a wet T-shirt contest in Coconut Park on the Big Island and ended up married to Charlie Owens.

He, on the other hand, had developed a sudden interest in photography so I decided to retreat to my room. The hotel was gorgeous—a swanky, but reverent old structure on a hillside overlooking the Atlantic to the south. There, with considerable trepidation, I opened the letter from   Lance.

My Dearest Lili, the Sugar of my life,

It's been a long time since I saw you. I went to work one morning thinking you'd be there waiting for me, when I returned. I had brought you some ginger lilies and heliconia blooms along with another special present which I still have. But you were gone and I was worried and deeply saddened. The children were upset and frightened and told me of your ordeal with the strangers in the van.

I didn't realize until you were gone how much I needed you, appreciated your every move, just your presence—the soft, sweet sound of your voice, the warm comfort of your breath against my body, your hand in mine or your head nestled up against my shoulder in the Porsche.   I missed seeing you playing with our children [the word 'my' had been crossed out and 'our' written above it], your arm finding its way around their shoulders before you were done. I hope and pray that it will be His will that we'll be reunited soon!   I trust to the Lord, Jesus Christ, that we will and rededicate myself and my voice to Him every Sunday—in supplication that He might answer my prayer and fill the longing I have for you in my heart."

From this point on I wept as I read the letter—that is when I wasn't laughing.

Why didn't I understand the omen of the Black Christ?

"Meanwhile I've been working on the cases of the bank bombing, Ephraim's murder and the credit card and loan fraud at the Bank of Barbados. Actually I now see them as one. As we suspected they appear to be as intertwined as soap on a rope— with the murder hanging like a pendant at the end.

"By now Elayne Headley must have told you that we were able to prosecute Mr. Baker and Miss Cumberbatch for credit card fraud and there were so many incidences of it that they will no doubt be living out their days in Glendairy Prison. The files you gave us were invaluable and allowed us to persuade them to plead guilty without your even having to testify. The fools had the files so well documented that there was little wiggle room left for them in explaining their wrongdoing. It turns out Mr. Baker was supervising the international aspects of the fraud through Miss Bangerter, whom we have not been able to locate since the blue building at the end of Broad Street burned to the ground. As nearly as we can tell the bombing was perpetrated by a group of radicals from Jamaica who were attending the University of the West Indies and it was only casually related to the scandals at the bank.

"I think Mr. Baker had a hand in, or at least prior knowledge of the murder, but we haven't been able to find absolute proof.

"Elayne did not know what I'm about to tell you. I was conducting a secret investigation which grew out of the information you provided about the gold smuggling particulars and your rendezvous with Mr. Musgrave. As you know we suspected him for some time but were not able to solve the puzzle until you gave us the last piece.

"Mrs. Musgrave was arrested while passing through Grantley Adams International Airport from Surinam on her way to London. Knowing you as I do you'd better sit down and grab a box of tissues for this is hilarious."

By now I already had the tissues at my side.

"She got off the plane during her layover and went to visit Mr. Baker in Glendairy before she caught the Concorde, which is why she convinced her poor husband to arrange a stop in Barbados. I say 'poor' husband because I think he worshipped her and had no idea what was going on between her and Winston Baker. Now she and Mr. Baker are both roosting in Glendairy, although I doubt they get to see much of one another."

"When she got back to the airport only a couple of hours after landing she failed to successfully pass through the metal detector. After several attempts and being searched the security people still could not figure out why the alarms kept going off. To make a long story short, someone had woven gold into her underwear and bra, apparently thinking it an insufficient amount to trigger the detector. But as you probably know our security has recently been upgraded. So there she was, 'a woman in golden panties and bra,' being brought into the Central Police station in handcuffs, like a common criminal.

"It's a wonder any of us around here are still alive because we've all been laughing so hard about it ever since that our backs and bellies ache. The *Tell It Like It Is* people on the Voice of Barbados will have fun with that one for years to come!"

Lance was right. I did laugh so hard that I cried, and cried and cried. I missed him and I loved him. *Is it possible to love more than one man at once? Why should I wonder? Men do it all the time.*
I dried my eyes and continued the letter.

"Then they searched her husband's suitcase and carry on luggage in spite of the fact that we knew he was a diplomat. We took the risk against protocol even though we might not be able to use any evidence we might find. We found gold jewelry, emeralds and even a small stash of cocaine. It turns out that gold was being brought into Barbados from northern Brazil and Surinam and some of it was fashioned into jewelry here while the rest of it was being cast into bullion and transported as freight.

"We could never figure out how it was being shipped out of the country, even though we had staked out the docks, until you confirmed it for us with your message through your lawyer. Then when you saw Mr. Musgrave in Guatemala City while he was supposed to be in Surinam, we were able to close in on him, as well.

"Because of his diplomatic status, we are not able to prosecute him, but have been assured by MI-5 that he has probably seen the great outdoors for the last time in years.

"By the way, thank you for reuniting me with the jewelry and coins that comprise the humble savings I've accumulated over my career as a policeman. I guess I don't have to explain to you why I don't trust banks. I apologize for accusing you of taking it. I should have known better and now recognize that it was a cheap shot. I think I lashed out at you because my feelings were hurt, when you left so unexpectedly.

"This brings me to the most important part of my letter and the reason I am sending it, instead of giving it to Elayne to deliver to you personally. I want to be sure it arrives safely. I also want to maintain the highest level of security and, quite frankly, I was afraid Elayne might open, read and attempt to reseal the letter. You always said she had a difficult time minding her own business."

That's for sure.

"We believe that we know who was behind the murder of Ephraim Whitney. Through the course of unraveling what we believe is a worldwide drug, emerald, gold and gun smuggling operation—not to mention money laundering—we have become more fastidious in our surveillance. Since Barbados Cable & Wireless, as you once mentioned, charges a king's ransom for an international phone call they get lots of allegations about over billing. You may recall they used to cut off their customers after eleven minutes and then play them a tape-recorded lecture about exceeding their credit limits. The unpopularity of that policy has in turn caused them to allow longer calls but to record them—to prove, if need be, the length of each.

"It happens that they made an audible tape recording of someone from Hawaii calling to say that 'two coconuts must be removed from the tree.'

"'Knocked down?' the recipient asked. 'No, one cut and the other pricked,' the voice on the other end replied."

"Now, cryptic as that may be, we turned it over to MI-5. They've been working with us to stop the smuggling and they were happy to get their hands on the tape. After turning it over to their top people they concluded what several of us at the RBPF already surmised—the coconuts were you and Ephraim.

"At first I was saddened by your departure. Now I am elated that you appear to have made it safely away, albeit to the same state in your country where the man who made the phone call lives. I fear that he may have already tried to contact you. His name is George (it's spelled 'Jorj' but pronounced Gay-org) Santini. Perhaps you know of him."

I stopped laughing and put down the letter. I was in shock. I took several deep breaths and picked up the letter.

"If he approaches you, you should avoid him. If you see him, or meet up with him or his agents, please consider that they may be armed and dangerous."

I was stunned. I couldn't have read on except that I thought he might say something about his children. I read through my tears. Then for some perverse reason I laughed. *Yes, I think you could safely say that George was armed.* Then I shuddered—this time for my own safety. I continued with the letter.

"I think we are fast on his trail and best of all I don't think he knows it. It may sound like we've got him cold. But in spite of what MI-5 had to say our attorneys and those in the states who would be involved in extradition proceedings tell us otherwise. 'Even though we can prove it's his voice and *imply* what he meant, getting a murder conviction on this flimsy evidence—or a conviction on any charges for that matter— remains speculative. It's not like having a confession in his own handwriting.'"

"So we labor on, my sweet—me with the almost unbearable desire of getting back together with you soon so I can share the clarity of the thoughts I now have about you—no—us. I will have a surprise for you when we meet again—a romantic surprise and I hope you will like it. Meanwhile suffice it to say that 'I love you'—there I finally said it so now you know what is in my heart.'"

Why didn't he say that when he was with me? If he'd ever said that even once . . .
Tears. Kleenex. And this time no starched white Bajan police uniform or strong, athletic shoulder to cry on.

"The children are fine but they miss you. They keep reminding me that the last day you were here was the last day the house was clean although Idalia is bravely doing her best to fill your shoes in that regard. Theo keeps asking me to write and tell you that you were right—he is now the champion of road tennis in all of St. Lucy. Emma is definitely in the worst shape over your departure. She just keeps saying, 'Shoogah!' and looking out the front door and the side window into the driveway for you. I don't think she fully understands that you are gone.

"Then sometimes without explanation she launches into a dance which I presume is the hula that you taught her. At that I usually start out laughing and end up in tears."

I know the feeling.

"Bye—or-as you say in Hawaii, aloha—for now my love, (It sure feels good to address you in this way and soon I will do so in person.)"

Lance Williams, <u>Chief</u> Inspector RBPF"

Hmm! Chief Inspector. Impressive. "What in the hell have you done, girl?" I said to myself. My first inclination was to feel sorry for myself, to wallow in self-pity, but *"No."* I said. *"It's time you did something intelligent for a change—a credit to your gender."*

Aunty Fay always said, "Ac'ing a foo' ovah a man is not a charactah flaw. Addahwise, no moa kids, ha."

But I was mad and I had to do something. *But what?*

I took the letter down to the lobby and thought about having copies made but I feared there wasn't time. George could return at any minute. I got an envelope and addressed it to Izzy. I knew that a man of his character had not opened the letter. I put his Kaua'i return address on it and made it out to his Honolulu office because that's where I thought he spent most of his time. Hurriedly, I took the time to delete the parts about "love and romance" with a laundry marker that I borrowed from the bellman. I didn't want Izzy's feelings hurt, anymore than I wanted the details of my personal life to be revealed in any public proceeding. I put a stamp on the envelope—one depicting one of those old churches in Leash-boa—scribbled 'I'm hoping you'll know what to do with this' across the top of the first page, put the letter into the envelope and dropped it into the hotel mail slot. I kept the envelope the letter had come in.

Then I asked for two blank sheets of hotel stationery. The concierge handed me two sheets but they had the emblem of the hotel embossed across the top. I said, "No, plain paper."

"Does Madam care how big the sheets are?" the man with a dark brown cookie duster Hitler-style mustache, asked.

"No," I said, "it doesn't matter."

"Very well, Madam," he said. He took the two sheets back from me and added a third. He reached into a box inside his podium, pulled out a pair of scissors and proceeded to cut the letterheads off the sheets. Then he tapped them against a nearby tabletop to make the sheets flush with one another, handed them back to me and said, "There you are, Madam—two sheets of blank stationery, along with a third in case you run out of space."

I could tell I was upset. If not I truly believe that I would have thought of cutting the letterhead off myself. I ran over and punched a button for the elevator but it didn't come and it didn't come. I punched it again and again. I was afraid George would return and catch me in the lobby and start asking questions so I took the stairs.

After I climbed the ten flights to our room I was out of breath. I put the stationery into the large ashtray that George had insisted on having for his Cuban cigars, lit a match to the paper and crumpled it as it burnt. Then I took the envelope that Lance's letter had come in and I burnt it, too. But I was careful that the flames did not devour the return address, only blackened it.

Then I went out on the tiny little porch adjacent to the room and sat on a white wrought iron chair. I looked off towards the sea and awaited George's return. The weather was crisp and the salty sea breeze invigorating.

* * *

It was well after seven p.m. before I heard George's key in the latch. I was just about to order dinner without him.

"Run out of film did you?" I asked.

"Yes, as a matter of fact, I did. The beach was gorgeous, the hillsides charming but the company dull and uninspiring. I spent most of my time at a little sidewalk café. I wish you had stayed and joined me."

By now I had had a chance to regain my composure but I was still furious less than one millimeter beneath the surface of my skin.

We ordered room service from the hotel menu and resolved that we should spend a quiet evening, just the two of us. The bellman came and started a fire in the fireplace.

"Fado music with dinner?" George asked. "The hotel will provide it if we ask."

"No," I said. "I think we should provide our own music," and winked at him.

He winked back. "Yes, my dear. That sounds lovely. Truly lovely."

I realized at that moment that George had never told me he loved me. I guessed that I had just been willing to assume it in his case. I hoped it wasn't the money that had blinded me. It could have been the power. The only man I could ever remember who was forthcoming with that proclamation was Izzy. Dear Izzy—bless his heart.

"George, do you love me?"

"Yes, of course," he said. "Why do you think I married you?"

I decided it best not to answer. I hated to think it was for my political stature and influence, just as Izzy had said.

The lights of the ships going in and out of the harbor in the distance were mesmerizing and the flickering lights of the lower hillside buildings made an appealing portrait. Part of me wished I could have dedicated the evening and idyllic setting to romance—with someone not necessarily present company. But I had set some goals. One was to see how much port I could get George to drink and the other was to see how many uses I could find for the port which was poured into my glass.

When his back was turned I watered the ivy behind me with port. When he went into the other room to answer an inquiry from the front desk I threw a glassful into the fireplace. I drank a little. It was sweet and fruity, just how I had grown to like it. I kept filling his glass and proposing toasts—to our agreement, to mutual understanding, to world peace—which he showed no hesitation in telling me was "wishful thinking and naïve—" to the environment, which we both seemed to respect and appreciate, to business success and to a long and lasting friendship.

When he went to the bathroom I opened the sliding glass door on to the porch and poured another glassful down onto the sidewalk. I thought I heard a distant yelp. I stepped back and quickly closed the door. For the next twenty or thirty minutes I sat watching the door and listening for the phone, thinking someone might complain. But no one ever did.

When he seemed sufficiently plied with liquor I got him to join me on the bed, luring him with promise of a special treat for dessert. But he had difficulty hoisting his mast. It showed signs of life at one point and I pretended to endeavor to assist him in its resuscitation. I tried not to

show my relief that all of our efforts were in vain. I hoped
he wasn't too drunk for the next phase of my plan.

 "George."

 "Yes, dear."

 "Do you love me?"

 "Yes, I already told you I did," he replied.

 "Do you have any business dealings in Barbados?"

 "Yes," he said. "I don't suppose that's any secret. I
have business dealings all over the world."

 "Then George. . . . George, honey."

 "Yes, Sugarplum."

 "Then why on earth did you make arrangements to
have me killed?"

 George did his best to sit up and compose himself
but I don't think there's a man alive who could have
shrugged off what he had imbibed. He reached for his
head.

 "What makes you think I had anything to do with
it? . . . I mean, uh, er-, I don't know what you're talking
about."

 "What about the coconuts?" I asked. "Was I the
one to be cut or pricked?"

 He coughed. "Huh? I don't have the faintest idea
what you're talking about. I didn't order any coconuts—
not in Hawaii, not in Barbados. I don't even like
coconuts."

 "You do know," I said. "They have a recording of
you arranging to have me and Ephraim hit."

 George was either a remarkably good liar, even at
fifty-one proof, or Lance had fingered the wrong man.
After all he had once confused Shirley Bangerter and
Elayne Headley when he warned me there was an Amazon
hit man working at the bank.

 George said, "Who's they? Who's Ephraim? And
where am I?" He looked around the room as if his head
were spinning and then passed out on the bed.

* * *

 We had one more day in Albufeira before it was
time to head for Madeira, the birthplace of one of my great-
great-. . . grandparents on the paternal side of my family.
Now I didn't know who to believe. I was confident that
Lance wouldn't lie to me but maybe he had gotten it wrong.
George, as usual, was very persuasive.

 He told me that people impersonate him all the
time—everything from dinner reservations to tee times on

the golf course. Knowing how to imitate his voice and use his name effectively could pay big dividends and it came as no surprise to him that someone calling Barbados had done so.

"But wouldn't the authorities be able to figure out where the call came from?" I asked.

"What sort of an idiot would make a call such as the one you described from his own phone?" he asked.

I had to admit that he had a point. I spent the rest of our honeymoon watching him, sensing his body language, evaluating every move he made in my direction trying to sort his sincere and honest gestures from those that weren't.

Then I looked at the brighter side. *What if George is telling the truth?* I *did* want to have children and my biological clock *was* running. It was at least half-past-ten on its way to striking midnight. Every year I waited to have a child cut down on the prospects and increased the odds that there would be birth defects or complications. Several of my colleagues in the mayor's office who waited to have children over the age of forty had underweight children, born prematurely. About half of the infants required surgery for one thing or another. I didn't want to get into extra innings and face that prospect. It wouldn't be fair to me or the child. I had experienced enough misery with Christian's last illness to last me a lifetime.

In the end I decided it would be unfair to convict George, even if just in my mind, on such flimsy evidence. I knew that feeling all too well.

* * *

By the time we got to Madeira I was so excited at seeing the birthplace of Marcello the Portuguese troubadour who spawned a tributary to my paternal genetic stream that I lost track of my concerns. My focus had changed to the beautiful mountain range and the city of Funchal.

We went hiking, which turned out to be my favorite part of the entire honeymoon. Breathtaking views. We returned to the city each evening to break bread and nurture our romantic relationship. Somewhere along the way I decided to try to make the best of the marriage. I couldn't make a judgment against my husband without conclusive proof, even though I resolved that there were some questions that must be explored more deeply once we returned to Hawaii.

On our last day in Madeira we slid down a hill in what looked like wicker lawn chairs on skids. Two men rode on the back and steered them, like sleds, while we laughed and cheered. It was good to let our emotions out and forget about our troubles. I watched George's expression each time he looked in my direction.

This man does love me. I can see it written on his face.

Chapter Twenty-One

I was glad to get back to the ranch to start my married life with my new husband. All of the high living and extravagance had begun to make me feel guilty when others in the world were starving. I was sure most people had never given that a second thought unless they happened to be the ones without food, and I had been one of those people.

I decided to fade from George's side for a while, let our desire for one another rebuild, and then approach him for a romantic encounter in a few days, when his desire for me would be at its peak. Even though I knew he was less than perfect I still wanted to have children and those children would have to be his. For all the phone calls and interruptions he didn't take on our honeymoon he made up for after our return.

There were dinners to which he had invited guests to which I was not invited but that didn't trouble me. I preferred, at least for the time being, to eat in my suite or in the lovely garden that extended between my suite and his chambers. He would usually call to make sure I wouldn't be offended or send me a note in his frilly handwriting to say that I still held his heart. That made me feel better about his absence.

The staff had saved a pile of Sunday newspapers for me and I was able to sit down and get caught up on all the word jumbles and number puzzles I had missed. I still had the list of account numbers I had copied while I worked at the Bank of Barbados and I hoped that working the number puzzles would one day make me astute enough to find a pattern in them. The word jumbles were on the same page so I worked them, too, just for the fun of it.

On the third or fourth day after we had returned from Portugal I decided to entertain him in my suite—sleep with him there—something we had never done. I also thought it was time to tell him that the pixies must go and that if we were going to be successful as man and wife we should act like it and share the same portion of the house.

I conspired with Mrs. McAfee and Mrs. Silva, the two older ladies on the household staff, to fix his favorite meal—roast beef, blood rare, and to prepare my suite and me in an appealing and alluring way. I primped myself for several days. Tanned myself in the garden—sequestered from the eyes of the helpers. Got a perky new haircut, had my nails done, got a facial—picked out the clothes, including lingerie, that George had most favorably commented on. I lifted weights to tone my muscles, cleansed my pores in the sauna, and did everything I could to be sure that my man's mind would be on me alone when we re-consummated our marriage and I asked him to discuss issues important to us.

When the bewitching hour came I put on his favorite see-through lingerie, took a chance that no one else would see me and snuck down to his chambers to seduce my very own husband and lure him to my suite. When I got there his door was closed and I knocked ever so politely.

"George, George, are you in there, dear?"

There was no answer.

I knocked again, only this time briskly. "George, George, it's me, Lili—your little Sugarplum," nauseating I know, but he had begun to refer to me as his "sugarplum" and I decided to go with it as a sort of special pet name for just him to use.

There was no answer at his door.

I picked up the house phone and called one of the pixies, Ethel Farmer. "Miss Farmer, where is George? Is he out this evening? His door is locked and no one answers."

"He's in his room, Ma'am. I'm sure of it. I just took him a large ham and pineapple pizza and beer that the delivery man brought, not twenty minutes ago."

I knocked loudly. "George, George. I'm tired of standing here like a fool in my underwear. Why won't you answer your door?" I got mad, turned around, picked up the most expensive looking vase I could find and broke it against the door.

Thinking he must be out after all and Ethel had been mistaken I turned to gaze out the window into the garden beside his chambers while I waited for him not to come. Just as I was about to turn my head and apply one last knock I saw Roxanne in the waning light of early evening, just as plain as if it were broad daylight. I could see her fair white skin was flushed red from her ankles to her widow's peak.

Just then George opened his door and I pushed past him to see if the bed was made. Of course it wasn't. "Been taking a nap, have you?" I asked.

"Don't you ever break into my chambers again!" he roared.

"I didn't break in. You opened the door. What was that rock headed pixie doing in here anyway?"

"Who?"

"Don't you dare be coy with me. I saw her leave by the side door."

He looked at me and grinned. "She was taking dictation."

I walked over and picked up her black nylons off the floor and held them about two inches under his nose. "Is that why she left these?"

"I'll do as I please. I'm the master of this house. Didn't you read our agreement?"

"You know I didn't and I'm not going to and this shit is going to stop right this instant."

"I'll say it is." He roared and opened his hand and slapped me across the face with his palm. I reeled and had to grab the bedpost to keep from falling. When I rose to confront him he hit me again, only this time with his left hand from the other direction.

He said, "Had enough? Well so have I. I'm keeping my end of the bargain so you take your *hapa haole* ass, go back to your room and mind your own business.

Just then, one of the men stuck his head inside the door. "Trouble, boss?"

"Nothing I can't handle, Lenny."

That was the first time George Santini hit me but it would not be the last.

* * *

After that episode I spent the next couple of days in my suite. I didn't want anyone on the staff to see my bruises. Not only was I embarrassed but they would also know I had lost power. I wondered where I had gone wrong. When had I made the critical mistake?

But then things started to go my way again when I least expected it. He dismissed the pixies, told me he had found good homes for them with nice masters who would treat them well and take them on lots of walks. It was on the edge of my tongue to ask him whether or not those homes were run by madams but I figured it might upset him and I didn't enjoy being slapped. At least he hadn't hit me with a closed fist. I like to think I wouldn't have stayed if he had.

I thought about leaving him anyway but then I got to thinking about Mimo, Aunty Fay and their needs that were being met by George's generosity.

Then he started to court me again as if we had never married. Came to my door, brought me flowers and presents, apologized profusely for what he had done and begged my forgiveness. We had purposely quit using birth control and each time he took me I prayed to the Virgin Mary—even though I had no intention of becoming Catholic—to intercede for me with her Son to allow me to bring forth a child. I even recited a few Hail Mary's from the holy card that María had asked Alfonso to put into the backpack the day I left Guatemala.

George had photographed just about every bare breast this side of Gibraltar but the customer I wanted for mine would have a small, innocent mouth, no teeth and wear diapers.

Things went on like this for months while I gradually let George back into my life and into my bedroom. Earlier on I had thought I wanted us to move in together, share a single set of rooms, but now I felt safer and more comfortable the way things were.

I was again invited to the dinner table with his friends and he became more open about his business dealings in front of me. He pointed out that one of the things I had agreed to was never to testify against him in any forum whatsoever. Izzy had previously explained to me, when it came up with my first husband, Charlie, that the marital testimony privilege was discretionary with the person who was asked to testify. It could be claimed or waived.

In my case if I waived it, I would lose everything he had given me in consideration of the wedding. That included the children's trusts, Aunty Fay's sporty new A-frame overlooking Waimea Canyon. The pedigree cats he had bought her when several of the old ones ran away in protest over her new house being devoid of hair balls. Mimo's house and Daddy's living allowance (although no one had ever been able to find him). And I knew Mimo would lose his job, which he loved, driving a bulldozer for Goodman Construction in Kaua'i. It gave him such a good feeling of self-esteem. These were some of the reasons I had decided not to leave him, not the most prominent ones I hope, but those nagging ones below the surface that you don't like to admit to.

I wasn't sure he could still take Mimo's house away, since it was in Mimo and Ruth's name but this was not the sort of man I wanted to defy. I kept thinking back to that "death do us part" comment he had made when I accepted his proposal of marriage. I began to wonder whether or not he had indeed tried to arrange to have me and Ephraim killed while I was in Barbados, as Lance had said.

When one of the union leaders or a businessman or even a government official would get too far out of line George would call a meeting at the huge koa table in our dining room and summon his men— "henchmen" might be a better word. After hearing from all sides there would be a straw vote of everyone in the tribunal, except George, as to whether the "problem" should be "worked with" or "eliminated altogether."

Once George had heard from his advisors he would make a sign. It was like the hand signal that one makes while playing blackjack. Brush his fingertips towards him across the table and the "problem" was to be "eliminated." Make a horizontal sign with his right hand like an umpire makes to signal "safe" and the person was "worked with" instead.

It took me a while to put this all together, but by quietly listening and watching the hand signals then reading the *Honolulu Advertiser* I could soon see how the finger tapping translated in terms of "stats." The offender would inevitably disappear or wind up in the morgue. George batted a thousand just by tapping his fingers and without ever stepping up to the plate.

As I watched this and thought more about it I became certain that George was not the sort of person I would wish to upset.

*   *   *

Once the pixies left and we were short handed I helped the maids with the housework. They were overloaded and I didn't want to appear like Ena Martin, whom I had once worked for as a domestic servant, and just become a lazy oaf. It felt good to pitch in and George didn't seem to mind or notice, I'm not sure which.

One of the things Mrs. McAfee complained about was that it was so hard to "clean master's ashtray," given all the cigar butts and ash. They would get ground down into the grooves, she said, and become "beastly difficult to clean."

"I'll do it," I said. "I've had a little experience in my time with master's dirty ashtrays." I was thinking of the one I used to clean at the Martins as a youth. I knew it was a nasty job but I also knew the older women would respect me for doing it. The ashtray was located in George's study.

I had never been in his study before. He had made clear that it was "off limits" to me because it was there that he did some of his most sensitive work. As his wife I respected that. But, as his maid I figured I had the run of the house.

Mrs. McAfee was right. The ashtray was a bitch to clean. I couldn't do it all at once and would take a break here and there to regain my conviction and composure. During those hiatuses I dusted. For the most part it was boring but then I ran across something in his bookcase. It stopped me cold.

It was a small blue book with a silver-leafed emblem of two leopards hissing at one another. I got so excited I had to run to the bathroom and come back. Before I did so I hastily put it back on the shelf.

George came in while I was in the bathroom and I had to hide in the shower, while he relieved himself and then left.

I couldn't believe it. I was astounded. For one thing I couldn't believe he was so stupid—unless that book was essential for the operation—so essential that he had to have it near him at all times—and for another I couldn't believe it had survived and made it all the way to Hawaii from Bárbados. *But, why here? Why would he want the book?* Unless he was more intimately involved in a lot more than I had guessed.

Then something dawned on me. *Why hadn't I thought of it before?*

Hurriedly, I ran from his chambers to my own suite. I grabbed one of the "love" notes he had written to me when he was trying to kiss and make up. I unfolded it and carried it tightly clasped in my palm. I ran back down the hallway to his chambers, looking every which way to make sure I wasn't being observed.

Swiftly, I thumbed through the book. Page two-hundred-nineteen—no. Page two hundred-ninety-seven—no. God, this book was full of information—and in the right hands I figured, very juicy. Page one-hundred-twenty-one—no. And there it was on page one-hundred-thirty-four and the handwriting matched exactly. His handwriting—the frilly script of a ruthless tyrant—was next to the amount of money used to try to bribe me.

I was so excited I had to go back to the bathroom. This time I decided to use my own. Begrudgingly and with trepidation about the book's safety and future availability I slowly and carefully placed it back where I had found it. I arranged everything around it, along with everything else in the room, as nearly as I could to the way I thought it had been when I entered the study.

No sooner did I get inside my own suite than George knocked at the door. "How about a little nookums, Sugarplum? It's been a hard day."

"I'd love to but I'm on my period," I said, groping for the quickest and easiest excuse I could find. George was not a man to ford the red sea.

"Oh," he said. "Sorry to bother you. I'll take a rain check."

How sweet! The truth was that my period was a few days late but I knew he had a general idea of when it was and would believe me in an instant.

* * *

For the next several days I was on the brink of panic thinking about how I might get my hands on that book and get it to the proper authorities. I was fearful it might get moved or destroyed. So when George said to Mrs.

McAfee, "Nice job on that ashtray but why did you quit in the middle?"

I stood behind him and shook my head at her profusely, praying she would catch my drift.   She said, "Well, I didn't—"

Then she looked over at me and appeared to catch on.

"I didn't have time to finish it, sir. I apologize. I got distracted and then forgot. Let me get to it right away."

"If you please," he said.

Later on Mrs. McAfee asked me, "What happened with the ashtray? Why didn't you finish it?"

I said, "I wanted to but I wasn't sure I would measure up.   You know how Mr. Santini is when something is not done to his satisfaction."

"I know, Mum. He can bite your head off."

"You don't know the half of it," I said.

Mrs. McAfee said, "Do you want me to clean in there? . . . I mean so he won't be so troublesome about it?"

"No, definitely not," I said. "I'll see to it myself."

"Very well, Mum."

* * *

In getting the book to the authorities I thought I would be the best courier. As much as I figured Tiny liked me I doubted he would betray his boss to that extent. After all he had just been his best man. And if he were caught he was more likely to get the finger brushing response instead of the "safe" signal I might get, if anyone could. I didn't think George would be stupid enough to have me eliminated if he wanted to keep his job as labor boss and maintain his public image. His constituents would sense what had happened and it had been tough going for him politically until I came on the scene.

How do I get that book out of there?

I decided to test some theories. First I walked to the end of the driveway and figured that if no one stopped me I would just go into Waimea, do some shopping and come back.

"Where ya headed, Ma'am?" The guard at the main gate asked.

"Why I was thinking of going into Waimea to get some groceries," I said.

"Just a moment, Ma'am. Let me get one of the men to drive you."

"Oh, but I can drive," I said. "Could you tell me who to see for the car keys?"

"Why Tiny and the chauffeurs keep them but I don't think they'll give them to you. Besides we have strict instructions regarding who can drive through the gate."

"Shall I call your husband? He can approve it."

"No. Don't bother him. I know he's busy. How about if I just walk into Hawi? I can probably get what I need there."

"I'd better call your husband," he said and reached for the phone.

I panicked but tried not to show it. "Ralph," (I could see his name tag.) "Ralph, I just need some Tampons and I'm embarrassed to send anyone else to get them."

He breathed a sigh of relief. "I know. Ever since Roxanne and Madeline and the girls moved on, I'll bet it's hard to—"

"You're right, Ralph, but they were all placed into nice homes. . . . with wonderful masters."

"I know, Ma'am. The boss (by now everyone referred to him freely, even in front of me, as "the boss.") told me. Ain't that nice. The boss is very thoughtful that way."

"I know what you mean," I said. "He's so kind and considerate or I don't know what I would do."

"I know just what you mean, Mrs. Santini."

* * *

I tried riding horseback to the edge of the property and seeing if I were followed. Of course I was. The man who tailed me was pretty discreet. But as I neared the edge I noticed the distance between him and me decreased.

An exception was when I rode near the ocean. No one interfered with my rides along the beach or the nearby cliffs. I was followed but no one tried to prevent the excursion. George must have given a special dispensation for such a ride. He knew how much I loved it.

I discovered a waterfall that I had not known was there. It sprang out of a lava tube and then descended two or three hundred feet over the cliffs to the ocean below. As the rainy season was now upon us falls were beginning to crop up all over the windward side of the island. The noise from the falls was deafening and I thoroughly enjoyed it.

I figured I might be able to ride all the way around the island by staying on the beach. The beaches in Hawaii are all public. But I knew my pursuers would never be far behind and I didn't want to discover my ultimate boundaries. Riding along the beach gave me a larger sense of freedom.

And I had thought a jury of my peers were the ones who might send me to prison.

* * *

Then I got a break. George told me at dinner one evening that he had been told by his attorneys that the civil case against me was about to be dismissed because the appellate court had ruled the enabling statute unconstitutional—as arbitrarily vague. There was one catch, however. The trial judge to whom the case had been remanded had decided that I would have to sign some papers to dismiss my counterclaim against the county for malicious prosecution. The truth was that I would have had a reasonably good chance of prevailing under the circumstances and the judge didn't want to end up falling into disfavor with the governor. Everyone knew he was vying for a trusteeship with the Bishop Trust.

When Izzy called I said, "I'd just like to get this garbage behind me. I'm not interested in the county's money."

"Are you sure?" he said. "They've put you through a lot more than just 'inconvenience.'"

"I'm sure."

George said that he had made arrangements for his attorneys to bring me the papers to sign. I told him that I insisted that I have my own attorney go over them with me.

"It's just a sheet of paper from what they tell me."

"Just the same I didn't read the last batch of papers I signed for you and look what that got me."

George looked puzzled. He didn't know whether to be angry, hurt or laugh.

"Just kidding," I said and reached over and barely touched his arm.

"I'm sure I could persuade you to sign," he said.

"I doubt it," I said and looked at him sternly.

He decided to ignore the line I had drawn in the sand and said, "Very well, then. Your attorney it is."

* * *

I would have signed those papers in the blink of an eye, even for George's low life law firm except that I needed Izzy to carry the ledger to places I dared not go. On the day when he was scheduled to come I took special care to look nice and hide my badges of shame.

I caked makeup under my eyes so that he couldn't see the latest bruise. It was my retribution for asking George where he'd been so late the evening before. The hell of it was I didn't really care. I was just trying to be social. I had given up trying to hide the beatings from the maids and the rest of the staff. But for one day I figured it was something I didn't need for Izzy to take from my doorstep to his.

I decided to have breakfast early that morning and eat a hearty one because I knew there was a lot to accomplish and I would need all the strength I could get. I wished Lance were there to fix one of his great omelets with onions and peppers and a splash of his father's hot pepper sauce spilled over the top. I might even put in a bay leaf. No one else was stirring yet, not even Tiny, so I sat down to work the math puzzle from the preceding Sunday paper. I was actually getting quite good at it by now.

There was a little historical quiz in the corner of the page so I took that, too. *Hmm! That's interesting.* This morning's quiz was about Lord Nelson. "When was the Battle of Trafalgar?"

And then it hit me like a volcanic eruption. I filled in the blanks 1-8-0-5 and I knew I had found it. I had discovered the code and realization that Ephraim must have come to just before he was murdered. I had looked at that list of questionable transactions at least a hundred times by now—not the ones with the math errors, but the ones I had found by checking the vouchers against the computer runs, according to Ephraim's instructions—and I knew the answer without checking.

Still I ran to my room and got the list. I put it on the desk in front of my make-up mirror and turned on the lights. I uncurled it and smoothed it out. Sure enough. There it was. Every single transaction had the numbers 1-8-0-5 in it. They were not necessarily in that order. Sometimes it was 5-8-0-1 or 5-0-8-1 but they were there every time in the context of a nine-digit account number. Sometimes the numbers were contiguous like 245180598 and other times they were spread out like 219870654. I underlined them to make them stand out and check my theory. Ephraim must have deduced this in an instant.

I had to implement my plan to get my hands on that book. If my theory was correct, then every number in the book would bear the same code.

An hour or so before Izzy arrived and shortly after I
knew George had gone into the kitchen to have breakfast, I
decided to sneak down and get it. The book was a risk that
I knew might cost me my life. But what was my life worth
now anyway? It was a chance to do something worthwhile.
Make my mark. Improve the lot of others.

When I got to George's room the door was closed.
I was afraid he might be in so I knocked gently. No
answer. I entered.

I went to where the book had been but it wasn't
there. I was on the verge of panic. I searched all over the
room but it was nowhere to be found.

Out of desperation I went to the kitchen to see if
George was still there. What was I to say to him? "Where
is the ledger that tells of all your transactions in the
Caribbean? No, I'm not thinking of that one. I mean the
one that has your handwriting in it acknowledging the
source of the bribe money in my criminal case."

I had no idea what I was going to say. Fortunately
he was gone and Tiny was just finishing up his coffee and a
biscuit. George was out in his fatigues running an assault
defense drill and was expected to be gone a couple of
hours. Perfect. But nothing without the book.

"Tiny, have you seen George using a blue ledger
book?"

He looked at me with a blank expression.

"It has two leopards on it hissing at one another."

"Oh, I thought those was mountain lions."

"No, Tiny, they're leopards. But I can see how
anyone could get them confused. Have you seen it?"

Tiny sipped his coffee. "I think the boss took it
with him into the bunker."

My heart sank. I knew I had no chance of getting it
from there. I didn't have the right artillery. They wouldn't
even let me in, especially if they were conducting
exercises.

Tiny put down his coffee. "Just a second. I'll go
and see if he left it in the dining room. Sometimes he brings
it to council meetings and he may have left it there. He
might have hidden it in the china cabinet." Less than five
minutes later he came back with the book.

I was jubilant but tried not to show it.

Tiny said, "What if he asks about it? What if he
asks where it is?"

"Tell him I have it, of course." It was the same thing I had said to Hans when he asked about what to do if he received another telegram from my pursuers. I preferred not to put Tiny's life in danger, especially since he'd have had no idea what for.

"Are you sure you're supposed to have this?"

"Yes. George's been going over it with me. He wants me to learn the business in case anything ever happens to him."

"That's the boss," Tiny said. "Always thinkin' ahead."

I hoped and prayed the exercise would last longer than usual and that George would not come back prematurely. I took the book to my room, checked three or four transaction numbers at random throughout the book. The code held. I was willing to bet that if this code were checked against all of the other books and records of the bank there would be no accounts other than the "funny" ones that used all four of those numbers in any sequence. This information in the hands of the right people would enable them to go directly to the transactions that should be questioned in the banks main books and records.

I desperately wanted to thumb through the rest of the book to see what else I could find but Izzy was due any minute and I had to get ready.

Chapter Twenty-Two

When Izzy came I took him straight to my bedroom. I could tell he was uncomfortable. "Izzy, you shouldn't feel uneasy. You've been in my bedroom before, remember?"

"How could I forget?" he said. I could tell he was not quite sure what I had in mind.

One thing Izzy and George had taught me was you never know who might be listening or watching. I had had a strange feeling from the very first day I had been in that suite and now I was wondering whether or not there were surveillance cameras hidden in the woodwork. I had not had time to secret the book away like I wanted to so I invited Izzy to come along with me while I changed.

The former Mrs. Santini had a set of panels with Japanese art on them that stood in a corner. I wondered if she had used them so she wouldn't have to undress in front of George. I stepped behind them and dressed while I talked with Izzy.

I had put the book under some of my dirty clothes and shuffled things around so that I could slip it down my back and under the belt of my riding breeches. What a tight squeeze that was. Then I put on a loosely fitting sweater over it.

"Lili, you're going to be hot," Izzy said. "And you're dressed for riding. I thought we were going to talk."

"We are, but I like the fresh air myself." I glanced around the room and Izzy immediately caught on. He was Mr. Paranoia when it came to listening devices.

"But, Lili, I didn't bring any riding gear. If you had called—"

I wanted to say, "You're kidding. Do you think George would let me make an off-island phone call?" But, I didn't. Instead, I said, "I meant to call you but you know how time flies."

"I understand," Izzy said, although I wasn't sure he did. "Here, Izzy, I had someone send to the stables for these." I gave him a complete set of riding clothes in his size. Since he was small I was able to get him the actual shirt, hat, whip and boots that one of George's jockeys had ridden in a race at Santa Anita the preceding year. The maids had sewn a panel on each side of the shirt to make it wider. It was bright yellow with a black number seven in a circle. I wondered whether or not Judge Henderson, of the Kaua'i Circuit Court, had bet on that race.

George was so tickled that one of his thoroughbreds was good enough to place in a race at a major track that he kept the jockey's uniform and horse's colors as a collector's item in a glass case in the tack room. In reality it had been I who got the outfit for Izzy. I broke the glass case and took it. In a few minutes Izzy would be sporting the same colors as George's jockey, only this time on Lazy Susan. I had long since graduated to more spirited mounts.

"Do you have your briefcase?" I asked.

"Yes. I never leave home without it."

He held it up from behind the Japanese panels where he was now dressing.

"Good, bring it along."

"Are you kidding? On a horseback ride?"

"Izzy I forgot to tell you that I have a doctor's appointment later today. I only have a short time for us to meet. We'll have to stop somewhere along the trail and have our meeting. I've got to be getting back."

I could tell he was looking carefully around my eyes. "Anything serious?" he asked.

I prayed that none of my blush had flaked off to disclose the bruises. "No, I think I'm fine. Just a routine checkup."

"Good. I'd hate it if anything ever happened to you."

"Me, too," I said. "Come to think of it we should bring my will up to date."

Izzy looked concerned.

"Just a precaution," I said. "You know I just got married and all and I want to be sure that Mimo and his children and Aunty Fay are still my primary beneficiaries."

"We can write a holographic codicil today, Sugar. That means it has to be entirely in your own handwriting. We can replace it with a formal revision later. Your premarital agreement allows that."

"Good. I'll grab a pen and paper. Will any kind of pen and paper be okay?"

"Everything for the court has to be in black ink," Izzy said. "But I always carry a black ink pen with me."

"And what about that mailer I asked you to bring?"

"Yes, I got George's facsimile saying you wanted the original, signed copy of this release to go directly to his lawyers today. So I brought a mailer."

Now it was my turn to ham it up in case anyone was listening. I looked around at the walls and said, "George wants this done in a hurry. So he'll be obliged if you get the paperwork right off to his attorneys."

Izzy came out from behind the dressing panels.

I laughed. He looked so cute in the jockey outfit. Miraculously the boots fit as Izzy was considerably bigger than the jockey. His riding breeches were left behind by one of the pixies.

"Are you ready?" I asked.

He ran his hands jokingly along the sleeves and elbows of his yellow jersey as though he had just won the feature race and smiled. He held up his arms, made two fists in triumph and tried to make his biceps bulge. "Yes," he said. "I believe I am."

"Good." I said. "Let's go!"

* * *

When we got to the tack room George was there.

"What are you doing here?" I asked.

"I was about to ask you the same question," he said.

"Izzy and I are going for a quick ride and I'm going to sign the paperwork on some scenic vista overlooking the ranch—a celebration of Izzy's hard work. We're taking along a bottle of Hans Kornell champagne."

George looked doubtful and then appeared distracted. "What's he doing wearing Jean du Lac's jersey and our stable colors?"

"He forgot his riding clothes."

He looked at a riding whip on the wall. I think he would have used it on me if Izzy weren't along. I could see from the look on his face that he was having a hard time suppressing his anger. I smiled.

I said, "I thought you were supervising defense maneuvers with the men this afternoon."

"I remembered I had some bookwork to do but I wanted to see how our new filly was coming along first."

"How is she?"

"A beauty," he said.

Our horses were saddled for us before we got there. While we were talking I had been leading them out of their crossties.

I gave George a big hug and kiss as passionate as I could muster. "Catch me after the ride?" I asked.

He seemed interested but I stepped back because I didn't want him to discover the book in my pants. I don't think he noticed that I had on a sweater in spite of the sweat rolling down my forehead. I quickly mounted Rusty Nail, a dark chestnut gelding. He was high-spirited and faster than the red wind. George must have calmed down because he came over and tried to reach his arm around me for another kiss. "Gotta go," I said. I gave "Rusty" a light nudge with my spurs and we were off to the rolling hills.

* * *

It was hilarious to see Izzy dressed like a jockey, especially in his thick glasses. He was a reasonably good rider.

"Spent some time in the saddle, recently?" I asked. I had remembered him as a clumsy rider but he seemed to have improved.

"It's Kiku's idea. You know how Japanese people enjoy western culture? Well, she saw City Slickers and fell in love with Billy Crystal so now we have to go riding every Saturday."

I laughed. "I'm sure it's good for you." I pulled alongside him.

I didn't know what George was doing or just what "bookwork" he had in mind. I figured I'd take a chance and enjoy myself while I could. We loped along in the rolling hills and the scenery was as beautiful as ever.

"I have to admit that you were right, Izzy."

"Right about what?"

"I'm afraid my marriage to George was not made in heaven."

"I tried to tell you."

"You did a pretty good job of doing just that as I recall."

We decided to climb the butte on which the bunker was located but a helicopter swooped down on us before we could get a good start so we decided to visit the ocean along the northeastern coast on the windward side of the island. I have always loved the windy, stormy parts of Hawaii.

I asked, "Do you think George is in cahoots with the governor? I mean is it all one big conspiracy?"

"No, I don't think so," Izzy said. "It's more like a division of territories, the slicing of a pie rather than an entire dessert in one serving."

"Izzy, what a great analogy. I think I got it."

"Only I think—in fact I know—especially after the letter I got from you from Portugal that George is involved internationally. I'm not sure the others are. In fact I doubt it. He's like the high stakes player in this game, like the guy at the no limit baccarat table. The others are probably just playing the nickel slots or blackjack."

"You're on a roll today, Izzy. I wish I could think of some math problems for you to help me solve."

"How about the Pythagorean theorem?"

"No thanks. I don't even know what that is," I yelled, as we turned to head towards the coast. We pushed our horses to a trot. I could see that we were being followed but it was by a lone rider and he kept well back. He didn't seem obtrusive and his following would not be evident to a casual observer. He would ride ahead for a while, maybe check the rocks in a lava fence or stop and check his horse's hooves, take off his hat and look back at the main house. But he was there—ever present, ever heading in our same general direction. I suspected that if we galloped, so would he, but I would have to save that for another day. This mission was too serious to experiment.

"How are things going for you with the bar association? Do they still have charges pending?"

"Yes, although I have a feeling they won't want to proceed once this case is dropped. There are too many big names just below the surface of the scandal. Too many influential people might be hurt."

"Are you kidding? Do you think it extends that far?"

"You never know where the tentacles of corruption are in this state, Lili. Look at the Bishop Trust. Who would have expected our state's finest citizens to misuse the funds intended for our native population?"

"I could smell that one from the cheap seats," I said. "Their seven-figure salaries were outrageous to begin with."

"Appointed by the governor and approved by the supreme court," Izzy mused.

"Go figure that one out," I said.

Finally we reached our destination—the waterfalls along the coast I had discovered a few days earlier. With the sound of water splashing against the rocks we could barely hear one another but that was my plan. I had heard of directional listening devices and wouldn't put anything past either the mind or technology of George and his men.

We set up office on the upwind side of the falls to keep the papers dry. We composed a will and I signed it, dividing my worldly goods and income among Aunty Fay, Mimo and his children. I left my horse, Rusty, to Lance's children. George had given him to me as a wedding present and Izzy confirmed that he was mine to keep or do with as I chose. I didn't know how he would get to Barbados but if he did, I knew Theo, Willie, Idalia and Emma would love to care for and ride him.

I signed the papers dismissing my counterclaim against the County of Kaua'i. That took only about thirty seconds. Then I showed Izzy the book.

"According to Inspector Lance Williams in Barbados . . ." I stopped to wonder if the way I mentioned his name would cue Izzy in as to how I felt about him but the water was loud and splashing. I had a hard time keeping the book dry. "According to Inspector Williams of the Royal Barbados Police Force this book has records for all major international money laundering transactions run through the Bank of Barbados during the last five years.

"There are no names but every major transaction is there and the account numbers are coded to distinguish them from legitimate bank business."

"Wow!" Izzy said, "How long have you known this?"

There was a light spray on the pages from the falls so I moved the book a little in an effort to keep it dry. "It took me almost nine months to figure it out," I said. "My friend, Ephraim Whitney, probably figured it out in twenty minutes. But, then again, it cost him his life."

Izzy could see that my mention of Ephraim's death upset me so he reached over and held my hand for a moment.

"Better not let that horseman see you do that," I said. "The boss might misinterpret it."

Izzy seemed unfazed and asked whether or not he could see the book. I handed it to him.

He thumbed through it. We verified several more numbers and, as no surprise to us by then, they all fit the pattern.

Izzy noticed the fold out page in the back—the one that I had been reluctant to open the night I shared flying fish with Mr. Baker before I ran into Miss Cumberbatch climbing his steps like an alley cat. Izzy opened the page.

"See there," he said. "This page was not a part of the book when it was bound. See how it was glued in later, almost like an afterthought."

"Or a supplement," I said.

"Yes," Izzy said. "That's a better way to put it, 'like a supplement.'"

He opened it, showed it to me. "What do you suppose this is?" As he did so a torrent of water blew in our direction and soaked the page. I blotted it dry with the kerchief from my hair.

There was a schematic of lines in all sorts of directions with arrows and boxes and letters inside. After many years as mayor of Kaua'i I could tell at a glance it was an organizational chart.

Izzy looked baffled. "But what about all the letters in there? They look like alphabet soup."

"Here, let me see." He handed me the book. I looked up and down the coastline but I couldn't see the lone rider. I was confident he was there but took my chances with the book.

I studied it for a few minutes while Izzy went into the bushes to relieve himself, while keeping an eye out for intruders. By the time he returned I had it.

"I've got it, Izzy. See here in this third row of boxes where it says, "BGI LDNAIS?"

He nodded in the affirmative.

"Well, at first, I thought that meant 'BGI,' as the three letter identifier for Bridgetown International Airport.
"What does it really mean?"
"Izzy, BGI stands for Big!"
He looked uninspired by my discovery.
"Izzy, that's Big, as in Big Island."
"So?"
"Look here. Look more closely." I have to admit that I was feeling pretty good about myself for now it was my turn to figure something out in a few minutes. See here, EEGROG IINNTSA.
"Yes," he said. "as if to say, 'so what?'"
"So, they're just word jumbles, anagrams. EEGROG IINNTSA is 'George Santini!' And look here! Look beneath those letters, it says, FRCTEEENONM that means 'enforcement.' George Santini is in charge of enforcement. Izzy, Winston Baker was a chain of command freak. I'll bet he did this. He kept telling us that the French and Spanish lost the Battle of Trafalgar because they were so poorly organized and unclear about who was in charge at every level. First Admiral Villeneuve failed to accept the removal of his command in favor of Admiral Rosily. Then the Spanish captains under him refused to follow orders. 'If it weren't for that,' he said. 'Lord Nelson might still be alive today.'"
"That's a stretch," Izzy said.
"I know. But, you know what I mean."
"I sure do," Izzy said. "Can you get me a copy of this book?"
"There are no copies," I assured him. "Just thinking that I might have had a good look at one of those pages made them try to kill me. This is not the sort of thing you keep a copy of," I said.
Together we worked on the word scrambles and did as many as we thought we had time to do, which weren't many. We identified the notorious Grämlich brothers. R.M. is now in Las Vegas posing as a dentist, but he's really in charge of LBNIGMAG, better known as Gambling, while his older brother F.W. remains in AOGBOT, better know as Bogotá in charge of the ICONCEA, cocaine concession."
Unfortunately some of the letters were smeared. For example I couldn't make out the name that went with the title "EREGLSNCOII," nor did we have time to work out the one that identified George's role. He was in a line

with others, identified as OOCPS. There were a whole bunch of "soldiers" down below. I quickly solved that one as it had just appeared in last Sunday's paper in much the same form.

I sensed we were running out of time. I wished we could work out the other names especially the ones near the top.

"What do you make of this 'M.F.' in New York?" Izzy asked. That one was easy. He was the "boss." The title was not even jumbled.

"He's got to be the big enchilada," I replied.

"Who do you think he is?" Izzy asked.

"It could be a he or a she," I said, resentfully.

Izzy refused to acknowledge his *faux pas*. "The masculine includes the feminine unless otherwise indicated," he parroted. For a moment I felt as though I were back at the Bank of Barbados receiving instruction from Mrs. Musgrave. "Who is it? Do you have any idea?"

"I don't know, Izzy. I'm sure there are so many 'M.F.'s" in New York, I wouldn't know where to start. Besides, it could be 'F.M.' Look. The ink's been rubbed out and written over. It looks like a recent change."

"Do you know what this means?" Izzy asked. "I mean—this chart, these numbers, this book. Do you know what it all means?"

"It means I may get some good out of that will I just signed."

"Oh, Lili." He came over and hugged me close and tight. I hugged him back. I could feel the cold water from the falls that had sprayed on him when the book got wet.

"Don't worry about me," I said. "I can take a lickin' and . . ." I stopped, while Izzy looked at me quizzically. "Oh just something I used to say to Aunty Fay when I drove around in that old station wagon that Charlie and I used to have. Seems like a lifetime ago."

Izzy asked, "What do you think we should do with this? I could copy the chart and some of the rest of the information but not all of it. It would take hours. How much time do you think we have?"

"I've had a chance to think this over for a while, Izzy. I think we should send the entire book to the FBI."

"That would be effective," he said, "but it's bound to cause you trouble. This is the sort of thing that George would likely miss."

"I can handle it, Izzy," I said, without having fully considered the implications. "What do you think will come of it if we turn it over to the FBI? I mean in the long run." I grew excited.

"I think they'll use this ledger and that organizational chart to drive nails into the coffins of George and his associates. I only hope one of them is not yours. It'll take a while, given the workings of the government, international political considerations, change of administrations and such. But in the end—I think you've got the principals in this organization by the balls and this will provide the necessary tools to castrate them. At least it will provide the governments of many nations with a 'hit list' of their own."

It was good to think they might end up like Ephraim—at least in one sense.

"In the meantime, Izzy, could you call my friend, Inspector Lance Williams of the Royal Barbados Police Department? Tell him about the account number sequencing—how it works and all. With that he can identify the affected accounts from the bank's own records. Will you do that for me?"

"Consider it done," Izzy said. "Is that why you're doing this? Taking this chance? Is it all for him?"

It was on the tip of my tongue to say, "Tell him I love him," but I didn't. I didn't want to hurt Izzy's feelings. "No, Izzy, I'm doing it because I think it's the right thing to do. They've hurt a lot of people and ruined many lives, not the least of which is mine and Ephraim's. Remember our pledges at St. Elisabeth's Russian Fort that night when we were kids. Is altruism so difficult to understand?"

"It is these days," he replied. "There's precious little of it."

"C'mon," I said. "Don't feel sorry for me."

"Oh, Lili," he said and put his arm around my shoulder. I could tell he was sad for me by the way he held me. I could also see it on his face. "Are you sure you'll be all right?"

"Don't cry for me, Izzy. I should have known better. My father was a bum and my first husband, Charlie, was a bum. Guess that's just the sort of men I'm attracted to."

"I resent that," he said.

"You're the vast exception. You and a man I met in Barbados." Neither of us spoke again for almost a minute. I bathed in self-pity. We stood and stared at the falling water, occasionally scooped a handful and splashed it on our faces.

"What next?" he asked.

"I'm glad you asked that. We'd better get going. Time may be getting short. If we take that book back to the ranch George may have noticed it missing and take it away from us."

"That would be a fair assumption," Izzy said in all seriousness—so Izzy-like.

I said, "I've been watching and I'm convinced there is only one man following us and I don't think he has a radio. I've watched him carefully each time I've ridden out here. I've gotten as close to him as I could a couple of times and I think it's just a guy on a horse."

"With a rifle across his saddle?"

"You've noticed that, too?"

Izzy nodded.

I said, "First we're going to change horses. Then we'll take advantage of the fact that there are two of us and one of him."

"Shall we rush him?"

I looked at Izzy as if to say, "What in the hell-"

"Just kidding," he said.

I said, "When we leave here, given the choice, I'm sure he'll follow me and let you go. I have no doubt about that.

"You're going to ride into Waimea as fast as you can and send the book in that mailer you brought. I handed him the business card with the FBI agent's address on it. Send the book to the address on that card."

He looked at it and stuck it into his briefcase along with the legal papers and the ledger. He tethered it to Rusty.

I said, "I'm going to take the long way back to the ranch and hopefully by the time I get back the book will no longer be in your possession. You take the first flight back to Honolulu, call the FBI and get some protection of your own."

"I have an old law school buddy, Richard Austin, who lives in Hilo," Izzy said. "I'll ask him to take me to Oahu on his fishing boat."

We hugged as we had as children after a day of play. Another I-never-want-to-let-go hug. For me these were happening altogether too often.

I handed him the whip.

Izzy said, "What about Rusty? You know I could be accused of stealing your horse. I could lose my license to— "

"I know," I said. "You have my permission, but in case that's not good enough, here's a bill of sale. It *is* my horse."

"Good piece of lawyering," he said. "I didn't know you knew that much about the law."

"I did learn a few things as mayor," I said. "When you get to wherever you're going just leave the horse with a note that says it belongs at the Santini Ranch. I have a feeling it will be returned."

"That's true. I doubt many of the local residents would choose to be considered thieves from your husband's point of view."

"Just you and me, Izzy. We're the damn fools." We hugged again.

"Go on, get out of here," I said, "before I change my mind."

Izzy turned to mount his horse. "Oh, what about my suit?" he asked.

"Just tell your wife," I joked, "that I insisted you take it off in my bedroom and you didn't have time to put it back on." I changed my tone. "Izzy, you may never see that suit again. That's one more thing I owe you."

He got on his horse and smiled. I could barely keep from laughing. His riding skills were adequate but he seemed to have considerable difficulty taking command of Rusty. I came to the edge of the falls and watched them depart. At one point he almost slipped off the horse. Then he managed to get himself back on straight, gave the horse a little swat with the whip and perched on the saddle like a jockey. I laughed until my sides split and then I cried. I wondered whether or not I would ever see my friend again.

I turned and looked the other way. The rider had come closer to make sure I was still there. But he hadn't become what one might call "intrusive."

Chapter Twenty-Three

I took the long way back to the ranch, through Hawi. I leaned to look at the beautiful Kohala cliffs and mountains as I loped along. I felt like the errant teenager, out with Daddy's car past curfew, who knew that she would be in trouble once she got home, but was having a good time and didn't want it to end. In my case there was no such car but there had been beatings I had gotten from Daddy for staying out late. The feeling, if not the act, was familiar.

I wanted to give Izzy all the time I possibly could to get away. Eventually I came to Hawi, and when I did, more riders approached, and I knew that time was short. I figured I had better try to get back to the ranch before they did to accomplish as much as I could before the book was discovered missing, assuming it hadn't been already.

I surmised that it hadn't, given the demeanor of the riders. They were altogether too calm to have absorbed news of the missing book. Perhaps maneuvers had gone on longer than expected. It was now nearly three hours since Izzy had left, bouncing around on Rusty's back. I was sure that word of his departure would be flashed to all hands on deck, now that my lone follower could communicate with the others.

I trotted up the path beside the ironwoods and mused to myself about all that had happened since I first saw them. I was a different person now. Oh what I would have given to turn back the clock, to have made different choices. I felt as though I had aged ten years in less than one.

As I rode through the whispering pines I thought of all the mystery they held. In the evenings I used to sit on the sun porch and watch them rustle in the moonlight while I gazed through them at the ocean in the distance. I looked up at the windmills and watched them lumber just as lazily as the day I had been chauffeured through the front gate for the first time.

I passed through the main gate and there was no reaction except for the tip of a hat.

"Howdy, Mrs. Santini," one guard said.

"Lose your companion?" another said.

"He's coming later," I answered, a response which didn't seem to phase anyone.

I quickly untacked Lazy Susan and put her in her stall and asked someone else to brush her—a task I normally did myself. I rushed into my suite. I had my own telephone but what purpose it served I had no idea. Just the same I hurriedly called 1-800-GOFEDEX and to my joy and surprise—I had never tried a toll free number before— the call went through. I found that package number 807912955017 had been scanned at the Hilo processing center and had already left the airport en route to the Memphis, Tennessee processing center nearly forty-five minutes earlier.

After I got back to my suite the strangest thing happened—absolutely nothing. By late afternoon I had grown tired of waiting for the firestorm so I did something to keep myself busy. I put one of the maid's aprons on over my clothes. After all, what was my proper role? I didn't want to think of myself as a whore as I still met my "wifely responsibilities."

I put my hands in the pockets of the apron and stretched them and then went to work cleaning and dusting. I stayed away from the master's chambers. I figured there was already enough unsettled dust in there from the cleaning I had previously done.

Then Tiny came to get me. He looked as though his mother had died and he'd just found out. "Boss wants to see you in the dining room," he said.

"Bad?" I asked.

He didn't have to say anything for me to know the answer but he did. "Bad as it can get."

"Tiny . . ."

"Yes, Ma'am."

"Don't do anything that would get you into trouble, not for me, you hear?"

"But, Ma'am."

I gently put my finger to his lips. "*¡Silencio!*" I said.

My encounter with George was not so touching.

"Where's the book?" he asked. "Where's the goddamn book?"

"What book?"

He smacked me. "You know what book I mean, you rotten bitch!"

"It's gone," I muttered, while my head quivered back to steady.

"I thought so," he said. "With that blood-sucking lawyer, Kawamoto?"

"He's already mailed it," I said.

He hit me again, this time with his fist clenched. I could feel Tiny grab onto me, partly to keep me from falling and partly to hold me back. It was like a procedure with them, each schooled in the next step. Tiny hung onto me and I prayed that he would continue so that he would not get into trouble, and I thought, You don't even fight fair with a woman. I could feel my adrenaline flowing. If I'd decided to break Tiny's hold I'm confident that I would have killed George. But I'd already been privy to enough murders and attempted murders in my life. I knew that wasn't the answer.

"Where did he send it?" George asked.

"I don't know for sure," I said. "I think he mailed it to MI-5, British Intelligence in Barbados." I wanted to throw him off track.

"Men, you know what to do. Get that book back, and pronto! Our entire operation depends on it."

Several of the men left at once.

He beat me senseless, not with the palms of his hands this time, but with his fists. I slumped in Tiny's arms. I tried to regain my strength and stand, just to defy him. And then, just like in a gangster movie, he put on brass knuckles. "Take this you lousy bitch!"

He hit me in the jaw. I felt it crack and my blood splatter. Several of my teeth flew towards the floor, and then silence while my teeth hit—not like rocks but with soft pinging sounds, like rainfall on a tin roof. The blood spewed from my nose and mouth. Onto the floor. Onto my clothing. Onto my white apron, where I knew it would turn brown and stain.

Tiny let go of me and I fell to the floor. I could see out of the corner of my eye that George, my lover, was about to kick me in the ribs with his combat boot. But Tiny grabbed him and said, "Don't do it, Boss. She's had enough. If you kick her, you'll kill her."

"Maybe then she'd learn her lesson," he said. He picked up a linen napkin off the dining room table and threw it at me as if that meant it was time to clean myself up and get back to work.

I became delirious and went in and out of consciousness as if in a dream. This time I didn't see Momma but a choir—a choir under a red and white tent in Speightstown, singing to the heavens. I was back at the People's Cathedral on the hill in Bridgetown with Lance as the lead singer, me cupping my hand to receive the bread and sip the grape juice of salvation. My brain spun wildly. A myriad of colors, stirred by the midday sun, formed a pinwheel of Kaleidoscopic flashes.

Now I was back in the Porsche, the yellow Porsche, motoring up Lance's driveway, only this time the children were clasping their arms around my neck, too. They were kissing me. We were a happy, loving family, as I had always wanted. I reached out for the dark hand with the wisps of curls that belonged to the love of my life. His hand reached to pull me up the rocky cliffs near Bathsheba. I could almost grasp it but not quite. Gradually it slipped from my fingers, just as Momma's hand had done in the rocks near Polihale—a recurring dream that haunts me to this day.

I came to and looked about me at the cold, harsh realities of life. *How could such an elegant dining room be the host of such ugliness?* My husband had gone. Tiny stayed long enough to ask, "Can I help ya Ma'am?"

I shook my head, "No . . . No, Tiny. You'd better get out of here before he gets mad at you, too. One beating today is enough." He looked at me with sad eyes and left.

I crawled on my hands and knees because I didn't have the strength to stand. One by one, bit by bit, I picked

up my teeth from the floor and placed them into the pocket
of my apron.

I cleaned up my own mess, cold and alone,
shivering on a hot sunny day. I wiped the blood off the
floor. The pain had not yet begun in earnest. I was in a
state of shock. I nearly collapsed before I was done and
rested sidesaddle on the floor.

There I sat, an abysmal failure—in the mate
selection process anyway—a prisoner in my own home
with the sentence already pronounced, "until death do you
part."

I wondered how I could have been so blind or
stupid or both. I could have blamed it all on the afflictions
I had as a youth—the abuse, the beatings, the scars that will
probably never heal. The deficiencies I may always have
in the capacity to make wise decisions, especially where
men were concerned. I knew that now. So I decided at that
moment, then and there that I would no longer look to men
as the ultimate answer to my needs but to a higher power—
a power I could always count on to guide and protect me.

I prayed to Jesus. I prayed that my life would some
day be a better one and that my life's ambition to do good
would be fulfilled. I prayed that I would one day be part of
a happy and healthy family. I prayed that I would become
wiser in my choices and more considerate of others who—
through my own selfishness and poor judgment—I had
unwittingly put in harm's way. And then I prayed for
forgiveness.

I gave my prayers a "chonce" to rise to the heavens
while I dabbed the rest of the blood off my face in front of
my makeup mirror with a cold white washcloth. Then I
locked the door to my room, sat down—grimacing with
pain—and planned for my ultimate escape.

* * *

A few days later, when I was able and the pain was
finally beginning to subside in my jaw, I read in a prior
edition of *The Big Island Gazette* that the U.S. Mail
dispatch from Waimea to Hilo had been "hit" by a group of
robbers. All the mail was stolen. It happened the evening I
was savagely beaten. When I had been confronted with the
loss of the ledger, I had been careful to use the word
"mail," over and over again, as a diversion even though I
knew Isito Kawamoto and his habits like the hair on my
head.

"Whenever it's absolutely, positively, got to be there on time," Izzy was fond of saying, "send it Federal Express."

It would have paid for George and his men to watch more TV commercials.

There was also a black and white picture on the front page showing a mysterious rider in a jockey uniform galloping along the main street in Waimea, along with the caption, "Fourth Leg of Triple Crown Comes to Hawaii."

I know George saw it and I know he knew it was Izzy. But you couldn't tell from the picture who it was and they didn't mention him by name. There was also an article about Izzy in the *Honolulu Advertiser* and the work he was doing against those who had benefited unjustly during the building of the convention center. It intimated that federal agents were protecting him and his family while he completed his important work to bring them to justice.

No prosecution of George has taken place, nor any of the people on the chart as I write this but I am confident it will be coming. I can feel it as certain as I feel the heat in the red wind that whistles through the enchanted pines. I watch those long ironwood needles and limbs swaying much more often than I used to, especially in the dim glow of moonlight, as I sit, ponder, meditate, wish and pray alone on the sun porch. There's not much else to do now as many of my already limited freedoms have long since been curtailed.

Other novels by this author:

Sugar: A Hawaiian Novel The prequel to *Spice: An Island Intrigue.* The story of a woman, Lili (AKA "Sugar") Kaleo, who rises from the vagaries of child abuse and domestic violence to become the mayor of Kaua'i only to get involved in a bribery scandal and face a criminal trial, thanks to her ne'er-do-well husband.

> Soft cover: ISBN 0-9667235-1-1 $12.95 US*
> Hard cover: ISBN 0-9667235-2-X   18.95 US*
> Audio CD: ISBN: 0-9667235-4-6   34.95 US*
> * Prices subject to change without notice.

Also available with a hand-painted Hanapēpē Falls graphic and/or author signed, numbered series. See website www.watertonpress.com, or call (800) 558-4102 for details.

Novels in progress by this author (EPD = estimated publication date): Monitor progress by checking our website and be sure to vote on the novel you'd most like to see published next.

Everything Nice: A Plantation Era Novel The prequel to *Sugar.* The story of some of the more colorful ancestors of the lead characters in *Sugar & Spice* in a plantation era setting. A sugar magnate spawns both the islands' once leading industry & the people who made it great. EPD: November, 2005.

That's What Little Girls are Made of The sequel to *Spice.* In it Lili is faced with the challenges of nurturing the theatrical talents of her handicapped daughter while raising her in a less than friendly environment. EPD: March, 2004.

Wake The story of a San Francisco personal injury attorney, Michael Flaherty, who takes his wife and two children with him to an American Trial Lawyers' Association meeting in New York City, knowing that his wife is planning a rendezvous with another man in Paris after the trip. On her flight to Europe, the plane explodes, along with a plot that leaves her husband as the prime suspect. Before long, he's involved with the daughter of a Jewish cabinet officer, who soon begins to wonder if he planned it. EPD: To be determined by reader interest & demand.

The Cock Crowed Twice The story of a Sacramento, CA real estate developer's wife, who concludes that her family's values must be reassessed, when she finds her all-star son dead on the first day of school. In reviewing the journal of one of her great great grandparents, she surmises that the dysfunction in her family is handed down as reliably as the patterns in the family china. EPD: To be determined by reader interest & demand.

To order books and/or register for publication notifications, discounts, please fill out and return the following (no purchase necessary) by mail or fax: You may also order by phone at 1-800-558-4102.

All books ordered directly from the publisher in lots up to one-hundred-forty-four are signed by the author.

Your name: _____

Mailing address*: _____

City: _____ State: _____ Zip: _____

Email address: _____

Phone*: (   ) _____ Fax: (   ) _____

*Optional, except for orders & the following for orders only:

Credit card # _____ Exp _____

Type: Visa   M/C   Amex   Please notify me as to the following:

_____ The publication of forthcoming books & titles

_____ How to register my book club & receive special discounts

_____ Author appearances and presentations in my area

_____ How to cross-link to promote related charities and causes

I would like to order _____ copies of

_____ @ $ _____ *

(*Prices are listed on cover & on page 344 and are subject to change without notice.) I understand there is a $4.00 shipping and handling charge on orders of less than ten (10) books. You may continue your order on an attachment, if necessary. Please enclose a check or your credit card information, and, if you are a California resident, 8.25% sales tax. You may use any of the following means to place an order: (800) 558-4102; Fax (925) 838-8034; mail: PO Box 847 Danville, CA 94526; email: Books@watertonpress.com; or place your order on the web at www.WatertonPress.com. *Mahalo!*

Acknowledgements

When I think of all who have helped me, the most difficult aspect of writing these acknowledgements is to not leave anyone out. Inevitably and inadvertently I will and for that I apologize in advance.

All of my novels begin and end with my story editor, Jacquelyn Powers, of Sedona, Arizona. Without her I'd still be wandering in the desert of empty, unfulfilling, disjointed prose. She's the one who keeps me "on track" and "focused."

Others on my all-star team of those who brought professional grade critiques and editing to bear included Ann Fields, a writer from Dallas, Texas, whom it's a privilege to know and work with. This also applies to Lois Lautenschlager, an English teacher at Bellefontaine Middle School. She still lives in Kenton, Ohio, where we both attended Kenton High School (Rah! Rah! for Kenton) and graduated in 1963.

Terry O'Meara served as an excellent fact checker and word choice wizard, while Deb Atwoods, MFA, one of my regular Thursday night writing group compatriots, graciously shared her insights by reading and commenting on the novel prior to publication.

Phyllis Taylor Pianka, whose kind, patient mentoring on a month-in and month- out, year-in and year-out basis has consistently shared her praise, experience, skills, criticism and encouragement on a basis so generous that no one would have a right to expect such a gift. All this was done at the head of the Thursday night group table, where my colleagues freely and, I hope, honestly, shared their criticism, suggestions and encouragement, as well.

Always echoing from the background are three great writers, Elizabeth George, Terry Brooks, and Bryce Courtenay, all of the Maui Writers' Retreat and Conference, whose mentoring, suggestions, teachings and insights are destined to echo and ripple through all of my writing forevermore.

My special thanks goes to Margaret Loveridge and her husband, Adrian Loveridge, of the Peach n Quiet Resort for their kind, patient and tireless efforts helping me complete fact-checking and cultural and geographical research on the island of Barbados. My appreciation also goes to my friends at the Bagshot House and Sea-U Guest House, who unselfishly shared their time and knowledge to help me make this a better book. Oh, yes, I don't want to forget Alfred Pragnell, who helped me with the local linguistics, colloquialisms and the dialect of Barbados. And to Sgt. Barry Hunte of the Royal Barbados Police Force for demonstrating the police force in action.

I want to thank Hau'oli Busby of Honolulu for her linguistic assistance regarding the Hawaiian language and Pidgin and especially for portraying the aloha spirit for me and then repeating its rendition whenever I'm at a loss. Likewise, I want to thank Mona Wood of Ikaika PR, Cheryl Ching of the Trinity Broadcast Network, and Jeela Ongley for their linguistic assistance, loyal support and encouragement over the years. These are all fine ladies that others would do well to emulate.

Then there are those eighty or more test readers without whose comments, perceptions, checking of facts and credibility enhancing suggestions this book wouldn't be one-tenth the quality that I believe it now is. I'll call them—along with those who asked to remain anonymous—the Menehunes and share my gratitude to them as a group. Penultimately, there's Carol O'Hara of Cat*Tale Press, who poured over my manuscript for weeks, editing the grammar, punctuation, sentence structure, word choice and logical consistency to bring the book to its current standard of linguistic excellence.

And, last but not least, I thank my wife, Terri and daughters Aubrey, Courtney and Tara Rose, who've been very patient and encouraging and without whom it would be difficult to see the sun come up each morning. *Mahalo nui loa, muchas gracias,* **thank you one and all!**

—Dan O'Connor, the author

Publisher's Note

It has been reported to us that there have been difficulties in ordering our books from online book vendors, such as Amazon.com, as well as U.S. mainland bookstores. Our books are widely distributed throughout the state of Hawaii, so there is no problem there. <u>Here are some tips for ordering</u>:

a. You can always order books directly from the publisher at WatertonPress.com, (800) 558-4102, or Fax: (925) 838-8034, often at a discount; always signed by the author;

b. Or from our distributor, BooklinesHawaii.com, toll free: (877) 828-4852;

c. If your bookstore doesn't have our books in stock (and chances are they don't, if it's not in Hawaii), they can order a book for you by contacting Ingram, the major U.S. book wholesaler.

d. At Amazon.com, for example (as of 9/4/02), if you list only the name of the author, it will not return any of his books. If you type just the word "*Sugar*," under "title" you will get 1,353 results. Waterton Press, listed as "publisher," WILL bring up our books, as will the ISBN. See "other books by this author section" and the back cover of this book for all current ISBN's, or visit www.WatertonPress.com for an updated list.

Thank you for supporting us and our products. It is NOT a given that all good books eventually find their way into mainland bookstores. Their fiction shelf space is generally reserved for books by the largest publishers, which is often paid for and/or reserved in advance of their books even being written.

Notable exceptions: Many Waldenbooks stores (e.g., Logansport, Indiana, where the author was born) and Barnes & Noble (Daly City, CA), near where the author lives are notable exceptions, as is the entire state of Hawaii. *Mahalo nui loa,* thank you very much to them (<u>without whom we would no longer be in business.</u>)

*—***Aloha,** *Stanford J. Waterton***, President**

Author's Note

My goal in writing is not to become rich and famous. It is to "make a difference." I try to do that by presenting compelling, dramatic stories in the context of important social issues.

In presenting those issues, I try to see that all salient points of view are represented through my characters, whether or not I agree with them. (Otherwise, I'd be writing propaganda.) I have no conscious goal to elevate a particular conclusion or hypothesis above the others, but rather to "get people thinking" about the relevant social equities. For it's my readers, not me, who can directly bring about the continuous change that is necessary to constantly improve the society in which we live.

I was recently chastised by a test reader, who said that I should not have broached the issue of the concerns the heroine had in *Spice* about the color of her prospective child, because "I had to put the book down at that point and stop and think about my views on that subject before I could pick it up again and resume reading the story."

Touché! If it weren't for this goal, I'd just as soon be driving nails or laying bricks or practicing law instead of writing.

I've often had readers say, "You should be on Oprah!" As though all that would be required would be for me to say, "By-the-bye, Oprah, do you have a moment for me to be on your show?"

Meanwhile, my wife and I have teetered on the edge of financial ruin, while I wait to be discovered. I was invited to New York by the representative of a major publisher to discuss the possible purchase of *Sugar*. What I went away with was the notion that, like Hollywood, the publishing industry is primarily interested in purveying the "sure thing" from tired authors, many of whom have long since made their last salient point.

If you believe in my work and its thought provoking qualities, then I ask that you help get the word out. Tell your friends. Pass your book around to be read by others. Mention my work to your influential friends, such as Oprah. Make sure your local bookstore carries my books. Follow up to see if they kept their promise to do so. Sponsor a charitable event. I'll offer my books at a fund raising discount.

If you do these sorts of things, I will keep my commitment to you to always write the truth as I see it, irrespective of the reaction of those whom it might make squirm in their seats, loosen their ties, or—heaven forbid— rethink a firmly held attitude or belief. *Aloha 2002,-DJO-*